Master of the Squirting Flower

Master of the Squirting Flower

Stories

Volume 4

Bruce Adam

Ara Pacis

Master of the Squirting Flower. Stories, Volume 4

Copyright © 2008 by Bruce Ormsby Adam.

Title page drawing and book design by the author.

Jacket photo, "At the Vermont State Fair, Rutland," by Jack Delano, September, 1941. Library of Congress collection.

First Paperback Edition, 2008

Ara Pacis Publishers
P.O. Box 1202
Des Plaines, IL 60017-1202
www.arapacispublishers.com

ISBN-10 : 0-9661318-5-1
ISBN- 13: 978-0-9661318-5-7

Library of Congress Control Number: 2008939523
Manufactured in the United States of America.

Contents

Master of the Squirting Flower

In memory of my father,
David Storrie Ritchie Adam
May 19, 1924 – February 15, 2002

He taught me courage

My Poorest Friends

I'm a poor friend to my friends. I'd had many dealings with this terrible neighborhood, riding the thin road from safety to the store. The manager was unfriendly. He took my business but never acknowledged me except with contempt. I'd known Ed the cashier for many years. I thought I could talk to him, but when I asked about the flyers I'd seen posted along the road, and on the walls in and out of the store, he wouldn't answer me. They were his. I knew that. He was buying up common date coins for some reason. I was just asking why. But he just sneered. At that moment, the manager walked in, and I said to Ed, "I know where you get your attitude, from him," timing it so that I could point and indicate the manager, just as he walked by us into the bathroom, but they both ignored me. I almost followed the manager inside because I usually hide my bike there, but I remembered I'd locked it outside in a safe spot.

But it was gone when I got there. Stolen. I should have known that would happen and taken it into the store. I just got lazy, and I got bit for it. It was hard to swallow, but what could I do? I looked around, sliding a door open on the store's loading dock, but there was nothing, and I closed it before anyone would see me. I walked to the corner where Jack and Carol, my poorest friends, and to whom I had been a poor friend, were waiting for me on their bikes. Carol rode to me and I started to tell her what I'd said to Ed in the store, but she rode past. Then came Jack, and I repeated what I'd said, and he rode past. I caught up to them and decided it wasn't an interesting story. I said my bike had been stolen, and they rode away.

From that point, there was a shadow across my mind. It hung like

3

a gaudy funereal drape over my mind, heavy and drab. It was the apparition of a mood, suddenly substantial, and as much as I wanted it removed, it was reminding me of something I did not want to hear about myself. Looking at it more closely, it had the sun print of a bicycle on it, not in a pattern that would appear in a child's room, but more of a marking that a bike had been lying on it in the sunlight, and the curtain had faded around it, only in this case, it was the bike that was the faded part, and the tapestry told me that the bike was missing, dead, but it was still real in my mind. I kept thinking about the replacement cost. I was trying to rationalize, telling myself that the parts were worn, that there were problems with it, and that I needed a new one all along. I told myself that those who stole it would never get any money for it because it was worthless, but it struck me that they may have achieved their aims just by taking it from me. I stood there staring at the white shape of the bike in the fabric, and when I turned away, the dark imprint was still before me like a shadow, but it was made of the fabric of the curtains, and there was a smell of death about it from hanging over open caskets for many, many years. I'm a poor friend to myself.

It was getting late in the day. The sun was just setting. I walked back to where Jack and Carol had been waiting, and there was an old Chevy idling. There were about five men inside. They looked like thugs to me. I tried to walk by them without showing fear, but I wondered if they would follow me. I couldn't shake the thought of them as I made my way back across town. It was an awfully long way to travel on foot. There were terrible sections ahead. There were no cabs in the area, and I wondered if I should just go into a building and ask someone for help. Perhaps I would see another store open where I could call for help. I didn't want to go back and ask Ed any favors. That's when I remembered the history I had with him. I'd put it all aside in my mind, but we had once been much closer, and we fought over a business transaction and didn't speak for many years. I'd been going to his store for several years, and our conversations had evolved from cold silence into somewhat cordial if not strained small talk, but I'd managed to put aside any memory of the past, at least while I was in the store. But I'd also set it back to square one with my angry comment. Maybe they stole my bike. It was locked, but they had metal cutters, and they could have brought it in through the back and hidden it. Why do I have no friends?

I thought of calling family to come and get me, but I didn't want them coming into the city where I was at this time of night. I remembered when I was young and used to walk through bad neighborhoods, but I could run then if I had to. I was more daring. Light from the first bad quarter I would have to pass through lit up the clouds ahead. That would be one raucous group to greet me, but I hoped they wouldn't notice me. I focussed on the clouds. Somehow the expanse of sky seemed much more extensive than it ever had before. All these people, none of whom I could see, hated me when I'd done nothing to them. They believed everyone like me should treat them a certain way, and beyond that, they couldn't blame themselves for how they would treat me. You can't love everyone, but you can be punished as a representative of a whole group that is poor friends with another group. We knew we should all be friends, but we have all been poor friends to one another, everywhere, even in family, only we were liable to be punished for it when we displayed concentrations of anger when our father had authority. We had to answer for it. I remember waiting for my father to come home, worrying that he might kick me around, bit to pieces like the lagoon minnow I put in a tropical fish tank. It flashed from one end to the other, terrified and ragged where even my hand reaching into the water from above to try to save it only made matters worse. All I could do was watch it die, the new pet I was so excited to introduce to its new family. I'd become its poorest friend, helpless and responsible, watching its fellow fish tear it apart down to its last tatter, its eye never changing, no brow to accent it and reveal emotion, but I could see the terror there, and in my own reflection.

Where is the hand that put us here? Will it reach in to save us as we hang like fruit begging for flies, or wait until we hit the ground and rot? There's flies either way. There is a mindless presence in nature, and an energy like light in the mind beyone recalling a sunlit scene. Is there light in the mind? Will it not be destroyed? My poor friends have all come to tatters for what they do not know.

5

Displacement Par Excellence

The machine that put me into the body of the 25-year-old black gangster worked too perfectly to be believed. My own mind was somewhere in the mix. I was conscious of the transfer, but the other men were totally deceived. I sounded like someone else. My every movement was who they thought it should be. My chuckle and gait were singular to their friend, and it was absolutely effortless on my part. I was laughing with them, calling them by name, and I knew everything that had gone on for many years, but the mind in control, somewhere in the back of the mind, was me, a white, 56-year-old man with no criminal experience of any kind.

But what got to me, what astonished me was having the whole night ahead of me, and all the boundless energy of being young, where though I'd been up all day, the plan was to go to the club and have some fun. Remembering that, I wanted to live it again, so I went beyond the parameters of the program and slipped out with them into the night. I knew which car was mine, and I drove. They all piled in and passed a bottle and drugs around. Before we got to the club, I was already high, and so absorbed in the persona of the man I was inhabiting that my mind slipped so far into the rear that I lost touch with it until the next morning. I danced, I drank, I got into a fistfight and won. I rolled into the driveway at the break of dawn and collapsed into my bed, and not alone, I might add.

I'd also forgotten how bad you can feel the next day after living it up like that, even in the prime of life, and it took a long time for the pounding of the door to wake me up. Agents entered, whisked the girl away, and sat me down asking what went wrong. "Whatcha mean what went wrong? Whatcha all doin' in my crib anyway? Whatcha want with me? I don't know you, I ain't done nothin', and I ain't sayin' nothin'!"

"You're not who you think you are," they said. "You're a criminal investigator. You were supposed to stay near the transmitter. Instead you walked away. You stayed away too long to restore the connection. We may have lost you in there. We're going to have to take you in to try to get you out." I told them to get their hands off me. I fought. I almost got away, but one of them clubbed me.

I woke up in a cell. Everything they told me was a crock I told them. I didn't remember nothin'. It was all a lie. If they had something on me, then fine, arrest me, but I wanted to see my lawyer, but they wouldn't give me that. I said it was against my civil rights. They told me to think, to look inside myself, that there was an old white man in there, his mind at least, that he was their best agent. They asked me to look around and see if I could find him, that maybe he was still alive. So little was known about the process they used to invade me, they said, that they couldn't be sure what had happened, only that they could do the extraction with that consciousness coming to the forefront and helping to make that connection. They were getting rough and insistent. I told them to go to hell, so they hit me again, knocked me out, and I woke up on a table, strapped down, with a wad of something in my mouth, cloth I guess, and wires all over me, and I thought, "Oh no!" just as I saw this guy pulling a switch, and sure enough, I blacked out. I went through that a few times and woke up in a bed exhausted, and these guys were looking me over, asking the same questions, getting the same answers, and that whole process repeated itself for a couple of weeks, and they threw in a couple of other ways to try to get to me just for good measure, but it was all for naught, so they finally threw me out, no charges filed, and let me go back with my gang. When I got my clothes back, I found the number of that chick and called her to come and pick me up. All the way home I'm thinking about that white man inside of me, that poor old white man. First thing I wanted to do was raise my glass and thank him for all the memories, and for all the strength that comes through government training.

Brushes with Death

I remember I used to walk to work reading books saturated with wisdom; not me, the books. I was really just a kid then, and I had no idea what was coming. Still I loved all that knowledge and wisdom, the writers leaving it all on the table. There were mothers dying, crop disasters, prison breakouts, abortions, you name it, and all the emotions that come with all that. It was a pleasant walk to the square, and I can visualize myself almost like looking down from a high hill, watching some poor bastard who doesn't realize his blind march is perfectly timed with a train just visible on the horizon.

But maybe that was just the time of becoming acquainted with ideas. After all, there's got to be a time of innocence and even a kind of stupidity when it comes to reality. Strange to think that we're even tuning it out when trying to absorb what it is, thinking of ourselves as somehow immune when we're completely absorbed in the tale of someone's demise. Oh well, there's a million of them, just like markers in a cemetery, and what can we do with all of them anyway but sort through and look for the ones that hopefully will offer us insight and entertain us a little on our walk?

That was me, and I remember the big stack of books on my floor, higher than my mattress because that was on the floor. I was a poor student then, just starting life on my own, and it was a thrill to just stand there day after day without anything terrible happening even after all those years of worrying what it would be like to move away from home and live in the big city. It was like standing on the high hill and having all the missiles fired from the valley miss me, for all I'd heard was how life was out to get me, and there I was, safe and secure, not a worry in the world, and my best friends were the writers of books, most of which were also trying to warn me, or prepare me in some way; yes, to strengthen me for what was to come.

I wasn't a frail child, but I'd had my brushes with death. I was hospitalized a few times, so sick that I had to consider the possibility that I might die without knowing what a full life might be like. I came out of those experiences probably a bit more vulnerable, more aware that reality was served to everyone in the same deadly dosage when the time came. I may have lost a step in the race for fear of getting sick from going all out, and I grew more introverted over the years, suffering from headaches that frequently took me out of the social context of the immediate family for days at a time. I was gregarious enough, but I became comfortable as a loner, and I developed a strong sense that I was going to be something someday, and I tried to make good use of my time. So when I became a college student, I tuned everything out as much as I could and tried to absorb as much knowledge as possible, which meant that I usually had a book in front of my face at all times.

When the train hit me, it wasn't so terrible as you might think. I don't remember everything, but as terrible as it was, the doctors said I was lucky. I was so absorbed in the book I didn't even hear it coming, and while it only knicked me, it sent me flying, and I didn't wake up for a couple of days. When I did, I had several broken bones, and at one point, they had me on a morphine drip, and when I slept, I had some amazing dreams.

There was one where I became a door-to-door brush salesman with Death himself. I wasn't a full-fledged salesman as much as a trainee, and he took me out on the streets to train me. He didn't so much as have a list of potential customers, nor did he go to every house. He would instead examine the disposition of every house, see what kinds of things were out in the open, things like kids toys or whether the garage was open and a gasoline can in plain sight. When he thought he had found a good one, he would knock on the door and chat with the lady of the house. He would show her a selection of brushes and engage her in enough conversation to determine when everyone would be home. Then he would set something up, some kind of trap, like putting the gas can in just the right spot so that when the husband drove into the driveway and walked into the garage with a lit cigarette, he would trip and the gas would ignite, killing him and burning the house down. Many other family members would escape the disasters he would cause, but he always got somebody whether it was a kid or one of the parents. Grandparents were easy prey. He would sometimes engage some old lady in a converasion about brushes and lure her onto the front step and get her to trip off the edge of the stair.

In the dream, I would just stand at a distance, usually just across the street, and watch him work the street. We didn't just do one neighborhood, but whole nations at a time. In any given day, making our rounds, we covered the whole world. He would get into a canoe on the Amazon and talk about how brushes would effectively remove all the dust in the boat, and within a few minutes, watching from shore, I would see several people stand and try to catch a snake. Then the boat would capsize and the piranha would simply take over. Everything I ever read in a book or a newspaper about how people died would be the same trick he would pull on his customers, and I when I woke from that dream, I felt like I had learned something, though I wasn't sure what at the time.

I recovered from my injuries completely, and a few years later, when I had finished school, I was drafted by the army. Now I do just what Death taught me and set traps for the enemy. I look for places where the signs point to his passing, and I place a charge. A short time later, I hear the blast, but I am already at work behind the command huts getting everything ready to take out the post. I also have my favorite places to sit with my gun and snipe, but no matter what I do, I never feel like Death in being immediately engaged but rather at a distance, like I am watching from across the street, but I do everything he taught me, and I do it very well.

Looking back on all my reading, I think the books served to prepare me for the pitches. In a ball game, the pitcher often throws you something just to set you up. The books gave me an edge, which is to say that while I know I'm being set up every day, I'm enabled to transend getting hit and participate calmly in terrible interplay.

Big Ben

I couldn't believe it was really my long-lost friend on the news. After all these years! Ben always said his fifteen minutes of fame would be spectacular. We used to walk down from the dorm to the square for coffee, and the subject would come up quite often because we were both so young, still in school, but we knew we had prospects. Something deep within us told us that, and we also recognized it in one another. That was the great thing. There is such utter warmth in the sensation of someone knowing you will realize your dreams. He made me feel that for a few months, and then, all at once, he turned on me and the world, and I never saw him again.

Then the news came on one night while I was doing the dishes. They talked about this man doing this ridiculous thing to attack a Prime Minister somewhere. He had some kind of lasso and was apparently trying to rope him in. Well, his throw was off. And when I heard the name of the attacker, I turned, and there was his picture on the screen. It was Ben, alright, only what, 25 years later? But I could still see it was him, same greasy face, same pock marks from a terrible complexion. It was coming back to me how miserable he was. I'd always remembered him as brilliant, but now I was seeing something more real, an underlying layer that had been more about him than all the other parts. I knew it was there in some ways, but I had tried to be a friend in such a way as to soothe that part of him. I might have known he would come to no good, but then I thought, perhaps I should use this as an opportunity to get in touch with him.

Well, that was a mistake. It was almost like he was waiting for me to do that. I found out where he was being held and got the phone number off the internet. I indicated that I was a long lost friend, and then came the 20 questions. It became obvious to me that this was considered a political matter of the highest order, and I had implicated myself as a suspect in a conspiracy. Simply by calling, I had put myself on the police radar. And since the foreign prime minister had been visiting, everything was being done to take care of things so completely in order to make a good show of friendship that it didn't matter to the authorities whether I was just an innocent getting caught in the mix. No, it even looked better to nab me and declare an even greater success in solving the crime. They figured out pretty fast that we attended school together, and Ben was no help at all. He said it was all my idea.

To the bitter end he said that. By the time I got to the jail where he was being held, he had concocted an elaborate but quite believable story of how and why we had plotted this whole thing out. They put us in a room together. This was our fine reunion, and I listened, and I denied it, and they told me to shut up and told him to go on. It went on and on, and it somehow sounded so familiar, and then it dawned on me that it was exactly like we had talked about one night on one of our walks, the idea of becoming overnight sensations by doing something ridiculous exactly like that.

I realized that is why I had felt an unusually keen interest in the story when I heard it on the television. There was something familiar about it even then. I suddenly blurted something about his never being any good at the rope part of it, that I should have been the one to throw the rope, that no matter how we practiced it, he never got it right. The police looked at me, then to Ben. He seemed a bit stunned at first, then a smile slowly broke on his face. Despite police pressure against it, we fought our way into an embrace. "Old friend," he kept saying. "Great to see you," I said as they pulled us apart.

Now we see each other at exercise time in the yard, just like back at school between classes. I'm not sure exactly how this "exposure" will help either one of us, but we are elated somehow that we have been noticed, even mistaken for something we are not, knowing that such a perception is like giving someone a suit in which to fly to a desired destination before removing it. The trick in our case will be to convince people that we have been misunderstood. We used to talk quite a bit about coming up with a plan that would take us to the next level when we get out, to take advantage of our being well known. People have a way of forgetting what you did and accepting you as a celebrity. But we're not the same anymore, really. We lack the enthusiasm of younger men, and we couldn't agree on anything. I wanted to do an extended slip and slide that the president would have to navigate on his way from the White House to the helicopter, just for laughs, and he wanted to have a hole somewhere along the way that the president would fall into. So now we sit around picking up gravel by the handful and shaking it out of one hand, or passing it between two hands until gradually we drop every last bit of it.

If that is a sign that time is running out for me, I hope that it is more about prison time because I want to get out of here. The way I now see Ben, I might have seen this tendency of his to want everything of me, as if I should be the one to pay for everything that happened to him, as though I'm to blame. We used to sit in the square and drink coffee, and he would always find a way to make me pay, and to borrow money on top of that. I never kept track, but I know how many cigarettes he's taken from me since I got in this place, cigarettes that he's selling to others and keeping the money. I was always willing to be used when I was young, and that was because of some inner sense that everything was right in the world. Now I just give it up because it doesn't matter. We could have continued to be lost to one another, and it would have been like we were just a few cells apart in the same block. We were always linked in some way. I don't know why. I don't want to know why. My life is the dirt that sticks to my hand when I drop the stones. My days are only visible under a microscope. There are the tiniest traces of quartz in the dust that my sweat picks up. These tiny particles make their way to things I touch, and someday someone will come and track my movements by these particles, and they will find them on the neck bones of my friend Ben after I pick the moment to end his life, and shortly after, my own, in keeping with our sacred, unspoken pact.

The Most Pedestrian

He was a reference librarian, but he wanted to be a leader of discussions, to start a topic by throwing out an idea that had so much meat on it that every dog within a mile would want a piece of it. Naturally, he would need to moderate the activity, hold the bone up and out of reach, and pick parts of it off so that each would have its proper share. He even relished the idea that they might all decide to attack him. That is where the metaphor broke down and returned to words. It was not about dogs and meat and biting the hand that feeds them, perhaps even mauling him. It was just words, and his greatest strength was patiently ignoring every insult, large or small. He had grown immune, perhaps invulnerable was a better word, to all critical activity against him. You might say he was better than anyone else in that regard, for he never descended to that level, never attacked anyone in any way, never insulted anyone, and yet it was true that it wasn't long in nearly every social situation he was in that criticism against him would erupt at some point.

As soon as that happened, he singled out the attacker, put them on ignore and went about his business as usual. This usually led to another attack, someone else to ignore, and it usually wasn't long before he found himself casually getting up and walking away from a meeting he had called. He would calmly go back to his desk and think no more about it. He just organized his papers, got the cart of books and started putting them away, and he politely answered questions from library patrons, helping them locate a resource on the computer and often did it for them, even to the point of walking them directly to a specific volume, opening it and finding the

14

right page. There was nothing but praise from the patrons. He was the most despised person in the library by everyone who worked there, but to anyone needing help of any kind in the reference section, feelings ran from appreciation to high praise for his professional knowledge and people skills. The town newspaper had written a story about his indefatigable facilitations, which he posted near the lunchroom. Someone smashed a fly on it, and there were food stains on it like someone spit on it, but once he'd posted it, he never looked at it again directly, only peripherally to make sure that nobody tampered with it. To him, it was his flag at high staff. People could walk by and ignore it because it was a free country, but it was the standard he set that made it the colors the library flew. He was the living manifestation of the purpose of the library as spelled out in its charter, in every charter. He lived and breathed that purpose, and the reward of recognition on the outside was all that counted. It was irrefutable, and all the inside animosity was mere jealousy, nothing to descend to or engage in, all to ignore, and truly, he just blocked it out like it wasn't there. Everyone started with a clean slate with whatever was next on his agenda because he kept no memory or ill will of any kind. It was simply business, and if anyone he supervised was late for work or failed in their duties, he was very strict in implementing whatever course of action was dictated by the employee manual, a copy of which he kept in his desk drawer, not that he really needed it because he had been there twenty years, and it hadn't changed much in all that time. It guided him to excellence in performance, and he had memorized it both in words and spirit, so he wasn't fierce or vindicative against those who may have been excessively rude on any number of occasions. If the book said to let them go with two weeks severance after a third offense, that is exactly what he did, and he never gave anyone he fired a second thought as they left for the last time. He interviewed people and chose those he felt would serve the library the best according to the precepts of the manual, and he didn't hold it against himself if they failed along the way. He just let the book do the thinking for him, and that was that.

But then one day while he was browsing the internet, he found a forum where people talked about books and reading along with a wide variety of related subjects in various threads. He lurked for a while, then finally joined and began to post his views. But rather than simply reply to posts, he started threads, as if to call people to meetings and be a group leader, a position with which he was comfortable in the real world.

But he discovered rather quickly that an internet forum is not the real world. People hide behind user names and do not often reveal their identities. Some people actually enjoy attacking others. Some write better than others. There's also a degree to which cliques form, and new members must establish themselves, earn respect of the voices before they are allowed to conduct the choir, so to speak. And he didn't do that. He just posted questions about the economy, made statements about the fate of book sellers that sounded to many like bold and false predictions without merit. Someone posted a picture of a man in a trance looking into a crystal ball.

He ignored it, but not in the same way that he did in the real world. He did not know who this was. He began to research the previous posts of the individual to learn more about him. He complained to the forum moderators in private messages, and their reply was that he should familiarize himself with the rules in the Frequently Asked Questions section. He opened those threads immediately and printed out all the information pertaining to forum rules on ethics and civility. He even made himself a nice little book to keep in his desk drawer next to his library manual, but he found that there was nothing to prevent members from attacking him, and the only way he would be able to win an argument was to engage in it, or walk away from it.

So he decided to ignore this person, and he started another thread about the economic woes, asking people what their experience was, and whether they were cutting back in their expenses in order to weather the worsening economic conditions.

Anonymous individuals began to pounce on him immediately. They said he was "trolling" for trouble. They called him a trouble maker, said he couldn't see that really things were far better than he suggested. So he cut and pasted an article from the online *Wall*

Street Journal that told of major companies cutting back as people eliminated certain types of purchases in order to save money. Quickly, the moderators demanded that he remove the article because it was copyrighted material. His response was to wait twelve hours and then edit it down to the headline and lead. He said it had originated from his paid subscription and now that it was old news, it was changed to citation only. That is when that irritable member who had posted the picture of the seer replied, *I don't understand. Are you saying that paying to read the articles also entitles you to also post them elsewhere as long as they are complete and unedited? The moderator's point was your posting it at all was a copyright violation.*

I am curious whether you are deflecting that and saying it's OK to post such articles as long as they are not modified. Did you shorten it only because you deem it now to be "old news?"

No offense, but reading your last couple of threads, there have been several moments where I have gotten the feeling that you just want us to listen to you spin your wheels.

He calmly replied that he had taken the article down because he wanted the thread to stay focused on major publishers and how consumer behavior in a troubled economy will affect them. He said that if the thread were to veer off into unrelated territory over the legality of the quotation and proper citation of copyrighted material for educational purposes, then it would no longer serve any real purpose and should be closed down.

The anonymous member replied at length: *Speaking for myself, I sometimes feel as though the proximity of the media affects us more than it should. Yesterday, my wife tried to remember words from a song along those lines, that people were so poor that…When the stock market fell/We couldn't tell.*

There is a degree to which I've noticed that my response to all things in the world is different now that I have my head in the internet on a daily basis. I see the news about tornadoes or hurricanes or fires every day, more than I did years ago when I only saw it at 5:30 p.m. when Walter Cronkite reported it on the news. Now I find myself clicking on the weather maps during a storm, reading the alerts for any flood watch in effect and even reading the National Weather Service's "Advanced

Hydrologic Prediction Service" for the river a few miles from my home. Things have always happened, but they haven't much happened to me, and now I'm worried more than ever that they will, I wish it were like before when things affected me when they happened, not before.

Without going into too much more detail, I feel the point's been made somewhere else in the thread that we are letting fear get the better of us by the degree to which we are letting ourselves become saturated in information that is clearly fearsome in many respects but doesn't exactly conform to what we would define as really impacting us directly. Even while the price of gas at the pump has made me cut down on my driving, I'm frankly not sure whether I am doing that to some degree because I have heard a thousand times that everyone is cutting back. I would honestly like to step back from all the focus sometimes, and I think the results of your poll are going to be slanted somewhat because you're asking people like me who all have their heads in the internet, which is affecting our objectivity. We are like towers that receive a signal and boost it before passing it on. I think I'm more level headed about things after a vacation, when I've been away from a computer for a while. I still get the news on the radio. I still hear about the storms and the economy, but I'm not so easily shaken. But you're not getting the opinion of the people who may have it in a better, more balanced perspective, at least not if I'm right that the internet is skewing our perception.

I remember when I was a child there would be a tornado warning, and we'd run for cover, and that would be once every few years, and we wouldn't hear about it or run until around the time it was necessary. Now I catch myself watching what the weather is doing when the storms are still in Missouri, observing those yellow patches isolated by Doppler radar and Weather Channel video as being so threatening, wondering whether they will be passing over my house with the same strength later that same night. I'm leaving politics out of this, but the same is true there, that there is an abundance of constant repetition so as to completely saturate one that he cannot think straight. Fear is the enemy here, which is what was stated earlier in the thread, I believe. The truth is that reducing anything to its proper perspective is the best thing to do, make molehills out of mountains, and the internet has a tendency to pass mountains off as the true state of affairs, when in fact, many things are really just molehills. If we stand back a little, when the stock market falls or anything else happens, maybe we'll be able to feel it, but we'll know it won't kill us, and we'll know that we'll get through it, and it's better to know in advance that you'll survive whatever comes (unless it kills you) than worrying it will do that before it does.

It pays to be prepared of course, but not overly so, and we don't need to think about things too much. When a man approached Confucius and tried to impress him by saying that before he made any decision, he thought about what he would do at least three or four times, Confucius replied, "Twice is enough." Fear has a tendency to drive people into making bad decisions, and if the real bomb shelters people built in the fifties are being replaced with mental ones, I hope I'm right to predict that we will find them to be equally unnecessary in the long run.

Then the moderator chimed in: *Oh, really? You took the article down because you want the thread to stay focused on book publishers and how consumer behavior in a troubled economy will affect them. You were asked to remove the article because posting it here infringed copyright. Had you not removed it, you would have had your membership on this forum revoked.*

He got out the forum guidelines he made into a book and searched for anything related to limitations on moderator power and the banning of members. What he found was that the moderators could do anything they wanted, that they owned the forum, and that anyone could be banned whenever they saw fit to remove a member. He also received a private message from the moderator that he was being formally warned as well as being put on a watch list for possibly having an agenda, and that no further deflection of any moderator concern or demand would be tolerated.

That word "deflection" sounded familiar, and he found it in the post by the member who had posted the picture. He had said, "I am curious whether you are *deflecting* that. Evidently, the moderator had picked up on his post and put the pressure on him as a result. From his study of this member's posts, it was obvious that he was somewhat of a trouble maker himself, but he apparently had the blessings of the moderators. He researched his posts much more thoroughly and printed them all out. He nailed down his first name and general location. He found that there had been several give-aways of book-related items, so obviously there were members who knew where he lived. He researched their posts, and by a stroke of luck came upon a reference by one to having the same street name and number in a different town in another state, which was 754 Washington St. Using his skills with reference books, he tracked down the exact building where this person lived and discovered it was a single-family home.

It was hundreds of miles away from him, but he picked a free weekend and drove there. He arrived in the early evening and drove by the house. There were children in the yard, and a man mowing the lawn. He saw this man as his enemy, and he didn't even notice the children. He parked around the corner, waited until the children had gone inside, then shot the man with a rifle as he was closing his garage. Then he drove back home without stopping.

The next day, he posted an apology on the forum to the moderators for not being more attentive to the rules of conduct and promised to observe all copyright laws. It took about a month before anyone posted a question regarding the missing member. Nobody knew why he had not been posting. People speculated that he simply had stopped posting and moved on as so many do on the internet. Apparently he didn't really have any friends at all. It was the same with the reference librarian he had killed about a year after he was hired. After that fellow "disappeared," he had been promoted to head of the reference section. He found the elimination of that one person was all he needed to tune all the other negatives out, and it turned out to be true for the forum as well. People still attacked him for his posts and his threads. Many said he was the most boring, the most pedestrian of all the members, that he just enjoyed hearing himself talk, that his opinions lacked any interest or depth, but he sailed along happily, and the moderators were happy with him too. He ignored his antagonists, and having memorized the forum rules, sent the moderators messages regarding any violations as he enjoyed watching others get sanctioned for not following the rules.

Master of the Squirting Flower

I hate the circus. All them freaks. But it was in town, and no surprise I got the call late that there had been a death. Turned out
to be pretty much open and shut. Of course the hospital will have
the final say, but it was no homicide from what I've seen. Could be
ruled a suicide, but I think it's more a "cause" of natural "cases,"
which is to say that someone drank too much, lots too much.

I guessed from the uniform that it was the ringmaster who met me
and walked me through the mud to the midget's trailer. I knew it had
rained a couple of days earlier and was humid, but the paths were
still pretty bad out back behind the big tents. "I guess the elephants
might have been back here," I said, but the ringmaster didn't crack
a smile.

The trailer was diminutive just like the man, with a small door
and everything, and there was a smell about the place I didn't like
having to get used to. It took a while. It was a musty, old-man smell,
like I remember when my grandfather had a room in our house
before he died. Hard to think of someone the size of a boy as an old
man, but I guess they said he was seventy something, maybe older,
but nobody really knew his age.

I immediately saw the framed picture on the wall, George Washington standing tall in full uniform, and I asked if the midget was an
admirer. "No," the ringmaster said, "he did have the same name, but
he always said that since Washington lived, the universe had
expanded so much in every way, that matter itself had expanded,
and we are bigger by far than the people who lived 200 years ago,
and he hung that picture in order to remind himself daily that he

was a bigger man by far than George Washington."

I really didn't understand what he was getting at. I said I'd be fine and he could leave. I started looking around the place, bumped my head once on a cabinet looking for another light. I saw it was filled with liquor, cause of death I was betting, but there were some clean glasses, so I poured myself one and started going through drawers.

I noticed there were lots of books, things like Pascal, Mann, Dostoevsky, Plato, anthologies of poetry, books of art, all kinds of high brow stuff. And there were interesting objects as well, intricate animals made of folded paper and things like that. There was also a lot of music, but it was all classical, symphony and operas, stuff like that. In the drawers I found grease paints that he would have used to make himself look like a circus clown, and a variety of the objects you'd expect a clown to have like a horn, a squirting flower, hand buzzer and other such things. I put the squirting flower in my pocket thinking I might be able to use it on someone at the station.

There was also a folder with many notes on how to prepare for various acts. Among the papers I found his notes on mastering the squirting flower, and it contained several pages of detailed information. I folded those up and put them in my pocket as well. In another folder there were things he'd written, some poetry and wild meandering thoughts I figured he'd written while he was on a drinking binge there near the end. It was dated just a week or so earlier, and it was rather long.

I have left myself open in the darkness like a bit of peanut butter in a mouse trap that has been set where I know the spirits run rampant and devour things like me, but my plan is that as soon as they bite, I'll catch one of them instead of one of them getting me. This is no joke, and I've entered into the last phase of my maturity, of having all my wits about me, so that this would be my last chance to take a voyage, to make the final discoveries in life, but because I am the head of a family, I cannot really leave the house. My life is boring.

On the other hand, there is no doubt that the discoveries are right here to be found. I know they lurk in my dreams. I feel them following behind me when I ride my bike around the local ponds to get my daily exercise. I stop and chat into a recorder, offering my impressions of what they may look like, how they seem when I imagine them, which is all I can do. There is no actual sighting. I can't see anything, but judging by various factors, using other means, I can do a type of subtraction and at least offer what I think to be a decent suggestion of what type of spirits they are, and these will serve all ages at some point. People will be able to say they have heard about the very things they are sensing through my writings.

So I wait here in the dark for something that lurks. And while I'm sitting here waiting, talking about these things with you, I have the sense that there are a few hundred things that I need to do. The yard behind the shed is overgrown with weeds, for example. I don't even want to begin to list the other things. I went into the kitchen this evening and turned on a light, and I saw a mouse jump. I had to set traps. I used peanut butter, which usually does well to attract them, and it's difficult bait to remove without springing the trap.

But this is summer, and usually I do not see mice at this time of year. They normally appear when it is cold outside, and every October I end up trapping at least a dozen or so within a few days. I do not understand what brings them here now, except for the fact that due to my increased interest in spiritual entities and such, I have developed a tendency to leave unfinished food on plates in the kitchen. Actually, to be honest, my place is quite a mess. But that happens when one is occupied by all things metaphysical, by dreams and the flow of spirit, which is wonderful when it is a consistent blanket. But when it becomes lumpy, that is, when the blanket of spirit breaks up into a mangle of various kinds of strange entities that can almost be sensed, then there is another whole world present that calls me out to explore it, yes, explore it, now, in my final chapter, in my overly boring hum-drum life, it is here. It has come to me as the very thing that I would go out to find, even if it took me halfway around the world, for it is the very thing that a man must seek in order to find himself, and so I wait in the dark for it.

But why do these petty, unfinished tasks keep intruding on my thoughts? Is it the bait of some spirit trying to distract me from what it knows will empower me when I catch it, even so much that I will become so strong that new eyes may open to let me see more than one is allowed in this world? This is what I want, but also, I can't help but feel that all

*those around me, everyone with whom I have had contact, starting with
my parents, never could have known that this would be my destiny, and
so they never knew that this should be something cultivated. There is no
manual or system for doing that anyway, and so all one gets is the book of
duty, the list of chores, the broom, the laundry, the dishes, the toilet and
the bathroom floor. Then there is what you have to do tomorrow or next
week, the promises you have to keep. All this comes by degrees and you
get more adept at it. In fact, the better you are at doing it, the more you
get heaped on you. You rise in your employment and become more valuable the more you can retain of useless information, especially if you can
remember what other people have to do, and create lists of things they need
to do for you and the company. You become their master. You define the
roles of everyone, but you lose your sense of definition of what life means.
You lose yourself in all the things that life has to offer, but you have no life.*

*All that has been said before. It might as well be on a greeting card.
"Congratulations on your promotion. Now you have lost one more cru-
cial portion of your soul." Yes, why are there no cards like that? But I lost
my train of thought. I was trying to lead up to the point of saying that once
you are so completely trained in the art of fitting into society in this way,
which is the way everyone is raised, then even when you go against the
grain as I have, and turn your attention totally to spiritual things, even
then, at your most fluid state, when you are most floating like a blanket,
uniform and flowing, there is a nagging sense in the back of the mind that
you are forgetting something, that there was an appointment to keep, or
that you are neglecting some task that needs to be done, the not doing of
which lessens you in some way, makes you lazy, drops you out of the social
network until you can pay your way back in with excuses and apologies
declaring a kind of temporary insanity. Nobody can accept the idea that
one can be occupied in the examination of their own thoughts and dreams
as if one is a farmer planting and harvesting. What a ridiculous idea!*

*I also was planning to mention that there is a sense in which this dis-
turbance, this sudden feeling that you are neglecting something breaks into
the flowing, peaceful blanket of spirit in such a way as to turn it into a
jumble of lumps. You lose that essential degree of finally being a kind of
receiving antenna and the screen of your mind turns to that familiar static between stations, like you have forgotten something more important,*

where your mind comes back surrounded by chores, each marked and known, and plotted into a chart so that they can all be completed in turn day after day. But within the mind there is a dissatisfied, nagging sense that this is not the purpose of your life, that you have just suddenly dropped out of warp into "other consciousness," that state of mind forced on you from childhood, that state of mind that brings smiles from all the other worker bees who can now finally fathom what your purpose is, what it is that you do, and they can now go back to sweeping the floor or clicking keys or sanding the deck, all thinking ahead to what they'll have for dinner and what they'll be doing for the weekend.

All I can say is that I'm more in that state of flux than here in the darkness sitting as bait in a trap trying to lure a spirit form that I know has been lurking and following me. Even my wife is depressed that she cannot get a reasonable answer from me as to what our plans are for the weekend. Other people already have their reservations months ahead for their winter vacations. Why am I thinking that has something to do with the mouse having entered my kitchen in the summer. Quiet. I think the form is coming for me, and that in a moment I will have trapped it.

False alarm I think. Another thing that frustrates me is the sense that I could just completely devote myself to what would obviously seem like lunatic ravings and never be done. Or I could just devote myself to one unfinished project after another, put my whole soul into each one, and never turn it into a semblance of what I feel is possible for it, never render it into anything so beautiful as the incomplete sense of longing, which is only present by not completing any project. It is rather achieved by lumping them all together into an impossible dream of accomplishment, and out of that, there is hope that I have reached a sense where the only project worth doing might gain one more letter or stroke of color or note on the staff. It is as though at that moment of heightened sense, the lurking spirits sense the light and embark on their mission to capture it, detach it from me, which to me feels like being snuffed and put back on track of the daily needs, when it is actually a theft of truth, if you will, a bite out of that one part of me that was at that moment richly glowing, which is taken from me, which is what I'm laying on the line here to attract them, and if I succeed, I will be left with a part of one of them holding it. Yes, I will feel empty, but the whole trap will have sprung. I will sense a loss, but the light will still be there, a little unexpected, like a mouse stealing in during the summer, perhaps because it knew that it would be unexpected. Are they that wily? I had not heard of such a thing, but I half believe it.

The other thing you should know is that the whole trap mechanism is also built around a third party being present, which is you. I have said "you" many times in this message. You have been singled out in that way, which you thought was a kind of technique, a device, when in fact it was part of the whole formula. It is like the old joke of building a better mousetrap. The spirit I'm out to capture is one that thrives solely on the light that comes as a result of the denial of all things petty. If you are in the least way intrigued by any of these concepts, then your mere presence poses not just a threat, but additional light and therefore bait in the trap. Thus you and I sit together in combined and shared light that draws in the monsters that would have us return to work in short order, leaving them to nibble on their bounty, our light, our recognition of the higher purposes, which come at the price of cleaner bathrooms, more orderly areas behind the shed, cleaner kitchens, and no mice except at times you'd expect them during the year. So the mice coming as a surprise is an indicator, yes, a sign, that all this is working, though the wife will say it only shows more what she was afraid of, and then you will see it too. It will dawn on you, what you were supposed to be doing, taking out the garbage or putting your dirty socks in the laundry, or brushing your hair and thinking of friends and how much you'd like to invite them over for a backyard barbecue and would next Saturday work out?

Doing that would leave enough scraps to keep the mice outdoors, don't you think? I can understand why you would need to get back at some point, but please don't let the fact that there is no fish to hold up that someone can take a picture of make you think that there is nothing to show for all I've said here. I can tell you that the flow of spirit has no facts to back it up. We have all the facts. We can pile them up. We can build anything we want. The spirits I'm talking about are made invisible by that. They thrive on that, depend on it. But if you remove yourself totally from facts, then and only then can you develop the eyes to begin to feel them, sense them as they lurk and follow you around. Over time some of the strange things in the back of your mind come forward by degrees and begin to make sense. They flow over the facts like a flood and begin to rise up, and facts don't float, they sink, so when you start to float on the blanket of rising water, and you must decide to float, not sink or drown, however the facts will try to pull you down. And if you do this a little, though having been trained rigorously through life for a factual life, you will never be very good at it, since not many people are doing it, you will know those who are, and you will also begin to draw in those who have a tendency to feel that the sense they have of things in the back of the mind is worth exploring, maybe so important that they might go halfway around the world to find out more, except they don't have to because it comes to them, only everything about life fights it, and people will fight you, and you'll lose people as you gain yourself, and you say and do things you've never done before because you're learning how to swim in spirit, and there's no manual for that, and if you get good at it, you'll start with a nagging sense that there is more, but you won't know how to see it better. You will sense light in yourself at times, and you'll feel the lurking come closer, and all at once, the light will be gone, and you'll be back in life tending to responsibilities.

Then, at some point, the darkness will be your friend, and some summer night, you'll make your way into the lair of the spirits, because really they're very lazy. They leave food all over the place, and they don't expect anyone at such a time. Mostly people show up only when life is sparse, when they are dying, and the cold is upon them. They are desperate then, and easy to dispense with. But I'm talking about a summer offensive, where the spirits are all lumped together, and even all the light they have taken is turned off for what is their night. And such a night where they can be so totally laid back can only come when they feel no sense of the "other consciousness," of one's sense that what one is doing is wrong, or when someone is thinking of what they have to do or worried about what one thinks about what they are doing. They will relax totally and even sleep, forming a peaceful blanket and forget to lock their doors when you are so completely trained the opposite way to merely go into that zone of light yourself, but call it night, and when you can become so furtive in what seemed so bright when you felt it in first instances that you can extend it like unseen energy, use it as a force, and not just take the scraps the spirits left out, but capture the entities themselves and become their master. But the only way to captivate another human being is to show them that such a thing can be done, to hold that spirit up at the end and say, "Man does not live by bread alone," and by breaking it and sharing it, laying it down in the darkness to let the never-ending light pour out of it like the X-Ray burst that goes through all flesh but nobody sees. And who is there to see this truth and light in a world of hard facts?

The body is a pool in a hard world, some would even say cruel, yet the world has no will of its own as an object. That is the domain of the soul, whose ultimate goal is to be unified with the fluidity of spirit abounding in the universe. The hard world is a world of facts, and when those facts go into the pool of the body, they displace the spirit, fortify the body against spirit, to make sense of the world, eventually blocking out spirit entirely, unless the spirit is felt and learned so as to displace facts. Then you float in the world fact free because all of the facts have become fluid, neither lost nor absorbed, merely part of the flow, where the world is all spirit, and the light is all spirit, and then you feel yourself waiting in the darkness as I am here. You're some kind of luminous bait that surely will be attacked, for the world wants to be rid of it to get on with its chores. It has no time for dreams and cornucopias of light. But it is exactly this radiation that has infected me, that I need to have cut out to be restored, for my wife is snarling at me as we speak, yesterday's work is all around me in a disorganized array. I cannot begin to think that I can ever line all these things up again and forget this curse of darkness and light into whose hands I have commended myself.

Is that what this is about? Now it is easy to dismiss. It is just worlds apart from all reality, words on a page. Here we have a trap set for a mouse, and now it is Christ Himself in his last gasp, leaving this world. Who would follow such a meandering mind as mine, believe there was any spirit or light here? I am just an ordinary man. You should forget about all this, go back to your regularly scheduled tedium and forget about that sense of glowing you felt, and your vacillation between that light and the darkness of the world. Think of it as either a wake-up call or a dousing blast, like looking into a flower that squirts in your face, and you take it, and you master it, and you make it your whole life.

I read through the whole thing and put it back in the folder. Terrible stuff. Made no sense at all. So I stuck my head out the door, bumping it on the doorway, and called to the ringmaster. I asked him what was up with the guy in the last weeks, that there were some very crazy writings. He told me that the midget had gotten on-line and was talking with some woman on the other side of the world, that he guessed he had maybe fallen in love with her, and she loved the thoughts he shared, his poetry and the stuff I just said was crazy, but apparently at some point he let the woman know what he really was, at the point when he thought really that she loved him for what was inside, but when she discovered he was a circus midget, she dropped out of sight, and that's when he went on the drinking binge and got out of control, ruined a couple of acts and had to be taken out of the tent. The crowd laughed thinking it was part of the gag, and he'd put something in the squirting flower and got it in everyone's eyes and escaped, and they found him later in his trailer, crying, but nobody thought he would take his own life or hurt himself.

I asked what he thought they would do, hire another midget to replace him? The ringmaster said probably not, that the whole idea was getting so non politically correct that they probably wouldn't fill the hole. In the long run, the circus was starting to die out. I told him I had a few things left to do for my report, and that I'd be out in a few minutes. He said fine.

So I went back into the trailer and looked around one last time for anything I could use. I found a gun, and pocketed that, but there really wasn't anything else. Oh yes, I took some of those wild and intricate paper foldings that were really amazing and put them in my jacket pocket. And I took the journal and stories as well, put them in my pants. And the laptop computer. I took that as well, for evidence. Then I just took my lighter and lit up a curtain. I waited until it really got going and ran out of the trailer, and I bumped my head really good that time, and I got outside.

The ringmaster came running up asking what happened. I said there was a spark in one of the lamps and there must have been some alcohol from a broken bottle of scotch on the floor because it all went up so fast. The trailer was really up in flames now, a total loss, and other circus people came out of their trailers to see what was happening, and they came as close as they could, and I could hear them saying, "Oh no!" and things like that talking amongst themselves. I asked what the big deal was, and they said it was a great place, that he was such a good musician and magician, a truly spectacular person who had interesting things and told such good stories, that it was a shame to see it all go up in flames like that, leaving nothing for any one of them to keep as a memento.

A few minutes later the fire department and a few squads came over, and they got the fire out, but it had gone up so fast, there was nothing left. People were crying, and the uniforms started directing them back in their trailers. I told them the place was a fire hazard, that the midget must have not used all the things in there because of a short circuit nobody knew about, and so unfortunately I just must have set it off without knowing it, and the place was damp with alcohol from his binge, and I'd put it all in the report.

I got in my car and as I started to drive back home, I could see them all behind me there in my rear view mirror, all watching me leave, all those freaks, the fat tattooed lady, the clowns, with nothing to live for, going around from town to town selling peanuts and jumping through hoops for laughs, such a bunch of losers. I watched them get smaller and smaller, and I suddenly understood the thing about George Washington. They were all getting smaller like midgets, and I was getting bigger, and it was all scientific.

Back at home, I poured myself a drink and looked at the stuff I'd brought home. The animals made from folded paper were still so fascinating. I put them in a bag and put the bag in a bottom drawer. On the laptop I found all kinds of correspondence with the woman they said had dumped him, and it was clear that the guy had a gift of the gab. I couldn't understand all the words he was using. They could figure all that out at the station. I got the squirting flower out and the instructions he had written. He had it all mapped out with drawings and explained the timing of it. I put it on my lapel and ran the bulb down my sleeve, bent my head to sniff it, lifting it to my nose, and squeezed. Bam, my eye was filled with something, and it wasn't water. It was excruciating. Then I remembered what the ringmaster has said about the flower being filled with something else, and I ran to the bathroom sink and started flushing my eye with water. It took probably fifteen minutes before the pain went away and I could see again. It was worse than tear gas, and I couldn't do that to anybody, at least not until I'd cleaned out every part of it.

I soaked it out over the next week, and I studied the instructions carefully from the papers I'd tucked down my pants. I learned a lot about how meticulous the midget was with his persona. He had carefully written out his whole act, not just the squirting flower, but everything about who he was, and he described it so well I think I could actually see him, like Charlie Chaplain. He had a thing with a fake bouquet of flowers, too, that disappeared, and he had explained everything so well, a person might be able to follow along and maybe master it, but I could also see that it would take a long time to get it right, and the only place to really do it was in a show like a circus, because where else could you do such things, really? And probably, at the time he was born, that was the only thing he could do, and he was probably orphaned or forced into it, but there he was organizing it like it was a chosen career, like Fred Astaire dance steps on the floor that he once followed, but no longer needed. And then I was thinking how in the end, he'd beaten the world, was maybe more normal than anyone would have thought, and the thing that eventually got him was also something normal like being rejected in love, when anyone who looked at him must be thinking what a sorry soul he must be to be a midget in a circus like that, that he must be so sad and be a drunk, which I put in my report by the way. The other stuff about being self-educated with the music and books and such, nobody would believe. But the flower was interesting. I'd always liked the idea of pulling a good gag like that, and now that it's clean, and following his instructions, I find I can now get water into a cup, well, some of it, from five feet away.

And I'm guessing he did the folding to make those intricate animals, too. That's something else I'd like to learn how to do, like maybe I could unfold one slowly and keep track of the steps with drawings so that I could go back and refold the animal, and then start with a fresh sheet of paper and do it myself. That would be worth doing, I think. I never had such treasures like that before.

Vital Connections

I've always been the one link in a group of friends that each remained connected to when the chain broke up, more like a key ring than a link, perhaps, because I hold them all even though they are not interlinked with one another. Even years later, decades later, I remember everything in the finest detail. Some people can't and won't do that. They don't look back. Even if they do, they may not be in the same emotional tempo, so if I were to call them and express emotion, they might not feel anywhere near the same thing for me. They might remember and say it was nice to chat, but then they would just go right back to what they were doing.

Me, I hold it all inside. I keep a record. I remember. And I know how life works in chapters, and I know how experience is meant to be intense for each span of time, and then we must move on. There is nothing like the taste of a slice of pie, bite by bite, but beyond a certain amount, it grows sickening. But kept within a limited number of bites, it can be so delicious. The same with a sunset, which is so beautiful, but if it were to last many hours, who would care anymore? I know all that. I understand it. And I've had my pie and my days in the sun. I know my life is limited and that my best years are behind me, but mentally, I'm right where I should be, and like I said, I don't forget things. I remember.

Now I want to mention that I have a friend who is going to die soon. He's younger than I am, and you could always see he had problems. You would say if you saw him that he didn't have long to live, and when he went to the doctor, all the doctor would give him was six months to a year. I had read about a plant in Florida, a tree with very big leaves, that might help him out if he got them in time. So, I got this big idea about having a last adventure for him. Neither of us had any money, so it was just about getting up and going there any way we could. We panhandled enough to get out of the city, and I called a few towns ahead of us and let them know we'd be coming through. I told them the story, and those who would listen published a little piece announcing where we would be on the main street or in the park. We would stand there and talk to people, do some juggling, talk about the illness, whatever anyone wanted, and in exchange, all we asked for was a little help to eat, sleep, and get to the next town.

Some people were very nice. They brought food. They gave us a place to sleep or money for a motel. They arranged for the bus ride for the next day's trip to the next town. Or they even called the newspaper in the next town to pick up the story and help decide a meeting place so that people could see my dying friend, learn our story and help us out a little.

But there were also people who came to gawk and criticize. They called us bums. They made fun of us. I could see them giggling. Now the teenagers and such I didn't care about. They don't know what they're doing anyway. But some of these people were older than either of us. They were downright rude. Once, we were accosted on the way to the meeting place by a gang who refused to let us into their town. They made us go a different way, and on a couple of occasions we were robbed and beaten. My friend probably lost an extra month or two off his life thanks to some of those people. I couldn't believe it. Well, I shouldn't say that. I just was flabbergasted at the moment, but if you asked me whether two such guys could make it all the way to Florida like that without encountering some crazy or rude people who didn't understand and who would try to interfere, I would have had to say that no, I doubted whether they could make it, but we did alright in the end.

The news actually got bigger and bigger as we went. The donations even increased. We stayed in better places, ate better food, and we were recognized by others along the way who gave us donations on the spot even before we got to the meeting places, like in hotels where we were staying. People would see us at a table, come up and say how great it was what we were doing and wished us the best, and they might give us a little something to help out.

This was a big piece of pie though to take bite by bite for so many days, day after day, and do it the way we did, town after town like that. It was exhausting even if we got sleep. We'd get up sometimes so tired that when we walked outside to realize how hot and bright it was, we'd lose our sense of time and space in a way. It was like an overwhelming cloud had surrounded us, and it was just morning, and the cloud was saying that it was betting that we wouldn't make it through the day, and maybe we had already checked out of the room and suddenly our bowels would start making trouble from breakfast, and I wouldn't know if his time was coming, and we'd be over at the hospital trying to get in to have him looked at, and for some reason I wasn't seeing straight because of the heat and the humidity and all the days on the road. I was thinking I needed a bowl of those large curing leaves myself.

Well, it went like that, you could say badly and haphazardly, or fine and friendly, for several weeks, and we covered a lot of ground, talked to a lot of people, repeated ourselves a thousand times, and got spit on and got some lovely home cooked meals. We had dogs chase us, even got bit once, got soaking wet from a couple of major cloud bursts, got put in jail once for vagrancy when a policeman saw us going into a train tunnel and thought we were up to no good, and I could go on and on about the various things that happened, maybe even fill up a book, but I didn't keep a record or a journal, nor did I record anything because I didn't use any of the money that way because a lot of the extra we got was either stolen, or we gave it away to others less fortunate who we would see along the way, which was another thing because we saw so many of those, more than I can tell, and sad as our story made me, there being so many others even worse off made me even sadder I can say for sure.

Well, long story short, we made it to Florida, helped by a truck driver who recognized us in Georgia and saw that my friend was on his last legs and that we wouldn't make it without a long drive of some kind, so he took us in, which was on his way, but he still went out of his way by a hundred miles or so to get us to the spa I had read about that used these leaves and made a preparation that might save him, but even though we got that far, my friend didn't. He died during the last night, and it was a big story when the driver dropped us off in the town, where I told him to, not the spa, but the town square and there the two of us were, only me alive, and they asked me all kinds of questions, some even suggesting I'd killed him by bringing him down such a distance like that, asking me how come I didn't have a job if I was so smart and things like that. It was all so much colder when there's a body, like people suddenly have to start probing, like they have a need while someone's dead to look for other souls to kill, like it is time for extermination, find another victim, put the blame on someone when they were only trying to help.

Now I said that my life was basically coming to a close anyway, didn't I? Yes, I think I did. I'm not saying I'm not somewhat healthy. I am. I could go a few more years, but I've lived the way I've wanted to. I've had plenty of things. I've had plenty of women. I had my day in the sun. Like I said, I made vital connections to lots of good people, and I was the binding agent, the one that drew people in who otherwise never would have connected if it weren't for me. Every one of them would only know what was happening in the lives of the others if they asked me what the others were doing. I realized I had this quality, that it's what made me different, and I called it the quality of making vital connections, but I learned that it's vital for them to have the connection to me. They didn't seem to need to be connected to the others I was connected to; only to me, but then there came a time where things really deteriorated in my life, when I lost my job and family even before I started living on the street, that people wouldn't have anything more to do with me. So it doesn't matter anymore whether I live one more year or five. I've done what I wanted to, and I tried to help my friend, and I'm glad for that.

And now that it's over, I plan to retrace my steps because I haven't forgotten anywhere I've been, and I'm going to go back on a killing spree and track down every last one of them that laughed at us or spit or giggled, or kicked us or robbed us and drove us out of town, not the kids of course, but anyone and everyone I recognize going back is going to get it good. I made note of them the best I could, and I'm going to do this in a way that won't be connected to me in any way, not at all, because there are no more vital connections. I've collected enough of those big leaves to make another concoction out of them that will kill you. That was the thing all along about the tree. It will give you life, or it will kill you. I came down to tap it for life, but it didn't work out like I wanted, so I'm tapping it for death, and when it's over I'll drink my hemlock, too, but I'm not saying that's the kind of tree it is. The one I'm talking about was in the garden, and I'm the snake.

Marie by the Time of the Tree

Marie learned she'd been carrying twins only when she'd already had the abortion, a fact that might have steered her in another direction had she known. Her mother was a twin, and when she was little, she always dreamed of having them.

She'd told a counselor after the abortion that she felt sorry that she'd never even know what the children would be like, that it would be harder not knowing, and the counselor said she'd spoken with some mothers who had lost children later on, when they were a few months old, and their personalities were developing, and these mothers expressed a feeling that suggested it was harder to lose them knowing them as people, that a loss at the beginning is easier than down the road. Marie didn't say anything, and had already started thinking, *Yes, perhaps, only I actually killed them, didn't I?*

The reasons for it were plain enough. She was really one of the rare few that had become pregnant without penetration, from extremely heavy petting. Her boyfriend promised nothing would happen. The chances were next to nil, but there she was in the end, the virgin Marie, carrying a child, two it turned out, only there had been no visit from an angel, and her Joseph wouldn't own up to the fact that it was his, nor stand with her, and so she took the advice of her parents and went to the clinic. But now, having done it, in pain and misery, wondered why God had let this happen to her.

That night she was thinking too much as she had before only this time she was doubled over in pain, in despair, looking for the answer through tears, knowing it wasn't there but asking for it anyway. All at once, something like a touch came over her, from without, because knowing her own self was centered in her mind. She felt a presence of some kind, right there with her, but of spirit, not body, and strange like the wind, yet somehow familiar, getting through to her, mingling with her spirit, not earthly but knowing earth in a way, for it flooded her with something she knew but hadn't felt in a long time, and she wasn't doing it herself, she was sure of that. The feeling it gave her was one of complete love and understanding, of why God loves us, of the human condition being pitiful in some way but great in many other ways. It said that we're all in the same boat but that God's love for us is universal, and our misery and ignorance, though it blinds us, is nothing compared to that love.

Marie understood, and she realized suddenly that she knew how to love everything, understanding it all in the instant of comfort God had just shared with her. The slight touch was so filled with love, and it was so much the opposite of her own notions, where anger and suicide had seats in the legislature, where it was common in her thoughts to hear them blasting against life in general, arguing that pain was necessary and good, and to fight those around her, push them away if they tried to reach her. That is how it had been, and she realized she had learned it from the world, that experience, the great teacher, had taught her how to hate. But in an instant, somehow she was filled with the truth of life, of the whole picture, was found in an exact opposite, in something she would not have reasoned for herself or believed in without outside assistance, for it was too uplifting. But at the same time it was not anything to dismiss, even in the face of just having been to the bottom of her soul, drowning in sorrow. This was another kind of flooding where she felt risen on another kind of tide. The touch may have been short, but lifted up, her sense of spiritual visitation was long, and so she could test it with wonder that it still surrounded and filled her with the familiar yet unexpected new sense of truth, and knowing it was written by God himself, that He had come, and that she was able to identify Him instinctively, and that where she had been, there could be no natural, sudden gush of the opposite so naturally, that a handful of sand in the desert doesn't by itself produce clean water, that the darkening in a coal mine isn't suddenly turned to light when conditions grow dark enough, that this didn't sprint from extreme pressures commanding not just a dose of the opposite in respect for not going too far the other way, this was more an instant removal of all that ailed her, at the moment when she, alone in her own ways and sense of laws of the universe, would expect to go fur-ther down the road to despair, except that she started drilling, that she reached up against the darkness and sent a little prayer for com-fort, and it came in such fullness that couldn't be denied.

She'd felt touched by God, made a witness, she was sure, and was instantly changed by it, granted a sense of God's love and now was filled with exuberance just to be alive, certain that love while diffi-cult to find was true. The new understanding afforded her in an instant a broad sense of the world's blindness to the truth, causing all of the woes that were its main legacy. Marie, realized that no one would listen to her because people who listen to witnesses might only become believers in her story and would still resist real change unless they had seen it for themselves. So man was doomed to blind-ness, but Marie had only to think of her entire life to forgive the world, for she was no different than anyone and had fit in quite well with her cynical exasperation and dutiful snubbing of any and all, looking out only for herself.

Marie's former boyfriend was not open for this revelation. She went to him, and so much poured from her, and she spoke with such authority, connecting religious matters she'd previously held to some degree in her head like so many academic arguments, into one sermon that did not move him. He told her he was happy if it made her feel better. Marie was not the kind of person to try to force any-thing on anyone. She believed inside that the comfort she'd been given while of a personal nature was meant to be shared. How could she hide it, after all, when she was totally different, changed inside? This was a renewal, and she dismissed his wall and called her friends and family to comfort them and explain that an amazing thing had happened. She'd lost children, and her heart was full. She had noth-ing to embrace but the cold hard facts of what she had done, and wasn't it amazing how her faith had bloomed? She credited it all to the Lord, told them of a God who was watching and listening, indeed ready to shower love on them all because He is love, and we hold Him back with what is in us.

They wondered at her passion, some seeing it as a fever of the moment that would pass, telling her to calm down, not blow a fuse, but she just said she was OK with it all and decided it was high time to return to church, because that was Gods' manifestation on earth of His kingdom, and there she would find the fellowship of His followers. That very day she drove over to the one in town right next to the big lake and sat down on the shore thinking she could walk over, have a talk with the pastor and probably be baptized that very day, but she felt she didn't need it. She had an inner peace that her twins were sharing in fullness the great love she had seen in part, and she thanked God for letting them skip the great confusion of life if that was His plan, and she prayed to be helped to see this life as beautiful as with the same love He'd shown her, prayed not to forget any of it, or sink to bottom if she faced such a hardship again.

Marie took a bike ride that spring and didn't see the emptiness of the season she'd come to believe was inherent in it before, where mother earth in renewal showed herself to be an old lady, having certain unpleasant smells she covered with perfumes so flowery they would be called cheap except it was the scent of real flowers. There had always been a kind of ruddiness about the spring, but now she determined it was always due to the emptiness of man in its midst, that it was the newspapers blowing around, the cracked concrete and oil stains, the dilapidation of houses, rust on cars, creaky staircases, that gave spring its emptiness, which summer's lush overgrowth and brilliance tended to hide, and there were also bugs she had blamed, but now they were a vital part of revving the whole world out of its long sleep.

In her new fresh start, Marie took the world in and saw it in a new way. There were dandelions everywhere, the hated weed freely growing anywhere it wanted, and there were some people who cleaned their lawns thoroughly of them, not a weed to be seen, and there were the ones who didn't talk to anybody, who held their noses in the air, Marie heard the wind in the trees and mistook it for the sound of a car coming behind her, so familiar was she with the sounds of the invading culture, so limited in identifying the sounds of nature budding up between the crashes. A man working for the city was sitting alone in a sewer being repaired, pounding his hammer unenthusiastically as if he were waiting for his partner to return any minute with the sandwich he'd ordered. Marie passed by on the way home fifteen minutes later and saw that another man had joined him, and they were both sitting on someone's lawn under a tree eating sandwiches.

She began to trust her perception. This new harvester of mind seemed to have a better effect of pulling in meaning from reality, she passed a garage attached to a house, open with rock music and a teenager working on an old car, a whole flood of remembrances of the loneliness of friends angry in their homes with their parents and uncertain about the future came back to her. She didn't see auras, but felt the meaning in situations that she confronted. Her inklings seemed more than bits of understanding or mere perceptions. They felt more like pieces of a broken hologram where the whole picture can still be seen because each part still has a grid on the whole, and totally was coming through to Marie as well, like a bug suddenly given the right antennae and instruments to use them in war, or memory of something never known restored and accepted in its place as a perfect fit. Marie felt whole and enabled, though she had not felt she was a fragment or crippled, only thought what she had been was all that was allowed, gritting her teeth against reality because that's all one can do given its terrors and conditions if one wants to live. That is, unless one finds God and then understands why God existing is such good news, and Marie's life was a case that when she didn't know God, nothing mattered, and now that she did, nothing else mattered.

Marie enjoyed to some extent the measure of her new-found capacity almost to control things. On one windy day she saw a gum wrapper, silvery and floating high in the air, perhaps 200 feet above her going this way and that, wafting higher in the elements with no sign of coming down, and she said to herself with certainty, *I will keep walking a straight line, and turn the corner when I get there and that gum wrapper will fall into my hand at some point, and I will not change my pace*, and it actually did, after she turned the corner, without changing her pace it drifted down blowing way off course and coming back, then up, down until it went right into her up reaching hand. But after she actually caught it and thought about it, it made her a little afraid to be able to do such a thing, and she wasn't ready to test it again, but she was rather more content to leave open the possibility that it was a grand coincidence of some kind, and when she told people about God after that, she didn't mention the gum wrapper. Even so, a part of her was delighted that God was empowering her, and even if part of her felt a bit spooked about it, not testing the power also left open the fact it might really be there, that she was capable of performing minor miracles. It validated something for her, like she knew that because it had happened, whether it would happen again or not, it proved she was special in a world full of terrible things, a world with a hidden agenda, where pulling strings and cheating were the order of every day.

Then one night several things happened at the same time. A friend who used drugs committed suicide, and another came down with appendicitis and was taken to the hospital. This same night, her parents were attacked on the street and robbed. Her father had been stabbed and was taken to the same hospital where her friend was. All these things happened within a few hours of one another. After getting home from the hospital, Marie couldn't sleep that night. She felt a gathering of evil, a convergence of terrible forces that were beyond her power to fight, something waiting for her in combination on the other side of a wall, waiting for her like it waits for everybody, only that night it had not taken her but had hit three people she knew well, almost like it had knocked bricks out of the wall to take a few prisoners, and now the whole wall was undulating, ready to fall on her. She imagined one of those bricks was for her, a large one. The wind took it up and was blowing around above her. Marie could see it and tried changing her direction and speed, but there was nothing she could do to avoid it. She knew no matter what she did, whether she took her eye off it or not, it would not fall harmlessly away from her, but come down hard and crush her skull.

The events suggested there was a wilful disorder in the cosmos, a consciousness that seemed to spare her only to let her know that it was there, watching because she was one of God's children, and when the time was right, would come for her with a vengeance. Much as she had been healed by God's light touch, these unrelated random things at the opposite end of the spectrum from Marie's dance with the gum wrapper knocked her very much off balance.

The next night, Marie took a late walk along the river. The river and the moon were great symbols in her childhood, pieces of her poetry, the only thing missing being love, which she found later through God. But now there was another piece she was seeking, only because the night before she'd been too afraid to sleep. In a small park on the river was a woman sitting on a bench, and Marie didn't care about propriety or what the woman might think. She just sat down and started telling her everything that had happened to her, but the woman got up and hurried away, and for how abruptly and wildly she had encroached on her space, Marie could not really blame her. She sat on the bench in order to think. Why would she do that to anyone, just sneak up after midnight and talk of abortions, revelations, suicides and a conscious force of evil? She looked across the river and recognized the tree that had stood up straight until a storm knocked it to the one o'clock position. It had come up by its roots, and the mound was still visible at the base of the trunk, but the tree had survived all these years. Beyond it was the cemetery where her grandparents were buried. They died in that same storm after midnight. The car went off the road and hit a tree, the windshield wipers still going, her father said later. It was another tree, once straight, but set in motion, and something was out there, ready to move the slow, perceived-to-be-broken minute hands to mark another catastrophic event that only a tree might experience. Storms change the landscape all the time, and people forget about it quickly enough. She'd always remembered her grandparents' love, not how they died. She got up and looked at her watch in the moonlight. One o'clock on the button. She cursed the tree.

Over the next few weeks, her father did not get any better. Then he took a turn for the worse and was ultimately put into a hospice room. Marie knew he had a strong heart, but she also knew he was

43

one of God's children mucked up by a lifetime in the same world, and she prayed that in the end all people would be blended together in a new mix where we will find beauty being all the same, made of the same stuff, not conscious of all the little differences, and she added, *Amen.*

Not long after that, late at night and in bed, she felt something like the strange touch again, only this time it was a powerful sense of the presence of her father in the room. She had been drifting off to sleep, and there was something like the familiar sound of his breathing above her, and he came to mind with such force that she was certain his spirit had just been in the room with her.

The next day she was called to his bedside as he was dying. Her uncle said her father had woken up the night before saying he'd been with Marie, and it was at the same time when she'd felt him there. Marie closed her eyes and sent her spirit upward in thanks, grateful that there were so much beyond her, not all of it comforting, but feeling blessed. Then she politely asked that everyone give her a moment to be alone with him.

Her father was in a deep coma now, on a morphine drip. She hoped he would hear her, but as she started speaking to him, an unexpected wave of emotion and tears overwhelmed her. Instead of talking with him calmly as she was trying, she blubbered incomprehensibly, and felt exasperated that she couldn't control herself.

He died a few minutes later with everyone in the room. Marie was angry at the force that interfered with her last moments alone with her father. She felt that the *God of Duct Tape and Sand* had sealed her mouth and irritated her eyes, and she was determined to remove all forces from beyond from her experience. So she said a kind of prayer, the upshot of which was, *Please just leave me alone,* then slammed the portal shut in her mind.

But at the grave the morning her father was to be buried, she happened to look and see the sideways tree in the distance, on the opposite side of the river. It was eleven o'clock, and the tree pointed to eleven o'clock. *I said leave me alone!* she hissed.

Late in the Game

M yrt wanted to know why Greta was always late. She asked
everybody, talked behind her back at lunch, but nobody
had any answers, none that Myrt could accept anyway. The best was
Sharon's comment that Greta was preoccupied, caught up in herself
and needed the appearance of importance that comes with being
fashionably late. Myrt agreed that Greta was certainly self centered,
but at bottom, there was absolutely no excuse for it. Myrt had been
taught to be punctual, and that's what she expected of others. Sure,
on occasion there were exigent circumstances, like a tree falling in
the middle of the road in front of your car, but the excuse had better be a good one, only Greta never offered any. She was always late,
and always held her head high, and Myrt couldn't stand that about
her. When Greta was late for lunch one too many times, Myrt left
the restaurant and didn't talk to her for two weeks. It didn't change
anything, but at least Myrt had gotten a message through.

For a long time, Greta lived miles away from Myrt, out in the
country, far away from the community, sharing a large house with
her husband, Richard, who had done well in advertising in New
York City. They retired in North Carolina, built the big house, and
enjoyed the pool and the country for a while, but they realized they
were too old to keep up with maintaining everything. New York had
been more demanding in terms of entertaining friends, but they did
not even like having people over. Greta didn't have anyone to clean
for her, so they put the house up for sale and bought a condo three
doors down from Myrt around the time they weren't speaking.

Gradually, they renewed their friendship, but Greta wanted to enjoy the fruits of having friends nearby, to make use of them, and so rather than put her dog in a kennel when she and her husband traveled, she asked Myrt to take care of it. Initially, Myrt agreed since she loved animals. Her own dog had died the year before, and she had two cats, both getting old as well. She thought it would work out well, and she was happy to be able to do a favor. But the day after Greta left, Myrt realized the dog had fleas, a bad case of them, and she worried about the condo and her cats. She ended up taking the dog to the vet for treatment, expecting Greta to reimburse her for the trouble, but they did not return as planned.

Greta didn't even call Myrt to let her know she wouldn't be home. She and Richard just knocked on the door one night a week late to get their dog back. Greta noticed the smell of the flea medication right away and asked what happened. She did not accept Myrt's explanation and proclaimed that her dog never had fleas to begin with, and she probably got them from Myrt's cats. Richard stepped into the middle of the ensuing argument and suggested that the dog must have had fleas or Myrt would not have taken it to the vet. Myrt had already handed him the paperwork with the date and detailing the degree of the infestation. He thanked Myrt for taking care of the dog and reimbursed her from his wallet on the spot. After they left, Myrt told her husband Ron that she wouldn't watch Greta's dog again but would gladly do it for Richard.

But a month later when Greta asked for the same favor again, Myrt said she'd think about it, but she was determined that Greta's dog would never stay in her house again. She asked friends what they thought, but it didn't matter what they said. There was no way she would watch the dog. Greta guessed that was the case and did not come to Myrt to ask whether she'd finished thinking about it. Myrt said Greta knew better about that, and should know better also about making people wait by showing up late. She couldn't get over it. Ron could see the stress it was causing her and told her to stop worrying about it, or it could affect her health.

But it was already starting to do just that. Myrt was already eighty years old, and though her doctor warned her that stress was dangerous to her health, she was not successful at avoiding emotional upsets. And it almost seemed to her that Greta was deliberately doing things to upset her. Why didn't she ask any of her other friends to watch her dog? Myrt knew the answer, of course, which was that nobody was as reliable. Greta knew that Myrt had very high standards and always gave her best, which angered Myrt even more because Greta's best was so much less than hers.

When Greta returned from her trip, she went to the vet to pick her dog up, but she arrived late and knocked on the window. It was a small town, and she knew someone would let her in and let her take her dog home. But they had bad news for her. Myrt had died. Greta was shocked to hear it. She went home and called her friends to find out what had happened. It was a massive heart attack. Everyone said she was very stressed, and a few of Greta's friends said that Myrt seemed to have been very angry at Greta in her last days, but they also said that Myrt was always mad about something, so not to take it personally. But Greta did feel very bad that she hadn't been more considerate of Myrt's condition, which wasn't obvious since Myrt was always pushing what great shape she was in. Everyone agreed that Myrt was amazing for her age, and Greta was tired of hearing about it. But considering how well Myrt appeared to be and what had happened, Greta felt a little vulnerable herself. She didn't do half of what Myrt did to stay healthy. She was only a few years younger than Myrt, but couldn't compete in any category, really. Myrt was just more competitiv, needing to win at everything, but now that was over. All that was left for Greta was to pay her respects, and she resolved that she would take better care of herself in honor of the high standards of health that Myrt advocated.

Myrt meanwhile, or her spirit, was lurking around the village in disbelief that her corporeal life was finished. She was interested in what people were saying about her, so she floated in and out of people's lives listening as they shared memories and the sadness of losing such a dear friend. People gathered at her condo with her husband to help him, and she felt happiness in realizing that so many people really cared for her, but nowhere was Greta to be found even though she lived just a few doors down. Myrt sailed over there and found Greta immersed in crossword puzzles and television soap operas. She began to follow Greta around to see when there would be any kind of indication that she was aware that Myrt had died. She wanted to hear what Greta would say, but Richard was out of town, and it was just Greta, her dog, the puzzles and the television. The phone didn't even ring. It was soon obvious to Myrt that Greta really didn't have many friends or much of a life, and so she sailed back to the evening gathering at her condo where she immersed herself in others' continuing, heartfelt reactions to her passing.

Ron was really in no shape to take care of any of the arrange- ments, but one of Myrt's dearest, younger friends Susan had already taken charge. She was planning a service for the following Sunday at her house in the country. There was discussion of what kind of service it would be based on what Myrt wanted, and it was planned to be more of a reception for friends to be together in her honor and memory. Ron said Myrt talked about having her ashes be mixed with the dirt in the planting of a tree, and they decided to buy a young myrtle tree sapling and plant it on her friend's property where anyone could come and visit it. Myrt was very content to hear how everyone only wanted to carry out her wishes.

The evening went very smoothly, interlaced with sadness and laughter, and just as everyone was standing up to leave, there was a knock at the door. It was Greta. She wanted to join the party, she said. Myrt was furious that Greta would show up so late and refer to the gathering as a "party." She didn't know what she could do in her current form to have any effect, but she wanted Greta to trip as she walked in, so she flew at Greta's feet, which had the surprising effect, it seemed, of causing her to fall. Fortunately for Greta, some- one caught her, but it shook her up enough that Susan walked her home. All the way Greta kept saying it wasn't the rug, that she'd felt something hit her legs. Susan said maybe it was a muscle spasm.

But in that moment, Myrt realized that she had a certain power to effect things. To test it, she flew out the door and into the branches of a tree, trying to make the branches move. There was nothing discernable until she felt frustrated, and then the branches seemed to respond. By focussing all her anger, Myrt was successful even to shake the tree enough that leaves fell to the ground. She wanted to use the power to do something to Greta, maybe to haunt her, but she decided to think about it first.

Over the next several days, Myrt's remains were cremated and arrangements were finalized for the service at Susan's house. Myrt spent most of her time following Ron around because people were more apt to discuss her when they were with him. She was surprised how quickly the subject had already turned to other things with most people. They were getting on with their lives. Someone else had died just after she did, which took away some of the attention, which aggravated Myrt as she wanted everyone to focus on her.

The day of her service at Susan's house started early for Ron, and Myrt was right there with him when he arrived at the house early. Susan and her husband wanted him there to make the day more comfortable for him. There were many places to walk and sit, and he wanted to be there to greet friends when they arrived. Susan took a phone call and said it was Greta calling to say that she would be there early in order to help out. They all had a good laugh about that, and that's when Myrt realized what she was going to do to get back at Greta. She decided that she didn't want Greta at her service and that she would do what she could to prevent her from coming.

So Myrt flew over to Greta's condo and was surprised to find her still in her robe doing a crossword puzzle in front of the television. Her initial reaction was to want to roust her up, make her get ready for the service, but the idea was to prevent her from coming at all, so she looked around to see what things she might do to accomplish that goal. It made her angry that Greta was doing nothing to keep her promise to get to the service early, so she felt she had the power necessary to interfere, but it didn't seem Greta required impeding. Still, Myrt thought sabotaging the car would be a good start, so she hurried under the hood of Greta's Lexus and ruffled things up the best she could, not knowing what the results would be. When she dashed back in to see what Greta was doing, she was in the shower. Myrt played with the hot and cold water knobs whenever Greta had her back turned, pushed the soap off its dish and perhaps extended the shower by a few minutes, but the service wasn't scheduled to begin for several hours, and short of knocking Greta unconscious,

Myrt wasn't sure she could involve herself successfully in a moment by moment assault without revealing her presence, which is to say make Greta wonder whether something or someone was present in the room with her. Myrt didn't want that, but Greta seemed oblivious regarding the interference thus far, taking it all in stride. Myrt knocked a drink from the dresser onto the clothes that Greta had laid out on her bed, ruining the ensemble. When Greta found it, she merely poured herself a new drink and selected something new from the closet. Myrt managed to push Greta's lipstick behind the sink, but Greta had several new ones in the cabinet. Myrt played many little tricks on Greta, but none of them seemed to work, and when Greta finally got in the car, she managed to start it and began driving to Susan's in plenty of time for an early arrival.

Myrt didn't want to do anything to force Greta off the road, and she was about to give up and fly back to Susan's house to enjoy the moments with those who cared for her, but then Greta turned off the road and started driving away from Susan's house. When Myrt was satisfied that Greta had a different destination in mind, she flew back to Susan's full of joy. She had learned that being joyful also gave her certain powers, which she expressed by running through the wind chimes. The hour of the service grew near. Myrt continued to ring the chimes until Susan called for everyone to gather by the tree. A long procession of mourners made their way from the house to the tree. People chatted as everyone assembled. Then Susan welcomed everyone and started her eulogy for Myrt.

About five minutes into it, Greta was observed to be making her way across the yard. When she got close to the service, she took a route along the periphery and took her place at the back of the crowd. Myrt had almost forgotten about her, and her mood changed from very peaceful to terrible anger. She sailed over the gathering and started swirling. For a few moments, Susan stopped speaking, and everyone waited for the wind to pass. Myrt settled down, and Susan resumed. When she finished, Ron said a few words and thanked everyone for coming. Then Susan asked if anyone else would like to speak. Greta raised her hand and stepped forward.

"Myrt is here with us right now," she began. "I know that's what everyone likes to think, but I really mean that she actually is here, and there have been a number of clear manifestations that can't be dismissed as coincidence, just like the sudden wind a few moments ago. For the last several days since she died, I've been terrified because Myrt has spent a lot of time with me, and she's been very angry. I've tried to calm myself by playing games and watching television, not to interact in any way, but I know that she didn't want me here today, and I'm late because of her. I said I'd be here early, and I would have been, but I felt she would only let me in if she believed she had succeeded in keeping me away." Greta paused and looked around at everyone. "I know most of us are about as old as Myrt was, but none of us was in such good shape. Our times are coming, and I've got to thank Myrt for finally helping me realize the meaning of friendship even at this late date. I came here to say to her and to everyone how sorry I am that I wasn't a better friend, that I took so much for granted. I should have given more of myself. I hope she will forgive me for coming up short, for always being late, but I never was as good as her at anything, nor as loyal, but I understand now, and I'm sorry that we all have lost such a dear friend. The last thing I want to say is that most of you know that I come from a strong scientific background. My father was a physics professor, and I have never believed in a spirit world, the occult, life after death or anything like that, but all that has changed for me."

As Greta finished, people gathered around and hugged her. Susan brought Myrt's ashes to the tree where she and Ron mixed it with soil and filled in the hole around the myrtle tree. When they held their glasses of champagne up to toast Myrt, she swirled in joy filling everyone with a sense of her presence. When a bird landed in the tree, Myrt dispersed. Soon, everyone went to the house to eat.

Later, Susan and Ron walked Greta to her car and thanked her for giving them a strong sense of Myrt's presence. Greta said she no longer felt she was near, then couldn't start her car. Ron lifted the hood, saw a part was missing and said the car wouldn't run without it and that it must be close. So he looked around and found it on the driveway. But by the time he fixed it, Greta was late getting to the airport to pick up her husband, which was no surprise to him.

Platform Father

It was breakfast, and they woke father up to let him know. His daughter Catharsis fluffed up the pillows while his son Denizen brought him the morning paper. His wife Miaculpa brought in the tray, set it down, and all three propped him up so that he could eat. Denizen opened the window to let some air in. Father yelled at him. It was obvious that father had given the room an unpleasant smell during the night, and only father was numb to it. Miaculpa went back to the kitchen to bring the coffee, and Cartharsis added the cream and sugar to taste and let him test a spoonful. He said it was perfect, and she was blown back by the strength of his breath.

After breakfast, they brought in the platform with the hole in it and carried him to the bathroom. There, father was on his own, able to care for himself. He called when he was finished, and they brought in the flat platform and took him to the bedroom where only Miaculpa stayed to help him get dressed for a trip to the beach. Denizen cleaned up the bathroom, sprayed and flipped on the fan to clear the air. Father said Denizen was making too much noise.

They carried father to the van on the car seat platform, which allowed him to drive the family to the beach. Again, father picked on Denizen, telling him to hold his end up straighter. Denizen asked whether he could drive, and father just laughed in his face. When they got to the beach, they lifted him onto the floating platform and carried him to the water. Father was much pleased and enjoyed floating on the water, looking out to sea. It calmed his spirit, brought nature back to his senses. Meanwhile, Denizen met with friends and complained about his life. He was entrusted with the rope connected to father's floating platform, and he said he wished he could just let go of it. All of his friends said they were unhappy with their lives, but Denizen felt his was the worst of all of them combined, saying his father was always on his case. Catharsis and Miaculpa laid out towels and started their long routine of sunbathing, which meant slathering one another with various sun blockers and tanning agents, then laying out and roasting their bodies, turning at intervals so as to ensure the results would be even.

While Denizen continued talking with his friends, he failed to notice that the rope had gotten wrapped around a rock. Meanwhile there was still slack between the rock and father, and when a jet ski crossed over and cut it, neither father nor Denizen felt the impact. Thus father started to float away, just when he started to doze off, and Denizen and his friends had gotten into some very distracting joke telling that so engrossed Denizen that he totally forgot how terrible his life was. Miaculpa and Catharsis were on their stomachs, their heads turned away from the beach, so they could not see father floating away.

Father didn't wake for a few hours, the waves were so calm, the breeze so pleasant. But the sun was hot, and he wasn't in the shade, so he was burning up, and he felt delirious when he woke. It was fortunate that father had insisted that his floating platform have a compartment with various necessities in case of an emergency. His thoughts were jumbled, but he instinctively knew that he must set up an umbrella. In a few minutes he had shade. There was also fresh water, and while his thoughts continued to make no sense to him, he was driven by a sense of what he needed to do. It was as if he was listening to a foreign language in his head, but it was a translation of what he was was thinking, which he knew first and instinctively despite the confusion of the words he was hearing in his head.

Meanwhile, back at the beach, a couple of hours earlier, one of the boys suggested that they toy with Denizen's father, perhaps yank him a few times to infuriate him, an idea that Denizen was quick to nix knowing his father's temper. But it made him look to see where he was, and when he couldn't see him anywhere, he pulled the rope as a means to locate him by connection, and he felt the strong, unexpected tightening caused by the rock. Seeing the rope floating cut just beyond the rock, he dropped the rope and alerted his mother and sister, who were fully baked to a beautiful bronze patina. All three of them bounced around like charged particles. They yelled to the lifeguard, who, after scanning the ocean and seeing nothing to concern him, looked down numbly, wondering why three people on terra firma were screaming like they were drowning. Once he understood what was happening, he called the shore patrol, and the search began in earnest.

Unfortunately, the tide had gone out rather quickly, and there was only one craft to perform the search, and they didn't get the time frame correct, so they confined their search too close to shore. Denizen couldn't stand just watching, and despite the protestations of his mother and sister, paid a vendor to rent a jet ski and went off in search of his father himself. He chose an angle guessing which direction his father had floated out to sea based on his sense of the steady, light breeze and set a course. Despite the fact that all trace of land soon vanished behind him, and the waves grew choppier, Denizen never second guessed his course, and he never thought of turning back. Finally, he spied an object on the horizon directly on his path, and he recognized it immediately, though it was just a dot, as the platform of his father.

When he reached the platform, he found his father engaged in enjoying a fresh drink and fishing. He had already caught several nice haddock and a cod, pretty good considering how tough they were to catch in those particular waters. Father was happy to see Denizen, and expressed wonder that he would have risked so much and come so far by himself in that way. He also told Denizen that he had planned to set up some kind of rite of passage for his son that he would go through with him, but he had been unable to decide what that would be due to that fact that the very nature of such a rite is that one go through it alone. Now, he said, he didn't need to consider it further because Denizen had managed to make the passage by himself, and had become a man that day.

Denizen smiled, and father threw him a rope that he'd gotten out of the compartment, which he had tied to the platform. Denizen tied it to the jet ski and proceeded to tug his father's platform all the way back to shore, basing his direction again on the angle of the wind to retrace his course. In due time, they recognized the tiny bronze-colored dots of Miaculpa and Catharsis standing on the beach, directing in line with the course, and they arrived at the very spot where Denizen had left without so much as having to make a single adjustment on the whole trip back. Father said that Denizen could have done it all with his eyes closed.

The shore patrol was amazed at the success of the effort and suggested to Denizen that there may be a future for him in ocean rescue if he was interested. Denizen smiled and took a card from one of the officers. They even helped carry the father's floating platform back to the van, where Denizen and the girls were going to transfer father to the car platform, but father insisted that they instead put him on the back seat platform, and allow Denizen to drive home. They were initially shocked, but it changed to understanding, and they smiled. This was Denizen's first platform, and he jumped at the chance to be strapped into it. Just holding those keys in his hand raised his spirits to a new level, and he thanked his father for giving him the opportunity to show his skills. Father laughed and said he'd just experienced that firsthand, though he joked that perhaps he was still delirious as a result of his ordeal. He did still have a headache, but thanks to his own foresight, he was able to forestall any chance of any complete collapse and so saved himself that his son could rescue him.

Once the story broke in the neighborhood, Denizen enjoyed even more accolades including a story with his picture on the front page of the newspaper. He was also invited to participate in the village's Heritage Parade, which by good fortune was scheduled for the following weekend. Denizen was the man of the hour, and cheered as a hero. They put him on a platform and carried him along the route where he waved to an admiring crowd. Watching his son from a platform on the curb as Denizen passed by, it was the proudest day in the life of father, whose name was Mortify. Never before had he felt himself so firmly set on such a sturdy base and so uplifted.

A Nominal Appendage

There really isn't any place for a literary essay to appear, not in any regular, daily publication like a newspaper or magazine. The content just doesn't generate any real interest or have a wide enough audience. It would be like a radio station playing sonic tones normally used in hearing tests instead of music. Three minutes of long beeps would not develop much of a following. That's the point, and a literary essay is skimmed more than studied, and whatever dialogue one might have intended, the most people take from it is the dial tone of a telephone without actually dialing in to be engaged with whatever is at the other end.

I know this from having approached several publications with a proposal to prepare a daily literary essay. One of them finally took me up on it, this paper, but it only lasted about a year before finally being cancelled, and this is my last essay to finish that voyage. During this time, I've enjoyed my cubicle in the office, the getting up for a cup of coffee and pacing the hallway trying to get an idea straight in my head, the chatting with the pretty clerks in the circulation department. It was an interesting life, but it was more like being a journalist than a writer even though I tried not to let that creep into my work. My colleagues were all on a different wavelength, and none of them treated me like I was one of them. I remember one time at lunch, one of the more grizzled reporters commented that what I was doing was like sitting in an empty building late at night waiting for a story, that the most I'd get was the sound of pipes, maybe a furnace shutting off; while they were off at a building on fire, mothers leaning out of windows holding their babies beyond the smoke that was engulfing them as it poured out in flumes and rose into the sky. I pondered that for a while, and someone else added that maybe it was the building I was in, that maybe I'd set the fire, or maybe my burned corpse would be found, recognized only by dental records, to which another said they would know it was me from crooked teeth without the records.

Every one of these guys had more than paid his dues. Whether it's behind the desk or on the scene, thirty years of digging up dirt must put a callous on the soul, I thought, or this was a kind of sense of humor acquired among the beasts and demons between file cabinets and mayhem, or this was just the process of initiation, my running the gauntlet, where a good deal depended on my response, even whether it was silence or a witty comeback. But what can a tenderfoot do to the veterans? It was more like being captured, being outnumbered, and the driving force of the mentality against me was part stereotype, part something to which I aspired. It was Hemingway with a dash of Royko, with a touch of Len O'Connor, another Chicago commentator I'd never met but would have expected to take my pie without asking, which is what followed as each guy left the table one by one. They stuck a fork on my plate, picked up a gob of something I might have eaten, shoveled it in their mouth, laid the fork next to me, and walked off. In the end, my plate was empty, and I had said nothing in response.

So my literary essay that day became my response. I wrote about being in an empty building waiting for the story that would come, that all these people in their rooms sleeping peacefully tonight would wake at some point to the sirens of the dive bombers, and none would get out before the stairways were engulfed in flames, and though the streets were filled with onlookers and a few fire fighters, other buildings had been hit, so there was little hope for the children held out the windows, and they would be dropped when the mothers finally lost consciousness, holding out as long as they could, while across the street watching at a safe distance, a gaggle of reporters made bets on which babies would drop first and actually forked out fistfuls of money and laid out increasing odds whether it would be the blond or the brunette, the screaming kid or the one already dead from smoke inhalation. And when it was just a burned out relic before morning, the fire out, the dead counted up and jotted in notes, they all herded into the Grizzly Bear Tap under the tracks, a safe haven from any air attack, and got some of their losings back in rounds bought by the "better better," who picked the correct last one to fall into the flames from the last mother to collapse, and when they were all good and drunk, they took turns calling the story in to the newsrooms, then headed home for a few hours sleep before stopping back at the Grizzly for lunch, which amounted to stealing whatever any unsuspecting customer had when he momentarily looked away for a second, and if he complained, he was booted out by management for not being in the guild, for the Grizzly, if nothing else, was an establishment of the third estate, the life's blood or mother ship of the soldiers of truth, the harbingers of all that is and the pallbearers of good taste on the side.

Meanwhile, out of that reverie, that slight dozing off into how that night of terror would be callously minimized by those who had seen it all and saw to it that it was delivered in the morning edition, I hear the furnace shut off, and there is total silence. The babies are all sound asleep. The mothers are at peace. But several hundred miles away, pilots are gathered in front of a map at a target briefing, the fathers of children in similar buildings where the poet is not allowed to sit in the silences, buildings not with guards, but chatty women looking for anything to tell to the police so that they might have a chance at the bigger apartment. When the bombs fall there, there are no grizzled reporters to lay odds, only poets somewhere to see the bigger picture, whether they were in a building that was about to be bombed, or tucked away in prison somewhere so they couldn't speak, locked in with journalists who maybe drank too much and offset the pain with a bit of callousness but otherwise got the job done, incarcerated for telling the truth, the poets, wherever they were, were as much as sitting in an empty building, that the world was just a building housing souls, and within all that has ever happened, or would ever happen was silence, and in that silence was another kind of truth, no better or worse for lack of fires and tragedy to speak of, just honest to goodness truth, which cannot be bought or borrowed or stolen, and once dispatched, never taken back.

I stopped there and thought that should about do it. I sent it off to the editor who was one of the guys ribbing me at lunch. I expected he would come out and give me grief, refuse to publish it, but it went in as is, and much as I expected very little response, I received none. Still, the next day at lunch, I didn't get the same ribbing, just a bit of silent treatment, but at the end of it, someone got up first to leave and came back and set a beer next to me and left. Another did the same thing. And another until I had about fifteen beers in front of me on the table. The first few seemed like a happy message of belonging and congratulations. The rest were like murder, down the hatch and into the patch, but I didn't think them capable really of such a deep conspiracy needing to be looked into for an underlying complexity of meaning. But if I was going to be one of them, I would certainly have to drink this many in one sitting, and get used to it. Or maybe the point was that I wasn't one of them, that I couldn't keep up with them, that an invitation extended in such repetition was also a wall put up to keep me out. I had made a choice of the silent building, not the blast, of the silent writing, not the news, and though I was mixed in the old gang, I knew I couldn't adopt their ways and stay the course of what I was doing, and I think they knew that, too, and much as they may have had against it, they were going to cut me some slack. Or finally, because I hadn't built up any resistance to that much alcohol in one sitting, whether it be through job experience, indicating how far I was behind them, or just from having manifold problems myself, it was their nice way of saying, Die, and putting a little money in it to attest to how serious they were about it. And so that was the end of my first few days on the job. Not too bad, but it was downhill after that.

Even during the first week, the editors weren't sure where to place my work, or how to design it. It was easy to mistake as a sports column with my mug shot and a byline, and if it wasn't going to be in the back of the paper where the sports section usually is in a tabloid paper. Where were they going to put it? It didn't really belong in the news up front, and it certainly didn't belong in the business section, so they did the only thing they could think of, which was to finally let it settle in among the editorials.

Of course, I had to be careful then to craft my essays in such a way that they didn't read like editorials. In one of them, I tried a literary-minded satire of an editorial, but it was misunderstood, or more fair to say, that nobody understood it at all because they absolutely tried to read it as such but couldn't figure out what I was saying. That sort of made my point in a way, that without some sense of what the editorial is about, a handle of some kind, there is a degree to which we can really have no interest, and once the shelf life of the moment is gone, and the situation is no longer a topic, then of course the writing is irrelevant except as an historical document. That was another thing that irked the editorial writers, which was another group extant from the grizzled reporters. Immediately, I sensed they were uncomfortable with the fact that here I was suddenly among them placing what some would argue were intended to be timeless documents among articles that would go bad quickly, sometimes the very same day. But it also struck me that some of these people were actually kindred spirits, far more intuitive and kind than the news gang in the sense that they were actually doing the same thing I was for the most part, only they were focusing their ideas on an event or situation, and that confused me for a while. I started to wonder what it was I was actually concentrating on. Because of them I had to ask myself what my subject was, and what I was trying to say. It wasn't always so easy to discern, like I had to forget that I even had a focus at all for the engine to start and follow its course, wherever that was, and that wondering what I was trying to say had the effect of cutting the engines, dropping me out of whatever flight pattern I was on and ruining the mood.

So I was there to think, but not to be aware of it, I would say, to get into the unconscious mode in order to create in high style what would grab the attention of my readers. Where would it grab them? I honestly didn't know that until about the third month when I started receiving letters from my readers, few that there were. I had gotten some replies early on, asking what I was doing or congratulating me for trying to bring something different into a daily paper, and there were even some literary minded folks who wrote to say that my work was beneath contempt, critics who felt I was merely sidestepping the necessary process of going through them, but the people whose letters started coming in around the third month were just your average folks who just read the essays every day, and after three months, they decided to contact me. I thought it was a joke at first because the letters specified something in common, which was a physical reaction to my work.

Some of the columnists get letters by the bagfuls, so when the mail room guys brought me mail addressed personally to me in handwriting, they made a big deal out of it, and everyone made a joke about it. In fact, people gathered around my cubicle waiting for me to open it and read it to them, which I did. To paraphrase, the individual said he enjoyed my writing but had developed a serious itch, which when scratched brought a good deal of pleasure, which was unusual because it was not in an area usually reserved for such feelings. Of course, when I'd read that out loud, there were peels of laughter. Even I could see the veiled attack, someone grabbing his crotch, perhaps not as civil as grabbing the throat and gagging, but I got the picture. After that, around the office when I walked by, some of the guys would start scratching their chests and making noises one naturally associates with extreme pleasure. I laughed it off, and just suggested they read my articles and stop looking at the pictures. A couple of weeks later I received another letter in what looked like a completely different handwriting that said as much the same thing, which I discounted on its being so similar, and I wondered if I was just going to start getting harassed. But there were return addresses on the letters, so I didn't completely dismiss the ideas. Looking the names up in the on-line phone directory, I also found the names and addresses to be real. At the same time of the arrival of the second letter, there were some attempts at humor, but nobody cared so much that I was getting mail. By the time the third letter came, nobody seemed to notice. The mail room guy was polite. He just handed it to me and went on his route, but again, I found the message to be very similar, only this one actually described an appendage, not as a real thing, but he said that some-thing must be there in order for certain things to be happening as they were. So he called it a "nominal appendage," a phrase that struck me, and by the time the fourth letter arrived, I decided to contact a few of these people and see if any one of them would meet with me so I could get to the bottom of it.

Every one of them wanted to meet me. I cleared my calendar for a day and met them each for an hour, six in total who had written by that time, though after that there were a few other letters, and I answered those with a letter in which I explained what I knew about the situation from having spoken with others who had similar experience. These interviews were all fascinating to me, and from them I extracted that these people were not having an isolated experience. They indeed described the experience in the same way, that after reading my essays, they had felt a new kind of itch, which demanded a special kind of scratching, one not easily achieved without the next essay, which they said brought them pleasure, though they couldn't always describe why. The essays had no good news, happy facts or interesting statistics pertaining to any area of study in which any of them were interested. The one individual who had described having a "nominal appendage" said it was more of a construct that was taking shape in relief of the itch, something to offset it, that at some point the essays created an issue, something never before experienced, and though the itch continued and was softened by further readings, there was an increase in the itch and the size of the conceptualized thing, whatever it was, that was growing increasingly successful at relieving the itch even though at times there may be a drought of input, so there was more a continuing sense of satisfaction than an untreatable itch. I was glad to have set up his appointment first, because when I spoke to the others, not all of them had considered that, but when I explained it, they said they understood the concept, several so much so that it was if a haze had suddenly lifted and a boat that was always there was revealed.

In any case, that was the most interesting part of having been able to run this experiment, however ill-conceived some may think it was. I may eventually collect the best of the essays in a book, I don't know, because even properly compiled in a form one normally expects of anything literary, there is little, if any, hope of any greater chance to reach a wider audience, except perhaps that group of critics waiting to be appeased, who think of themselves as holding the keys. But I have learned that it is more interesting to me personally to think of what I do as an exercise of fishing, as it were, of trying to catch people and giving them an itch, and perhaps, quite possibly, even the nominal appendage that eventually grows along with greater and greater discovery, and not for nothing, but offering tremendous personal satisfaction. In any case, there is nothing more I can do here in this paper than say thanks because my limited success was not enough to keep the column going, only enough for me to know that it was worth doing. I decided not to even tell the editors here about any of these events, deciding rather to reveal them here, but even that is bound to escape notice because I learned a while back that most had stopped reading my work entirely, except for one guy in the newsroom who came forward and told me about the itch. His nominal appendage is now the size of a yacht, and he sails and goes off on pleasure cruises every weekend, even at the expense of his marriage. Yes, his wife left him, but he actually thanked me for it. Go figure.

Woman's Leg Syndrome

The way Johnny Pepper explained it to me, I understood quite well how one thing can be mistaken for another at a distance and then become quite clear when it comes closer. I still do that all the time when I am driving with many objects, but it's especially true with tire fragments because there are so many of varying shapes. Usually my mind sees it as some kind of sad case of a dead animal, and then I see it's a tire. A shirt on the road, or a bag on the side of the road, it all appears as something else, quite clearly though, until proximity brings home the proper perspective.

So when Johnny told me what he had seen, I understood it perfectly, but at the time I did not realize he was not speaking of an isolated incident. He said that he was passing an alley and looked in and saw a woman's leg sticking out between two garbage cans, with room behind there for the rest of the woman, but it turned out to be a collection of other objects, just bundled together in a way that looked like it was a woman's leg. I told him I did that all the time, and he laughed and said it was such a strange thing.

A couple of weeks later, I was with him when he pointed to some trees next to the church. "Do you see that over there?" he asked.

"See what?"

"That woman's leg in the brush, with the shoe with a bow."

"No, I don't see anything," I replied, but I'd forgotten about the other conversation, and my mind was racing that maybe someone dumped a body in the brush, and I was reluctant to move closer.

"Oh, it's only the light and shadows playing tricks," he said. "But that woman's leg pops out so often. Why does she do that to us?"

"What do you mean, to us?" I asked. "I didn't see anything."

"But you said you did when we talked before, remember?"

"No, I said that I've thought I've seen plenty of things that turned out to be common objects, but I've never seen a woman's leg."

Johnny was quiet and said he wanted to go home. On the way I was thinking that he saw a leg so often that he thought it must be normal, and now he was upset thinking something was wrong with him. "Johnny," I said. "It's OK to see things like that, as long as when you get closer you know what it is you're really seeing."

"It isn't like that," he said. "I never see anything except a woman's leg, and it's the same leg every time, and she's wearing the same shoe with the laces tied into a pretty bow, and the hem of the dress is always the same pattern, too."

I told my dad about it, and he said it was just Johnny's imagination playing tricks on him, that something like that would pass, that it was just his age, his emerging interest in girls probably. "Did you guys ever look at pictures of women on the internet?" he asked me. I didn't want to admit it, but he was able to gather from the way I tried to cover my smile that I had. "Johnny's probably just done it so much that it's gone to his head," he said angrily, "so don't you do it anymore, now go to bed." And he slammed the door shut on me.

It was the first time I ever layed in bed thinking about a woman's leg. I tried to figure out what there was to look at, what someone would like about it, and I couldn't really see anything there, really. A few nights later, my dad was watching television, and there was an old movie in black and white with lots of dancing, lots of guys picking up girls with one knee bent and throwing them up in the air and catching them, their dresses flying up and revealing attached, patterned bottoms no different in size and shape than panties but passable as shorts under a dress. It was interesting to see so much leg, and I believed these were legs that were starting to match my imagined sense of legs that Johnny Pepper was seeing.

A day or two later, Johnny and I were wandering the mall after school, and he froze, pointing to a store window across the mall. "That's it over there," he said, "the pattern of the dress." We walked over, and it didn't change as we got closer. It was a fabric store, more antique stuff, new old stock, with bolts of cloth in the window. Johnny stared at what was a kind of off-white background bedecked with similar images of clumps of pine needles with cones. It seemed something more appropriate for curtains than a dress, and I said as much. "No," Johnny said, "it's the dress on the leg. I swear."

So I went in and asked, and sure enough, it was for curtains, and when I asked if it was ever made for dresses, the salesperson said no. I left and told Johnny that it was for curtains, not for dresses, and he said it didn't matter. He knew what he was seeing. "But what you're seeing isn't real. Even you know that," I told him.

"But now I know it is real," he said.

I didn't need my father to assist me in the logical explanation. I suggested that Johnny probably saw such curtains in somebody's house, or maybe he even saw a real leg coming out of the curtains like that. "That's it," he cried. "That's it!" But he wouldn't say anymore about it, which bothered me a little because I'd helped him reach that discovery, but on the other hand, I figured I would find out in the near future because Johnny usually told me everything, and this was something important.

But it turned out to be in another category by itself because he wouldn't spill the beans. I kept after him, but he even started to distance himself from me. He stopped knocking on my door to walk to school. He sat somewhere else in the lunchroom, and when I tried to talk to him, he just said to leave him alone. So I did. I had a lot of other friends, and I was always busy doing something, so I never sat back and worried too much about it even though it hurt at first that he had shut me out. At the end of the school year, Johnny moved away, and I heard his parents had divorced.

About a year later, my parents split up, and it was the first time I learned anything about what had been going on for years. My mother had been meeting with Johnny's father for years during the winter for a few days when she was supposed to be at an extended teacher's conference in Colorado. She always made the trip because it gave her a chance to visit with her mother in Denver every year, but the truth finally came out that she was also fooling around out there at a condo owned by Johnny's father's company. It turned out the curtains were the same as the pattern that Johnny and I saw in the store, and the reason Johnny wouldn't talk to me is that his parents were breaking up at the time because I'd help him remember something he told his mother about, which was that he had gone to Colorado with his father when he was little, and though he had gone to bed early, he heard a noise, got out of bed and saw a woman on the couch with his father. He said something, and the woman stood up and pulled the curtain around her, but Johnny could still see a leg from where he was standing. Johnny's dad figured he might not have seen anything, and he assured Johnny it was only his imagination, and Johnny tried to accept that, but the memory was triggered later, though he didn't know who the woman was.

His mother did, and she called her husband on it, and when it all came out, she left him, and Johnny overheard a conversation that made him realize it was my mother, and so he was too ashamed to talk to me anymore. After his mother left, Mr. Pepper went out of his way to break up my parents' marriage. He came over one day and told the whole story of everything Johhny saw, which I overheard, but my father said he was no dummy, that he'd known about the affair while it was going on. My mother was shocked to discover that, but she had in fact called off the affair some years earlier when my father had mended certain unexplained ways that were apparent contributing factors in her having strayed. So it was a no go for Mr. Pepper, who did not succeed in making a quick, lateral move.

Meanwhile, Johnny had gone away with his mother, and one night a few years later I gave him a call and told him I knew about everything that happened but that it didn't bother me. "Nothing happened to you," he said, "and I certainly didn't do anything to you that you should say I'm off the hook for now."

"I'm only trying to say, Johnny, that we can be friends again."

"No we can't," he said. "I only had the problem of seeing your mother's leg when I was with you. And now, even talking on the phone, I can see it again through the window out by the shed."

"Yeah, with a shoe with a bow in it," I said. "You think you're so screwed up. I'm wearing the shoes now," and I hung up laughing, but looking down at my shoe, I had tied an usually pretty bow.

The Moth Eater

I remember first hearing of the moth eater when I was doing research through newspapers on microfilm at the Boston Public Library. As often happens when I am looking up specific stories, some other story strikes me as it would looking through any newspaper, and there's something about reading through old papers that makes me realize that nothing has really changed as much as some would have us think. As a kind of snapshot of life, without looking too closely at the stories to determine the clothing or level of technology, there is much the same going on now as ever.

And there are also some things that just stand out more than others, strange stories, and the moth eater struck me in this way. It was the story of a boy who started eating moths as a baby and was continuing to do so as a teenager, and the paper was printed just before the start of the Second World War. At the time, the moth eater was about 14 years old.

Another strange aspect to the story was that though they mentioned his name and where he lived, throughout the piece, the story referred to him as "The Moth Eater," almost as if he were some kind of act. Well, it wasn't on the front page, more of a feature piece, but I also considered how this type of notoriety would not necessarily be welcome by the family, that if it had been my child, I might have preferred to keep it under wraps, but the way it was presented, this individual would devour as many as he could catch, and he left the light on outside the back door just so he could spend a couple of hours in the evening catching moths to eat.

I read the whole story, and I felt a bit strange after doing so, that

68

I took a break and went into Copley Square for a walk, and I stopped for a sandwich and a cup of coffee. It was a beautiful day as I remember it. The sky was full of big, puffy clouds. I remember thinking a lot about moths, but I didn't see any in the clouds, by which I mean that I looked at the cloud formations, but I mostly saw faces and animals, not insects. It made me realize that I really never saw many insects in the clouds.

My own experience with moths had been fairly unusual, I thought, since I had even raised them when I was a teenager. As a boy, I first heard of the majestic Luna moth from a boy who claimed he had caught one. I saw pictures in a book, and in those days I was running after anything I could catch, snakes, frogs, butterflies, but given that moths are generally nocturnal, and my parents didn't leave the outside light on long and called me in before dark most nights, I honestly had never seen a luna moth, though it remained on my short list of creatures I wanted to catch.

I did manage one night to catch a Polyphemus moth, and I took it into my room and kept it there overnight. In the morning, I saw it had laid eggs on the window sill, tiny hassock-shaped pills in abundance. I took some time to study the mother a bit before releasing her into the darkness that evening. She was a beautiful little creature, with antennae like leaves from a tree, and two wonderful black eyes surrounded by fur. It was easy to imagine this was not an insect but a tiny being with many feelings because she actually started shaking in fear when I kept her from flying off my finger by cupping my palm over her. I found it very endearing.

Some days later, the eggs hatched, and I managed to keep a good number of them alive by giving the caterpillars plenty of fresh leaves each day. I stripped the maple trees in the yard of just what they needed, and by the time they were full grown, they devoured everything I gave them each day, down to the stems. Finally, after they spun cocoons, I put them outside for the winter. In the spring, I watched them hatch out, and never once, during the entire process, did I ever think about eating them in any stage of their development. I guess I was not a moth eater.

There was a clear picture of the boy in the paper eating a moth.

I didn't know how distinct an impression it made on me, but it was ten years after I'd stumbled on the story in the library that I happened to be in a rest stop somewhere on the Massachusetts Turnpike with my family. My son was just starting to show the signs of disobedience one expects in a teenager. He was 13, and I must say, he was trying my patience more and more every day. If I was tired, which I was when driving all day, complete exasperation wasn't uncommon for me. I had told him that he could not buy any more pop from the vending machines that day, but he'd already gone into the rest stop ahead of me and done so. When I saw him drinking the soda, I exploded, and there was a secondary reaction from my wife directed at me for displaying so much emotion in a public place. She was generally upset with my parenting methods with my son, but I felt that as he was just beginning to emerge as a man that he needed more strong guidance than ever, but my wife felt I was way out of line with my dictates and anger.

Once angry though, I certainly didn't want to listen to her, so I told her to be quiet and continued railing against my son, demanding to know why he would go to the vending machines like that after I had made it eminently clear that he was absolutely forbidden to do so. Just as I was in the middle of my tirade, an old man stepped into our midst. We were in the central area of the rest stop, in the middle of the heaviest area of traffic, but people were walking around us. This man came right up and stopped. I turned to him and said, "What, do you want to watch me hit him?" suggesting that he had come closer to see what we were fussing about. Then I noticed he was holding something in his hands. It was a giant Luna moth, and it was the first one I had ever really seen. I thought he might be wanting to give it to us, but when I extended my hands to take it, he pulled back as if to say, "It's mine."

"You know, sir." I said, "You really shouldn't hold it like that for too long because moths have scales on their wings that are necessary for flight, which come off easily as powder when they are handled incorrectly, and as you can see, it's already all over your hands." He didn't react or say anything, but started to walk away, holding it with two thumbs on top of the body, and eight fingers underneath to keep the wings spread. My wife resumed her argument, but I kept watching the man going the other way. He pushed through the doors on the other side of the rest stop. I said to her, "He was holding that moth wrong. He's damaging it. He'll try to let it go, and it will flop around because it lost too many scales."

"That's what you're doing as a father," she scolded. "What effect do you think you're having, rubbing the scales off the wings of a boy like that?" The comparison startled me, hit home, and I suddenly felt a higher, longer term impact of my temper than I had ever previously considered.

But I couldn't think of anything to say on that matter, because as we had started walking to the doors on the opposite side, back to where our car was parked, I was filled with the idea of what a strange encounter we had just experienced. "What was that all about with that guy?" I asked her. "Where did he come from like that, and why did he just walk up to us like that?" She didn't know. Then I suddenly remembered I had seen the face before. It was The Moth Eater, sixty years later. I was absolutely sure of it. I gave my wife the keys and ran back the other way, through the rest stop, the doors on the other side flying open as I flew out to try to find him.

I got there just in time to watch him place the body of the moth carefully on his tongue and close his mouth over it. He turned his head and looked over at me, and I could see the wings sticking out either side, so large they nearly covered both his cheeks. Then he went airborne, flying up and out of sight over the trees behind the rest stop. Moments later the wings fluttered down not far from me. I picked them up carefully, the first time I had ever held complete wings of a Luna moth, surprised they were still intact, and took them back to the car and gave them to my son who pressed them between pages of a book he was reading. There was still some powder from the wings on my fingers, which I caught myself licking once I got back out on the road.

Bragging Point

My shack was on the lake first because my father scouted this land when it was unexplored territory for the most part, full of swamp and ten miles from the closest gravel road. He happened upon it when he was hunting pheasant and the ground was frozen, which is when he found the lake, and when spring came, he wore his hip waders through the swamps, and when he fished the lake, he decided to find out who owned the property and make an offer.

Well, forty years later, my shack is the oldest like I said, and I still have the sweetest spot on the lake, right on the point, but my fool mother got most of the land in the divorce settlement and broke it up into pieces and sold it, which is where I got all these neighbors not one by one over the years, but suddenly and all at once during a construction boom a few years ago, and every one of the houses is modern and decked out in every way, and they all have boats, and none of them live here all year round like I do. I call my place a shack because that's what they call it, and some of them even want me to rebuild because I even keep my property looking as rustic and original as it was when my father trudged in here, so there are swamps and tall grasses in the expanse of acres that are all mine, and that everyone has to drive through and look at when they come in here, which is what they want to modernize, take away, because they think I'm hurting the value of their properties.

Well, the bottom line to me is that the day my father explored the area, this is the way it looked, and it's the way he wanted it to look, and I intend to keep it that way. I don't even mow the yard around the shack, and I don't do that for spite, but because there's a natural beauty and continuity to the whole perspective down the hill and around the point until you get past the trees and beyond my stretch of land, which is where you can see the development, and if I mowed or took the trees down, I'd have to look at all of that, so I do everything I can to avoid having to do that, to maintain a living sense of what this place was like before they all moved in, but again, I don't do that out of spite but out of respect. This place was here as it was long before them, and it's a very nice shack, and it will be here, still holding the point, long after they are all gone, and I want the heartier seeds I have here, which are the indigenous plants, to take over all the junk grass they hauled in as sod or planted to make this look as much like the suburbs as possible. That's what it is to them, and much as they're trying to get away from it, one would think they wouldn't try so hard to make it look so much the same.

My father sure made that clear in his day, and I liked trudging through the swamps with him to get here, and I wanted to stay there because I didn't have to mow the lawn. He let me lay back and do what I wanted, fish, shoot guns, whatever I wanted, and I've also had to fight hard to keep all my rights on my property, and I've succeeded only because my parcel of land is as extensive as it is.

Some of the richer residents are after me to sell because they see a windfall if they can acquire it, divide it up and sell it. With my parcel alone, there would easily be another fifteen or twenty homes because I have about a third of the lakefront, and every one of them from their side has to look at me from every spot of their property even though from where I sit I don't have to look at any one of them, and after what my mother did, there's no way that I would do anything to change that. In my mind, every one of them is my mother. Every one of them represents the same greed, the same desire to ruin a wonderful thing. They probably sit and wonder how many pieces they can break my property into. Actually, I know they worry about that because I've seen some of the proposals at the county seat, which they've run by to determine in advance whether they can use the water lines to provide service to so many new homes without requiring a tower. As it stands, the wells do the job, but one of the owners is an engineer, and he said they might need a new system depending on how many homes they got out of my property, so they drew up some plans and took them in for a feasibility study, and then I got wind of it because one of the county underlings came out thinking this was some kind of a done deal. Well, I certainly played along to find out as much about it as I could. I even got a copy of the plans by saying I had loaned mine out to someone who had later moved out. Anyway, I know what they're up to. And what they found out astonished them, that the value of my land with its perfect placement and long entryway besides the lakefront land, and the hilltop and ravine, the two ponds that none of them had even seen, and the wilderness area, or I should say former wilderness area that my father got condemned in an amazing reversal of eminent domain, which I don't really understand, but he had a friend who pulled some strings for him and got some stretches of land out back that my mother didn't even know were connected, but they're mine, and what they found out about them, what they learned was that if they could finagle it all away from me, they were going to need a lot more than what they thought, a major loan, but if they could get that, to the tune of millions, and develop all of it, they would have themselves an amazing windfall the likes of which they had never dreamed about. So they came at me with lowball proposals, and I rejected them, told them to get off my land, and then they even went public, saying one man shouldn't have so much, and you know what? All their work, greed and bellyaching drove the price up so far that it's more than tripled, and I still won't let any of them near it. I caught a couple trying to sneak around to take pictures, and I got my shotgun and fired up in the air and scared them off. I got it posted, no trespassers. But it's also helped me as I'm recognized as one of the richest men in the county, land-wise, and I noticed the ladies have noticed, and I do have plans in that direction because I want a son to enjoy it and keep it like it is. But already one of the girls is a niece of one of the owners. Can you imagine the gall, and the patience? Mine's stronger. I'll wait them out. And I'll have her sign a prenuptial that she loves only me, and she won't get anything if later she decides she doesn't.

Stinky Links

This golf course used to be just your every day landfill before it was turned into a golf course, and then for many years it was just an average course with the occasional gas pipe burning off the methane from the churning underworld of continually rotting garbage. I recall my second round following a two year hiatus, and I didn't recognize the layout. "Oh, it changes a little every day," the friend with whom I was golfing told me, "and if you haven't been here in two years, you'd notice the difference."

It was true. There were hilly areas I distinctly remembered were formerly flat. There were also several spots that seemed dangerously close to steep drop-offs. They were considered hazards, but I thought you might lose more than a stroke if you were to lose your footing in some places. But after the round, I admit that I felt a certain degree of elation at having managed to survive what was a totally new course, replete with dangers, along with a continuous, not at all pleasant order. Honestly, it wasn't a strong feeling, just an inkling, as if I had been in danger, and all the while I knew that directly underneath me lurked the combined discards of an entire society for the better part of twenty years, and it was boiling and changing like the center of the earth. I promised myself I'd come back and do it again sometime soon.

But again, work got the better of me, and my wife had another child, and when I did get around to golfing, it was always closer to home. It was five years before I ever thought of going to "Stinky Links" again, which is what everyone called it, but when I called a friend who was an avid golfer after so much time, he just laughed and said, "Just try to get on that course. The waiting list for a tee time is months unless you take one close to dark. The place is absolutely awesome."

I was curious, so I called for a tee time for the following week, and they warned that the sun would be down by the time I finished, and that I would have to sign a waver that I was doing it at my own risk. I agreed because I'd seen the kinds of drop-offs they had, and I put a flashlight in my bag to take care of the last couple of holes.

All was fine when I got to the course the next week. I was not able to find anyone to golf with me, so I signed the waver and took my clubs out to the tee. On the way, I fell twice, not because I am a klutz or was dizzy, but I could feel the ground moving. I soon learned that the mountain of garbage was in a liquefied state, and the whole course was in constant movement. It was actually undulating in slow motion, but as I stood still and watched the horizon, I could see I was rising in one place faster than the sun was setting. Every hole was different by the time you got to the tee than it was for the golfer in front of you. There were crevices opening and closing, and stretch bridges placed over them so that you might cross if you were quick about it. There were several markers along the way indicating there had been fatalities, and as dusk settled in, I could hear people ahead of me hooting it up. Some were screaming. I thought they sounded like false, drunk screams, or they were just trying to scare me, knowing I was behind them, but I knew nobody was behind me. I knew by the seventh hole why nobody would take a later tee time. The flashlight became useless. I was no longer golfing but crawling my way on ground that was swelling and sinking. Twice along the way, the ground burst open near gas pipe torches, and emerging gasses exploding, lighting up the course long enough for me to make some headway. I caught up to and passed the party ahead of me. Leaving them behind, I feared I had put them in grave danger, particularly as I had trouble putting out on the last hole. By the time I got to my car, it seemed like the whole mountain was heaving, and I drove down the hill fearing I would go off the road. The next morning I called for another dusk tee time. There is nothing more exhilarating than where day meets night.

Cloud School

I remembered Dennis from what I used to call "Cloud School." It wasn't what one would expect to have their kids learning in separate classes on Sunday while their parents were in church services. My mother put me in the Sunday School thinking it would be a religious education, but they talked about leaves and trees, identifying insects, and every week showed us a new kind of cloud and explained how to recognize it. They turned off the lights and used a slide projector, ran through the clouds we'd already talked about, then showed us a new one like "Cirrus."

My mother really didn't understand why I was calling it "Cloud School" when she would drop me off. I remember on the last day I was even at that church, Dennis was brought in as a new student. I remember it well even though I was only seven or eight years old at the time because the day before I had gotten a terrible sunburn on my shoulders from not wearing a shirt on what was a very hot, sunny afternoon, and this was another hot day. There wasn't a cloud in the sky, and I remember Dennis coming in late, too, and why he was there because a couple of days earlier, we were shopping and found him crying in the store. My mother stayed with him until she found his mother. It turned out they didn't live far from us, and my mother suggested the two of us boys might play as I didn't have any friends, and she also mentioned the Sunday School.

So evidently, she was taking my mother up on the offer, but when the slide slow started with the clouds, Dennis became violently ill and started throwing up all over himself. One of the teachers went to the church to get his mother, and mine came, too. Dennis and I were both removed as my mother was helping his mother with the situation. The cloud slide was still on the screen, and Dennis' mother exclaimed that was the problem. For the first time also, my mother connected my calling it "Cloud School" with the pictures being shown, and she realized I was getting more of a scientific education than a religious one, so that turned out to be my last Sunday School experience at "Cloud School."

Meanwhile, my mother learned more about Dennis having an extreme condition of reacting violently anytime he saw a cloud. His mother said she did not fully understand it but told my mother that it only began after her husband had killed himself a couple of years earlier. I overheard my mother telling my father some of these things. I didn't really even understand the word "suicide" until she said that the man had shot himself in the head.

I found this very disturbing, and I was a bit uncomfortable playing with Dennis at first, but he turned out to be more fun than my other friends because his mother gave him a lot of latitude. She also wasn't home all day, and she left him alone. Dennis always wore a cap and had been instructed to keep his eyes looking ahead, level or on the ground, but never to look up to the sky, and my mother told me while I was with him to keep a watch out for any clouds, and as soon as I saw any, to get Dennis inside at once. But there was a series of bright, clear days without a single cloud, which now makes me wonder at the irony of discussing clouds on those Sundays when there really weren't any to be found anywhere in the heavens.

One day while we played, I asked Dennis about his reaction to clouds. "My mom said my dad was allergic to bees," he answered, "and she said that one day he stepped on one and got all puffed up, and it also made him so sick that he threw up all his insides out, and that made him very light, but he was still so completely puffed up that when the wind blew, it picked him up and carried him up into the sky like a cloud, and she said he's a cloud up there now. He's up in the clouds."

I could see that by even talking about it he was feeling sick. But I had to ask one last question. "So why are you throwing up every time you see a cloud?"

78

"Because I want to fly!" he snapped. "I want to fly with my dad!" And he cried.

Those were the days of my youth when I thought I could fly. I remember an element of spirit that has stayed with me all these years, not always present, but it continues to define me in a way. I recall running out of Cloud School into the sunlight so that I could again feel my shoulders burning under my shirt. I was carrying things made of construction paper we had drawn and glued together in Cloud School. I don't know if any of them were clouds, but I wouldn't doubt it.

I recall an enduring sense of being alive in those days. I don't know how else to explain it. It was of curiosity, and of fulfillment, and desire, and of wanting to run, and not understanding why I had to run out of breath. A part of me understood a sense of there being enough absolute energy for all things, and I had trouble accepting that any of this would end in the short term, and that all of it would expire in the long term. So I understood how Dennis wanted to fly, not in the same context, but in general he was speaking of something I had felt when my mother told me that one day my life would end. It came as a complete shock to me. I had never questioned how my life had started. It all seemed to make sense naturally. But I had never even considered that it would end.

That summer seems long in my memory, but it was very short. Dennis and his mother soon moved to Arizona where the sky stood a better chance of being clear more days. My mother told me later that they actually bolted, left the premises in the dead of night behind in the rent, and that losing her husband had made the woman's life very hazy was the way she put it, so when she said it I thought of poor Dennis going away in a cloud, that his life was taking place inside a cloud, that no matter where they went, he would never know what a clear blue sky looked like.

But there was another incident that comes to mind whenever I remember Dennis. I was on my way to see him, and I was in the middle of the street when I heard him fighting with his mother. I could hear the two of them yelling at one another. I don't remember what they were saying, but I do remember Dennis got away with saying more to his mother than I could. Dennis came outside and slammed the door shut and stood there. He did not see me. Slamming the door had the impact of infuriating the wasps in a hidden nest behind the coach light above the door. I remember seeing them swarming all around Dennis who raised his arms up as if to greet them when he saw them. It was like he was saying, "Take me," but when so many of them landed on him and started stinging, he danced around trying desperately to shake them off before running back into the house screaming. His mother got the hose and sprayed the nest down, and Dennis watched out the door, looked at me, looked above my head, saw a cloud and started to throw up. His mother told me to go away, and I never saw them again.

And then the house was empty. I went over the day they disappeared and looked around the back yard. There was a cool breeze, but it was still hot and sunny. Out of the habit I developed when I played in his yard, I kept looking up at the sky, and on that day there were lots of clouds. I knew the names. I'd gotten that much out of Cloud School, and I knew I would die someday. I'd picked that up somewhere as well. But that was something I didn't want to know. What I wanted was to run with boundless energy and feel renewed, and feel almost that I could fly, as if I had the wings of an eagle. Why didn't they teach me how to do that? I looked at the clouds and looked for the shape of a boy's father. Maybe every boy's father eventually went up there, and that was what clouds were, but we gave them names instead so we didn't have to think that way. Yes, maybe we puffed ourselves up too much but weighed ourselves down at the same time so that there was no danger of getting swept into the sky; no hope and plenty of safety.

I went back to my house that day and watched the clouds slowly drifting over my head, huge and utterly silent. Before me was the last remnant of our play, a five-gallon bucket filled with the most vile stew that had ever been gathered and stirred together. Dennis was sometimes allowed to play outside on nights under a very gray sky. His eyes would adjust, but since there was no great distinctionof shapes, he did not get sick for some reason. A few days before he disappeared with his mother, Dennis and I were playing outside on such a gray night. He got an idea that we should gather anything we could find that was awful and put it in the bucket. My mother had three cats, and they used litter boxes outside. Dennis took sticks and began pulling out the solid waste from gravel and putting it in the bucket. He went through the garbage looking for rotting food. We found a dead bird, and he put it in the bucket as well. We ran the hose into it, then left the hose running to the side. Worms came up, which Dennis grabbed and threw them in as well. He asked if there was anything in the shed we could use. My father kept paint, gasoline and pool chemicals there. Dennis told me to get some chlorine tablets, and when I came back, he was peeing in the bucket. "Drop them in," he said. There was an immediate reaction, and the bucket started foaming, and the smell was terrible. Dennis took a stick and began to stir it up furiously. I had only been following along, not knowing what we were doing. I asked him what it was. "Grunt," he said. "We're making grunt." I was surprised he had a name for it.

My father was away on a business trip, and Dennis had left me with the bucket of grunt. I knew everything that was in it, and I wanted it all to go away. I had to do something with it before my father returned and found it there. I could barely lift the bucket. I couldn't carry it without it sloshing all over me. I wanted to take it somewhere in the yard to dump it, but it was so awful. It was all I could do to get it over to the bushes where I dug a hole, then dumped it in. Everything we'd put in poured out. It was disgusting.

I was never quite the same after grunt. I didn't eat well, developed migraines, grew skinny and overly sensitive. Sometimes I walk out on a beautiful day, look up at the puffy clouds, and I recall Dennis, the grunt, and I feel like throwing up. Yes, I still reel when I recall how the cloud billowed invisibly from that madly-stirred, noxious concoction and how sick I got when we were pouring it out.

Grounded

I wanted to go sailing again, which is to say be the captain of the ship, not necessarily to ride into a storm of any kind and put others in danger. I'm merely saying that there is a risk to being flexed in certain ways while other parts go flaccid. It's my tendency to use myself up for the sake of what lies on the other side, but I get caught up in the processes of the voyage. Whatever is out there will only see my sails if I do everything right, and having done it before, it's not about the thing I bring back. It's about managing the ocean.

I don't mean that I can ever control the sea. More ships have gone down than can be counted, and one can make every preparation down to the last detail and still not make it due to an unexpected sequence of events. That's my point. If I haven't made myself clear, it's that discovery is the object, but in the end, what is discovered is not in the objects brought home, if that makes any sense. I'm trying to say that a passage is made clear. The object is only a kind of tree on the other side. Let's say the moon serves in the same way. What did the Apollo missions actually discover? What did they bring home? A few rocks? Is that all those missions mean?

It was the fact that they actually made the trip, and the way it was done, that makes it fascinating. Years later, nobody would think of doing it the same way. There would be a different ship, one to get there faster perhaps, one to land in another fashion, and get back to earth using different equipment. But it would again be a matter of the actual consciousness involved. The moon would only be a dock again, a tether onto which one throws a rope and heads back giving it all the rope it needs so that the measure of the journey is made across space, that there is a discernable proof of the conquest or the establishment of a marker in what was once an impossible dream, or in what was once the stuff of dreams.

What is the actual stuff of dreams anyway? Isn't that what is being removed? Or is it something else? Why probe the darkness or the unknown at all? I always find it humorous when I read the stories of the frontier disappearing, like it's considered a process of looking under rocks for whatever is there, and as soon as man has covered all the ground, there is nothing left, and nothing returns.

The darkness is more fluid than that. It comes and goes like the tide, and each day that it rolls in, it pulls things out with it never to be seen again. We stand on shore and wonder about it. We look up to the stars and wonder, not about the stars or how far they are, but about the darkness. We wonder how to remove that. We have discovered that getting to the moon did not remove our doubt. We now may easily project that getting beyond the solar system, even to another planet, though it may allow us to expand our range, will not remove the darkness. We cannot so easily do that.

The darkness is so completely without equal in terms of the force of its sheer presence that space and the ocean are just places to take a walk in which we may take our fill of it in a way that gives us a sense that the darkness can be overcome, that we can beat it somehow. We put ourselves against it, and we come up with the ring. We hold it up, and our compatriots cheer our victory, and then we say a few words in memory of those who didn't make it, and then we go home to our soft beds, grateful that the children are sleeping soundly, and we think again of what we have actually accomplished, and we suddenly realize that we have done absolutely nothing in any way to control or curb or soften the tide of darkness that continues to roll in and out, taking things with it on its every visit, every day.

We recoil at the prospects and count our blessings, wonder at our good fortune and why we are so lucky to survive, and then we do nothing as time passes but observe the nature of things. We sit in the yard and watch the children swim. We take care of the pool. We clean the filter, screen the leaves out and make the water as clear as it can be, all the way to the bottom. We sweep the patio, and we mow the lawn, and in essence, we do our duty, small as it may seem, because that is our lot in life. We have to believe that the tiny little bit that we are actually doing to put the cans in the recycle bin each day will actually contribute to the ultimate saving of the planet, that the darkness previously content with rolling in and taking things from it will one day not decide it's time to take the whole thing with it, leaving as dull and blank a ball as those resoundingly cheered when photographs taken by a passing probe appeared line by line for the first time on the computer screen.

No, I am grounded, to be sure. That is what I was saying. To set sail is not in any way within my power. I cannot gather the crew because everyone's on a ship already sailing together, all at odds, in a kind of mutiny of partitions, unable to agree on anything at all, and careening into the darkness that is more than ever chipping away at it. Faced with the prospect of annihilation, of obliteration, of cataclysm and catastrophe, it gives comfort to some to not put the cans in the recycle bin, and to others, conglomerates larger than a powerless individual, it gives good reason to catch the last of a species in the ocean and get top dollar for the delicious sushi it will make. There is a kind of darkness taking over where the jungles used to be, the ones that were removed in order to remove the sense of darkness. It is the same kind of darkness where the oceans used to be full of life, the same oceans that were fished out because they were so vast and endless, so utterly beyond us that to have any effect was a sense of pride after centuries of never making a dent in the vast puddle. Finally the dent will not go away.

Now I am afraid that what I said about managing the ocean will be completely misunderstood. Here I have made it sound like managing the real ocean is the issue. Certainly it is an issue, but the greater one is managing another one. It is one thing for everyone to look up at once the moment that a blazing ball of fire crosses the sky. Where will it strike? People grab one another for comfort, grimace and wait for the explosion. Who will it take? Who will survive? How will we build the launching place so that we can send up such a blazing ball for all to see? Who will provide the text that will be read for the actual moment that the ball is launched? Who will write the music that will be played over the whole world when the ball is sailing? Who will manage the sound controls so that the music does not drown out the actual sound made by the blazing ball as it streaks across the sky? Who will set up the towers to play the music so that it can be heard at intervals around the whole globe? Who will make sure that everyone is attentive, awake at the time, outside to behold it live, and not merely in some dark room watching it on television? Who will ensure that everyone knows the true level of danger of the event? Who will explain that it won't just be a few killed in some random spot where the ball happens to land, but everyone on the planet because the planet is just a ship, and the blazing ball is about to put a hole in it, and the ship will sink into the ocean of darkness taking all hands? Who will do that? Or the better question is why would anyone do that when it's been done?

The fact is that the music is already playing, and everyone can hear it even though the sound of the ball is deafening. It was already launched, and it is sailing through the sky, aimed right at the side of the ship. Calculations are that it will hit the ship right in the magazine, and the resulting explosion would be heard around the world if it wasn't the whole world being exploded. Isn't that funny?

But what's funny is that I'm not interested in any of that. That is actually not the darkness I was originally talking about. I was talking about another trip I wanted to make, but I do not have what it takes to make such a voyage. I have no hope of cutting through the darkness I am talking about. It is an ocean of darkness, but it is all in our heads. What we have to do is manage it, not like the veritable ocean we should be managing. I am talking about managing ourselves, by grounding ourselves, together, all at once, in reality, which includes this irrational darkness that has gotten the better of us, that is tearing us apart.

My problem is that I already died somewhere along the way. The darkness overwhelmed me. I had a choice to take a bit of poison every day, which was the only thing that would give me the energy needed to make the journey of discovery of the thing that would be worth leaving a path to find, that my trip would allow others to go there without danger, but that I would die on the very day I would discover and isolate it. I chose not to make such a voyage on that basis, and I have lived tending the pool and the lawn, considering that to be the lot of everyone, and that I should be satisfied and content, and that all else is vanity, and the darkness is too great to have any hope of doing anything to have the slightest impact even if it is painfully obvious that change is necessary. And I made those choices because I saw my life as a burning ember that was limited, of course, to the time it would burn. I feared that the ember would die too soon, so I buried it in such a way that I would extend my life by making it burn longer. So I took care of myself, and I watched over myself, but I lost track of the ember. So many years went by before I even remembered it, and I was initially fascinated by its duration and congratulated myself for having gotten so much more out of it than I could have dreamed. But then I considered the darkness in my heart and began to have doubts. I went and dug up the ember and found only cold ashes, and then I knew I had been dead many years.

So take everything I say as coming from a dead man. I am grounded because I am buried. You would say I am alive. Alright then, I am buried alive. What's the difference? The ultimate issue is whether anyone out there is alive. If there is, there is nothing wrong with taking advice from a dead man. Don't let that bother you. You can do something. The rest of us who are dead cannot. We are done. The question is how many of you there are. Only the living can honestly answer that. My greatest fear is that only a few are living, and they will consider this, then make an examination only to realize that everyone is dead but for a few, and that the world has been commandeered by the dead who will not give up control of the ship, and since everyone is dead, there is no use trying to talk to them because there is no hope of waking the dead. And so the only thing to do as one really alive is to look at the darkness and not fear anything about it, but rather take internal steps to reach that point across the darkness and make a path clear, or, simply knowing it's clear, go there in one instant by the simple management of it, which comes instinctively after a lifetime of faith that despite all the dead, the inevitable end is the beginning of light.

My Father Knew Your Father

So they say there is something like six degrees of separation, and we're all connected to everyone else on the planet, but sometimes I believe it's less than that. To discover that my father knew your father just blows me away. Hard to believe, but true.

I was just picking up here, getting everything arranged like it was before I got here, when I happened to see a familiar spine in the bookcase, a scrapbook with the same markings from my dad's outfit in the South Pacific. At first I figured it was probably just a Navy-issued binder, something anyone could find at the time, but still, when I first saw it on the shelf, the first thought in my naturally suspicious mind was that you had stolen my father's book, and then when I got closer and I saw "USS Lexington" on it, I even felt anger. I even took my gloves off when I couldn't get a good grip on it to pull it out, but by that time I didn't care.

But upon opening it and seeing a strange name, Haylon, in the front, and snapshots I'd never seen before, I realized it was just a coincidence. A lot a boys from this area served on the Lexington. I remembered reading a story about it that my father clipped. I wonder if your father's name was is that story. My father was in there prominently. Oh, I see it's here in the back, pasted in. I guess your father kept his scrapbook going longer than mine did. There are lots of blank pages and envelopes full of pictures never mounted, and they have nothing written on the back. This one's much more complete and detailed. I'll bet I could use this one and figure out quite a bit in my dad's. I won't mix up any of the pictures though.

I've looked through my father's scrapbook many times during my life. There were times I felt I'd missed something, and he would have made me feel that way to hear him talk about how everyone came together after Pearl Harbor. My mother always was the talker. She said he went off and joined as soon as he heard about it. All the boys did, she said, and they were unhappy if they couldn't get in. She said his parents had to sign some kind of permission form because he wasn't even eighteen yet, but he wanted to go. In a way, I've always yearned for that kind of correspondence, that kind of drive, but we moved from place to place when I was young until we finally settled here, but I never had what you had. I can't believe all this stuff you've got. I can tell lots of it came from your father. It must have. Look at the old radio, for example. That's one of the old ones from Germany with the Mahogany. My mother always wanted one of those. She said my father had one before the war but his brother took it. We had a small one, but the tubes kept frying out, and she used to try to fix them, and there was a neighbor who used to tinker with it, but he moved and it finally just broke, and we got a small television. But yours still works. God, I'd love to carry that out of here if I could. What a load of memories that brings back even though they're not mine. I mean, they're my memories, but still, I'd rather have one of the smaller ones because I remember that from growing up, though my dad did have one of the big ones like that before the war. That would fill in a gap maybe.

Flipping through this scrapbook I'm starting to recognize some of these people. And look there, it's my father! I've never seen that picture before. My gosh, there's a whole bunch of them here in this whole section. My father was a friend of your father! They knew one another. I can't believe it! They're laughing in almost every one. Seems like everyone is. It's the same in my father's book. I guess it's because they're all still so young here, fresh out of high school. There's one of my dad holding a whole branch of a banana tree, loaded with bananas. He's got nothing on, and he's holding it like it's growing out of his crotch. That was life in Hawaii when they had shore leave. He kept a journal and wrote stories of his experiences and one of them was of a guy who had a circumcision due to some kind of tropical jungle rot. The guy was in his 30s, and my dad said the hospital was all men, so the guy could walk around naked except for the circumcision bandage, which looked ridiculous, wrapped all around his privates. Well, my dad wrote that the ocean was right outside the hospital, and there was a pier that went way out, and he went out one morning as my dad watched out the window, and he went out quietly all the way to the end of the pier and started to pee, and he broke the silence with his screaming. Can you imagine that scene? Hilarious! I always loved that story.

I see here there are lots of faded polaroids, looks like they're from after the war. That always gets me about polaroids. People liked the new technology because you got instant results, but the pictures weren't as stable, so we have all these shots of the family that have just been ruined over the years, while my grandfather's pictures are clear and sharp. I see your father must have gotten a couple of promotions. Here he's an officer. In these other pictures near the beginning, he's just one of the enlisted men. What, was he some kind of smart guy, or did he know somebody? I can see why you have all this stuff. I'll bet he got a better job than my dad would have gotten. You just have so much. Did he drive a truck over and dump it on his driveway? I guess you thought you'd have an even bigger truck to drive over to your kid's house when the time came. Oh, I see, your dad went to college before the war. He must have gone in pretty high up and made ensign early on. He must have had it made all along.

Looks like there was some kind of barbeque going on, maybe some kind of reunion for the boys from the Lexington. I see some of the pictures were taken inside. Oh look, there's your radio, and the window looks the same. Hey, these pictures were taken in this house. I guess your dad didn't need to drive a truck in. Haylon just handed it over to you. Maybe you never were able to get a decent job, and you just lived with him, only you justified it as taking care of him in his declining years, so you thought you deserved all this stuff. I guess you were lucky to be an only child so nobody would contest you're getting everything. Not only was there so little for me to get, I had a brother and sister fight for every last thing, and about all I got were my father's war things like the scrapbook and journal because nobody else cared about it, but when I look at that stuff, I get all caught up in it, swept back to times I never lived.

I wonder though, if your father knew my father and they were such great friends during the war, and it is obvious that your father stayed connected to all his war buddies, while my father is not in any of the later pictures on the ship. I recognize most of these same guys. It must be after the kamikaze hit the ship. I was only two at the time. I didn't even remember it. Oh, here it is. There's a whole group shot of all the guys including your father, at the cemetery here for my father's funeral. No that couldn't be. They must have still been overseas. He was shipped home. This must have been afterwards. I guess they all made it out here after all. Oh my gosh, there's my mother in the picture, and that little guy is me. My god, I'm in your father's scrapbook. Unbelievable. But why didn't anyone stay in touch? Why didn't I know you when I was growing up? Why did my life have to be so awful and yours so full of things I never had? We just went to different high schools. I might have known you. I wish something else happened to bring us together to prevent this.

Look, I'm sorry, but when I broke in here, I'd been scouting the neighborhood for a while. You left too many lights on, and you never were home, I thought. You should have moved around more, let me know you were home before I broke in. I can't believe the bad luck. They said my father saved a lot of lives before he had it, which is probably why they all came to visit him and meet my mother. He probably saved your dad's life, and now I've taken yours. For what? I thought I wanted all this stuff, but I don't care about it except for the scrapbook, which I've already touched, and the radio. All this other stuff when I pawn it will never make up for what I've done here, but I'm telling you, it's a war. My life has been a battle. It all evens out. My father saved lives. I take them. I never had the advantage of knowing him. Why do people have kids when they know they might die? I have two myself. I'll take good care of the scrapbook. I'll combine them, I promise, but I'll have to burn them both, extinguish the memories of their lives before my kids grow up and start asking questions. So I'll say goodbye to you and your dad Haylon. Farewell.

A Man of Chalk

There was a time that my flesh was fluid, flexible. I don't know exactly when it changed though it was recent. In my mind, I'm just as fluid as I ever was. I mean, I remember what it was like to not give it a second thought, but at this point I don't know what it means to have an unconscious thought. Every waking minute I'm consumed by the fact that I'm turning into chalk.

I remember when I was a kid there was a field in another county, quite a distance from home, but it was close to my church, so if I got as far as the church, it was just another couple of miles, and I used to ride my bike there specifically because it was a place that was totally unexplored. There were no houses anywhere around, and it was still a frontier prairie, never disturbed, which made it great for catching all kinds of reptiles. I captured snakes there and brought them home where they always escaped. There was a stream on one side, and I used to turn up rocks to expose crayfish. I brought many of those home, but they never survived. I tried to make a pond for frogs I had caught, but I didn't realize that the hole I dug wouldn't hold the water. I walked away thinking the frogs would be fine, but the ground just absorbed the water, and I couldn't find the frogs the next morning when I was shocked to see my pond had dried up.

On one of my searches through that field, I happened to find a trilobite, a real fossil, only it was very fragile. It had all the detail of a petrified fossil, but it was made of chalk. I looked around for others, but I couldn't find any. Naturally, from what I learned in school, I tied the discovery to the fact that the area was once an ocean, and that the trilobite had died where I found it, but that was millions of years earlier, and it boggled my mind. I kept the fossil in my room, but I had a little brother, not that he did anything to it, but our room was generally cluttered, and much as I wanted to keep it, I never put it in a box for safekeeping. It just got lost, or so I thought, because I finally remembered what happened to it in one of those rare instances of memory surge where things you haven't thought of for decades come back all at once like diamonds out of a volcanic funnel. I remembered that I'd eaten it.

I did remember some of the details of why I did it, which was that after determining that ingesting chalk would not harm me, I held my nose, chewed it up and swallowed it in order to link myself with prehistoric times. The age of dinosaurs had always fascinated me, particularly that the several ages spanned many millions of years. It is thought that as a result of a higher percentage of oxygen in the atmosphere, creatures actually grew quite large. Even insects such as the dragonfly were enormous compared to those we have today.

I imagined as I downed it with a chug of *7-Up* that I was empowering myself with a type of oxygen pill like the ones that *Robinson Crusoe on Mars* was given by his man Friday, an escaped slave being hunted down by humming flying saucers with powerful beams. I loved that movie, and looking back, I wonder if I knew about the environmental issues that are hounding us today. I don't remember anyone really talking about the planet dying in those days, but eating the trilobite seems more of an act of survival in that sense. I was looking at it more as an act of acquisition of traits, I believe. I wanted to visit those days like the boys in *Journey to the Beginning of Time*, which was another program that had sparked my imagination a few years earlier, a tale of boys following a river that was taking them back to the age of the dinosaurs.

All silly stuff, I know, but it takes me away from another reality that is hard for me to digest, which is that I am turning to chalk, and now I wonder whether the trilobite has anything to do with it. When I say it takes me away from another reality, I mean that it's so unreal to me that I prefer any fiction that can carry me away from thinking about it, but as I said, I'm consumed by it every waking minute. There is no relief.

I first noticed it as a hardness typical of chalk, which is that it is also a softness, one that feels hard but is easily scratched. I feel quite resilient in some ways, even stronger than ever, but I also know that as much as I push, I'm also wearing away.

My main issue is one of leaving some kind of mark. I know that I can take my shoes and socks off and drag my feet down the street and feel no pain while leaving a long dry trail. I wonder how far I would get though. I don't know if when I reach my knees that I would be able to keep going, but to stop would mean coming up short. I mean that literally, for I would be that much shorter, but I can only control my movements, dragging one side or the other, as long as I can manage to move my hips so as to drag one side and then the other in a walking, dragging motion.

I could easily waste my fingers one at a time in finer lines, and then go to the wrists, then the elbows and probably all the way to the shoulders, but when I am just a trunk, what will I be able to do except use my back against someone to bend and shift and make useless, unimpressive, undistinguishable marks.

I was thinking it might serve me better in the long run to keep one leg, at least enough of a length of it to prop me into a focus. I mean that with one leg, I could drive myself along and remove half the side of me. I could hold my head up for that. I could continue to do that on my back, but being on my stomach would be trickier because I would need the toes to force myself along, and if they don't have a grip, or if I don't wear a shoe, I might lose my foot in the process.

So having considered all the ways that I might leave myself unused in the process, or have plenty left but lose the driving force or controlling mechanisms and therefore reach unintelligibility too early, my plan would be to use one leg to the knee and one arm to the shoulder first, probably my left arm because I'm right handed, and maybe my left leg, too. I'm not sure of that, but there's no way to experiment and run a test first.

The most important aspect will be to at least experiment, perhaps using just my little finger on my left hand, maybe just half of it, in order to gauge the effects of loss on various surfaces. I need to choose the type of canvas or paper that will give me the longest life. I believe I may have to perform some kind of sketch of the whole project, but I could do this in scale so as to not waste myself, and then I could ramp it up to the full scale model and only then put myself totally into it. So what I need is some kind of overall plan for this one essential work, my statement, as it were, and map out the various parts by the thickness of the lines and total coverage so as to choose what time and what part of my body to use to fill that in.

There is also the consideration of how to go from one step to the other without smearing something I had already finished. I would categorize myself as being a somewhat hard chalk, not anything like a pastel, more brittle and prone to longer life, but still, any chalk is just a powder once transferred and is easily smeared or washed away. So I must save one hand in order to spray finished areas. I was therefore considering that I may need to put my back into it and do some of the major background areas first and spray them down, and do the outlines over that, being careful not to lay it on too thick, or the outlines would be lost in a sea of similarity. But if I save the trunk portions for the end, I won't be able to spray the final work, and in effect, I'll just be rolling out of control all over what might have been a masterpiece had I mapped out the steps more carefully and not left a randomly sprawling hulk in charge.

All of this is the easy part, for I'm sure I can map out the steps once I have the idea for the project. But what will it be? I need a concept appropriate for the medium, a work that can be achieved using broad strokes, where the effects are achieved more as with shades as in something done in grayscale, and I'll need to practice that. I honestly wonder whether I might make a number of test lines as with my finger here, an elbow, a knee, my whole side, and sliding on my rear end, and examine the marks in order perhaps to have a sense of some scenes that might be more easily rendered, or more to the point, be brought to life naturally by the shapes I make as I take my life toward its conclusion through the work.

One thing I want to avoid along the way is any consciousness of what I am doing exactly. The point is to lose myself in it in such a way that I will be discovered. The irony is that one is rewarded for surrendering oneself beyond any need for the approbation of others. That point of unconsciousness is actually instrumental in enabling one, or of catalyzing the necessary mindset of delivering what is within, not just in thought, but what is known as the utmost, that sense of being at the edge, a point where the mind is at its peak in terms of actually being alive, something that can be sensed when it is achieved as it leaves a mark, almost like a trail, as one moves along, and it delivers the sense that it was both natural and purposeful even though it knew at the time that it was on its way to an expiration, which means it was a song of life in a way, of joy in the face of the ultimate end. So it was directed not at the self, but in universal terms, at the whole chain of being, which includes everything that has ever lived, including the lowly trilobite, long since extinct, which has also given me an idea.

The thing that struck me to remember that I'd actually found and eaten the trilobite was seeing a cloud in the sky that was shaped like a trilobite. It was a series of cirrus clouds that wind had obviously blown through as it had the appearance of waves in sand, and these waves were its ribs. I watched it as it moved slowly across the sky. Yes, that will be my work. It's all one color. I can get a blue background like the sky. Most of the lines are thick. I can do those with my body, then outline them with my fingers, and it's possible to do this in segments without overlaps and smears. The trilobite is a perfect subject. I was thinking space and glory and universal concepts, but all that has been done, and this is an extraordinary subject that everyone will be able to sink their teeth into. I only wish my canvas could be the sky as it is in my mind, spread out over all time, not covering but revealing all the ages, but I am a man of chalk and can only deal in imitations of a sort though made of me entirely.

Burke's Note

Raymond Burke wanted to tell the story of his life, the first half of it anyway, assuming he would live another forty years, and discharge all the memories to preserve them, which was doubtful. But what were the incidents that dotted his experience but so many disjointed scenes from various previous eras, not unlike what goes through the mind at the onset of middle age? He wanted to tell the truth, but everyone it might hurt was still alive. He used to feel his life had meaning and potential, that telling his story would give his life meaning again, but it seemed just another way of living in the past. As he thought of writing his life story, he was swamped by the flood of memories that washed him on the shore of the island of the sirens where he was being picked to the bones with remorse for what was lost and what was going to be lost.

He realized that no one would find interest in the incidents that engulfed him, and he saw no thread to connect them, no plot to give the story interest. It was only his life story, void of historical merit or charm, and perhaps it was for that reason that he wanted to turn inside out and scream, for promises that were unfulfilled. Despite giving the best part of his youth to hard work, the road ahead looked much harder than the one behind him. It may have been dangerous to look back so as to all but corporeally return to it, but there was something else that beckoned him. What was lost in the here and now, a belief in life, a joy for what was to come, was the essence of his spirit as a boy. He could almost bring that spirit back from his sojourns in his home town daydreams. Almost.

Since he'd become so preoccupied with his own history, knowing how generally uninteresting it was to others, Raymond was making comparisons to the history of the world, to the life of Caesar and Alexander, to

*the upheavals, wars, plagues, great murders, romances, artistic under-
takings, and everything else he could remember though he'd never really
liked history. So it wasn't surprising that he couldn't remember much of
Alexander and how the Alps fit in except that they were crossed and that
elephants had been involved, but as to what that meant to Raymond particularly, he couldn't say. He wasn't questioning why the events had been
recorded. He could rationalize that. It was just an early newspaper headline, the story being that Alexander had top billing for a long time in a
nightclub act a long time ago, and so his name comes up along with varying degrees when someone's doing a retrospective of performances on life's
stage. It was so natural too for Raymond to entertain himself with reviews
of men whose followers carved them into marble for today's museums.*

*He understood the reasons how and why history is recorded, but there
was something missing in it that might touch him the way he recalled his
own life. The way that he'd hit the ball over the fence twenty years before
still had impact. If Raymond was in the right frame of mind, he could even
smell the high school hallways or locker room. The humid air by the
lagoon where he kissed Sally was fragrant again with her breath, the
breeze cooling their wet, clinging skin as their arms unfolded from one kiss
into the next. Raymond wondered what would become of those realities.
They would die within him unless he could give them life, and since the
past was becoming the only thing that had anything of promise and fulfillment, he wanted to carve it into a form that others would say surpassed
the likenesses of Alexander, make people remember those details because
Raymond's present was as dull as cleaning up after elephants lumbering
through mountains toward some conquest soon to be long forgotten.*

*While Raymond went back and forth on excursions to the there and
then, the here and now was rapidly losing its hold on him. He wasn't
motivated enough by the fact that the present moment of the past may
exude riches later. He needed the now to have the same meaning and
power, and whatever meaning it had was obscured in light of the past
being preferable, more valuable. Raymond wanted to preserve what had
been real but whose reality was now only within him. But how?*

*The feeling was strong, but it did not blind him from recognizing that
it wouldn't be very interesting for anyone else. It was enough that his
whole spirit called on him to do something, anything, to extract the whole*

world living only in him in such a way that it was out of him entirely into a new form, that it might be digested and live again in anyone at any time, long after he was gone. Though it was an act of preservation, it wasn't the same as a selfish wish to live forever. Even he recognized when he scanned the world within him that he was just a minor character. A strip of litmus showed him his true color was right in the middle, average, within normal parameters. But there was another, immeasurable, unsearchable aspect that frowned on knowing that. If he could extract something of himself into a new form, it would need to be like cream that rises to the top, and the success of the extraction would be enough to cauterize the wounds of being a nobody. That would be the fall-away husk.

The world that Raymond would save would contain the best of him, but vestiges of Raymond himself might be visible as when the cameraman is visible in the mirror. But imperfections stemming from Raymond's being the one to tell the story would be acceptable as glare seen when a camera lens is directed at the sun. Raymond felt that for the most part he'd be out of the picture, but at the center because his life's essence was being captured. It would happen as a planet takes shape around a sun, the light source being the universal memory of shared experience. He would only be studied himself finally in light of others whose lives were shaping up in orbit around a source of light, and he would be that source for some. They would say their inner lives made sense. It was pleasant to know that this essence was there within him, but it made him all the more painfully aware of how little actually revolved around him in his life. If anything, Raymond's attempt to make sense of the past would help others deal with why he was revolving around himself. They would see how it was necessary not to help him cope because it was killing him either way.

Whenever Raymond spent time looking directly at himself in the light of the past, he was merciless on returning due to having to deal with so many imperfections even if they were normal at his age. He was chewing away at himself like acids in an empty stomach, while others his age seemed to be enjoying their lives. He felt that he was alone in a crisis of a meaningless present dwarfed by a past full of wonder.

But until he got it out, scenes from the past continued to cascade over him like drops from a faucet in torture. There were many times he wished he could make it stop, and so in a way that is opposite to telling a story in order to preserve it because it is loved, there was a sense in which Raymond Burke wanted to tell his story to get it out once and for all, to be rid of it like an odious malignancy. Meanwhile, the present provided its own constant pains. Each new day called for its resolve to get through it, but being sick of his life, and tired of living in the past, he needed to do something once and for all. The memory of skating or sleeping under the stars or hunting for snakes relaxed his anger against society's elephants that flatten the day-to-day Alps of promise, but the same feet of those elephants stomped on him every day, and the command was to clean up after them.

Raymond grew tired of puffing up the vistas, of crawling into them like a suit in the hope that he'd reabsorb a lost essence that once made him believe in life. Even the hope of relating the tale of having found it again, the dream of offering it as a gift that would mean everything to everyone, was waning. Yearning for fullness from the fountain in the world left him empty, just as it always had, but surveying the past to quench his thirst only brought him back in the desert of the present. But again, he had found a source in himself that would deliver itself continually and whatever happened, would never run dry. But he had to act.

And now it is up to the world to determine whether the fruits of Raymond Burke's search through his life have any value. Obviously, no one gives a damn about cards dealt, hands played or cheating. Winning's what counts. Cry babies don't belong in the game. All losers want their stories told. But it's no longer possible to leave the life of Raymond Burke to the oblivion from which it springs, for he has created a new well. Look within it, and you'll see yourself. Dive in, and you'll find yourself.

Having finished his suicide note, Raymond quickly hung himself. What he didn't write was he was angry at his wife. He'd gotten fired six months before and still had no prospects. She'd told him as she left for work to get out of bed and look for a job, or she would divorce him. He was going to do that, but then he had a moment of lucidity, a succulent, almost sticky sense of the inevitability of death, a grasp of reality he would normally have shaken off for having things to do, promises to keep. But the vortex seemed to present an opportunity to complete himself, and so he started the note, which went so well that he fell right into the rope without a second thought.

Next, Please

There comes a time for turning the page after a difficult time, but sometimes the page itself seems too heavy to lift or has hardened almost into permanent flooring, much like the bricks along the Appian way, still serving their original purpose a couple of thousand years after they were set in place. I have been waiting for a new chapter to begin for quite some time without success. Even after a vacation, there is direct linkage and continuity to the old days, not any kind of new beginning, but it must come at some point. It must! If it doesn't, well, it just means the end of the world.

The basic problem is that the world is coming to an end, and as long as that is the case, there is no turning the page since this is the last page in the story. It is just a couple of paragraphs from now that the words come to a dead stop, followed by "The End." Of course, that is just a metaphor, but everyone seems to know the end is coming, and the whole world seems resigned to it. Each person feels unable to do anything about it as larger forces continue unabated that are causing the end to come. These forces, it turns out, are made up of thousands of people, individuals who know they are part of causing the end, each feeling impotent to do anything to stop it. In short, the whole world believes itself impotent to do anything, and so it is business as usual. If you really want a metaphor, think of the planet as the body of an ostrich where the head is buried in itself, unable to look at how it is suffocating itself in itself. How sad!

It's easy to see how it's impossible for the world to come together on matters of religion and politics, but the issues that are bringing the end to the world are extant from either of those. We could make

100

a list of the things we absolutely need to do in order to save the planet, things that everyone knows we can do, but we cannot even make a list for some reason. It is as if our hands were tied. We all can agree, but for some reason we cannot find a way to reach ourselves all at the same time to initiate anything along the lines of a stoppage or cessation of activities that are leading us to destruction.

Strange, but the best we can muster is a kind of artistic statement, an expression in a form that can be installed in a town square or make the news, putting everyone in mind of the obvious fact for a moment as they walk or ride the train to work. There is way too much garbage, so a work of art made of garbage, perhaps aluminum cans, might be interesting. The air is polluted in many cities, so perhaps a meter with a needle twenty stories high to relate the degree of smog, the worst being when you cannot see the needle, and at the base, a passageway of clean air long enough to clear the nostrils so that the city smells are apparent on the other side.

All of this is fine and serves a purpose, but it really isn't motivating anyone to do anything. It is more like intellectual enterainment or a serious joke, the kind one makes when one knows he is dying but still has all his wits about him and a good sense of humor. Yes, it is interesting that there is so much garbage and dirty air. Thanks for the permanent reminder. But wouldn't it make more sense to just make the statement that the end of the world is at hand, or at least prepare a work that goes further than merely reminding us of problems without solving anything, perhaps something to scare us?

What I envision is a monument that visitors from another planet will discover when they arrive and find no human beings left, something that will welcome them to a world still full of much life that will accept their presence fully, which we could never have done. The monument would make it clear that the visitors should be grateful that we are gone since we would never have welcomed them. Rather, we would have tried by our very nature to destroy them, the very same tendency of suspicion and distrust that we relied on to destroy ourselves. The only way we could welcome them would be to be gone because we were a problem to ourselves, so much that we couldn't even tolerate ourselves, and we would rather force everyone to be like us even when they already were virtually identical. At bottom, the differences between us were superficial, but they were so ingrained and internalized, and we were so limited that we could not abide in the end by anyone thinking along different lines than we did, nor can they tolerate us. Meanwhile, as we fought, the things we could change went too far to fix.

All I can do is wander in my thoughts. I see the whole world as not being surrounded by space, but under a canopy that is many thousands of feet high. At the very top of this tent there is a falcon on patrol. It is flying so high that it isn't visible to the naked eye. No one even bothers to search for it with binoculars. They merely trust that it is there. All day long while we go about our business, worrying and bustling, arguing and being inordinately silent about our fate, there are birds dropping out of the sky. I see it happen all the time. I am standing on the street at lunch in my suit. I look very nice, and I notice another dead dove slowly twisting as it plummets, already dead. I say it plummets, which suggests a great speed, but at the same time, its descent is slowed by its wings still catching the air, but it is dead all the same. Those who watch and are willing to talk about it say that the dove flew too high, and the falcon nipped it. The bird drops out of sight, and then the feathers follow. I have heard that it is just the bones and feathers that actually hit the ground. The actual meat is in the stomach of the falcon, which is always growing, and always staying out of sight, patrolling ever higher, but still those doves keep going up there and getting nipped, which is to say devoured. They are falling all the time. Soon there will be no doves left. It is somehow in the nature of the bird to seek its own destruction, and the falcon, after all, is a bird of prey.

On the last page of the tale, it is time to choose a new leader. Despite the gravity of the situation, old methods are in use. There is no mention in any of the candidates' speeches of doves falling or the brutal falcon in the air. During the speeches, and especially at the end of each one, people applaud, but I keep saying, "Next, please. It's time we turned the page." But it ends right there with no pages left, just people on worn, ageless tiles under a falcon's shadow with feathers wafting slowly as cinders from a distant fire.

City Job

Ten years into the city job, I finally got the first leaf under my neck. My father predicted it would take at least twenty years of putting up with the daily baloney, but I learn quickly, and anyway, after ten they really couldn't fire me anymore without having an extremely good reason, like catching me dead to rights in some act of municipal treason, but I played within the bureaucratic boundaries like no other. My father got me the job the year he retired, which made it hard for me since nobody would let up on me after he left, saying how I only got the job because of patronage and nepotism. It was true. The superintendent owed my father a favor, but everyone had the same story. We were all there to do the time, and some weren't even there. We took turns punching them in.

When I first saw the leaf, I tucked it under my collar and went to the men's room and pulled open my shirt. It looked like ivy was starting to bud on my chest. I got goosebumps, and they didn't go away. The next day, there were little sprouts on the top of each one. I was thrilled. Pretty soon I was totally covered with leaves. Now I could do anything, go anywhere with absolute impunity.

I learned quickly how to manage the effect of releasing the garden to fullness or retracting it to a corporate state. Whenever there was a visitor, I was just your normal guy in a suit doing his job. But as soon as it was clear, I released the undergrowth and practiced making my way around the office without being seen. It was not as easy as I thought it would be as I don't know how many times I'd pick a spot only to discover someone else with greater seniority already there. I had to learn how to recognize when a spot was taken, and some of these people were so good at camoflage that they were virtually undetectable. Still, in the end, I learned the most important trick of all, which was to be able to blend in and flow almost instantly back to my desk in full retraction so as to appear normal, and I mean I could do it in a millisecond from anywhere in the office. I had discovered that I could hear everything that was going on just by tapping in. It was like once I had blended into the wall, my eyes and ears were everywhere all at once, and no matter where I had settled in, I could pull out at any point, even in my cubicle, soon to become an office. Yes, once I had mastered that, I was one of the elite. Only a few were ever known to have that ability, and I just seemed to be a natural. I learned I could cover more than several floors and do the same thing, even over others who were blending into me without knowing that I was even there. So of course it wasn't long before I was head of a whole department.

My father would have been proud to see how I'd mastered the art, but I believe it just sinks in over time and manifests itself, almost like it's already in the walls, and one accumulates it like doses of radiation that alter the cells, planting new information that allows one to mutate into a new form of corporate entity. There obviously is no book on it. It only comes through experience. My father spoke generally of things along those lines, but I can't say I ever really understood until I bloomed, and once that happened, there was no stopping me. For years I languished under the impression that a city job was a dead end and harbored dreams of doing something more important with my time, but once I had the power, I became locked in, fixed in my element, and I honestly felt more comfortable there than I did at home. Even though retirement is many years away, I dread it like nothing else. So what I do is stand in the tunnels waiting for the trains and let them pass. I linger there and absorb the fumes, the noise and the darkness. I've already made it home several times faster than the trains can get me there, just by becoming the walls. One day I won't so much retire as extend my range. I'll own the whole city, every tunnel and rooftop. I'll be everywhere at once listening to everything. I'll pick all my spots and expand my range, cover the whole world, and nobody will know I'm there.

The Shell

When a man pushes too hard for reasons pertaining to his deepest need to be whole, he sometimes searches for ways to reach his goal more quickly, and sometimes these paths turn out to be quite destructive. In Derrick Langley's case, he found a drug that helped him, but it was addictive, and though for a while it proved to facilitate his need to achieve, bringing him closer to his goal, which in many ways was simply to provide for his family, at some point he started taking a step back each day and his purposes seemed to grow ever more distant. He even began to focus more and more on the drug itself, when to take it for maximum result, how to shake off the hangovers and headaches without taking more of it, and it was then that his family started to notice the changes in him. His temper flared more quickly and to unexpected heights when he was initially asked what was wrong. He declared the subject a dead end to everyone's surprise. Of course, they backed off, but at the same time, they began to watch him.

When they started doing that, he had a dim awareness that he'd gotten off track. He looked at the calendar and realized it had been weeks since he'd actually done anything productive. He knew the drug had taken over, but he was too embarrassed and afraid to admit anything and tell his wife that he needed help. He remembered why he'd started using the drug in the first place, and decided it wasn't the drug's fault, that it was rather his own lazy nature getting the better of the gentle facilitating effects of the drug, and he had to start pushing again.

This is the point at which Derrick began to push too hard. He

105

stayed up later and got less sleep. He grew more silent and bellicose at the same time, retreating from everyone and exploding on every confrontation. Everything anyone said or did was wrong and perceived to be against him. But he was genuinely trying to do his work again, to make his life meaningful and to prove himself. But what he didn't realize was that all these things combined, including the drug, had softened and weakened his shell to the point that he was quite on the verge of popping through, and that's what finally happened one morning when his wife started nagging him after he got out of bed late demanding coffee and breakfast.

Derrick didn't feel anything unusual. Even the level of anger seemed normal to him, and while it wasn't the biggest explosion, all of his outbursts had so weakened him that his inner self actually began not just to protrude but to extrude at various points all over his body. He was wearing pajamas, so the red, puffy, wormy, muscly things were only visible on his face and hands. His wife started screaming. He didn't know what was wrong until she told him to look at his hands. He screamed too when he saw it. He went to a mirror and was horrified by the sight of the fleshy protrusions. He didn't know what it was or what to do. The children rushed in to see what had happened and screamed as well. Derrick's wife put them all in the car and drove him to the hospital, but at a stoplight about a mile from the emergency room, Derrick jumped out of the car and ran into the woods.

He didn't know what was happening to him, and he seemed to know instinctively what he had to do. He remembered the place where he'd transformed into a man some twenty years earlier. It was a hidden place, something never spoken of and hardly remembered. Instinct takes one there at the time of metamorphosis, and immediately afterwards, the entire process is hazy. Derrick didn't know exactly where he was going, but the places seemed familiar. After running several miles, he came to a clearing full of husks the size of men. He passed some young men in a daze leaving the area, freshly emerged from their shells. He looked around, and there were thousands of these shells. Many had fallen and broken. The shards were somewhat large on the surface, but underneath were much smaller and more smooth. Even deeper, the consistency was as fine as sand. Beneath that, there was rock composed of the same material. As he stood there, several boys entered the clearing, took a position and seemed to freeze there. There were some boys still in the shells in the middle of the process, and he saw some young men coming out of their shells. They ran when they saw him.

He trudged around looking for the spot where he'd emerged, fearful that his shell was long gone. Then he remembered he'd chosen a spot almost in a cave, an enclosure with an overhanging rock. He found a familiar crevice, more like an opening, a place he could not squeeze through but through which he was sure he had emerged after he came out of his shell. He picked up some shards and sharpened them on the rock, took off all of his clothes and began to cut off the protrusions from his chest in the hope that it would be enough. He abraded those he couldn't reach by rubbing his back against the rock until they were gone. Finally he expelled all the air from his lungs and tried one more time to squeeze through. He panicked for a moment as he became stuck, and the adrenaline kicked in. He pushed with all his strength just as he was losing consciousness and fell out the other side.

When he woke, he was staring at his old husk, the one he'd left behind when he first became a man. Fortunately, it was intact, nor were there any others in the area. It surprised him that after so many years, so many thousands of transformations, he had chosen a spot that nobody else had ever seen but him. There were no shards anywhere, no sandy bottom. If the husk had even fallen, it would have been smashed. But for the first time, he wondered why he hadn't changed out in the open. Were there other enclosures like this one where other boys equally self-conscious had done so as furtively, as if ashamed of what was happening? He didn't know much about the process, and he realized the entire clearing was so far out of the way and the experience so hazy that it never mattered, and he shouldn't be thinking too deeply about it now. He needed to lose himself in a new process, a kind of reversal, in order to undo what happened.

Slipping his arm into the old husk he realized that he wouldn't fit. The protrusions made him too large for the old shell, and so he had to start cutting them off one by one. This was a painful process that also made him realize that everything he was removing had become a part of him since he had transformed into a man. He was still generally the same size and stature except for what he needed to remove, but he was sorry to do it for having acquired it slowly over time. He wondered how much of it made him who he was. Soon the floor of the little cave was covered with little shards of himself, all the wormy, fleshy extrusions he had cut off. The first ones already seemed to be shriveling. As he cut of the last one, his mottled shell came off, and he eased himself into the older one of his youth. The process itself put him into a kind of trance so he did not know exactly what he was doing or how he was doing it, but like finding his way through the woods, it all seemed familiar.

A few hours later, Derrick found himself on the side of the road where he jumped from the car. He started walking home, and it was not long before he got there, only it was the house where he'd grown up, and both of his parents were dead. There was another family living there. They recognized him and told him where he lived. He walked there and knocked. His wife answered and started yelling at him for making her worry, but she could see he wasn't really listening. Also, examining him, she saw that he was intact. She asked what happened, where he went, but he did not remember anything. He didn't seem any worse for the wear, and seeing him again removed much of the anxiety, so she let it go. She made dinner, and he went to bed early.

In the weeks that followed, there was something different about him that put distance between them. Within a year, she had packed her bags and left. She took the kids with her. He never resumed his work, never forced himself to do anything due to a strange inner sense that he might hurt himself, that he was too fragile, and it would be the end of him if he did so. It was as if he believed there was no room for him to expand in any way, so he never grew after that. He spent all of his time passing his time without any consideration that life was a thing to be taken seriously, that it matters what one does and how one performs and how important it is to push as hard as one can, risking everything in order to succeed.

Janus

When Bojan Usnik came over to play ball, he was moderately sensational for the first few years of his contract, and because he was a gritty player who scored and never backed down from a good fight, the fans loved him, but I always thought he was two faced. They even called him Janus, combining the last part of his first name and the first part of his last name, but nobody excpt me ever connected that to the mythical representation. He ended up playing for many year, then retired into private life for a while, which is when I got to see how he really was.

When I was old enough to drive and attend games, he was still in his prime, maybe just starting to fade. What surprised me was how the fans fawned over him, even buying his food in the stands. That's right. Not only was his making money from his contract. He was milking the fans by selling bad, cheap food at your typical arena-inflated prices. I never bought anything that I knew he had anything to do with. I remember also that he never liked signing autographs. He also didn't much like giving interviews after he was the star of the game. He'd say the usual drivel about trying hard to get the win and walk off to the showers. Out in the parking lot where the fans were waiting, he'd just drive away without waving.

Then came his retirement. I used to drive by his house. Word was you weren't even to slow down or look his way when driving by his house because he totally wanted his privacy. All the residents of our village knew about it anyway, and I could understand that part of it somewhat, given the fact that some folks couldn't help honking and waving once they knew where he lived, and being such big fans they might drive all the way from the other side of the city just to say they saw him in his yard. Whenever I would say he was a mean guy the way he treated the fans, people would just say he was hard-nosed on the field, and hard-nosed about his privacy, and he was just being Janus. What got me was they didn't catch the double meaning.

Well, Janus had health problems after he left the game, and locally the newspapers were always talking about his being hospitalized for this or that. He really had the sports media's sympathy in those days, but what I remember was the huge signs he put up just outside the arena advertising his new lines of shoes and other things. Still, the fans seemed to love it, and they even sold his products in the arena, though thankfully he had gotten out of the fast food business.

Then there was word that he was falling apart. It became big news very fast. He started losing his fingers at first, then a whole arm. Some of the fans thought it was related to how hard he played, and they gave him lots of credit for that. Then it was revealed that he'd had a disease since he was a kid and played through it under careful medical supervision. Once again, his stock rose in the eyes of the fans. He also didn't get to play as long as he'd wanted, and it was due to his condition. This affected his lifetime stats, so when it came time to elect him to the Legion of Legends, he was denied entry for not having played enough games, which many fans found ridiculous because it was not a measure of success when he played and was only institutued after he'd retired, almost as if to keep certain people out. There were many famous stars of yesteryear who were in for playing fewer games, but some said the leagues had expanded to the point that this was a necessary move, and it had been voted in by the board of regents, none of whom had ever themselves played, a point which also agravated the fans greatly.

But what I remember is how Bojan waited by the phone in front of cameras for that call to select him for special abilities, which would allow him entrance despite falling short of other standards. Every year it was the same thing, one or two players might make it, and the local press would show up at his home, and he'd let them in and wait for the call that never came, and he would wave to the fans outside the window, which surprised me for how I knew how much he really hated the fans. Meanwhile he started losing his toes, and a leg. Then he had another operation, and people thought he'd die.

That was when a movie about his life was released. The fans seemed to love it, but to my mind it was just another ploy to get him voted in the next year. He survived the operation, but lost the other foot. About that time, he started showing up at the arena and stopped into the broadcast booth to say hello and stayed the whole game giving his opinions. He started doing it once every six games or so, then started showing up almost every game, and then suddenly he's the assistant announcer. The fans really liked it. But to my mind, he sounded drugged all the time. He was not a good speaker by any means, and I figured that must have been part of the reason he avoided interviews after the games. But here he was again, back in the game at a different level, and when I would listen to the games, I used to keep count of all the mistakes he made, and I tried telling people about them, but nobody cared. They were all just happy he was up in the booth, what was left of him anyway, waving to the fans, and then going back to the microphone and misreading the various plays on the field, mispronouncing names and making a fool out of himself. And at the same time, he continued selling his legacy, talking about the days when he was a player, naming his achievements, letting the main broadcaster give him kudos, reminding the fans where the film of his career was currently playing and saying at least once or twice a game what a shame it was that he hadn't yet made it into the Legion of Legends.

I told everyone I could that he would never make it in as a broadcaster, and every one to the last agreed with me, but they said he wouldn't make it in on that alone, but along with all his other achievements in the game, being a beloved broadcaster on top of everything else might just be enough to get him in. On top of everything else?! I couldn't believe it. All I could see was the food, the shoes, the shooing people away, refusing interviews and autographs, the waiting by the phone, and the movie; and I'm supposed to see the bad broadcasting as a cherry on top? What kind of backwards argument was that, I asked. They said I didn't understand that he was a part of the history of the team, a city hero and a true fan himself.

They all said I didn't know him, and nothing I could say could convince them that I knew him better than anyone else.

Meanwhile, his health was always deteriorating but seemingly never contributing to winning over the votes that counted when it came to giving him special dispensation to enter the Legion. Still, he never let up on reminding everyone who he was, what he had done on the field in his glory years and waving that last arm of his whenever anyone whistled or called to him, or during any breaks in the game. The fans saw him as a true fan of the game, the team, the city, and especially of them, but nobody knew his real motives as I did, how much he despised them and was only using them.

But there's one thing I must say that I appreciated about him, which is that no matter what part of his body had fallen off, he never mentioned it or complained in any way. I was so pleased that he didn't milk that, cry about it, ask for sympathy, or tell everyone how much pain he was in. On the contrary, it was obvious how resilient he was, how happy he was, but then he was probably drugged to the gills, and who knows whether a side effect was to make him appear to be a decent person. Perhaps the drugs even made him think he enjoyed what he was doing and that he liked the fans. Perhaps he even laughed when the process of disintegration began to speed up, when he started losing everything at once, it seemed, and in a matter of no time, he was reduced to a small heap that had to be carried in and set on the table. He could still see out from that though, and express the same dull glee and appreciation, still call out his achievements and do commercials, but I'm not even sure if he was more than a head and an eyebrow in those last days.

There was a tale of a man who did very bad things and went into seclusion for many years. Then the world needed a great man, and they looked and found this hermit reduced to a ball of hair, and he had achieved inner greatness, enough to save the world in his day. But here was an athlete who came at the world overtly for his own aims, and the fans put still him on a throne and carried him as he needed to be carried, and they did it because he once carried the team. I still don't get it. The man is obviously a failure and is being punished by an angry God, and nobody can see it but me.

The Ivy

I told my wife I wanted to retain the yard for the children when we bought the house, and she agreed, but by degrees she slowly took it over with this and that planter, an arbor, a garden and finally a fence that took away the ball field that they had only just begun to use, which took away my dream of pitching to my sons and teaching them the game. She scoffed at the notion, saying there were parks for that, nor would she listen to any reminders of the promises she'd made. She said there was room for a pool, but all that meant was I'd have to keep up with maintaining the clarity of the water, and every year it was a battle against the encroaching green.

The pool was just there to take away my focus from the rest of her efforts to take over the yard, which was only half the plan because she was busily at work as well to make the inside her domain. I'm not quite sure how she managed taking it over, but I only have the one room, my office, to call my own. She calls it a mess, and appeals to me to clean it up, but I've managed to keep her out of it for good reason. Meanwhile, she maintains her vigil in the yard. There are swings dangling from the branches of the tree, but they are decorative, not things that the children can really use. She worries they will kick a ball into her flowers, so there are no balls to be found anywhere in the yard. Every so often when I'm screening bugs out of the pool, I remember my vision of the yard and wonder how it's come so far from that. Then one day I caught her with several ivy plants that she brought home from the store. I nearly exploded when I saw them, and I forbade her the right to plant them anywhere in the yard.

113

I tried to explain my awful experience as a child when ivy over-whelmed us. She didn't understand the story, took it all as hyperbole when I described it as a war, that there were ladders, fire and axes, spraying and several temporary engulfments. I saved my father once when he fell into the ivy and was almost lost for good. I remember greasing myself and going in with a machete. I found him and cut my way out, which began a new zeal for the destruction of ivy. That may have heightened the passion of my description, but there was no exaggeration whatsoever. But my wife yawned and said she would buy some trestles for the ivy to climb and that I should not worry about it. I should have recognized it was just a ruse, but ivy starts out very slowly. It takes time to connect to wood or brick and develop roots and its thick interweave of branches. I thought it would be a simple matter of simply patrolling the yard on occasion and rip the ivy from wherever it had grabbed hold, but the times I went out to do that, it was simply on the trestle, small and inoffen-sive, and I mistook it as another plant, a type of ivy that had no power to affix the hideous suction cups that take hold like small pox and refuse to be ripped down. My wife's green thumb also made it seem a pretty addition, and when we sat on the patio and she would praise the look of the yard, there was a degree to which I would have to agree with her. I was affectively sleeping on duty, and I didn't realize that everything was just ramping up to speed, and once out of first gear, it would all get ahead of me.

Meanwhile inside the house, she was playing the game that the mess was all my fault. Of course, I bought the children lots of toys to play with, and like all children, they do not play with the toys for long. My wife wanted to get rid of all of it, she said, to make room for what things they would acquire in the future, which was a lie because she kept trying to curtail any purchases of new toys since they wouldn't play with toys they already had. Every so often, she would start rearranging an area. When I would say it was unneces-sary to throw anything away, she would go out and buy new storage units. We ended up with storage units all over the house, but I did not notice that she was quietly bagging up a few toys a week and throwing them out and replacing them with knickknacks and all the various items she had collected from yard sales. This all happened in the upper rooms. My domain was downstairs. It was my haven though she called it my dungeon. It was also my blind spot because it was maintained to deceive me. I saw everything there in place, and it lulled me into believing that no changes were taking place.

But things were changing at an alarming pace. I didn't have many things, and as I said, she would often go about cleaning up an area, making it her own, which meant she had to eliminate things that were mine, things she knew I was saving, which she'd started telling me I should throw away years earlier because I wasn't using them. But I would say it was my house, too, and I had the right to save whatever I wanted, and it didn't amount to much.

Then, at some point during a marathon cleaning exercise, she would come into my office in tears. She would act as if she were having some kind of a horrible breakdown. She would cry and say we needed to get rid of things, or she would die. I wondered at the excess of emotion, whether it was hormones, but having seen a slow building up, I would be fooled into thinking it was perhaps a real reaction to something very important to her. For a moment, I could see all reality as fleeting, and so all my things stored in the back rooms were expendable, totally unimportant. So I would promise her I would get rid of them, that her happiness was most important to me. She would thank me and later apologize that she didn't know where all that emotion had come from, letting me justify it for her, and then she would ask where the boxes were that I had promised to throw out. In time, she brought them up herself and asked whether these were among those I had promised to throw out, knowing full well that they were among the very few things I had put away. It was all so little considering the life I had lived. She would put them out on the street, and before the garbage truck came to take them away, someone would have come and taken them because it wasn't junk.

This went on for years until I had very few things left, all of which I staunchly refused to dispose of despite her emotional entreaties. I kept them all in the office and warned her to keep her distance, that it was my last refuge. With all those things there, without any storage units to contain them, the place was a mess, and whenever she stuck her head through the door to ask me something, she would turn up her nose and exclaim that I was a pig, that the place was horrific, and I would yell at her to get out. Over those same years, my efforts to protect my office made me overlook what was happening everywhere else. It was as if by putting all my protective resources into that one place, I had taken down the guard everywhere else, and so she had made all the upper rooms and the yard her own. When I started taking care of the pool, I battled algae, which always turned the water green by the end of the season. But over time, I had mastered the water, and effectively kept the water completely clear. Again, in the yard, I was kept busy in the center keeping something clear that didn't have anything to do with everything else going on around me. I didn't see that the ivy had taken over and was growing on the fence. I would screen the bugs out the pool, pull out the filter and hang it in the arbor on a pole and spray it with the hose. I even had to push the ivy out of the way, but I didn't notice that the ivy had taken over. In my mind, it was just that nice little plant on the trestle that had just gotten taller. How could I have gotten so carried away, so distracted, to have lost all my natural sensibilities that I'd learned while growing up?

Then she came knocking on my office door one day in midst of one of her emotional outbursts about the office. She said she could not live like that anymore. She collapsed onto her knees and grabbed my legs, weeping miserably on my shoes, begging me to do something about it. That's when I looked around and recognized what I'd been saving for what it really was. Everything I had saved from her and the garbage was actually a defense against the onslaught of overgrowth that had taken over the rest of the house and the yard. Of course she wanted to get rid of it. It was the only thing left that could stand against her, and it was plenty enough to win the battle. I shook her off and asked how she could be so concerned and pathetically emotional given the fact that she never spent any time in the room. I told her to get out and never again say a word about it or I would dismantle the upstairs shelves, throw out all of her knickknacks, spray the yard with herbicide and tear down the fence. She wiped her eyes in disbelief and left, slamming the door behind her. I knew there and then that I'd declared war.

I left the office and went upstairs to try to talk to her, to bring it down from red alert, but I could not find her. I went out to the yard, and that's when I noticed the ivy had taken hold as it had over my father when we did battle and I finally saved him though we lost the house. I went down to my office and found her there bagging things up. "So it is war! Alright then," I shouted grabbing an axe and making my way upstairs to do my own chopping. On the way, it all became clear to my eyes. The whole upstairs was hers, divided and organized with all her things in her personal way of expression. Out in the yard, I started chopping at the ivy, but I was so agitated I let myself get too deep within the branching to notice the ivy had me and was constraining my ability to effectively swing the axe. I tried to get out, but the vines held me back. That's when I noticed the pipes protruding all along the periphery, and I realized the pool was merely the source of water diverted for the sake of the ivy.

And now I am lost, and I know she has finally won. I can see her through the leaves carrying out the only defense I had, things I had been saving for years. I turn from calling her to help me to swearing at her, but she ignores me either way. There is nobody here to help me as I did my father. The children are all away at summer camp. I fought it. I said I wanted them home, but she said there was nowhere they could play, and she didn't want them tearing up the garden. I should have wondered then why it was so important that I keep the hose in the pool. I should have wondered at the size of the water bill, but she took care of all that. I realize now that I was just being used from the very beginning. When I met her, it had been so many years since my fight with the ivy that I'd forgotten its true force and the importance of staying vigilant. If I was ever going to have had a handle on it, it would have been to keep the yard from becoming hers, but I let it go, and I am to blame for falling asleep.

I stare out of vines knowing this will be my last look at the world. This is the nightmare view I never thought I would see. I swore I would not follow in my father's footsteps, yet here I am, an even greater fool though I never thought of him that way before. I can see my wife through the leaves. She's doing something with the pool, shutting off the water that runs to the ivy, for what purpose I cannot tell. Then I begin to feel it. Having lost its source, the ravenous plant turns its attention to me. I can feel it begin to drain me. Soon I will be a part of the entire perimeter. Perhaps I will electrify the ivy and protect my family, turn my back on the outside world and attend to them with every fibre of my being the perfect husband, charging an otherwise wild nature with a loving, superior human element of red blood racing through photosynthetic veins, alert to all danger day and night. Or perhaps my wife was sending me a message that the pipes are now clear to the pool. I try to wiggle my toe toward the closest opening. I can feel her waiting for me to pop up in the middle of the clear water and take me in her arms again, glad that I have returned into the fold. Evidently, I am becoming delerious. I must maintain clarity as I scribble out these last words.

I cannot even hope that anyone will find this desperate note I write since I am inside the fence and cannot fold it into a plane. To her, it will look like a ball has found its way into the yard, and she will dispose of it. How can I ever hope that it will blow out anyway to be seen by other eyes than hers? In one last realization of the futility of it all, I crumple it in my fist and flick it out of the ivy. I relax my hand, but I can no longer move it. The ivy has covered me all in stillness now, holds me and my bones immobile, even compensating for the bulge I once made. All is in smoothness now. The whole length of fence flows in a fine, uniformity of green.

Transphobia

I always thought of Judge Balenz as nothing more than a woman whose only power was that of great bluster, and that she used it to hoodwink people into thinking she had some kind of edge over them, that she was smarter, or had more courage, or was worthy of being a judge, a position for which I never once thought she was fit, since I had seen her up close a thousand times while growing up as a neighbor and playing with her son. I found her to be a skittish, self-absorbed frail little thing who cried when she didn't get her way. I knew her long before she had any political ambitions and always wondered where it came from, and then I figured out that she knew people and eventually got appointed to a position. As she gained in stature and respect in the community, she also got full of herself. I remember she'd always been rather abstemious, never eating much, probably because she was so nervous all the time, but once she had a little power, she took hold of it and began to relish in life's buffet. She grew fat and pompous by the time her son and I were in high school, and that's the thing Nick picked up on. He became an arrogant snob himself and began to use his mother as a ladder. He ended up going to an ivy league school and marrying a nice girl who was much too good for him. He moved to the east coast where her family was prominent and took a job in her father's firm. But he'd bring her home at Christmas, and that's when I met her. She took a shine to me, and one thing led to another. He found out about it after about seven years, and then she divorced him. They had no children. She never took up with me after that. I may have been her type, but I had no connections.

What I'd done to Nick was just the last straw as I'd taken just about every girl he ever had away from him. He was somehow braver about approaching pretty girls, but I would take the fish off the hook so to speak. I knew he carried a lot of resentment about that over the years, and after his divorce we just stopped speaking. I didn't see him for twenty years. His mother prospered in her career. I'd see her on television quite a bit, advocating this or that cause or speaking on behalf of this or that candidate. She was very political and filled with that familiar bluster that everyone thought was just a natural gift of spirit, but I knew that underneath it all she was once a frail little thing who cried when she couldn't get her way.

I used to hear about Nick through the grapevine, and one day friends started asking if I'd heard how sick he was. They said he had cancer. It was a shock to me, but there was no way I was going to contact him at that point, even if he was going to die. Then it just so happened that I was walking past the courthouse just as Judge Balenz happened to be coming down the elaborate marble staircase in her robe, plump and regal, gesticulating with great affectation as she spoke to several men in suits following her. Then she noticed me and pointed as if to freeze me in my steps. She reached the street, said a few words to the men who then dispersed laughing nervously. She turned to me and began speaking like one of my elementary school teachers, like she was my boss, full of that bluster that did not suit her. She spoke about her son, betraying no emotion, laying it all in my lap, telling me that I had always been his friend, that he needed a friend at this awful time, that I could make a huge difference, and that I should go to see him. Then she added something with an extra dose of bluster as if she wouldn't have been able to push it out unless she had lost all perspective that one gains from being equal to others. She said that at the very least I owed him that after all the things I had done to him. I answered simply that while I was sorry for Nick, I was not on trial, and it was not her place to say such a thing. She fumed at that, like she didn't ever remember what it was like to reflect on a comment and maybe offer an apology.

She warned me that a day might come when I'd come before her like so many others, and I should worry if I didn't take her advice seriously. She said I was thin-skinned and what she said would sink in quickly even if I acted like it bounced off, and she warned me not to forget to whom I was speaking. I wanted to insult her for wearing her robe around while other judges left theirs in chambers when they went to lunch, but I fell back on my mother's teaching that I should respect my elders at all times, and so I said I would try to make some time to visit Nick.

She didn't saying anything, just glared even harder at me, and then she turned and walked away. Then I remembered I didn't know what hospital he was in, so I called out her name. "Joyce! Joyce!" She must not have heard me in the sounds of the traffic, and as she was getting further away rather quickly, I yelled "Joyce" a few more times at the very top of my lungs. I could tell she had heard me, but there was something in the way she reacted, the way her shoulders moved, that told me she was shuddering, and before she'd even turned far enough around to where I could see her face, I knew it was about my having called her by name in public like that, in front of all those people, when she was all about the position, the respect, and there I was, to her just another little man, but even smaller as I was just that kid who lived next door who was always over getting popsicles and using her swings in the yard and sometimes throwing sand her in son's eyes and running off while he cried for her.

When I did see her face, it had already contorted beyond recognition. I knew instinctively by the way she stood there that this was not a good situation. It was almost like a boiler was about to blow. She was changing somehow. Her face was starting to wrinkle in a strangely symmetrical manner, beading up. Lines of demarcation were forming. I felt like I could hear something. It was almost like a humming. It wasn't from the street, but from her. I sometimes feel in moments of fear that I can hear the sound of my own blood in my ears, and if that were there, it was combining with what I heard from her, and already I was starting to back peddle, slowly at first, then faster. Then I saw what looked like she was expanding. It happened quickly, but I saw it in slow motion. She suddenly burst open. Her robe fell to the ground. She became a great swarm of hornets, every one of them homing in on me. I was already at a full sprint. I may have looked back once to see in a split second how it took off after me, or maybe I imagined it, but I knew I had little time before it caught up to me. I got inside a building across the street and thought I'd beaten it. I watched as the swarm covered the windows, and then I felt the sting from one that must have gotten in with me. I slapped it, but it was too late. The hornets swarmed there for a few minutes, then flew off back to the robe where the judge rose again and composed herself. She waved to several admirers, shook a few hands, then started walking again, off to some high priced lunch where only the right people are allowed.

I could feel my neck was swollen, but I realized how much worse it could have been. I decided I'd better see Nick as soon as possible, so I went home to start calling the various hospitals to find him, and I hit it on the first one, which was the most obvious choice as it was close to where he lived. I went up to his room directly. He was sitting up in bed reading some philosophy book about dying well. He grimaced when he saw me, closed the book and asked what I was doing there. "I bumped into you mother, and she told me in no uncertain terms to come over here and see you like I owed you or something." I was never one to mince words, and I realized how much animosity I still held against him. Back when we started college, before he was married, he used to come home on vacations, each time more affected, each time just that much more superior to me and letting me know it. By the end of his four years becoming better than everyone else, I was primed to screw him any way I could, and I realized standing there looking at him that this was why I moved in on his wife, winked at her, spoke to her at parties with a certain subtle musical inflection that was calling to her, inviting her to smile first, and come after me later.

I could also detect that Nick's demise seemed totally tied to her, that he had truly loved her, and I felt the little boy was still in him despite having acquired the finishing school veneer, that there was more of the sandbox in him than the exclusive college club. I wondered if perhaps he put it on for them and only brought it home out of habit. It's not uncommon at that time of life to separate out of blindness. As the river takes us in different directions, we do not have the ability to honestly understand how we are all changing. We take the changes too much to heart without reflecting how much we have changed as well. We hastily close chapters in life that would otherwise be continuous and connect with the present. I realized that Nick and I were still just children even then. At least I knew how immature I was, but I didn't like thinking about it. I wanted to move on. It was too late to make amends anyway. Too much damage had been done.

I asked him whether the philosophy book was helping him beat his fear of death. He said it was a dead-end subject, and he laughed. I told him I was not afraid of death and because of my studies in Transphobia could even bear the fears of others if they would let me take them on. He said he'd heard of it but didn't know much about it. I explained that if he would relax and let me take his hand that his fears would pass into me, where I would expunge them. So I took his hand and told him to relax, to let his fears out, but I felt anger coming through him into me, and of all things the anger of others against me was my greatest fear. I felt my chest surge. I saw he was looking at me like his mother but without the same definition. His wrinkles were growing smooth, but his grip on my hand was growing more tight. I tried to shake loose. He would not let go. "So you think you can just screw my wife and ruin my life? I see you have been stung," he said. "I can feel my mother in you now."

My chest was heaving. I felt like I might be having a heart attack. Then I heard buzzing, and I felt something crawling under my shirt, then around my collar. Suddenly hornets were flying around the room. Nick began to laugh. In one clean jerk, I broke loose from him before being totally torn apart into a complete swarm. But those hornets that had come out of me began to chase me, but for having missed lunch and having run myself out earlier, I was no match for them, and they caught up to me as I ran out of the hospital, stinging me one after the other. It struck me how they were a part of me, and as they died, something was lost in me, something like the conscience I had never had. Yes, it was like my own conscience had finally found a way out and was chasing me down to administer justice no matter what the cost.

123

Twin Darknesses

Lester Higgins took up painting at a later age than one usually would expects one to do so, quitting his job and leaving his wife in order to be able to devote all of this time and energy into his new career. Neither the job nor marriage was all that satisfying or difficult to leave, so it wasn't as traumatic as heart attack experts would warn. He also changed his residence, but if he were given a physical exam, it would show that all these moves had done him good. Lester never felt better in his life, and he was driven to make all these changes by a vision he had of the artwork he would produce, along with a sense that it would be extremely powerful as well as successful. He was already somewhat familiar with the feeling since he often had ideas for inventions, but they never went anywhere. The difference was that Lester had never studied art nor did anyone ever say that he had any talent, but one night he dreamed that he understood everything about painting and woke with a sense of his mission. He went to the grocery store for the last time and turned in his resignation. Then he called his wife who he knew was having an affair and told her he would not contest the divorce any longer. He felt relieved and contacted a friend who was a real estate agent about getting an apartment in the art district in the city. He moved into a loft two weeks later with plenty of supplies. He had a large savings account and never had any children, so he was able to buy lots of materials to get started. He set up the easel, took an already stretched canvas out of a box and got started right away.

The theme of his first work was a desert landscape with a two-headed dog. Actually, this was the general idea of every painting that Lester planned to paint. One after another, they went on the easel and came off. The landscapes were all very simple and naive. There was very little to say they were not cartoons. He always drew the horizon line in black. Even the sun was usually outlined in black. The landscapes were not ugly, but they were not in any way special. One would know from given elements the kind of landscape one was viewing. His deserts always had a cactus or two, and so on.

The dog with the two heads was drawn in various ways. Sometimes it was sitting. Sometimes it was drinking out of a bowl or a stream. Sometimes it was climbing a mountain or crossing the snow. In one of Lester's favorites, it was swimming in the ocean. The dog with the two heads was Lester's leitmotif, and he painted it again and again. It was always a black dog, a labrador. He used some gray in order to show its eyes and mouth. The teeth were always very white, and there wasn't much to say that the two heads were in any way opposed. If one looked happy, so did the other. If one seemed in any way angry, so was the other. He generally painted the two heads in identical fashion, more as mirror images, than to depict them in any way as having any duality. He also had a name for the lifetime series of paintings. He called it "Twin Darknesses."

Around the time he was nearing completion of his hundredth painting, Lester received an order of a hundred frames, all the same. It took him a while to frame them all, but after he'd done seven or eight, he'd memorized the system and went through them rather mindlessly. He also took pictures of a few of them, mocked up several posters on his computer and took them to a printer who perfected them to Lester's satisfaction and then printed several hundred of each. Lester also left him pictures of all the paintings and a text file of descriptions and prices for a catalog he wanted printed.

Lester took them around the city and posted them wherever he could, and then he went about making his loft look like an art gallery. In a week, he had gotten all the paintings hung up the way he wanted. Several boxes of catalogs arrived several days before the opening. He hired a catering company to bring wine and cheese on the night of the opening, and then he just sat back and held his breath for the miracle he knew would follow. Then, just as he dreamed, on the night of his opening, the crowd streamed into his gallery to view his first batch of the Twin Darknesses series.

There are mysteries in the universe for which laws to explain them will probably never be isolated, but even without such laws, the mysteries often show themselves in ridiculous ways. Many scientists assert that everything is finite, that everything will be destroyed when the universe ultimately collapses on itself. They say that the sun will go supernova and destroy the earth long before that. Some say we will destroy ourselves long before that happens, but they add that everyone on the planet will be dead of other causes before that, so everyone goes about as if there's plenty of time.

As they go about doing various things like attending art openings, people like to use words like "eternal" and "truth." Each individual seems to think his own ideas and reactions are more on point than others. Nobody can explain the mystery of why certain forms of art have become parodies of themselves. Nobody knows exactly why it happens that some people proffer their silly views without ever considering how they measure against the history of ideas. Everyone knows why the very idea of a gallery opening is so appealing more for the wine and cheese and the mingling that goes on, but nobody can explain why so many artists are so tedious, or why there are far fewer famous artists in all of time than people who believe in their great genius who attend a given opening on a given night.

Lester's opening was a great success in terms of the wine and cheese, but it was not attended by the respected downtown gallery community. The loft he rented was smack in the middle of a starving artist community, and when they heard about this opening, it didn't matter who the artist was or whether the work had any merit. It was a chance for them to eat and get drunk.

So by the third hour or so, the party was in full swing, and some of the guests were getting a bit out of hand. There was one who introduced himself to Lester as Henry Matisse just to prove to his friends that Lester had never heard of him, even though Matisse displayed a love of black outlines in many of his paintings. He was right that Lester did not recognize the name, and then the small group of students discussed the question of whether something can have merit when it is done independent of another's work, even many years later. They left when one of them became sick.

Lester overheard many unkind comments about the two-headed dog in every painting, but he'd anticipated that and understood how young people would make fun of it. He also realized that none of the experts and reviewers had shown up, and he was disappointed not to get an expert opinion or even have a chance to read a review in the morning. He reasoned his opening had been too far off the beaten track and resolved to have the next one in the gallery zone.

As he was pondering this, a woman sauntered over running her finger over the rim of her wine glass and asked Lester if he knew about the collection of physical abnormalities in the *Peter the Great Museum of Anthropology and Ethnology* in St. Petersburg, Russia. A massive wave of interest in the perfection of physical beauties manifesting themselves in this woman hit Lester hard, and his voice cracked when he said that no, he hadn't. He cleared his throat and took a sip of wine. She told him how the dogs reminded her of that and suggested he continue with the theme but explore different treatments. The exact phrase she used was "expand on it." Then she sauntered away nibbling on a cracker. Lester looked at her up and down. He only took his eyes off of her for a minute to speak to the caterer, and when he looked up, she was gone. He searched the loft high and low, but she had evidently departed. After that, he was so completely absorbed in the thought of her that no matter what he was doing for the rest of the evening, it was like she was standing there holding a cracker to his lips for him to nibble on.

The next day, all Lester could think about was how to find her again. He went out to breakfast and asked some of the students who had attending his opening, but nobody knew her. After a week of failing to establish any lead, he resolved to take her advice and hope she would attend his next opening, so he expanded on the theme. This time around, his works were much more inventive. One of them was a landscape painting, but he sculpted the two headed dog made from the neck up out of plaster of Paris and placed it so that it protruded drooling from the landscape into two large bowls on the floor below. The idea was that it would keep two water bowls filled for pets. He also did many paintings in reverse, meaning that he filled the canvas with the image of the two-headed dog, then painting landscapes as if reflecting on the fur. In the last weeks before his second opening, he did other kinds of paintings and only signed the paintings using the two headed dog as a signature in the lower right corner of the canvas. In another, he did a cityscape, but the new moon was a black dog with two heads curled up into a circle like the animals in bottles in the museum in St. Petersburg. He had searched the internet and learned a great many things about the exhibit, thanks to the mystery woman, and it opened his mind not just to many possibilities but to what he was trying to say, which had never mattered before since the vision of the works only gave him a mission without an explanation. Now he was thinking about the permutations of his work, exploring the variations, which validated the vision, but there was an emerging degree to which it meant nothing if he could not know who she was, and it was beginning to expand.

He realized this even more on the night of the second opening when she did not appear. Many of the right people did, however, and he received some interesting reviews, and he was glad he took the advice of the gallery owner who suggested due to limited space that he go with the strength of the newer works and not display any of the paintings from the first show.

The second show was successful, and it was all thanks to the mystery woman, from a single comment she had made. But he was terribly disappointed that she did now make an appearance. He made sure to mention her when he was interviewed by critics during the show, but none of the reviews mentioned her. He moped around the loft for a week letting the dishes pile up before he hit upon an idea that would carry him to the next opening, which was to incorporate a woman into the works in some way as the owner of the two-headed dog. He also started placing messages in the personal section of the newspaper in the hope that she would read it and come forward.

During this next period, he felt that art was the only thing keeping him from deep depression. He threw himself into the work and thought he was able to forget her, but the works themselves were all about her. One of the more powerful ones had a stunning canvas of a landscape of a dark street at night. Protruding from the canvas was the shoulder and side of a woman wearing the dress as he remembered it. Her profile was painted, and the sculpted part stopped at her waist. The arm of the figure extended fulling from the shoulder, and in the hand was a leash. On the floor five feet to the left of the painting was a statue of a two-headed dog tied to the leash as if out for a walk. In the woman's other hand was a wine glass.

But as the months wore on in this phase, Lester grew increasingly obsessed with the woman. He began to lose sight of the clarity and objectivity of the two-headed dog as the predominant symbol. The woman began to take over. In one work, the woman is seated on a veranda, as always with her signature dress and wine glass, but there was no leash or sign of any pet. The clouds were paw prints, however, which Lester brushed in as depicting the continuing presence of the dog, but more in an overriding spiritual sense. In another painting, the skies had turned dark, the paw prints ominous, and there was dog poop falling everywhere, piling up on the streets and alleys. But the lights were on in one window in a high rise, and the woman was clearly visible in her dress drinking a glass of wine.

In the last weeks of this phase, Lester began to add messages to the paintings. "Where are you?" he painted on one. On another were the words, "This is not a woman with a wine glass, but it looks like her. Where is she?" He also did a self portrait with a dog's head on each of his shoulders with his own head in the middle. Scratched in his forehead, dripping with blood, were the words, "Where are you?" The dogs tongues are lapping at the blood.

The gallery owner expressed some concern as to the meaning of the works and asked Lester whether he was trying to use art as a means to find a real person. Lester had learned much about "artspeak" in the years since he started painting, and he answered that of course he wasn't literally trying to contact a real person. He explained that the paintings were an expression of the longing within existence for something that cannot be obtained, that while we live in an environment of falling feces, somewhere there is a pristine creature who receives all our love though we cannot reach her, and though she is alone, she is also complete within the context of the art, but only given that longing, just as ugly wires cross the landscape are only allowed to remain due to the messages going back and forth. In the paintings, the only thing that mattered was that she was there. As long as she was in the paintings, it didn't matter whether or not she received the message or sent one back. Her presence meant that life was worth living despite the ugliness and pain.

Again, Lester's show was a success, but the mystery woman did not make an appearance. Someone asked Lester why the dogs had disappeared, and Lester said they hadn't so much disappeared as they had taken up the brush, that they were on the other side of the painting rather than within it, that this was the curse of art, that one begins with an idea that may be in some way disturbing, but it is presented in a pleasant setting, and everyone has a good laugh about it. But then the image gets into the blood. What's disturbing is felt, and one grows increasingly aware of it, and then tries to make sense of the world, paints in order to find peace. But there is no peace. And so in the end one looks for beauty, which is real, even if temporary, and you, the painter, are her dog with two heads, the twin darknesses. One head is the darkness of the world, the other is the darkness of the self, and beauty is the only light, the one thing that keeps the dog alive. It never lived before it saw that light. Before then, it was a blind beast, and even though it knows it is a dog, and the whole world is a kennel, beauty makes life worthwhile.

The man bought one of the paintings for fifty-thousand dollars. Lester had arrived on the art scene. He was able to start selling his original batch of landscapes for a pretty penny as well, but he didn't understand any of it. He had gone off track. He had changed, and he felt all he learned was there was a great new kind of emptiness that he would have never known if he hadn't become a painter. Now everything make sense to him. Art was his reason for living, but he wouldn't go so far as to say it was for everyone. He wouldn't trade it for anything, but he wouldn't recommend it because he envisioned a monster that taught him about beauty, then traded his soul to become that monster in order to keep beauty in sight, but however close, it was always just out of reach, a necessary arrangement of dark separation for both artist and master.

Night of the Frogs

Stepping outside tonight, I felt a strange crunch under my shoe. I could even hear it. I looked down, and there were beetles everywhere. I don't mean little ones running around, nor the clumsy flying June or potato bugs. I'd never seen these before, and they were quite big, and they were everywhere, all over the driveway, sidewalks and in the street. It looked like an insect emergence, infestation or migration of some kind.

I rolled the windows down as I started the car. I turned the radio off so I could listen as I backed the car into the street. The tires went over the beetles, which popped with a loud crunching. I drove down the street slowly, watching the beetles, listening to the crunching. They seemed to be amassing quickly, covering more ground. I reached the corner and tried to brake before making a left turn, but the car kept going. I thought it was sliding on the beetles, but the crunching had stopped. Then the steering locked. I tried spinning the wheels, but all at once the engine went dead. Obviously they had crawled beneath the undercarriage. I could see they were covering the hood of the car and crawling up the windshield. I looked out and could see they were starting to cover everything completely. The street grew darker as they blocked light in the windows of the houses. They were all over the light poles covering those lamps as well. I could still see the moon through the window, but it was just a sliver. All I could do was sit and wait for whatever would come next. They were carrying the car. I could feel it moving.

They had to have been unified in some way as army ants, but I'd never heard of such of thing with beetles. I did have an experience many years earlier with frogs. I had been on the highway at night in a storm. A bridge was out, and I had to take a detour. I quickly got lost in back roads along a stream. That's when I saw the frogs. There were literally tens of thousands of them, and I couldn't help running over them as I drove along. I rolled down the window and could hear them squishing. The rain had stopped, and the road was black and shiny. I had always thought it was due to the fact it was wet, but now I realized I was riding on a bed of beetles. I had been lost a good hour before I happened on the frogs, but once I started running over them, it was only a few minutes before I found my way back on the road. Looking back, I was so absorbed in pity for killing frogs that I wasn't watching where I was going. I must have thought I was making turns, but I was actually being directed by the frogs. As I was tying to find a path away from them, they were actually assembling on the backs of the beetles to help me find my way out of the woods.

What that meant, of course, was that the beetles had finally come for me. I always felt the day must come, and here it was. It was about a mile from the river, and that's the direction they were taking me. They covered the car, but they do not fit like puzzle pieces, so I could see enough between them to know where I was. Even though they effectively reduced the light to extremely low levels, I had lived in the area all my life, and I knew exactly where I was and how much time I had. I was frightened of what was to come, but there was an eerie beauty about the way they covered everything. I don't believe they were actually carrying me along by walking. I was going too fast for that. I believe they were undulating me there. Linked together, they were pulsating so as to carry me along like sliding a passenger down a sheet out of an airplane, raising and lowering their bodies in a pattern that directed me toward my ultimate end in the river. I considered all things to avoid it. I didn't want to die, but I knew it was my time. I made peace with myself and accepted it.

I could see the river was close from the approaching green. The frogs had formed a welcome mat to take me home. As the vehicle reached the transition point, I could feel the familiar squishiness again that I remembered from running them over, and I felt elated as they slid me the rest of the way on their slippery backs.

Public Faith

Having decided to make no attempt to increase my parcel of years on earth beyond what was allotted to me, I make no apologies for the decisions I made that isolated me and put me at risk. This did not stop me from insisting that my children visit the doctors and dentists and follow whatever was deemed necessary for their general benefit, but I had sworn off all medical assistance and made no effort to set any kind of example in that regard. What I gained was a sense that my remaining time was more compact and full of strange wonders. I felt that I was welcomed into a society of ethereal beings that hovered around me and gave me strength through powerful visions, which included seeing myself amongst them in fantastic settings impossible to adequately describe. Having these visions only validated my decision to not follow the ways of the world even though I would not recommend anyone follow my path. If anything, I would strongly advise against it as it takes a specific type of personality with special aims to make such a tradeoff as I have. It is a comfort to realize that fifty years ago, everyone lived like this, so I have only abandoned certain modern modifications to the generally recommended lifestyle, and most of my ancestors lived long and normal lives without fearing consequences that everyone seems to worry about nowadays. In many ways, I feel I have only cast off fear and doubt and am living in ways that man was intended to live and did so successfully for thousands of years. In any case, I do it more out of my sense of religion, out of a strict sense of faith, than for any other reason.

The reason I'm explaining this is that my faith was recently brought into question, not by others but by me, at a recent gathering to which I was invited for religious purposes. Naturally, I assumed that those inviting me knew my positions and contacted me accordingly, but this was a false assumption on my part, and I only learned after I'd already arrived that these were people of an entirely different faith, one in which I am not even mildly versed. I arrived, handed the host the wrapped gift I had purchased for the occasion, and looked around. That's when it began to hit me that my gift was entirely inappropriate under the circumstances.

I went all out and made a contribution of a beautiful gold star, very ornate, and very detailed with various kinds of silver and gold and precious stones, believing they would be very appreciative of it, but I see from the rituals and symbolism at the party that the star is not something they embrace, which is putting it rather mildly. I watch the host put the box on a shelf with the other gifts. I consider taking it immediately, but someone recognizes me and walks over to introduce me to the rest of the party.

I talk with people for a while, then smell some very strange but wondrous aromas emanating from the kitchen. They are the very kinds of smells that I have dreamed when I have dined with the ethereal friends I mentioned earlier. I excuse myself from a conversation and make haste to the kitchen in order to help out with the cooking if I can, dip a spoon into each pot to taste the various dishes and hopefully steal a recipe or two. I find a cookbook on the table, and the hostess happily points me to the appropriate page, which I begin to copy. The smells that fill the kitchen create an atmosphere that is the poetic equivalent on earth of the perfect ether of heaven, and as soon as I start thinking that, my ethereal friends arrive and surround me. I tell them they cannot stay, for they are neither right for the situation or representative of my own beliefs for that matter. I accepted them as a result or benefit of certain decisions I made as a matter of faith, but they are anything but religious in any way. I justified them as acceptable in my life due to the fact that certain aspects of life are allowed even if contrary to all that one holds in faith because the world is a complex place, full of contradictions. One must know what these things are, even in some way embrace them as a part of life, knowing they are still essentially rejected and will ultimately be abandoned when death comes and one becomes resoundingly whole in the next world.

One of the beasts made a comment about the gift I brought, and I tell him to pipe down, but I'm actually grateful as I'd forgotten to take care of the matter. Reading my mind, the entity asks why I don't just let them have it as it is, the logic being that if ultimately it is the right faith, it may have a certain impact in the long run and bring those who see it around to the right way of thinking by its subtle spiritual influence. Another ethereal being suggests that as soon as they see it, they will appreciate its monetary value and simple go about taking steps to alter it so that it will be appropriate for their faith. That idea hits me the hardest because I went to all ends of the earth to acquire it. The star is actually a priceless, one-of-a-kind piece that I cannot allow to be hammered into another shape. Who knows since they hate the star that they might hack it to pieces despite its being made of precious metals embedded with gems.

I realize it is inevitable that this beautiful object will certainly be destroyed, and I start stirring the marvelous vegetables into the stew on the stove, the aromas begin to further clear my mind, and I begin to believe I am reaching a clarity of thought I have never achieved previously. I begin to think I shouldn't have perhaps given it up to anyone, that in a sense doing so was a watering down of my own faith, that a better gift would have been to bring spices that the chef could use to prepare another dish like those in progress, only I did not yet know of the recipe book or that the food would be so fantastic and the center of my attention.

I also realize that I'm just a spice in the mix at the gathering, nothing quite so astonishing as the ethereal beings who have joined me, and nothing that would improve on any of the time tested concoctions which were inspired centuries earlier though coming to fruition at the moment, in their final stage of boil, soon to be served to the general pleasure of the entire company in the dining room. I am rather just a common spice like salt or pepper, but by mixing in with this whole group, and second guessing my approach, being indecisive as to what I should do, and being unwilling to stand up for my own faith, I have completely lost sight of what I should be doing, and in order to know what that is, I must begin again to shed everything and consider who I am, what I've done. It is the only way I know to extricate myself from an overall state of confusion in which I am unable to categorize or assert my faith. Only when there are no categories, only me, can I rebuild my awareness of the truth.

Meanwhile, everyone at the gathering is exchanging favorite proverbs and passages from what they consider to be holy texts, reassuring one another that they share the common discovery of the correct answers for the meaning of life. I feel all kinds of of gravity waves pulling me in various directions, but the actual state of my mind in terms of the choices that I made isn't as easy to disseminate when I consider the other people floating around me. So many ideas all declaring they are correct becomes in itself the actual dilemma that we face. And given the nature of the ethereal entities, the choice of whether to sin or not to sin, to go this way or that way, is not so clear cut. Then I start wondering about the face of evil. From when and where does it start? With witches and demons like the beings who keep me company? They can be tamed with good food. But what do they serve except to throw me off course, meaning there's a right way they do not wish me to take. Why would they be external for me and not others? Perhaps I know too much. Or is it just me creating all these dilemmas and confusions?

Anyway, I decide that I need to steal the star, my gift, so I return to the pile of boxes and take what looks like mine. It even has the card taped to the top. I hide it under my jacket and leave just as dinner is served. How sorry am I to miss that? But when I get home and open the box, it isn't a priceless star at all. It's already been altered though I don't know how that was accomplished in so short a time. What it looks like is a kind of ocean shell with a delicate mixture of metals and gems, just like the star, and it is so beautiful, natural and organic, and it seems the very kind of thing that I should settle for as my public faith. It's so very nice I feel I could live with it as a symbol for my inability to organize, categorize or explain my confusion, and the ethereal beings, their bellies full, applaud my decision and say how much is suits me as I tie it around my neck.

Closing the Outposts

I extended my range for many years, and I thought I could keep it all, but there came a time when I realized I must unwind my positions as they say. So I went about determining where the furthest outposts were, figuring I would start there and work my way in.

I did not realize how vague one could be naming their locations. The mere fact that I had outposts so far out in the distances shocked me. But my days of youth were quite amazing in that regard. It all began to come back to me a little at a time as I studied the documents. It was a wondrous time of general expansion, and I must say I had a gift when it came to establishing a presence. But when I left home for the first time, I really had nothing. I just set my course for the best university with steadfast determination to break down the doors of that outpost using only my genius as a key. But the door proved to be thicker than I had anticipated, or more to the point, my head was thicker than I thought. It was a failure I will never forget, but it motivated me and determined my course of life.

I'll never forget the one true friend I made in those days, a kindred spirit who recognized that I had the perception but warned that the real issue was whether I could get it out. At the time, I did not know exactly what he meant since I did not foresee any problem getting it out. Since I had the perception, which ran through my spiritual veins like blood, I could not see why I would not be able to tap into it any time I wanted, but my friend's words proved to be quite prophetic. I spent the next twenty years realizing that the mind was like a chamber with rock on either side that must be polished into a mirror surface. That takes many years and much patience to accomplish. Then one needs to let the light of one's mind into the chamber, and add to it over time, and there is no way of knowing how many years it will take until there is enough power in the perception bouncing back and forth in the chamber to pass through the mirror in a concentrated form of perception. It is a slow process that many abandon along the way. I never gave up, but it was costly, very costly to continue, and I gave it everything I had. Along the way, I established hundreds of outposts so that when the perception came through, these far off establishments would receive light and become locations in the cosmos, so it comes as a great disappointment now to have to close them, but at least I will be taking advantage of a rare opportunity to relive a very interesting part of my life, a time of utmost faith in myself and my abilities, and follow once again the path I took as well as review my progress. I am hoping that I will learn something along the way. I mean I hold out what some would call a vain hope that I will still be able to fulfill my great ambition. I know it sounds silly, but old habits die hard. I was blind but enthusiastic, and I had goals worth achieving, worth believing in, and I still believe in them now, that it is worth the effort even if one ultimately fails. All the perception within me says so even if I never do manage to send it out to the furthest reaches.

I know this may not make a lot of sense, but that is the result of the perception remaining within. I have been going through my old papers in order to find ways to explain it better, and I must say I am not happy with a discovery I have made. Even if it facilitates my progress or benefits me by permitting me to finally understand better how my way was blocked, it is hard for me to swallow that my life could have been different were it not for my so-called friend, the one I mentioned earlier, who I realize now was no friend at all.

I am so angry to discover that his real motive was to keep me from ever getting my perception out that I have made it my new goal to find him and destroy him. I located papers that indicate that he had access to my probes and turned my outposts into derelicts when they had been formulated to each be an oasis. What I learned was he closed them down after I had opened them, which meant cutting off the life source, and so they died, and as I started out in the furthest reaches, he managed to make his way inward, and he now holds the combined energy of all those points that were my discovery. He has positioned himself in the university, has its full weight behind him, and once again I must go there and make my case to regain the outposts, essentially reopen them, which at my age troubles me though it would be nice to see them all connected. Still, all those years of my youth were wasted as my belief in my own prowess slowly evaporated when strength was actually present. I should have lived a great life and been fulfilled. But I will have my revenge.

At the university, I found that his room was locked. I knew immediately that there was going to be a problem because his door was huge. I would estimate that it was twenty feet high and ten feet thick. Even after all these years, his associates recognized me from pictures he had posted behind the front desk, and they refused me admittance. I was told that he was on a sabbatical, and that I would not be able to see him. Several trucks drove up to the front of the building to begin building further barriers that would be finished within a couple of weeks. If I could not find him before then, I might never succeed because I learned the entire campus would soon be off limits to me, and a new wall with gates was also going up. I never realized the power I had given him, and the fear. That was his weakness, and I would need to prey on that.

In the limited time I had, I had leaflets made and dropped them from planes as I flew to the distant outposts. These were advance warnings of my intentions, an announcement of my presence, a full disclosure so that there would be no misunderstanding. I reinvigorated every outpost, got it open and running again. Standing at the furthest reaches of my progress, I looked out and wondered why I stopped so short of the endless possibilities that were out there, so as long as I was there, I purposely extended my range beyond even my own wildest dreams, and these were pristine areas, already enlivened and organized with what I would call a living sense of my mind, probably due to the influence of my light, which had been shining there for a time before the disruption. What surprised me was actually how far I was able to go out and see how far my influence stretched. It was plain to see that the perception was already in progress. I just lacked the faith to realize it and be comfortable having established a domain. As far as I had gone to establish those furthest outposts, because I was young at the time, I really was a coward in many ways, leaving the area as soon as I could without making an examination of the possibilities. Now I was able to understand, and it did something to me. The insights bounced back and forth within me. I was able to look at myself under an intense, inner light, stare at myself in multiple mirrors polished over a lifetime, and for the first time, I realized that light had changed from diffuse into a highly organized form. The chamber could no longer hold it, and it poured out as perception and established outposts beyond my wildest expectations. The extent of the range is astonishing, and I do not need to go out there to ensure they are open. The connections are too strong to tamper with.

All I need to do is work my way back toward the center, opening the outposts along the way. Each time I reopen one, there is a surge of perception that extends the furthest range to a previously unknown limit, and any delay only prepares the terrain in advance, organizing and invigorating it, and stamping it with my perception.

So with much effort, and over a long period of time, I finally manage to restore all the outposts. Though I achieved this as an older man, I must say I did not feel any less energized doing it than I did when I was young. As I reached the gates of the university, I found them open. A formal request was proffered to draw light from the array, to which I naturally gave my consent. My affiliation was never in question in my own mind. I learned through the surge of concentrated perception that it was being locked in my own chambers. Polishing the mirrors and planning to close the outposts kept me apart from the system. Now I was a part of it. Even my old friend's door was open to me, though I found it to be far less imposing blown off its hinges. I had gotten the perception out, but I worried about how self-destructive I was for so long that a whole set of outposts had opened on the other side of the spectrum. Messages poured in that they would stay open night and day to suck the life out of me if I ever felt the need. One side of me said they provided balance; the other said close them down, but strangely I lacked the perception for how to get that done or didn't want to do it.

Then, in a short time after I'd abandoned them, the dark outposts began to connect among themselves. I could feel them turn on all at once, almost like a gravity wave pulling me. The result was a long day of a drenching rain where I slowly developed a mind-numbing headache. I sought relief from powerful pain killers and drifted into a peaceful acquiescence to both sides of the spectrum. As the hours melted away, I melted, too. I began to feel myself pooling into my boots, so I took them off while I could. My clothes felt tighter, and as my fluids sloshed away from my bones and collected in my lower extremities, I managed to get most of them off and step into the back yard before my skin gave way, bursting open and releasing my essence into the pounding rain. Part of me followed the flow into the gutters, while the rest of me made the effort to climb the water-fall into the clouds. Another part of me went into the soil through holes the worms were making to escape the flood.

From these various vantage points, I was able to make a simultaneous survey of the elements. In time and by degrees, I separated further and further and touched every part of the heavens and the earth, each atom established an outpost so it was all one beacon in its own way, beyond right or wrong and passing no judgement.

Sometimes I feel trapped in a far outpost of a forgotten empire, locked behind a tall, thick door with standing orders to hold my ground until relieved. I've often felt the need to abandon it, to shut it down because it is obsolete. Every fiber of my being says that I do nobody any good to maintain this outpost, that the world has evolved beyond needing it, passed it by, forgotten that it even exists and that it is my job to give it up, to close it and others like it.

But, my old friend, with no knowledge of your whereabouts and no courier to collect this, I think of you because you understood me when I needed it most. The memory of those days lights the whole outpost and gives me strength to defend it with my life. Some, whose mission is to close the outposts to keep the perception from getting out, will recognize the light in the distance, but they will have no chance against others who will see it and wonder to the full extent within themselves how to test the limits and extend them.

Straining the Well

As children we were told that our people were determined to live outside the wall before it even went up, that the wall had a long history of coming down but the last time was too long ago to remember. The wall appeared to all of us as being far too high and imposing to imagine anything could destroy it, and we lived not only in its shadow but in constant danger as anyone who got too close was quick to learn.

Living outside such a city, one learns to turn adversity into opportunity in order to survive. I discovered quite young that there were blind spots along the walls. I knew where to stand and not be seen by the guards. We knew the ground there was more fertile due to waters from the surrounding moat, but there was a ten foot stretch of land from the wall to the moat, and we would swim the moat at night and plant seeds in the blind spots. The guards never realized the wall was feeding our people. We harvested the fruit and vegetables regularly, pruned the trees and replanted, and managed quite well despite regular patrols on top of the wall and one particular guard who taunted that he knew what we were doing.

I never believed it myself and thought he was just talking to keep himself occupied to pass the time in what was surely an extremely boring duty, but I never tested it by responding. When any guard was present, I waited against the wall in the blind spot until I saw the signal from the well that he had moved on and that it was safe to swim the moat. Using this system, we managed for years to have no contact whatsoever with anyone within the walls.

One evening, however, I took my son with me in order to train him in the art of managing the blind spot gardens. I warned him to stay close and not to do anything where he could be seen, but he was at the age of distrust in the stories we had told, and when my back was turned, he stepped beyond the safe perimeter. Instantly, an arrow whizzed from the top of the wall and struck him in the shoulder. I was able to pull him into the blind area by the legs an instant before a second arrow whizzed into the ground just over his head.

I pulled the arrow out, ripped off a piece of his shirt and had him hold it over the wound, but time was of the essence, and so I put him on my back and went the opposite way along the wall, a route to which the guard was blind. Friends were waiting to take my son across the moat. I doubled back to the blind area to draw the guard's attention away from them. I stepped in and out of his sight and dodged several arrows and saw his face. When reinforcements arrived, they poured down buckets of refuse. One of them dropped a bucket which bounced into my proximity. I picked it up, followed the blind route along the wall and sank into the water of the moat where I cleaned out the bucket and made for the other side.

It took several weeks, but my son survived. It was far more dangerous to attempt sorties to the wall to tend the crops, and we even pulled trees out in the areas compromised for fear they would grow into sight if left untended. Even so, guards along the wall were able to determine where the blind spots were and posted extra guards there, and over many months, each successive blind was compromised and lost. It was a blow to our culture, and we turned to rely more heavily on what we could harvest from the well.

The problem there was twofold. First, the well was in plain sight of the wall though it was generally regarded as being out of range, but now that we tended to gather there, the arrows started flying, and occasionally someone was hit. Second, the well was originally a sewer that we had managed to obstruct in the hope that we might make use of the water in time, which in fact we succeeded in doing thanks to an indigenous plant growing in the well that effectively strained the water in the well. It was also a source of food.

The bucket came to good use also, and for a short time, the well kept us alive despite our loss of the fertile areas next to the wall. But we were being monitored, and when suddenly the well plants began to die and our people began to take ill in great numbers, we realized that they had apparently worked through the obstruction in a deliberate and effective campaign to poison the well.

So many of our people died. So much pain and sorrow. It forced us to move further away from the wall and dig a new well. What surprised us was how so much water was always there, but we had never looked for it before. A few of the plants above the water line had survived, and a short time after we transplanted these, they were growing in abundance in the new well. We even used the bucket from the old well. It served to remind us of good times and bad.

Over the next several years, the old well, which poisons had turned into a sterile place, became a holy place for our people. At first we kept a fire going there, assigning someone to tend it each night. We believed that our spirit and fire were stronger than their wall, and we turned the old well into an altar where our people would gather to listen to our elders tell stories of the history of our people, and then we would pray together.

Then one night we were surprised by the sudden movement of the stone that made up the table of the altar. There was knocking. Someone was underneath. We prepared ourselves for conflict while removing the stone, only to discover several people emerge from what they considered a tunnel to freedom. They wanted to defect and be a part of our society, not as refugees but willing participants.

In time, there was a steady, nightly flow of people leaving the old walled city through the altar of the old well, so many that some believed they were straining on the well. I was put in charge of maintaining the tunnel. I installed and changed candles at intervals to make navigating the passage easier. One night I was surprised to see the face of the guard who had shot my son among those leaving the wall behind. My first thought was he was there to put an end to the exodus, but he was carrying a child, and I realized he was leading his family. In a way, his arrow that nearly killed my son had started this, but I said nothing of it as he passed. He may have even had a hand in poisoning the well, which led to the building of the altar, but I could not fault the man.

A Great Sea of White

My boss asked if I was ready to prove myself. I answered in the affirmative, so he told me I should handle the presentation to the directors. I thanked him for the opportunity, then wilted in my office as I realized I was not up to the task. I drew a huge blank, a big sea of white, a kind of office snow blindness in the face of needing to come up with an idea. The only thing I could think of was getting out of the office. I wanted to run away but considered that to face the obstacle, I should take a first step toward it, and as I needed materials, I decided to drive out to purchase supplies.

As soon as I left the parking garage, I knew someone was in the car. I looked in the mirror and saw it was Sharon, the wife of my boss. She winked at me. I didn't know what to do. I turned the corner and doubled back to the building, got out and opened the door for her, but she was not there. I bent down, looked all over the car, but she was gone. I knew I hadn't imagined it, but I didn't understand how she left. I returned to the car and started driving for supplies, and she was back. This time I asked what she was doing there, and she said she it was because she knew we wanted one another. Once again, I turned the corner to double back, but when I looked in the mirror, she was gone. I reversed direction again, and she was there again. I did not know what to make of it except to doubt my sanity, so to make sure she was real, I reached back and asked her to take my hand, which she willingly took and placed it on her breast. I started to swerve and pulled my hand back. I asked again what she was doing there, and she said she wanted to complete me.

I turned the car around and went back to the office, and just like the other times, she disappeared. I sat there worrying about my project, about the supplies, but mostly thought about Sharon, about what it felt like to touch her, and whether any of it were real. I wondered whether I had even left in the first place. I looked at the clock. I'd only been gone about 20 minutes. I still had the rest of the afternoon ahead of me. I could not sit there doing nothing, and I began to wonder what would happen if I drove all the way to the supply depot. Perhaps she would disappear on the way back. Yes, that was it. She was only there when I was driving in a specific direction. I could still get the supplies, and she would be gone on the way back.

So I went back to the car and started all over. I drove to the supply depot, and again, she was there, but now she crawled over the seat and sat close to me, nestled her head in my shoulder and rubbed my chest. I steadfastly continued on the journey to the supply depot. I had no intentions of turning around this time. I tried to think of it as not happening, but it was certainly real enough. By the time we arrived at the depot, she had gotten me quite excited, I must say. Rather than park in front, I drove to the back and parked along the fence by the loading dock. I held her close and kissed her deeply, and we swam together in a big sea of white. I'd never felt so excited or as passionate as I did until it occurred to me that anyone in the depot might recognize either one of us, so I broke off the embrace, started the car and drove to the front entrance. I said I'd be right back, went in and purchased all the supplies I thought I would need for a project for which I still had no ideas, then returned to the car.

She was still there in the front seat. Just seeing her made my heart race. I sensed she felt the same way, and fearing she might disappear, I drove a different route back to the office. About halfway there, she told me to make an unexpected turn in another direction. It was the first of many turns before we arrived at her house, which of course was also where my boss lived. I considered the situation. She wanted me to come inside with her, but half the afternoon was over. My boss had a habit of leaving early. Obviously, he could walk in on us, but I found that idea slightly intriguing and decided I would rather be with his wife than worry about the project, that I would rather take a risk of losing my job and have no shot at the opportunity, to never prove myself to him, than to not finish what had started, so I followed her into the house.

She was very deliberate as if there were no worries. She made us drinks, and we sat on a couch sipping, talking and finally kissing. I carried her upstairs, and we spent the rest of the afternoon together. As evening approached, I feared she was far too calm and patient. I hinted at leaving, and finally she consented. We dressed and went back to my car. As I was about halfway backed out of the long driveway, her husband pulled up behind me, blocking my way. The only thing I could do was start driving back to the house. I was in a panic, wondering if I was a dead man, but when I looked in the mirror, her husband's car was no longer there. So I started to back up again, and again, it blocked me. Again, rather than confront him, I started driving back to the house. We went back in, and I spent the next few days there, fearful that he might walk in at any minute, but he never did. On the third day, I got up with a clear idea of what I wanted to do in the project, so I went to the car and retrieved the materials. Then I spent the day completing it while Sharon rubbed my shoulders and made me coffee and sandwiches. By evening, it was complete, and not too soon for it was due the next day.

I was so satisfied with the result of my work that I'd made up my mind to stop worrying about my boss. I did a three-point turn at the house so I wouldn't be backing the car up, and I drove forward down the driveway to the street. There was no sign of her husband. Sharon stayed with me all the way to the office, but after I parked, she was gone. I went to the meeting, made the presentation, and it all went perfectly. My boss promoted me after that, saying I'd proved myself quite satisfactorily. He even said he thought I didn't have it in me, that he honestly expected me to fail in the make-or-break situation.

That didn't sit with me very well, but I quickly became absorbed in my responsibilities. My boss went up the ladder completely out of sight, into what seemed a great sea of white from my vantage point, while I took over the department. As I had risen through the ranks, I found that the hardest thing for me to do was delegate various tasks. Many members of my staff were fully capable of running the

147

presentations, but somehow I did not want to let go. I still enjoyed the rides to the supply depot with Sharon, but then she told me she was moving to a more exclusive, gated community, and it would be impossible to see me unless I had access to the company's Florida condo. With so many people using it, I could only hope to get it one or two weekends a year, at least until I was promoted into the upper echelons, and when she stopped appearing in my car, the work grew tedious, so there came a time to begin training someone else.

However, I was a little reluctant to go in that direction because I'd started dating a wonderful gal, and it was becoming quite serious. We married that following June, and I felt like the luckiest man in the world. We bought a house and spent our time decorating it and filling it with furniture. But happiness can be quite intoxicating, even blindingly so, and a part of me knows I should have kept doing the presentations myself, but the great sea of white beckoned, and so I finally delegated the responsibility to the most promising young man on my staff. Naturally, he expressed gratitude in the meeting when I gave him the assignment, but I knew he was lost.

Then I sat back and waited for him to leave. I watched through the window as he drove back and forth obviously confused by something. So I followed him to the supply depot. I could see that someone was with him in the car. I saw he did not park in front but drove instead to the back of the depot. I tried to follow, but my car died. It would start, but it died when I moved forward. I found the car ran fine as long as I went in the opposite direction. I knew they were going to the house, but I couldn't drive there either. I couldn't even get out and go to the house on foot. I did block him as he tried to drive away from the house. Then I went back to the office and waited for the presentation, which was great like I expected. In several months, I entered the great sea of white with great fanfare. Now I spend four weeks a year in the condo, two with Sharon and two with my wife. It's a wonderful place. A great sea of white sand stretches into the great sea of green under a great sea of blue. We walk the beach until discomforted by the great falling sea of darkness, a sensation of being watched and followed, so we turn around, put the condo in sight, which evaporates our fear in a great sea of lights.

The Metabolism of My Enemy

There are some people who enjoy stirring things up. That's me. Tonight I went out after midnight for supplies. The only store open was five miles away. I bought some coffee and eggs for breakfast, some smokes and a bottle of scotch. On the way out, I see this fellow on a cell phone. He's coming into the store. Looking him over, I drew from my database of native dances and went for the throat. I would call it "Cell phone dance of the idiot who looks like me with an egg finale." I danced, then emptied the whole dozen on him and made a clean getaway. To my mind, that's what human interaction is all about, especially given the fact that the situation is hopeless. I'm talking about the ability of people to relate in any way.

I know he would have refused if I'd opened the scotch and offered him a slug. He'd have taken me for a bum, which I'm not. I know the specifics of his culture and what kind of person he is because I'm the same way, and I hate it, so I take it out on my own kind because that way, nobody can complain that I have any prejudice. I'm as sweet as can be when it comes to anybody of any nationality or religion that in any way differs from me. I'm a model citizen in that regard, and it doesn't just stem from the fact that the full acceptance of others as equals is being stressed in society today. I was raised that way. My mother taught me to accept other people. She never said anything about accepting myself though, and she wasn't particularly accepting of me either. I came out of my family with as low a helping of self esteem as a person can have, and I'm fully aware of the depth of my resentment for such an experience. But I go out of my way to be kind to everyone who's different from me, and it's so diverse where I live in the city that I'm nice most of the time. But as soon as I see anyone who is from my clan so to speak, I go ballistic for no other reason than I can't be accused of a hate crime. Sure it's hate, more like self loathing, but it's also a loophole. It can be called an assault I suppose, but nothing worse, and the law can never get to the bottom of it or see that justice is served because there's no precedent. I'm just doing it to exploit the loophole because everyone assumes you're going to be nice to your own kind, which makes the law racially biased, wouldn't you say?

That is my way of stirring things up. I take it seriously. I'm even well known in the community for mistreating my friends and family in such a compelling way. I bow and open doors to strangers from afar, then stick my leg out and trip my cousin's kids, then push their faces in the ice cream. They know who I am. They don't press charges. They appear at my door in clothes they don't care about, knowing there's a good chance those clothes will be ruined by the time I get through with them. I've explained it to everyone, and whether they agree or not, the message is getting out. Or is it? I slam everyone in the tribe, not outside of it, and everyone finds that compelling. No? If you're inside the tribe, and you don't care, I'll be on you soon enough. You'll get your fair share. If you're outside the tribe, why should you care? If you know me, you might hardly be able to believe what you're hearing about me since every time you've ever encountered me, I've been nothing short of absolutely respectful in every way. But if you do come to believe that I am a terror within my own community, what skin is that off your nose? That does not bring your blood to a boil, does it? As long as you get more than your fair share of kindness in every way when you are in my domain, that is all that matters, isn't it? I want that you should sleep well and digest everything you eat and feel no stress or discomfort. I want your metabolism to be at its best in every way, just as is preached loud and clear through all the airwaves. But I'll tell you this. In no way will I let up on my family and friends. I'm taking all the lies out on them, purifying them, extracting all the darkness and evil and turning it into a comforter that will help you drift into stasis and eternal hibernation.

A New Face for Constance

Edward heard his mother say that a woman looked different, more radiant, and that she glowed when pregnant. But only his sister Annie received further elaboration on the subject, for when their mother saw him in the doorway, she closed the bedroom door in his face. "But," she went on, "if you should get pregnant before you marry, you'll get a whole new face, and it won't be a pretty one." While Barbara was giving her daughter another full dose of the absolute truth on all matters pertaining to womanhood, which was mainly about warning Annie never to let any boys touch her in any way and to guard her virginity at all costs until marriage, Edward went outside and wandered around to the back yard with an eye on Carla's garden through the bushes next door. There were strawberries to which he was allergic, but he found them so delicious he couldn't resist. They were worth the hives, but he had to be careful not to get caught and deal with Carla's wrath. She'd already caught him there enough times and warned him about the consequences of getting caught again that he surveyed the situation very carefully before slipping under the sticker bushes. He ignored the strawberries, which were in plain sight of Carla's kitchen window, and feasted instead on the black raspberries in a blind spot on the side of the garage knowing he wouldn't have a reaction to them.

When Edward came into the world, the houses were already situated to make for an interesting childhood. He had no natural sense of borders, so he didn't understand why he couldn't walk the length of the street behind the backyards. There were no fences in the early years. The houses were still going up when he was born, so by the

151

time he was seven or eight, it was still generally wide open, but some people were older, sensitive to children wandering around. On the other hand, this was just after the war, and the baby boom was in full swing. Carla was older herself and was a war bride. She got pregnant shortly after she met her husband, who was older, too, while he was stationed in Germany. He decided to marry her and bring her back to the states, and they only had the one child, Constance, who was one of the older children in the neighborhood, five years older than Annie. But being neighbors, they played together, which was fine with Barbara as long as Constance didn't reveal anything to Annie. Barbara made that clear to Constance, then went back to bombarding Annie with warnings about the danger of boys.

Meanwhile, the houses remained fixed in their right angles to one another, the sticker bushes grew without Carla ever trimming them, and Edward's excursions through passages he had made were also curtailed by his growing interest in other activities, although he always knew when the fruit was ripe. He outgrew the allergic reaction to strawberries, and much as he loved them, stayed out of her yard. He and other boys discovered rhubarb and peaches behind a church across the street. The old priest did not mind it when he saw them climbing the trees. He enjoyed watching them be boys.

The yards grew less cluttered with baby toys, tricycles became two wheelers, and the sounds of baseball cards held in place by clothespins clacking on the spokes filled the air. At night there were games of hide and seek, all ages participating, but Annie did not see Constance anymore in their shared, favorite hiding places. Constance was off to bigger and better things, to high school and to dating.

One day Edward caught wind of another conversation between his mother and sister only this time he was old enough to put his foot in the door when they tried to shut him out. Constance was pregnant, and Annie was receiving instructions that under no circumstances was she ever to have anything to do with her again. After warning her of the consequences, so that she would not appear to be a hypocrite, Barbara took Edward and Annie through the bramble between the yards, scratching her arm in the process, and knocked on the door. Carla let them in. Constance was there, as well as the boy who fathered her child. He was sitting in Carla's husband's easy chair looking uncomfortable. Constance looked like she had been crying. Carla asked what it was about, and Barbara explained that the children were not allowed to see Constance any-more, that this was the last time, due to bad influences. Barbara then took a mask from her purse, walked over to where Constance was sitting, and applied it to the young woman's face. "There Con-stance," she said. "Now you have the right look for what you've done. Annie will never be like you." Then my mother walked us back through the bramble and scratched herself again.

After that, they didn't see Constance, only someone wearing a mask. The mask had power that extended to make others around her look different as well. Her boyfriend Steve was made to look like a criminal who had come from a strange and distant high school where upperclassmen prey on underclass innocence. Under the influence of the power of the mask, Carla became a neglectful mother and her husband a heavy drinker. The houses maintained their angles and proximities though, so Annie required a daily dose of Barbara's effective, "Banish the thought" treatment, which filled Annie's mind with every aspect of sexual thought that a young girl can have, Barbara making sure that nothing filthy was left unspoken on the subject of maintaining purity, though she had covered this same ground many times over the years. Annie had heard it all before, beginning when she was in kindergarten.

The kindly priest visited Carla in the hope of bringing them to church, but Carla didn't want any part of it. She and her husband were planning the unthinkable, to have the baby aborted, and she didn't want a priest to make her feel guilty about taking such a step.

All anybody heard was that there wasn't going to be a baby. Carla wouldn't answer the question as to how there could have been one, and suddenly there wasn't going to be one. She didn't even offer a plausible explanation such as it was miscarried. It was as if she want-ed to leave it so ridiculously up in the air as to stupefy the mind until it realized that something terrible had happened. Nobody saw Con-stance for many weeks. It was as if Carla's whole house, which was turned at a right angle from Barbara's, had solidified an invisible

153

wall that extended along the angle of variance so that no mind or body could probe the lives next door. The bushes also grew thornier and higher that summer. Edward couldn't even get through the old path to the black raspberries when they were ripe. The house became a fortress in a compound, the row of hedges its impenetrable wall. Rumor had it that Carla's husband was drinking more heavily than ever. Edward could still see into the yard from the roof, and when he went up to retrieve a ball, he noticed that the grass had not been mowed for weeks. Thinking it an opportunity, he went over and knocked on the door. Constance answered, wearing her mask, in a night dress, and invited him in.

Edward entered a world of wonderful smell and forbidden femininity, knowing that from his mother's eyes, he had come too far. He was so much younger, but she became something like a strawberry or black raspberry or maybe a peach or a stick of rhubarb in his mind, and he hadn't even come through the stickers to the source. He remembered all the times they'd played before she went to high school, how friendly she'd been, how nice a neighbor, and the accumulated sense of that became a kind of crush, activated by sympathy simmering out of his mother's exaggerated judgement and constant haranguing, that and an overwhelming attraction to her new, more beautiful face. Constance agreed that Edward could mow the lawn for money, which is what he asked, but suddenly he said he was happy to do it for free, and Constance took his chin with one hand and lifted it gently, smiling at him, disarming him completely.

He started mowing the lawn, but his mother caught him and called him back. He said he had to finish, but she said no. Edward looked at the windows hoping to make a signal. The next day, he was playing baseball in the street and hit a ball through one of the windows. The other boys ran, but Edward stood his ground. Carla dashed out, made a beeline for him, grabbed his arm and dragged him into the house. She held his head over the sink and began washing his mouth out with soap. "Not finish the lawn, will you? Break a window, will you? Ruin my garden, will you? Well, let me put a new face on you!" she snarled, smearing the soap up his nose, in his eyes while jamming the bar down his throat.

Latimer's Flight

Someone working for the airlines must have gotten a nice fee for tipping off the newspaper as to what flight the eccentric and recluse writer Alan Latimer would be on. They even had the seat assignment and were able to plant me next to him, and my job would be to interview him without him knowing it. I tried to look as much like an ordinary business traveller as I could, to blend in with the background but appear professional enough to engage him in a conversation, perhaps one that wouldn't even require that he reveal his identity. Merely acquiring a sense of his views on a number of subjects would be fascinating to our readers. I also had a camera to get his picture if possible, but I wasn't sure how I was going to do that. I was seated all the way in the back of the plane where the bathrooms were. The best angle for a picture would be to move forward, but I couldn't think of any reason why I would need to do that. I was getting a bit ahead of myself, and it seemed, so was the plane. It started to leave the terminal, and Latimer wasn't seated.

I moved to the window seat, to his seat and looked out. We were departing the gate, but there was unusual activity on the tarmac. A door opened on the side of the building, and an airline attendant backed out pulling an old man in a wheel chair. At the same time, an older style stairway made for tarmac use was being towed to the plane. This one had a wheelchair lift installed. It took a few minutes to get everything set up, but I could see the old man riding up in the seat. I realized that it must be Latimer and got out of his seat.

In front of the plane, a stewardess folded the wheel chair and carried it to the back of the plane and set it not far from me. I waited

155

to see how they would handle the old man, but from what I could see, only a young man boarded the plane. He poked his head into the cockpit and chatted with the pilots for a few moments, then showed the stewardess his boarding pass. She led him all the way back and pointed to the seat next to me. After putting his jacket in the upper compartment, he apologized to me for having to ask me to get up for a moment so he could squeeze into the window seat. He brought his briefcase with him and set it on the floor by his feet. We fastened our seat belts, and in a few moments, the plane backed away from the terminal and lumbered toward a runway where it waited for its turn before finally taking off.

I decided not to say anything, at least not for a while, hoping that he might start a conversation with me at some point. It was a coast-to-coast flight, and I also knew from the tipster that he was flying to the funeral of his only brother who had died the day before of natural causes. That was how his flight plan had leaked out, though I was still surprised at the level of caution and secrecy employed to get him out of the terminal at the last possible second and onto the plane. I pretended to read a magazine from the back pocket of the seat in front of me, but all the while I watched his every movement, hoping to pick up something to add to my story.

Latimer looked out the window, staring into space, during the entire takeoff. Only when the seat belt sign went off, and the captain made an announcement that passengers were free to move about the plane did he snap out of what seemed like a trance. He reached down and opened his briefcase on his lap. I tried to get a glimpse of everything that was in it, but he only took out a book. He didn't sit back and read it as much as study it like an object. I could not see the title without turning my head, but it wasn't like he was trying to read it. He was rather feeling the surface, fanning the pages, smelling it; giving it that sort of treatment. Finally, he opened it and started paging through it, but again, it was evident he was not reading it. I finally decided to make some kind of move so I could turn my head and look without appearing to be doing so out of interest or curiosity in him, so I put the magazine back in the seat pocket, stretched my arms up and yawned, then turned my head to the right as if doing so to stretch, and then turned it all the way to the left, where I was able to glance at the book. It was something he'd written, which suddenly made me realize that he was treating it as if it were a new title, but I knew he'd not published anything in years. If this were a new book, anything I could find out about it would make the entire story a sensation.

Then Latimer surprised me by asking me where I flying. The truth was that I was coming right back, and I hadn't even considered inventing a plausible reason for the trip, so I just said I was heading out for a convention. Before he could ask me the next obvious questions, my mind was racing to create an elaborate fiction, but he didn't ask me. Instead, he said that he'd noticed I'd been reading a magazine but had put it away, and if I didn't have anything else to read, would I mind reading his new book. I could not believe my luck, and I tried to act as natural as I could. "Did you buy that at the airport?" I asked. "That's awfully considerate of you, but I don't want to take your brand new book before you've had a chance to read it."

"It's a book I wrote, not out in stores yet," he replied.

"Oh, you're a writer? How interesting," I said. "What's it about?"

"Well, it's largely a history, a commentary, I suppose you could say, but I'm an historian, and most people find history boring."

"Not me," I said. "I love history, especially the ancients."

"Then I think you'll find this interesting," he said, handing the book to me. It was a fairly hefty volume.

As I opened it and starting leafing to the first page of text, I noticed he was shifting in his seat. It surprised me to think he was uncomfortable in any way with what he had written, or that it mattered what I thought, but then I remembered my own feelings when someone was reading one of my articles at the newspaper. It's a strange mixture of satisfaction and trepidation, the latter stemming from a fear that the whole piece is terrible somehow. I knew that Latimer's work was great but never expected anything as wonderful from a history, which was not a genre he had worked in previously.

The story had me from the beginning, except it wasn't the details he was relating that I found to be exciting. It was what they conjured in my own mind. It was as if I was reliving aspects of my own

157

life. Incidents in the book reminded me of similar experiences I'd had, and even in the first chapter, my own life dominated my thoughts. It was almost as if his book was a mere catalyst for awakening my thoughts, as if a key had opened a door in the back of my mind through which memories poured in. I saw my mother as she really was. Something that had been lost when people close to me died was restored, and I was so mesmerized by seeing my own life pass before my eyes in such clarity that I lost track of the time.

I felt that telltale first sign of descent and looked up in shock that four hours had passed so quickly. I looked over and Latimer was sleeping. Sunlight on his face made him look much older. I set the book down and literally pulsated with excitement for the story I would write when I got back to the paper. Hopefully I wouldn't be held to task for ignoring Latimer for the whole flight. I was already dreaming up excuses for that blunder. Here he was friendly and talkative, and I hadn't taken advantage of him in any way. I figured if I was lucky he might even give me the book, which would compound the questions further as to why I hadn't interviewed him when I could read the book at my leisure at a future date.

In a few minutes, the plane landed. Everyone was asked to stay in their seats until the plane was at the gate. The stewardess came back for the wheelchair. Latimer got up, took his briefcase and got his coat from the compartment. He said goodbye to me. I handed him the book, but he said I could keep it. "Don't you want to know what I thought of it?" I asked him. He shook his head, no. He looked much older to me, limping while he followed the stewardess. I would have liked to have offered my condolences on the loss of his brother. Another stairway with a chairlift was towed to the plane, and after Latimer descended, he was helped into the wheel chair and whisked away looking frightfully old and frail.

When I'd gotten off the plane and into a seat at another gate for my flight home, I took the book out to continue reading, but it was no longer the amazing history, just an ordinary dog-eared collection of his best stories, which I'd always found strange and compelling but useless. I picked up a section of a newspaper someone had left behind on a seat next to me and pondered my fate.

Resonations

There is a place on earth where we will wind up when our lives spin out of control, taken over by drugs or insanity, when we are irreclaimable and vile, when others have given up on us. The worst areas are characterized by a strange build-up of a waxy substance that appears to accumulate in the corners. I don't notice it when I'm in the dregs, but rather trying to work my way out of them. It is almost like the graffiti, equally depressing. There are many kinds of blockades to exiting the bottom world, giving one a feeling that there is no way out. But of all of them, whether economic or gang related, nothing strikes me as more depressing than the sooty wax in the corners. It is something that gets under the nails so you cannot claw, and in the mouth so one cannot speak.

I hit the mother load of this stuff after my last binge of pharmaceuticals sent me tumbling not just to the bottom but through the floor. Everyone gave up on me, and one day I woke in the streets where there were stalagmites of this stuff. Looking up, I realized I was under an overpass where there were matching stalagtites. I shuddered and realized where I was, knew that I was having a moment of awareness like a window that might be my only chance to escape. Next to me, starting to awake, was an old friend of mine, someone I'd tried reaching when he was dropping to the bottom. I never had any success with intervention, but I guess we'd found one another in the waxy build-up. I used to drive my car through this area looking for him, insulated by the big engine and tinted windows. I always had plenty of gas and slowed down rather than stop at red lights. Always keep moving was my motto. But that also

159

translates to the lifestyle under the bridges and in the alleys. We kept moving. I stood up and saw cars just like mine increase their speed just at the sight of me. One honked, rousting George to his feet. I looked at him and could hardly extract the memory of what he once was, although from my memories of our youthful carousing that became the foundation for his fall, I rediscovered a sense of him, the personal quality that made me want to be his friend.

He started talking about getting the light for the car, It apparently was the project we were working on together in our shared insanity. He kept pointing to the passing cars claiming it was the right model and year, a '52 chevy. I figured out that we had to find a police car, rip off the top light and install it on a '52 chevy, and then we would make our getaway back into the old life we knew. I saw the social services building and told George I knew where I could find the police lights. He followed me into the building. The floors were slippery from the wax. Drunks were walking in, smelly and uncomfortable from having wet their pants in their sleep. The hallways smelled of old urine. I told George to have a look around, and I went where I remembered the social service counselors worked, and I saw someone I recognized in a shabby box he had turned into an office. I told him I was experiencing a lucid moment, perhaps a window to recovery, and he said it was a resonation. I didn't know what that meant. He said that all of us were intact in some way no matter what the level of damage, and that there were familiar sides, seemingly healthy aspects of ourselves resonating out of that. He said it was the inverse of the place in which we lived, that there was a part of us that remained pristine, no matter how small it was, and it was the negatively analogous to the waxy build-up in the real world, and that it was this material that resonated a saving signal, but often it was too late to do anything about it. He kept talking about it, saying things like there was a part of us that God has made to stay intact, the part of us He knows, loves and will salvage no matter what happens to us, or what we may do to ourselves. He said that every human being is a singularity, a kind of living black hole into which flows all the spiritual matter of the universe, and once it is collected within a singularity, it collects in dimension or creates new dimensions. I'm not sure of the exact way he put it, but it was beginning to sound preachy and extremely annoying, and I needed to go to the bathroom, which was the light at the end of the hall.

I didn't notice any of the wax anywhere, just bugs. There was one with wings on the floor that I tried to kill by snapping my shirt at it. Each time I hit it, it made a noise like an animal. I kept hitting it, and it kept making very strange, plaintive cries as if it had feeling. Suddenly it changed shape and became a small injured mammal. I let it go. George came in and said he'd found a whole fleet of '52 chevies on a lower level. He led me down several flights of stairs, and sure enough, there they were, an entire fleet of them. I realized why we hadn't seen any on the street. They had been effectively removed from circulation in order to thwart our escape. What was not clear was how to bring one to street level. I told George we might want to convert another kind of vehicle, that a '52 chevy would be noticed even after making it look official. George blurted something in wax and spit it into the corner. I realized then that the wax contained lost information and why we lived under the highway where it dripped in constant resonations.

I dipped my finger in the wax, rubbed it on my forehead and waited for an understanding of facts to emerge. I began to understand how much I had misunderstood, how far off I was when judging people. For example, I always assumed that my brother's wife had a natural dislike of me, that she was a difficult person, but I realized that my brother had told her stories before she met me, poisoned her mind, and my way of handling the troubles with her were ineffective because I could not see the underlying reality of the situation. My blind spot became visible, and it extended so far across the span of my life. It was so black and round, and I was going in circles on its opaque surface, trying to see the meaning of life through it, to force life to fit my obscured view. That is how I had become so lost.

I wanted out of the city, to get out from underneath all of it, to see and think as I had as a boy. I started to cry. I felt something at my side. It was the small mammal I'd mistaken for an insect, trying to comfort me. No, George was eating it, and threw me a piece.

No, I was suddenly aware of another resonation that put me back in mind of the correct view of things. It was not a waxy substance, but a combination of soot and snow, plowed a week earlier and pounded with splashes of dirty slush every time a car passed under the bridge. In other cases, it was just the crumbles of brick from buildings falling apart. Something in me made me think of it as the accumulation of verdigris, and my mind had turned inward, aware of the dimensions forming within the singularity, but real life is spent locked out of easily entering that world. Locks are put in place so that one cannot revolve into what seems like madness. To some like me, it can appear to make more sense, to explain the other side, and being there lifts me out of the banal sense that life must mean more than having a car able to withstand the ride through reality and its derelicts, have tire treads able to keep from sliding on the grease. But I had gone too far and gotten lost. The resonations were calling me back. I had to go, but I did not want to leave George.

I tried to reach him, to remind him of the old days, but he was too far gone, and he was there due to other causes like one of Saturn's children, one he'd finished eating and swallowed, and here he was being digested, hell bent on restoring order with a '52 chevy made to look like a cop car. He was a part of me, and I wanted to ride with him, but I'd gotten too long a look, become too fascinated with the inside core as it was formed, taken what was only imagined as real for having told me something, but what, I could not say. I could not carry it out. I could not draw the car or explain the wax, describe the insect or the animal into which it metamorphosed, nor even George. I couldn't make him real or bring him back with me. I had to leave him there and ride the next resonation out.

So I waited, and the soot and snow became wax, and we commandeered a chevy, put a light on it, then needed a siren, so a woman joined us who could scream like one, and we lived in that car and avoided capture. But finally the resonation came. My eyes cleared, and I said goodbye to the inside of the singularity, to dimensions under formation, and made my way back to the world, to doing things by rote, happy to leave it to those more enabled, whose shards of soul are more resonant, enabling them to explore deeper and reveal gleams of greater cogency.

Averting the Pin

My wrestling coach surprised us one day by coming late to practice and telling us that while our team had not been doing well in meets, he had discovered a little secret at church the day before that he planned to implement considering we were off to a losing season anyway. It seemed like every guy was getting pinned, and it was starting to get to all of us. So he said, "Boys, we're going to throw in the towel, so to speak, and not worry about winning for a while. We'll totally concentrate on not getting pinned. Now we've had drills on that, and you know a few things about keeping from getting pinned, but it hasn't been keeping it from happening. So we're going to start over, and we're only going to work on that as if it's the whole point of wrestling, like there's no other reason for being on the mat, to keep from getting pinned, and if you spend the whole match on your back and don't get pinned, it's a victory."

We couldn't believe what we were hearing. The whole match on our backs? "What was the secret you learned in church?" James, our heavyweight, asked the coach. "Yes, what?" we all chimed in.

"Well, when I was playing softball years ago," the coach replied, "there was this guy who couldn't hit. He'd come up to the plate and hack at the ball, his face muscles all ready to burst, and he'd use all this force and emotion, but he couldn't get the ball out of the infield. We'd all talk to him about fundamentals. We'd show him how we held the bat, how we used our wrists, and he'd acknowledge it somewhat begrudgingly, but he'd still go up there and never hit the ball like you'd expect someone who was a student of the game.

"Now that was years ago, and I hadn't seen this guy for years.

Then yesterday, I was sitting in church with my wife listening to the sermon. Everything was quiet except for his voice reverberating through the sanctuary. We were all very attentive. Then, suddenly, on my right across the aisle, there was some kind of commotion. Everyone around me stood up. I didn't at first, thinking there was a mouse or something, but there were strange sounds, grunting and thudding, and it struck me that it sounded like a fight. So I stood up, but I couldn't see over everybody, and then I saw two men going at it fiercely, throwing punches as if to kill. I mean their face muscles were so constrained, and there was so much hate in their eyes, and they threw their punches with so much force that everyone in church was trying to back off to give them room.

"Then I recognized that one of the fighters was the guy who had played on my softball team. I would say that I had never seen him more incensed except I saw the same look on his face every time he swung the bat, and as he went to throw a punch with all his might, the other fellow just clocked him, and he went down hard, instantly, unconscious, his head hitting the side of a pew on the way down, which could only give him a knot on the back of the head because he was already knocked out. He went down on his back in the middle of the aisle, and the other guy went down on top of him carried by the force of his punch. The guy on the bottom had both shoulders down, and being a wrestling coach, the thought struck me that he was pinned since I'd seen the same scene so many times, only not in church, not with people in suits, and then it hit me.

"I realized that this guy had been pinned his whole life. I know you don't know what I mean by that, but let me try to explain. Imagine that we all spend all our time on our backs in life, figuratively speaking, and we have one shoulder down, but the other one is off the ground. Imagine that all the wiggle room we have in life, the thing we call freedom, which encompasses our ability to make choices and go about our lives in pursuit of happiness, is all tied up in those few inches, and despite the fact that the weight of the universe, the facts of life, the fact that someday we will die, is all pressing down, we somehow manage to stay calm, meditate, and find happiness even knowing that at any moment our whole world could collapse in a disaster that would force our free shoulder to the mat and close the gap. Even so, we go about as if that wouldn't happen.

"Now I'm saying my friend there who was knocked out in church never had that gap. Both his shoulders were down when he played softball. And both his shoulders were down before he hit the floor. I saw something quintessential that linked his swinging a bat at a ball with throwing his fist at a face. There was no gap, no composure, no ability to experience calm under pressure and manage any such moment gracefully. Already down and counted out, we are not in the game or match but chickens without heads going through motions. Without the gap, without keeping that one shoulder up and off the mat, we have lost before we have begun.

"So what we're going to concentrate on going forward is letting ourselves get put on our backs, and then frustrating our opponents to use all their strength for the better part of six minutes to get the other shoulder down. Trust me, I'll have you able to read a book with your free arm, or eat an apple, while he's wearing himself down. You'll expend a lot less energy, and before the match is over, you should have plenty of time to turn the tables on him. He'll be so exhausted, he's likely to thank you for it. You'll learn more from being on your backs than any other position because it's analogous to the very position that life has you in whether you see it or not. You don't need to see it or accept it, just put it to use."

And so he trained us not in take-downs and reverses, but in how to keep one shoulder up to avoid being pinned. He had elaborate schematics for every way of avoiding having both shoulders held down simultaneously. The legs were highly useful in pulling up just far enough. So were the head and neck. Agonizing as it could be to struggle in various ways for the better part of six minutes, we became a team that never won a match, but never had a player pinned.

I think about the wisdom of the coach a lot now. So many years later, as humiliating as it was to lose so many matches at first, none of it matters now except the essential of keeping one shoulder up at all times, or rather, to remember that the gap is the space in which meaningful life takes place. I've kept in touch with many of my teammates over the years, and every one to the last feels the same

165

way about it. It was an awful time, but like wearing braces on the teeth, straightened us out somehow, prepared us better for what was coming than anything else we experienced.

I remember how I hunkered down before the storm surge of the hurricane. I had my oxygen tanks and gear, plenty to last through the twenty feet of water and the fifty foot waves that came in that morning. My home has an airtight compartment when I need my dry space, but decided to ride out the bulk of it wet.

I wasn't the only one who decided to stay, but realize I'd be the only one who makes it from the look of things. At one point, during the worst of it, I heard some tapping, and got the scuba gear on and went down in the water and out the front door. It was a one of the neighbors, drowned. He'd gotten caught in the cable wires on the side of the house, and the current was knocking him around. I brought him in, but he was gone. I saw others floating around, but I couldn't do anything for them.

The world became a different place for me after wrestling, but I was prepared for it by learning not how to keep my chin but at least one shoulder up. The way to survive is not about being able to counter every move the world had in its playbook, but to let it grab you and throw you around, and to ride out, whatever it is, on your back. All of life's lessons are learned from that position, but one must never become part of life's butterfly collection, never let the pin go all the way through both shoulders on the mounting board, never let the little identification card be added underneath. From the moment I learned how not to wrestle, I learned how to swim, for there really is no air in the world, only water surging in and out between everything, seeking out every living thing, marking it for eventual mounting, isolating its weakness and coming back for it.

But cruel as the bottom of the sea is known to be, indifferent and unforgiving of the least ignorance and weakness, it can do nothing against the one universal counter move by which we ultimately survive. Even on the surface, I understand the dead man's float, but I never forget the depths. I live on my back, and use my arms, legs, head, neck, whatever serves, to keep one shoulder off the bottom at all times. It's nothing to be near the bottom or to touch it, but it's everything for the bottom to take you, both poles at the same time, your positive and negative charge at once. That must be fought at all costs, for then one is short circuited, then there is electrocution. The heart stops, and the match is over, and one becomes part of the butterfly collection. So I highly recommend eliminating the dangers of life by giving in and letting yourself be ground into the bottom without yielding that one last and necessary charge that will complete the circuit and shut you down. Frustrating fate is far more effective than circumventing it. Be comfortable in its grasp. Let it pile drive you down and push you around, then compel it to recognize that it cannot pin you down. That is not victory in wrestling, but it certainly is in life.

I've always wondered about one thing though, but it's hard to put into words. The coach was in church when the fight broke out, and whatever caused the two men to go at it overrode the importance of maintaining some sense of decorum and respecting the sanctity of the place. It would almost seem that you would only ignore that if your life or the lives of your family were somehow at stake, and that you would defend them, perhaps even kill to do so, despite being in a place where killing is not countenanced. When I visualize the man going down after the last punch, I somehow see him lose some kind of last bubble of undiscernable space where his shoulder had not been touching, though in all senses nobody else would have granted it to him, and as if there is some kind of unwritten law of comfort, that when we are about to lose everything, we will cease being witnesses, his eyes and mind were closed so as not to feel the blow on his head, or experience the humiliation of losing the fight and perhaps his whole world. So the church at least grants comfort to the soul, though in life the whole experience may be one of suffering, of being unable to do what others can, of not being coordinated but always judged as being less, and flailing against that, knowing it isn't true, but ultimately being shown by better fists with a bigger shoulder gap and confidence in making the kill that one is less, essentially a loser. And all the times I stayed on my back until turning the tables and pinning my opponent, I felt like I was cheating, so I moved under water to remove the bubbles and gaps.

A Lump in the Head

The lump in the head is a bit like a giant planet making all kinds of demands, using gravity to pull everything toward it. All it is is a troubling knot of something that just needs to be said, which is all that is required is to get the lump out of being the center of attention. But it evolves into a kind of consciousness wrapped around itself, and it wants to be entertained. So it demands that a city be built around it to be at its beck and call, and the lump settles in, becomes part of the landscape, and the city, too, goes through permutations of a rise and fall, and ultimately takes on a life of its own that has its own goals and protocols that are at odds with what the lump wants. There comes a point where the lump begins to realize it may soon be absorbed and forgotten, and so it asserts itself with all its power and calls forth the dance of the spoons even though it means that the lump has to get up for the first time, to go to the theatre and sit in a front seat where the spoons dance, then fall off stage, each clipping a small portion from the lump, which goes away angry and disgusted. Outside the theatre, it hails a cab, and the taxi swerves in too close to the curb and knocks a little bit off the lump, and the lump is so upset that it goes down the stairway into the subway to catch the train, but when it tries to go through the turnstile, the turnstile goes through the lump and takes another chunk out. And lo and behold, by the end of the journey the lump in the head has been totally broken into bite-sized pieces just little lumps in the throat, that go down easy, piece by piece, in the proper order, and the noise they emit is exactly what needed to be said that all started out as a lump in the head.

Ruth's Tumor

The painting Ruth completed for her friend Dave was a landscape with bright strokes of white clouds over the ocean, only a tiny bit of which could be seen. There was a small cottage with a single tree, a few rolling hills , and a stream in the foreground with an empty boat. On the banks, boats were lined up against a fence, and a sandy path led down from the gate following the stream. There were other boats beached on the opposite side of the stream, and a sailboat upstream that appeared to be making a landing. Those clouds suggested a great wind, and several of the brush strokes suggested the wings of a bird gliding over the hills.

Dave said it was wonderful when she presented it to him. She said she was calling it, "Ruth's Tumor," which forced Dave to lower his chin and look at her over his reading glasses like it was a joke. Ruth wore a bandanna to cover her bald head and hide the bandages from her recent operations. They both knew she wasn't going to live much longer, and Dave wasn't entirely sure how to respond, so he looked back at the painting when she didn't meet his glare, and again proclaimed it wonderful, then thanked and hugged her.

He said he'd be right back and went into the garage for a hammer and nail, then hung the painting in a prominent, open area of the main wall of the living room and said it would hang there for the rest of his life. They then sat down to dinner and finished with coffee on the patio. Ruth wanted to sit on the stoop by the back door. She wasn't feeling well, and liked to sit near the ground at such times. Dave sat with her and looked up at the sky. There were no messages. His sense of the meaning of things wasn't clear, something like a radio that has lost its antenna and can't find a station. He was actually hoping to see some clouds, even expected they would be there looking just like the clouds in Ruth's Tumor, and then he caught himself connecting that word with the painting, thanks to her calling it that, and he was done for. He knew that from then on, he wouldn't be able to look at the painting without thinking of her brain tumor. He didn't mumble anything, but he shook his head, and Ruth recognized it as his way of rolling his eyes, which she never liked. She'd gotten him to stop doing it, but he only succeeded in adapting it to an unconscious shaking of the head, which he had never done before that, and the head shake was a habit that she'd never been successful of breaking in him. It made her cry, and Dave caught on immediately and shook his head the same way again, more out of frustration, inner eyeball rolling at himself for his insensitive stupidity, especially embarrassing for the fact that he'd been thinking of the title of the painting and thought she may have intuited this. In fact, it was only that this was one of her pet peeves, but in Ruth, there was a transformation from what was usually frustration for one of Dave's quirks into regret that she would soon never have to deal with it again, and in a flash, everything about him was endearing, and she took his hand and rested her head on his leg, and as she squeezed his hand, Dave realized that she was weeping about something much more deeply felt, something that included him for comfort, and he put his other hand on her shoulder, alternately patting it and lightly rubbing a small circle.

As the sun was beginning to go down, it wasn't long before the mosquitoes were biting, so Ruth sat up and said she should be going. Dave drove her back to her apartment and said he'd call her the next day, but he got word in the morning from her son that she'd been taken to the hospital during the night. Dave wondered why she'd called her son and not him, but it was more important that he see her, but she was already gone by the time he got there due to a massive hemorrhage. Dave spent time with her son that day, helped with the funeral arrangements and stayed through the wake and the burial of his friend. Ruth was married to Dave's best friend Henry who had died a few years earlier, and Dave's wife Barbara divorced him around the same time, saying she was cutting off a tumor, which hurt him deeply. But since they had spent so much time together as couples, Dave and Ruth just continued the tradition of getting together on Fridays. He sat in the living room looking at the painting she'd just given him, "Ruth's Tumor," thinking how her tumor, due to complications related to its removal, had just killed her. "Why had she named it that?" he wondered to himself.

He stared at it for a long time, studying it for some kind of message, for a reason why she would have connected a pastoral scene like that, with something that would kill her. Could the scene have been something she had visualized, that it was not adapted from a photograph? Perhaps having the tumor had stimulated some kind of creativity. Ruth was Japanese, and there was something very Japanese about the style in which it was painted, and yet there was something very much singular to Ruth herself, as she loved the sea though she hadn't seen it much since she left Japan as a little girl. Perhaps it was a scene from memory, a place she remembered. The longer Dave looked at it, the more anger he felt. It almost seemed the clouds were kicking up to hold him back from entering the world of the painting, that the boats on water blocked the path, and the boats in the water blocked following the river. The hills blocked the ocean, but if he were to enter the painting, where would he go?

He began to look at the cottage. Perhaps that was where she lived, where she thought of going when she thought of dying. There were tiny windows on the white walls, not very well placed on close inspection due to her not having had a particularly steady hand those last weeks, but from where he was sitting, it was all so peaceful and natural. The scene stemmed the tide of his anger. He went in circles a few times, from thinking of her tumor, feeling the anger that she died, demanding an answer, feeling blocked, then seeing it as a simple, beautiful pastoral scene that calmed him down almost like the sea would. Standing there, maybe in his own cottage looking out a window, there she was across the river safe and sound in the house. The wind was strong on high, but down below it was calm with no sign of a storm. The little bit of sea that could be seen on the horizon was blue and deep, almost separate from the river,

171

not in any way taking away from it or drawing it. The boats seemed happily anchored, waiting for someone to get in. There was the one close to his window, and the other one, the sailboat further up, now looked to him like it was slightly pulled up on sand. There was a color differentiation that he'd not noticed before. "That must be her boat," he heard himself say, which woke him from the reverie.

Dave stood up and stretched, feeling his muscles had settled into position from sitting too long. He went to the bar and made himself a drink, looked back at the painting, held up his glass and said, "To Ruth's Tumor," meaning the painting, and took a sip. For the first time, the idea of the painting being referred to as the tumor or even the tumor itself did not bother him. If anything, all the time she wore that bandanna, she'd worn it well. It complimented her appearance the way she tied it on her head. He would never think of her as having anything terrible that killed her when he remembered her in what was designed to hide the baldness and bandages.

From the new vantage point of the bar, and with the scotch beginning to flow through his veins, he saw the painting for how it complimented his room. It was as if Ruth had managed to select colors from swatches of the color of the paint on the wall, from the curtains and the furniture. He walked around the room picking things up and bringing them to the painting. "Yep," he would say when he found the color. This was a painting of his room, only everything was all stirred up and rearranged into a scene from her mind. It was like she took the view of his room, made it into a view of where she would live in eternity, and from her vantage point, she could look right into his room from across the river, and this amazed him. Did the tumor teach her to paint this way, or was it all in his mind? Was the painting a tumor turned into a healing object, neutralized, changed from an invasive obstruction into a welcoming portal? The river in the painting seemed suddenly alive. It was the carpet he was standing on, putting him right next to the boat. The land was cut-up drapes, the sky the same color and pattern of his ceiling. Even the cottage was a small porcelain miniature Ruth had given him for Christmas the year before. "I'm not a tumor," he realized, and he sank to his knees and cried for the loss of his friend.

Under the Barge

I always had a dream or fantasy of standing on a bridge with only scant moonlight to discern shapes, in trouble, being chased and cut off on either side, cornered, and just by chance a long barge is at that moment just beginning to pass under the bridge. So I take the only chance I have, put one leg, then the other over the handrail and time a jump onto the barge, which is actually massive, carrying an entire village of people who live in thatched huts. I fear breaking my leg, but surprisingly, the landing is soft, on grass, in a clearing, and I stand up and see the huts, and hear around me in the woods around the river, the gathering forces that were seeking me converging on a dead end, unaware of a barge silently slipping away.

It is just an image, but I find it compelling for some reason. I rewind it to the bridge, and I can even discern the tops of the huts that I hadn't seen before. It almost seems the whole village has been scooped up and placed on the barge, every stick and blade of grass intact, and despite the danger, it is finally sleeping. My sudden appearance goes undetected, and it almost seems like I can sleep, that the pressure is gone, that I have escaped, and as I repeatedly consider the scene with the dark night and slight light of the moon, I soon fall asleep without ever seeing what lies beyond that scene. The pressures of the day seem to melt away, and I drift out of whatever concerns that might otherwise keep me awake.

It's been many years since I first imagined this scene, and it's lulled me to sleep too many times to count, but lately I've been considering the barge in the light of day, as if standing before it on the dock, able to take a long look at its shape and construction, seeing every detail except that from my new vantage point, I cannot see the green huts or anything the barge is carrying. It is just too tall, and I am just too low. There is not enough dock either to walk around and make a survey. I can only examine it from the front where it is almost next to my nose. I can reach over and touch it, and looking up, all I see is the wall of its outer hull. I am blind to all else except a swath of sky and the sun, the glare of which instantly blinds and forces me to look down again into the waters lapping against the barge, which are the waters of my life, and of sleep.

I realize I have stuck my neck out from underneath the barge for a moment, and I have created the barge over a lifetime of worry and concern for every detail in my waking life. It is as if I have let things come over me and grown cold to them, so cold that it has transformed it into a blanket of crystals, not quite a sheet of ice. I see it as if I have submerged myself into the waters of life and let my worries become a blanket that I pull over me and up to my neck like one who has gone to bed and is trying to go to sleep. But what I've created is the barge, and I let it slide over and cover me up except for rare instance when I am somehow able to separate myself from it, which often happens when I get a terrible headache and must stop everything I'm doing and go to bed. Then I see it all before me as one who examines a ship closely on the dock. The high wall of the barge that blocks my view is the pain of the headache, and as it recedes, so do I beneath the dock and the waters as I resume my routines and take on the daily pressures that I face.

When night falls and I go to bed exhausted, when I pull the covers over me and lay the back of my hand on my forehead, released for a moment but still trapped in worries of what will come, I stand on the bridge again surrounded on all sides. Perhaps it is the bridge to the next day, or to the next life, but as the barge passes underneath and I jump, I feel safe and sound, and as I hear the sounds of everything chasing me down going in the wrong direction, I smile and lay my head in the grasses next to thatched huts of an entire community whose memory will never be wiped out when it finds a new place to thrive. By the time the village wakes, I will be underneath it effecting repairs, and when it sleeps, I'll rejoin them.

Water Man, Desert Woman

Water Man was mostly a collection of water molecules and a variety of dust and minerals he had picked up along the way of his journeys that took him everywhere in general and nowhere in particular. He ranged far and wide, dripping deep into crevices, flowing out in a stream and evaporating into the clouds until collecting together to fall to earth again as rain and begin the process anew. Water Man did this for years without complaint.

When we think of life, we imagine gradually tiring of constant motion, that it would grow dull, and there would seem to be something missing, but even with the changing to ice, to water and to vapor over and over, and doing it in so many places, Water Man was content. It was not in his nature to somehow wish to stop. To stay in one place was not a desire deep within him. Perhaps he felt a certain restlessness at times, but he never considered there was any alternative, no reason to think that anything else was out there waiting to change him, and his intuitive reaction was that to freeze or flow or vaporize was fulfilling. He did not want more.

Water Man was static in that sense, but he was also growing in another sense, beyond the acquisition of minerals and minute dust particles along his way. If anything, he had exchanged as much as he'd picked up, dropped off this thing or that thing and taking whatever came along. He'd carried rocks from many miles as part of a glacier for example, and when he broke off and became part of an iceberg, and finally melted in the sea, the rocks he carried merely sank to the bottom of the ocean, and he was not set up to secure them or worry about their well-being. He had no feelings one way or the other for anything like that, but he was in fact developing a greater sense of himself, a coming to consciousness of himself.

Had he never experienced any such sensations of this kind, what happened to him ultimately would have seemed to be a random event, and it would have happened without any memory of it, spectacular like an event in space when planets collide. But when one is conscious, one learns new information that falls in with the rest of the spirit, which then undergoes a recombination of sorts, and it becomes a new thing slightly different altogether from what it was.

And so, it happened that he found himself on one of his many journeys in the middle of a desert in an overnight rain, freakish and rare for that part of the country. He prepared for quick evaporation when the sun came up, but he felt the earth move around him, as it were, as the sand he had penetrated took a more firm shape. It actually stood up and thanked him, in a feminine voice. Water Man inquired to whom he was speaking, and she identified herself as Desert Woman, and somehow he felt he had always known her.

"This is my spot," Desert Woman told him, "but somehow I know the reason you've landed here is because of me, you have given me firmness for the first time, an ability to finally stand up and not just blow about reforming the endless dunes. You've completed me."

"And you have given me a basis, a foundation," Water Man replied. "I feel no need to seek my own level. You've completed me."

They spent the last hours of the night together, but as the sun rose that morning, the union they had formed broke down. Desert Woman floated away in particles that rejoined the dunes, and Water Man quickly vaporized and rose high into the clouds, alone again in the way he'd always known it, without lonliness, but aware of another presence that he'd never known, satisfied to have touched upon it on his endless travels, and hopeful that at some point he'd encounter it again. And so, as he rained and washed into the crevises, flowed out of the caves, freezing, melting, and evaporating into the skies, Water Man took pleasure wherever he was and dreamed of a sandy opposite, of being solid, yet without form, able to form mountains yet smooth out to a flat plane, something like him that could count time not in droplets but in endless grains.

The Dragonfly Placenta

When we were boys, my parents sent my brother and I to camp every summer. I was four years older, and tiring of all the silly activities in the last years. I was almost as old as one of the counselors, and I started heckling a bit when she was giving demonstrations, and she cornered me later to remind me of camp policies, and when she grabbed my arm, I felt a wave of excitement go through me, and she changed in that instant before me into an object of great interest. She must have detected something because at the instant I felt it, she let go of me and went on in to dinner.

My brother and I had beds across from one another, and I could not sleep that night. The moonlight was shining in the window on my brother, and I could see he was asleep, so I got up and checked the other boys, and they were all asleep, so I quietly went outside for a walk. I hadn't gone far before I saw someone else walking, and I knew it was the counselor. Denise was her name. I hid behind a tree, but she walked right for me, and I knew she must have already seen me, so I stepped into the open to take what was coming regarding camp policy. The moon was behind her, so I couldn't see her face at first, but when she got very close, I could see she was smiling. She walked right up, put her arms around my neck and kissed me. After a few minutes, she asked me whether everyone was sleeping, whether it was safe to go to my bed, and I said if we were quiet, then it should be alright, so we crept in and slid under the covers and started kissing. I remember going almost into a trance with the unbelievable passion I felt, and losing all sense of where I was, but at one point I opened my eyes during our embrace where I saw my

177

brother sitting up in bed, watching me with astonishment. I've never forgotten that awful moment of my last year at camp.

I grew up to become an artist, and I'm not sure how or why, but that moment of seeing my brother with his eyes open became the basis for deciding that art was something I wanted to pursue. It may have had something to do with getting caught, that art is not just any kind of device but a way of fooling people into a certain way of thinking, or better yet, a way of catching them in their current way of thinking and making them ashamed. Art plays a kind of practical joke, performs its jest, and generally speaking receives praise. Most individuals are good sports, but not necessarily groups of people. Somehow, when people are in the position of thinking for others, art is often seen in an entirely different light. Groups sometimes behave as if they know better what is good for people. Art is often blamed for going too far, as if we're meeting strange women outside and bringing them into a barracks of brethren and waking them up with forbidden embraces.

I suppose there is some truth that artists sometimes do try a little too hard to get a rise out of people, but it isn't always the case that we expect the results we obtain. It's hard to be noticed, and truth is an often ugly and boring subject to present on its own terms, so it is dressed up and paraded in the open as something it isn't, but the idea is that with careful thought, the truth will finally be recognized by a thoughtful audience, perhaps just one thoughtful individual, and not akin to a brother sitting across the room, shocked at witnessing something to which he had never been and should not have been exposed. Instead, the witness recognizes the entire scene, the whole story, and sees the presentation including the brother on the bed as a remarkable moment for the older boy, for experience in general, that the incident falls into the category of events of passage that every human being has. Certainly, in that sense not all of art is for children, and that is the point I am making.

I would admit to having taken certain liberties, to following certain modern traditions that have a certain shock value, but not shock for its own sake. Again, at least in my work, the shock is for the sake of truth, though some may not understand it at first and connect my work with those things designed solely to shock. I can live with that. I'll never forget during the birth of my stillborn daughter how the doctor stared at the placenta. I was in the operating room for an extended period, and I took note of that. I wondered what his interest could possibly be. I was in shock at having endured hours of waiting for my daughter to be born, knowing she would be born dead, and through my grieving eyes to see the doctor pondering the placenta made a deep impression on me. It reminded me of the time I was painting the house when I was sixteen. I was on the ladder scraping the gutters, and my arm was killing me. My father and grandfather were both in the house, but they checked my progress often, and it almost felt like the entire assignment to paint the house was a deliberate attempt to mold me into a man, that they had decided it was high time that they forced me to do something that no man enjoyed doing but that all men must eventually face doing, and painting was it. They would come out in bad spirits and criticize my efforts, point out spots I had missed, call me weak when I complained I was tired and lazy when I asked to take a break.

Toward the end of the day, from the top of the ladder, I saw a pair of dragonflies land on the patio, one on top of the other. Seeing dragonflies close up is very unusual, but here they were mating, and I wanted a closer look, not out of any prurient interest at all, but simply because I have always had an interest in nature, so I slowly and quietly stepped down the ladder so as not to scare them away, and I crept as close as I thought I could reasonably get and made an examination. I was down on my knees and elbows when my grandfather flew out the backdoor and blew his stack. When he told my father what I'd been doing, they had a field day with it, and I heard about it for years afterwards, how instead of executing the duty at hand, I chose to watch bugs screwing. They would bring it up at the dinner table when friends were over who I'd never met before. I suppose they felt it would help me become a man to eviscerate any lingering sense of dignity I may have had before them. I grew to resent all of their instructions. My grandfather's world became one of old Europe to me, the failure of peace and the bleeding out youth due to World War I. My father's world was the Second World War, and

179

I thought as much of what his generation had done with the planet. Neither one seemed to have any sense of what could be gathered into much-needed insight and presented as such, nor was either one particularly interested in anything out of which they might glean some important inkling of the nature of the world. No, both were totally content within themselves as to the nature and standing of the world out of which they had come and in its present state, and quite frankly, they both made me ill.

On the other hand, I was young, and I've since learned that during those formative years, the brain isn't even fully developed, and it's somewhat natural to have such feelings for one's elders. But I detected deeper meaning than that in my own rebellion. I began to study art and became fascinated with its position in the mind and in society. It seemed to be a thing the least interested in the mindless party, and yet it was the thing most likely to probe the most effectively as well as to poke the most fun. It was the one thing that arrived without an invitation that could not be rejected, and saw the thing the most clearly. I began to see the party, if I can call it that, as necessarily having something like this present, that whoever is present, however dignified and stately, without something to bring the whole into focus and either make everyone look ridiculous, equa,l or turn the whole event upside down, the only other possibility was that the party would take itself seriously, which is unacceptable. So I began to talk back and be disrespectful to both my father and grandfather. I made it clear I wasn't accepting any further molding by them and would avoid becoming like them at all costs.

I left home then at an early age and moved to the city and the neighborhood where the artists lived. I found it be a dirty place. I found artists to be thieves and liars, or at least those pretending that they would be artists. What was most amazing to me was how much reliance there was on their family, how important it was for them to convey that their father or grandfather was this or that important individual as if it gave them added respectability. Everyone sits around talking about what they're going to do and what they will be and repeats everything they remember that anyone has said that makes them sound like they're smart, but in truth, there's nothing interesting about any of it. I spent lots of time in the various galleries looking for truth in the images or presentation, but I found that everything being done was about shock value. Shock is compelling by itself, but I knew it must have more in order to be art. The individual is somewhat pleased by shock, and the group isn't bothered by it. In order to qualify as art, however, the group must feel it's being made to look ridiculous, equal or that the status quo is being turned on its head, and though it will dispassionately declare the work socially unfit, what it really feels is threatened and outraged.

So when I started my work, I tried to use materials that had not been used before. I took the idea of the social dinner party to heart and took parts of tuxedos, bow ties and shirt cuffs, and arranged it on the dish of fine china in the center with a full service of forks, spoons and knives, and the gravy was red paint spattered on all of it to indicate blood. Everyone saw this as being too obvious, and I took it down. When my fellow students were so perceptive, I knew I was on the wrong track. I wanted to be more elusive than that.

Around this time, I met a nice girl and became absorbed in a relationship. We decided not to marry since we'd only known one another six months. She was pregnant, and I thought it was the best way to handle it. As I mentioned earlier, the baby was stillborn, and that is when I got the first idea that I thought worthy after watching the doctor examine the placenta. I managed to obtain the placenta after convincing the hospital that I planned to bury it where I would plant a tree in my dead baby's honor, which I had heard was a tradition of sorts with some people. But I had other plans for it. I used it, with great difficulty and emotional stress, to produce a pair of large dragonflies, one on top of the other, just as I saw them. I worked a foundation of fired clay onto the surface of a canvas and secured it to the back. On this I fastened the dragonflies, and then I painted various men in the act of examining it. There is a man of science in a white jacket who is studying it. Behind his back he is holding a dragonfly collection. A soldier in WWI gear who looks like my grandfather is pointing a gun at it, about to shoot. There is a newborn child dead on the ground, its umbilical cord stretching to "The Dragonfly Placenta," which is the title for the piece.

Well, when my girlfriend's mother read the story in the newspaper that I had actually fashioned the dragonflies out of the placenta of her daughter, she had a fit. She drove into the city and convinced her daughter to come home with her, which surprised me, but in some ways I knew I had crossed the line although the painting did meet with some critical success. The mere fact that it outraged so many of my peers and "the group," as it were, pleased me to no end, though I was still extremely upset at the loss of my child and my woman, which more than offset any chance I would feel good about the success of my work. I realized that in many ways I was doing it for myself, and that I'd chosen my subject, even had the idea for it, out of shock at what life gave me. Nothing I could present would ever be as shocking to others as what I'd actually experienced. This consideration challenged my view of art, and I began to formulate a metaphor for the best kind of artist as one who has taken in all that life offers with an extremely open mind, then all at once has the experience of being flattened, not in the sense of actually being compressed, but more analogous to a building that all at once has all of its various floors mixed together on the inside as if being tumbled in the rotating cylinder of a dryer where all things are equally in the front and center or buried under all other things in proportion to one another, which renders them altogether ridiculous, equal to one another and constantly turning upside down from one instant to the next. In this metaphor, the mind is able to pick and choose from any moment of life because it is all in the same swirl.

A few days alone, and I couldn't muster much energy, not even to take my dirty clothes to the local laundry, let alone take them out of the washer and put them into the dryer, I took public transportation to the apartment of my girlfriend's mother to have the necessary confrontation to get her to come back with me. On the way over, it struck me that what I was thinking as I was about to face an irate mother was a little too much like I felt whenever I summoned the energy to create a new work of art. It was like I was on the verge of arguing with someone, of justifying myself, and of winning. How many times had I stood with friends in front of famous works in the museum, arguing over what the artist was trying to say as if a given work was an easy answer, and yet how many different answers there were. It was almost as if I knew the answers were simple, and yet I chose a method of couching them so that they would be next-to-impossible to extract, as if there would be great pleasure for anyone in that. As the bus neared the apartment, I saw two men on a corner that reminded me of my father and grandfather, and it struck me for the first time that I was no different than they were, just fighting a different war. I too had my causes, my points of reference that I'd actually longed for a chance to explain to a child. For the first time, I felt sorry that I had done so much to disappoint them. I wished instead that things could have been different in the entire nature of things, that people could connect so as to infuse another and share a sense of what is inside. I decided to listen to whatever my girlfriend and her mother had to say rather than go in expecting to boss them around and force them to see things my way.

When I got there, I was surprised to be allowed in so easily. Her mother left the two of us alone and went into the kitchen. Denise started to cry that her mother didn't want me to see her anyone, saying that it was really all about religion, that her mother was saying that everything I stood for was against their faith in God. As she kept saying, "The church this," and "the church that," my mind was drifting into thinking, "Oh great. I've got to beat down religious principles here. It's all about fighting religion, putting my beliefs against others when I don't really even share that particular faith or that particular denomination, but there I am fighting the bishops and fighting the priests and fighting the mother church that someone's mother, who doesn't have even a basic concept of theology, has set up as a main line of defense against me." I was thinking so much about how ridiculous, unequal and turned upside down everything was that I was only picking up what Denise was saying in phrases. "What you feel in your heart has pulled you away from the church... you have fallen away from the church... has yanked you away from the church... you've put your head ahead of the church." I finally interrupted her, took her hand just to stop her from talking. That quieted her, and then I waited and considered not what to say, but I rather felt the surrounding swirling of my thoughts, which wanted to say this:

Let's examine that. What is it that you really want to do here? Do you want to be with me, someone who knows what you just went through, who lost a child with you, or would you rather please a bishop and the stone statues that line the front entrance? How can I fight the church? Is that really what this is about? Does anyone enjoy pleasing an institution that supposedly stands for spirit to the evisceration of spirit, or of the freedom to live? We have a chance to knock down the things lined up against us, the ducks of convention, squawking at us. One of them is the church, as we didn't just walk by them. We did it. We knocked them down. We made a free path, only now we've got more of these things squawking at us, though maybe it's a different species of duck.

Now it's your mother and your sense of responsibility to everything you learned that was largely designed simply to mold you, the ideas that a family throws at you as its tradition, what fathers and grandfathers tell you they were, what you should be, when they were victims or pawns of their age, frustrated and disabled to live their dreams, and that comes in with the teaching. They say do this and that because we tell you to do it, and don't shame us. They take you to church to fortify it, throw religion into the mix and use it to cause fear, and tie you to a pattern, which is your denomination, like a Scottish tartan, that distinguishes you from others and blends you with your own kind. But what you don't realize is that it sets you up to put you at odds. It's inevitable that you will face something you want and maybe love, but to choose it will render you disloyal to your heritage, to your special blend, that all together is just national garment amongst many. And to the degree that you work on that level, you may please some, but at the same time betray your heart. In the end it never comes down to giving up everything one has for another. The forces back down and accept your choice. One has to prove oneself strong enough to give up everything, leave everything behind, and when nothing can stand in your way, then people give you the room you need, and hold onto you, and so will the church. Ultimately, it embraces you, or is supposed to, even for making choices to live outside of its walls. The people that love you, like your mother, are the people you love, so the faith and the religion have nothing to do with it because they're not pulling us to God in this sense. They're just trying to keep us from doing something they deem wrong against them, save us not from sin but from doing them wrong.

It's a big thing to have a life. It takes big choices, and against the weight of that, a mother can seem a little thing, and so she needs to make the picture bigger by putting your choice against the backdrop of the grand scheme of things to show how small a decision it is in the hope you will abandon it, though you must consider you're not falling into a pit by coming with me. After all, you have the rest of your life to make it up to God, and even to discover the path to Him, a path that should lead out of your childhood, not back into it, and so I've come to bring you home.

What I finally said was, "Your mother is trying to protect you. That was her job, but it's mine now. She thinks I've made some bad decisions, and I'm sorry that I've upset both of you in my trying to make a statement. If she can't forgive me, I'll have to accept your standing by your mother and her beliefs."

Within the hour, Denise was on the bus with me back to the city. It upset her to think that I would agree with her mother or leave her there. The fact that I would face them both was enough for her to decide to get out, and indeed, she'd had enough after a few days and wanted to be with me for all we'd just been through, and she needed to deal with getting through that, not examine the principles in her faith through her mother's point of view.

When we got back to the city, we went to dinner and talked about moving forward together, even uncertain about what we faced, particularly as to the reversal we'd already experienced at the outset. Still, I maintained a very calm and confident demeanor, much as I always had, but I felt as if my mind had been compressed and was spinning so that everything was exposed, which I found was a good thing, and made me believe that if I could sustain it, then I could freely draw from it, and my work would be impressive.

But that night I had a very disturbing dream. I was the father of a young boy who had been very sick. He had been trying to sleep on the floor and was getting a little bit better, but it was obvious from his fetal position that he was still experiencing a great deal of discomfort. He also didn't like the light in his face, and his face had the same chalky pallor of the stillborn child. He was trying to move his head away from the light, but he couldn't turn over, so I was telling everyone the light needed to be moved or turned out, while they wanted to leave it on, even to make it brighter to add warmth, and their solution was to give him something to cover over his head. At the same time, they wanted to put a pillow under his head so that he would sleep in what would look like a more traditional position, essentially making them more comfortable with his appearance.

Suddenly we were in a carriage on a bumpy road. It took my worry to a higher level as I thought it was ridiculous to try to help him sleep as sleep was impossible on the path we were traveling. As the dream progressed, the child was bigger and getting better but I was still having to shoo people away who were rolling around in the coach, trying to be an influence. Soon he was standing up, making it obvious that he didn't appreciate my not listening to those trying to help him. He said I was hurting him, but I told him that everything I did came from a desire to help. I said I loved him, and I hugged him. Then I said that if it were my father and grandfather, they would be telling him to sleep, that it was time for bed, and he laughed. Then I turned and saw a statue I had made, and I feared my son would see it. I asked myself what my family would think when they saw it. I was looking at it for the first time though I knew it was my creation. I was viewing it as I would any work of art, not knowing what it means, but trying to honestly react and understand it.

My immediate reaction was one of disgust, as one waking up in surprise to see people making love with abandon across the room where he was sleeping peacefully. The statue was all that was left of a prostitute who had died years earlier. Somehow, though it was in every way a statue, in the dream it was still alive, and as I moved in to get a closer look, the statue was inviting me to take part in her professional offerings, to pay for an experience with her. There was a sense in which she was saying she would allow me to step back and adjust, to give me time for the consideration to become more appealing. If I was filled with any desire, it was only to know how such a thing could operate. How was it possible that anyone could approach it on any level of desire? But I knew that in this world, extreme, unwanted things rejected in the mainstream operated with some success, beckoning wayfarers to their doom like the sirens.

This statue, this prostitute thing, had ridges on the sides of the legs, and I wasn't sure if they had grown there or if they were always a part of her, but I knew it was something evil. As I walked up and looked at her, it seemed there was something like a nylon pulled over her face. Maybe it was all the years that had washed down and softened the features of this statue, but it sensed the desire in me to understand it better, and it was able to amplify it, and so when it felt my desire and my emotion, my curiosity came to life and scared me. It then spoke with a very welcoming voice. It said, "Yes. Come on in." It was like she was saying, "I'm still here. I'm still lurking. I don't know how, but maybe you've activated me, and now I'm here night and day for your needs. I'll take you into my chamber where we can be together," which I knew would be like going back into wherever she was from, which was not only the wrong of previous times, but contained the death of all those ages gone by, including all the desires I ever had that were wrong, which I realized in the dream were only dormant, though I suffered to see the kind of thing that wakes them, even if it was just a dream.

When Denise and I were having breakfast the next morning, she asked why I was quiet. I said I was groggy from sleep and needed coffee, but I was considering how all of the images seemed somehow to connect with my experience, all the way from my brother catching me in an inappropriate embrace at camp to my suddenly catching sight of a horrible living thing, and after one has been through all the rites of passage, it takes quite a thing to provide the shock. I thought how it was funny how if there's nothing for a time in life to do the trick, a dream will come along and do the honors. I've kept feeling that I had a double life, that I was in bed with the statue, which is just a symbol, but I'm also my brother across the room, awake to my own sin, aware of what isn't just beckoning me, but to what I've prepared myself for, to what I've committed myself, which I've damned myself by creating, for this has all the earmarks of my handiwork. It is the real placenta on bronze, bringing what has died, what should be buried, back to an unnatural life, all for the sake of going against a couple of soldiers who became fathers when they were done fighting, who tried to save me by putting the fight in me

187

when there was so much peace that life was too boring.

I remember when my little brother woke up and saw me in bed, I traveled into him and saw myself through his eyes, as I thought he saw me, and it changed what I thought I felt for the girl, reduced her to a statue covered in a sweaty material, making it ugly, far short of love. She became the Virgin Mary in urine, a work I might have done had I continued on the course I was on, and which I understand in the sense of what we go through in the world, how godly things are subject to the atmosphere we create, but I decided not to be an artist like that, not one who seeks to bury truth under an aura of shock. There's a sickness of looking through sickness, a difference between choosing something or keeping it at a proper distance.

I dismantled "The Dragonfly Placenta" and buried it, planting a tree on the spot in honor of my dead child, which I understand is a tradition for some, and though it is not for me, I did it for closure, because painting starts with scraping and ends with sweeping up the chips, but the result is a surface that endures the weather and protects one's home, and so I paint like my grandfather and father taught me, though I continue to study nature as well, on the side.

The Army of the Dead

I had a dream that I'd been walking along the beach and found the body of my brother. In death, he seemed round and fat. In life, he was thin from hunger. Now his stomach rolled out of his open shirt, and he looked relaxed from having enjoyed meals without worrying about enemies and food shortages.

Strangely, the dream provided a visual explanation for what had happened. I saw my brother and Osim fighting. Osim stabbed him, and my brother fell in the water. I watched Osim drag the body onto the sand. Then he stared not at the body, but out at the ocean, seeming to absorb everything in a wide survey. I stepped up and asked him what had happened. Osim said that "the dog" had killed himself. I said it was not a dog but my brother. Osim said we were all brothers, but to die by the hand of Osim was a righteous death. "I am calling out the army of the dead," he declared, finally turning to me, and there was no skin on his face. The shock woke me.

I heard snoring from the couch across the room, and then I remembered. Osim was back. He'd returned the night before from the desert as I happened to be standing before my hideaway. He stirred for a moment. The couch was too small for his long legs.

Father had warned me that life as we knew it could only be threatened by one event, which was Osim's return. As long as he was gone, we were not at risk. But the last three years, even without him, had been violent for what he'd started. The whole country had suffered since he disappeared. Father and I had managed to survive but not without scars. We all hoped the violence would end in time, but the acts of terrorism initiated against the inner sanctum by

189

Osim persisted in his absence. He was declared dead, but there were many reports of individuals disappearing. A few reappeared. Most did not. Then we heard reports that whole villages were being burned off the map by a large independent army. There was little we could verify, and few that we could trust. Some said Osim was leading them, but I knew if he were alive that he would hang back in a hideaway. All we knew for certain was that Osim had been raised to the level of a sacred, dead leader, a martyr, and that he was still the motivating force behind the underground terrorist activity that many supported without having any clear idea of what any of it was for. Osim was a hero for the blind. I always believed there was a very good chance he was alive, managing operations from some hidden location. Everything had his mark on it, even the rumors. Terrorism had been on the rise, but preparations for the annual caravan had a way of causing that. All the officials from the inner sanctum being together like that made a tempting target. The cliffs were cordoned off, and visits to the desert plains below were restricted. Now Osim had returned near the anniversary of his disappearance. But why?

I got up to check on father who was slumbering peacefully in his room. When I returned, Osim was up. He apologized for the surprise of the evening before and asked how father was doing.

"Very sick," I told him, and then I realized he'd called him father. "That's the first time you've ever called him that."

"I refer to all elders in this way. A great deal has happened in the last three years, such amazing events. I admit I held grudges against you both for some things that happened when we were growing up, but I'll forgive him because he's ill, but you I'll only forgive if I can count on you now. All is in the past, and a new future's waiting."

I thought Osim meant that he'd forgiven father for being strict, but he was that way for both of us. "That was just his way of disciplining you," I said. "He doesn't need or want your forgiveness. You should rather thank him, and beg his forgiveness!"

Osim laughed. "How little you understand of anything. You would have me think that the way one treats an adopted waif is equal to what you received as his real son. No, I didn't deserve any of it, but I understand now that my father's death was necessary, and

190

I've managed to ascertain facts from days long before you and I were even in the picture. We were both victims, you know. Father too."

"You would like to think that this world is as it should be," he continued. "You were born into a system like an egg sac hatching on a leaf, and you've no concern for the root of the plant or whether it is sick. You accept the nature of things whether or not things are counter to nature. You've been so wrapped up in your personal life and emotions that you lack any outward sense or capacity to understand the politics, but at the same time, you cannot help it. The inner sanctum has made it so for everyone."

I tried to interrupt but he stopped me. "Until you have a notion of the whole picture, try just once to forbear reacting and making terrible mistakes. Today marks the dawn of a new age, and there's nothing you can do to stop it. I'm willing to add that if you listen, there's a chance you'll grasp what has happened and have a hand in setting it straight. Are you interested?"

"I don't know what you could possibly tell me that would change my opinion of you or anything you have done. You've been a deviant and disrupter all of your life. Nothing has ever been right for you, and one can reasonably understand why you would feel that way. None of us received a normal set of circumstances. But as long as I can remember, you've been nothing but a torment to me personally, ruining my life every chance you get. I suspect you're here to keep that tradition alive."

"So I've ruined your life, have I? My, how these three years have left you swamped in the same self-indulgent primordial slime in which life crawls. Time to come out of the gutter into the light. The truth of our lives doesn't sit well with any of us. That is sure. But my intention is to deliver the facts straight, to set the entire country back on its original course. Should complaints be set on my doorstep or pour like acid into the inner sanctum? We must act together once and for all."

"Frankly, Osim, I don't care what you do. Nothing you have to say will change anything. You're a dead man already. I suppose you should be allowed your last words."

"Whatever you say, but if these be my last words, they are words

191

for all who follow to live by. We must never be suppressed again and stand by while hope is buried. I am proof it never dies."

He told me the story of the three years he was gone, admitted to all the raids, to leading an army from a secret place. I worried about what was coming. I had no doubt that it would be as earth-shattering as he claimed it would be, and I was certain it would concern me as well, but that made the confrontation little different than any time we'd locked horns. It always turned out that mine were made of paper, his of ivory or steel. Mine was the shorter end of the stick.

Osim said, "When we were born, the country was in a terrible war, but by the time we were old enough to understand anything and learn about it, it was over. All we heard were lies, but we accepted the history. What reason would we have to doubt it?

"Actually, the truth is that we never won the war or repelled the invaders. The war was lost, the inner sanctum formed and filled with our enemies, and we were cut off from it hanging half-severed from the tree. Such a limb doesn't die as quickly as those cut off completely. It withers slowly, but it still dies in the end.

"Let me paint the picture for you exactly as it was, but briefly. The era before we were born was intensely political. The politics turned into a civil war. Religious influences were battling against an increasingly secular society. The name "inner sanctum" still suggests what it actually was long ago, the center of a deeply religious society, but they retained only the name and burned out the faith.

"The secular faction drove out the religious fighters and performed the first solidification of the inner sanctum wall, but religious forces were at work while we were growing up, modifying the hideaways as a means to attack and destroy the inner sanctum."

"That is ridiculous," I interrupted. Everyone knows that the hideaways are aligned to protect the country. The guns have always faced the desert, the only direction from which anyone can invade."

"You are mistaken. We were all misled as to the history of the hideaways. I assure you that this is just the beginning of many discoveries that will shake the whole nation. Also, you fail to take into consideration the possibility of an invasion from within."

"What else did you discover, then?"

"For one, I found that at one time hideaways had openings that faced the inner sanctum as well. I was able to verify this from documents I obtained during a visit to the inner sanctum where..."

"You visited the inner sanctum? But that's impossible. When?"

"Later. Let me finish one thought at a time here. I verified from documents in the inner sanctum that the hideaways were armed and aimed at the inner sanctum. Later, after the war, the backs were closed and once again the openings faced only the desert. It was thought after the war that they should be used to protect the nation from outside attack, but due to poor policies in the inner sanctum, they fell into disrepair. It was thought dangerous to leave guns that we might use, so armaments were removed.

"As for personal matters of that era, both of our fathers lived in the inner sanctum before the war. Did you know that? They knew one another, having worked together in a variety of matters. They had differences but were on friendly terms. That was the way of the political system. Your father sympathized with the secular extremists, but would have lost position to join the movement. My father was a religious leader and was therefore considered expendable.

"Basically, your father played his cards well enough that if the revolution did succeed, he would survive. His place in the secular party was safer, although to the secularists, he was nothing more than a tepid collaborator, unwilling to fully follow the beliefs of his own society. After the war, when power changed hands, he survived, but as a reward for collaborating with the secular state, he would only survive if he let himself be used by the new authorities, and so he collaborated with them as an informant."

"That's outrageous! You're just hateful!"

"You might think so, but not against your father. I don't see any law against surviving. We did not live in those days. We have no idea of the fears they faced. What did my father gain by dying? How can I paint a picture I didn't see? If I say that thousands rushed here or there and were shot down, or that hostages were taken and put against this or that wall, will you believe me when I show you the spot, or will you say there is no sign of blood that washed into the ground? If I take you to the bullet-chipped wall where fifty died, will you call it normal wear and tear, or the effects of children throwing rocks? I don't know how to convince you of these things, but the history wasn't recorded properly, and isn't reportable in a fashion that would please you, and even if it were, you'd think it some drama scooped out of a vivid imagination attempting to distort the present with lies from the past. I'm saying the present is the lie and that we are all doomed unless we act now."

"What do you plan to do, Osim? I find this very upsetting. What you're saying about father is ridiculous. He can't even defend himself. He's lost his mind."

"That was the effect of the torture he endured when they tried to procure information about me from him. He was blamed for not properly informing when there was really nothing he could have done. He was appointed my guardian because of links with the past, for knowing my father, because it was felt that I should be watched for any inheritance of what might threaten the country. And yet they planted the seed. Not my father and not yours. He was blamed further for having gotten soft for having raised me, for harboring a state enemy. Can you believe that? After all those years, which they told him to do, he was charged with harboring a state enemy. They wanted to destroy him after he followed their law to the letter. Their law has no spirit, but they said he should have seen it coming and known what to do.

"My father was put to death for crimes against the state. Yours became a state pawn. The state further fortified the inner sanctum and has treated all outer residents as enemies of the state. Survival was possible in the new order only if the laws were strictly obeyed, and to ensure that there was no threat from any given community, informants like your father were planted to detect any divergence from state policy. Any deviance was weeded out, but if the community was infected, the village would be destroyed. The foundations would be left behind as a reminder, but strict silence would need to be maintained so as not to raise a revolt. By degrees, the population would be reduced outside the inner sanctum to one that posed no threat. In time, though it might mean that all communities might vanish, the inner sanctum would hold the country intact."

"Are you saying that the ruins where we played as children were not ancient, but thriving communities of the recent past?"

"Isn't any of this believable to you? Haven't you wondered about any of it, the authorities, the war, the ruins, why we all live in hide-aways in the faces of the mountains overlooking the desert? Does nothing I have said strike you as plausible? Would I make it up?"

"If it served your purpose," I answered. Why don't you just invade the inner sanctum? Obviously, that's what you're here to do. What do you need me for, anyway? Food and shelter? I hope that's all."

"Actually, there is more, but it doesn't really matter. I'm trying to bring you in before it's too late, to give you a chance that your father never had. Generally speaking, you're innocent of any wrongdoing. You're just ignorant, that's all, and because you're my brother, I wanted to come here first. But now I find that you're more one of them, and that you think I've been out there destroying my own kind, riding out of the hills, burning villages."

"I don't know what you've been doing, Osim, but changing the nation isn't likely. And don't count on me to help you. You're a dead man as soon as you're seen, that's for sure."

"I've made it three years, haven't I?"

"But you won't make it three days now."

At that, Osim just came over and shook me. He slapped me several times and threw me into a chair. He was seething, unaware of how he'd filled my mind with new pictures and strange confusion.

It was almost too bizarre to accept, but how could anyone concoct such lies? The story of our people was hundreds of years old, and even at that beginning, the land was divided between those who lived above, and those who lived below the ground.

According to Osim, there was a religious persecution in what was an empire in ancient days. Even many centuries before that era, there had been a great deal of digging to acquire building materials. Over the years, countless subterranean tunnels were created when the land was mined. At the same time, people were persecuted and driven underground. They lived in the catacombs and continued digging, eventually creating an underground city spanning many square miles, and a central area now known as the inner sanctum.

The refuge in the catacombs became a thriving community beneath the one above that sought to root them out. They extended the tunnels, building rooms, tombs and chapels. The catacombs became the sole refuge of all who sought to live a free life, and over the centuries, many millions of people lived and were buried there.

At one point they were abandoned in an era when society actually did for a time relish freedom. The tables had turned, the despots were overthrown and religious kings replaced them. But these were the days of inquisition, and Godly kings can also be cruel. Those who did not properly believe in God were weeded out. The catacombs became prisons extending beneath the inner sanctum itself.

Osim told me that when he was a boy, although he only had very vague recollections, he had actually lived beneath the catacombs with his mother who was one of many prisoners there. He had to digress a bit here and tell me about his experiences in the inner sanctum, which I was grateful to hear, but his tale was somewhat blended with the vision of the inner sanctum as it had been when occupied by the religious authorities.

Entry into the inner sanctum that Osim visited, from where he was able to procure such amazing historical information, was strictly regulated. Even thousands of years earlier, the tradition was the same. The inner sanctum has only been open to the ruling class, whatever it may be. By the time Osim gained access, the inner sanctum already had a bloody history of switching hands, but the exact number of battles was unknown as history was suppressed.

He described to me how he first managed to stumble into a channel, a passage into the underground network that led directly beneath the innermost recesses of the inner sanctum itself. He had found a tunnel in his hideaway shortly before his disappearance. He first found a tunnel that led to a wall and seemed to go no further, but using the same tactics that helped him discover the tunnel in the first place, he found softer, filling stone, and after great effort, managed to break into the glory of an unknown channel in the great catacombs themselves.

Nothing could describe his great wonder and surprise. He was careful to return to the hideaway and ensure that no one could follow him should he be missed. Then, he spent months exploring and mapping the tunnels, feeling a vague sense of recollection, almost as if he were breathing amniotic fluids in the womb again.

It was clear that this elaborate network had been deliberately blocked. It was so vast that it rendered the inner sanctum vulnerable. Where Osim entered, it was apparent that there had been some effort to erase the religious references wherever possible. Obviously, a great many people had taken great pains to desecrate every religious symbol they could, but as Osim explored further, it was clear that the effort was abandoned. It was too overwhelming. There were far too many chapels, and the passion to destroy must have dissipated due to the sheer enormity of the task. There were many skeletons and skulls as well. Osim said that no human being can cut through the heart of history without finally being haunted by it.

It was a long way from his hideaway entry point that the real nature of the catacombs truly came to light. Osim felt he was suddenly surrounded by a congregation of everyone who had ever lived before him. He was the only living being in a multitude of millions, bones of every generation, all of whom craved to smell the desert but who preferred darkness to capitulation, whose presence proved to him something enormous in the human spirit to believe freely. Even if self-imposed incarceration be the only alternative, it was gladly accepted. Given skeletons as neighbors and winding tunnels for streets, still they looked forward to life everlasting, just as they seemed to look down at Osim as he held a torch aloft surveying the magnitude of a cruel history.

At times, he would return to the hideaway and ponder, trying to resume his life, but the questions of destiny so perturbed him that he pressed forward, against all else. Past the Great Hall of Skulls, as he came to call it, Osim encountered an undiminishing deluge of open graves. He said it seemed a sacrilege that the graves were open, until he considered that he had actually entered a network of tombs underground. It was a greater blasphemy that people had to live their lives on ledges carved out of stone that would be their graves.

Finally, after many months of adapting to the experience and painstakingly mapping the tunnels, Osim reached the area of the catacombs near the inner sanctum. Again, during the approach, there seemed various signs of desecration of one kind or another, but it wasn't immediately clear which symbols were targeted. On the one hand, there was an apparent attempt to wipe out any memory of religion; on the other, recent state symbols were vandalized.

Then Osim actually found an area that reawakened a sense of certainty to his recollection. Bars and cells in the tunnels. Still, there were skeletons. It was horrible to see how prisoners had been left to starve and die. As he surveyed the prison and its hundreds of cells, he cried, for he knew this had been his birthplace, and one of these cells was the grave of his mother. No wonder the inner sanctum, the world at large, wanted these secrets to remain buried.

What struck Osim particularly was that the truth was crying out in the form of millions of skulls, not that there was any one cry, aimed simply at a shared desire while happening to be persecuted, but that throughout history, for some reason there were ideas that were persecuted, and this system of catacombs was the result.

Whatever their differences in life, they were all just bones now. Their very sameness was the very foundation of the nation that wished to conceal it, and yet it weakened that foundation. There were millions crying for their story to be told, and yet those living preferred to ignore the macabre reality even though the tradition of destroying people was continuing.

In the many, many miles that Osim had traveled in the catacombs, something made up of quiet pleas from every skull he passed was born. It wasn't that he served the idea the bones might have died for, but to serve the idea that there should never have to be such a place as this. The collected appeal that Osim felt was to somehow open the catacombs to the world for proper acknowledgement. But while he felt empowered, he felt curiously mortal, weakened to a sense of futility because of all those who had died though they had a cause for which to live, dream and fight. How was he to change the world when for thousands of years, so many were just so much fodder for the mill, dust on the floor of the grindstone?

Again, he returned to his hideaway and surveyed the desert, wondering of his life and the state of the nation. He said he tried to accept things as they were. People seemed to be occupied in the enjoyment of life. Children were playing in the ruins just as he had, but wasn't the presence of the inner sanctum beneath them indicative of an imbalance, a deranged arrangement? He couldn't shake the feeling of a song, a chorus from below, chanting for retribution and reinstatement. They cried to be an army of the dead to fight against an army of the living, dead inside. He felt impelled to return to the catacombs and go further into the mysteries.

On this next journey, he went beyond the prison and found that there were actually fewer tunnels. He wasn't sure why, but he believed he was going to somehow find an access to the inner sanctum. There were actually just so many dead-ends, but he persisted. Perhaps the same techniques that were used to conceal tunnels had been employed here. Although it was tedious work, this theory paid dividends as Osim was able to find and excavate a hidden passage of softer stone that finally opened directly into a large room that seemed a base of a wall of a chamber in the inner sanctum itself.

Not knowing what to expect, he deemed it necessary to proceed with the utmost caution. There were no doors, and yet there was only this one wall, and so he tested every area for a sign of weakness. Finally, on one portion, there was a sign that some of the bricks had been removed and replaced. Over several days, he very quietly scraped the mortar until he was able to remove some bricks. Gradually, he was able to make a passage and squeeze through. He'd extinguished his torch in advance of even removing the first brick, and was working in total darkness. Now that he had entered, he still replaced the bricks though he was feeling around absolutely blind. Finally, he lit a match and found that the chamber contained all manner of discarded military gear and uniforms. What did this mean? There was also a door which proved to be the point where Osim was able to gain access to the inner sanctum. He opened the door slightly and peeked through.

He was soon to learn that there was nothing about his appearance, dressed as he was, that would merit his fear. He traveled around furtively, carefully mapping as he went, and for a time saw nobody. Finally he heard a hubbub of voices and entered a great mall bustling with activity. There were hundreds of people like himself. All the women wore maskss, but Osim was dressed like most of the men, and so he was able to enter unnoticed. The area in which he was walking with the crowd was below a ledge reserved, it seemed, for a more haughty class of person. Osim observed that more ordinary citizens were required to live beneath the level occupied by the more dignified, ruling class. All manner of life existed on various platforms. The lowest was most ordinary. People entered their homes on this level, and attended to their needs. Osim could see that although there were fewer people on the next level, that the situation was the same for them. Standing back, he saw there were levels above as well, and then he saw that he was in the Hall of the Spires, the part of the inner sanctum visible above ground but protected by a huge fortress. There were levels all the way up.

Nobody paid any attention to him. Simple observation helped him absorb a sense of the customs on the next level. Their feet were just about at his eye level, and he watched them closely. All of their manners seemed affected, and it was a simple matter to become acquainted with their curious pretensions and varied gestures. By exploring the inner sanctum, he found areas little traveled, and managed to climb to the next level. He admitted to stealing clothing that allowed him to walk freely in higher levels. By merely mimicking actions he had observed from below, he managed to portray himself as one of many lower dignitaries. One rule of thumb was never deign to look down on the lowly multitude. Keep looking up.

By degrees, Osim managed to quickly work his way up into the inner sanctum hierarchy, and even managed to access the archives. He made a long story short, and simply addressed the fact that through a series of subtle machinations, he was accepted as one with proper right of access. It was apparently a simple matter of acquiring the dress and attitude of those several levels above the archives and descending to the archives.

It was in the libraries of the inner sanctum that Osim made his most startling discoveries. First, he was able to ascertain information regarding the life of his father, including diaries. There were terrible truths in these texts, but he told me everything. The first matters shed light on the life of his father and the kind of society that existed before the war. His father had been an inner sanctum high dignitary and minister of the faith, but had become involved with a woman of lower birth. She loved him above all else, but when she became pregnant, Father Osim was determined to avoid scandal. The catacombs had been used for years to purge the souls of sinners, and while his actions would warrant punishment, he did not want to feel the tickle of the whip.

But the woman had to be punished for her shame, and Father Osim had her agree to live in the catacombs and endure the shame for his sake. He promised to attend to her needs, and to the child's.

To this promise he was faithful though he continued to live out his bureaucratic lies until the sanctum was overrun in the war. In the purge of the prison, the woman said nothing of Father Osim. The connection was discovered, however, and she was judged to be of high religious association and thus was sentenced to die in the purge. Her child was spared, exiled to the outer boundaries.

Father Osim delineated these matters in his diaries. It was also noted in the last entries that despite the fact that his sins had never come to light in public, the forces that had overrun the inner sanctum found such corruption in the hierarchy that none was to be spared. Father Osim became a victim of the same purge that took the life of Osim's mother, and his bones were probably somewhere in the prison section of the great catacombs below.

I found it interesting that Osim would divulge such details to me. All the years he lived in his hideaway as a young man, he'd seemed to me to be doing nothing more than idling, contributing at times to the strange, mutant maturing process of young people. This new, information put him in a different light. It made me think how my own life had its secret side, as with my dreams and sordid affairs, but his secret life had an emerging noble quality, while mine was destitute and cramped, still demanding to be kept secret.

Continuing about his father, Osim added that in the last diary entries, his father, who had for years been nothing more than a bureaucrat of a ruling religious tyranny, had ironically come to some sense of understanding in a religious perspective. Osim reached into his shirt and pulled out some tattered pages that he claimed to have torn from the diaries of his father from the inner sanctum. I found it curious that he should not hand me pages to read that would reveal his father's rationalizations, justifications and hypocrisy, but rather those in which he sought light and wished to redeem himself.

As I read the pages of the diary that Osim had handed to me, I thought the passages tedious and sought ways to interrupt, but Osim insisted that I continue. He said I could benefit from seriously considering the enigma that his father's life posed. When I finished, he asked me what I thought of the last entry.

To be buried in the catacombs is an honor for one whose bones are sent there as mine will be, judged guilty by man but nevertheless forgiven and free. It would be absurd to request burial in the catacombs. I would not choose it, nor recommend it, but there will be symbolic exoneration in the company of bones. From beginning to end, and ever after, I was and am just one of the great race of man under God, ever and always under God.

Obviously, I said, his father had not been buried in the catacombs. "That," he said, "was done deliberately in order to dishonor him." Then he left the room for a moment. To my shock, he carried father from his sickbed. I protested vehemently. Father was in no condition to be moved. What right had Osim to disturb him? "I want him to know that all is forgiven," was all that Osim said.

"Forgiveness or not, there's no reason to move him," I objected. Father was babbling insensibly, but as Osim lowered him onto a sofa, father looked into his eyes with a clearing gaze. He smiled, then grimaced and covered his face with his hands, whimpering, "Please mountains, fall on me."

There were no answers to questions, just new mysteries. Even Osim's carrying around religious documents purported to be his father's was criminal for the content alone. His having acquired them in the manner described, if true, was just a further felony.

I began to shout so loud that my father moved his hands from his face to cover his ears. I admit that Osim was not shouting. He was trying to talk quietly, but his choice of subject matter, the forgiveness of my father, based on the nature of what he had divulged previously, was unacceptable to me. I could only imagine what he had unearthed regarding my father in his search of the catacombs and the inner sanctum. I didn't want to hear any more lies.

But Osim was calmly insistent, and gradually I gave in and listened to the rest of his tale. I had stopped yelling, but father continued to keep his hands over his ears, and he punctuated Osim's story with his incessant babbling.

Osim said he understood that it was going to be painful for me to accept, but that my father's life was equally marred in the crisis of a generation earlier. When the invading forces had entered the inner sanctum, my father was also a high dignitary of the faith, a few levels beneath Father Osim. But he was a dignitary nevertheless, one marked for execution like all the others. He and Father Osim had been friends, father being a sort of protege, one that Father Osim had been grooming for high places, but in the chaos of the invasion, father killed a soldier and changed clothes with him. He was captured and would have been executed but he was found to be more valuable in what he might divulge of inner sanctum secrets.

The forces that invaded the inner sanctum came bearing a grudge. Some of their leaders had escaped imprisonment in the catacombs and weren't out merely to turn the tables. They wanted revenge. Father was obviously more interested in his own skin than in saving others, so he was quick to point the finger in the direction they were looking. Father Osim had confided his greatest secret to father, that of having an illegitimate son living in the catacomb prison with his mother, and when father revealed this to the provisional military government, they received the information with great delight. What better way to prove the necessity of bringing down a religious government than to parade one of its leaders as corrupt. Father Osim was made an extraordinary example thanks to father, and his name became a mockery in the nation. After his death, despite the obvious religious awakening, even those who survived the purge were glad to see his grave devoid of any religious marker whatsoever. The new regime would only tolerate ancient religious symbols, and generally, even most of these were being gradually obliterated by the new consensus.

Again, father was given a reprieve, if an exile to the outer boundaries could be called that, and finally the child Osim was placed in his care as an ironic reward for what he had done to the boy's father, and the boy received nothing from his real father. The story didn't hold any water in my opinion. The notion that the inner sanctum was taken over in that fashion, and now housing a new generation of bureaucrats was unfathomable to me.

Osim could only advise me that truly this was the case, that he had encountered numerous examples of pompous behavior throughout the inner sanctum. For example, no lesser dignitary could turn his back to a higher personage when leaving the room. The highest dignitaries had flames burning on their heads whenever they were in mixed companies. The offices of these highest dignitaries were equipped with special air blowers to cool their heads while the flames burned. Young boys served as acolytes to light them in the morning and put them out whenever needed. How these highest dignitaries treated these young boys was not to be described, according to Osim. The inner sanctum that was saved from religion had reached a level where it needed to be saved again. It was either that, or the entire nation would soon be absorbed, and by absorbed, he meant destroyed. The erasure of religion so pervaded the inner sanctum that they actually had an echo chamber of prayer, a small room where a visitor was allowed to speak to God, only to have his words bounce back off the walls. It was the inner sanctum's way of saying that prayer is useless. Visitation to the echo chamber of prayer was mandatory, and everyone knew that all comments were monitored, just in case one might actually say something in a manner to suggest there was hope of the words passing through the walls. Those listening actually feared signs of faith, and promoted its rejection and at the same time worked incessantly to detect it. It was also a way to bring down dignitaries who had fallen into disfavor since it was easy to prove one had spoken an actual prayer in the chamber.

When Osim paused in his tale, I urged him to continue. It was true that I was looking for contradictions, weak points I could attack, but I was also fascinated at the construction, almost as if I were witnessing a great ruins assembling itself into a thriving city out of ashes. My mind drifted from time to time into an intellectual reverie, an examination of details he described. Such drifting was momentary, and I missed nothing of his descriptions. He began talking of the war around the time we were born again, about the hideaways once being aimed at the inner sanctum. Those who had escaped from the prisons in the catacombs had rallied people that lived on the outside. They had occupied the hideaways and modified them to attack the inner sanctum at the fortress and the exposed spires, and yet, there were problems. They really weren't sure there was enough ammunition to dent the fortifications of the inner sanctum, for the inner sanctum seemed to have been built to withstand such a bombardment. But according to accounts Osim had witnessed, there was apparently some despair in the secular ranks, but those who had survived the horrors of the catacombs pressed onward, or quite frankly, downward. The hideaways proved to be safe quarters against any patrols from the inner sanctum, and they also provided a hidden means to explore internally, just as Osim had done when he was living in his mountain hideaway.

Apparently, it didn't take long for the secular rebels to tap into some of the tunnels of the catacombs. Osim's own excavation through the softer rock had merely been to rechannel through material used to fill in the tunnels made by the rebels. Their work had been much more difficult. They mined through solid rock, and they used precious gun powder to blast through some particularly hard stone. Finally, they reached the catacombs, and what they encountered in religious symbolism was met with outrage. These rebels weren't aware of the fact that they were about to encounter thousands of years of history of bones, and by degrees, they tired of desecration as the sheer enormity of the past surrounded them. They had their own purpose after all. The catacombs were merely a tunnel that would hopefully provide them with a means to infiltrate the inner sanctum and attack it from within. Thus, they were ordered to conserve anger and energy, to ignore the religious symbolism and save the fight for those in the inner sanctum.

By the time they reached the catacomb prisons, they had already decided on a plan. The leaders knew how the prison operated, and they had every reason to believe they could overpower all the guards without being detected. Those who lived in the inner sanctum would have nothing to do with anything in the catacombs. The guards themselves were of the lowest sort, and those who weren't sympathetic with the cause when the rebel forces first appeared exchanged places with the prisoners being released, who had all been neglected, effectively become prisoners of war no matter what they had done to be sentenced to the tombs, and most were in terrible condition. Horrors too awful to describe stared at the rebels. Most of the prisoners were mere skeletons dipped in skin, too weak to be moved. These semblances of living beings were more like the bones in the catacombs than the living, and the way that they were piled on ledges, just as the bones from hundreds of years before, tore at the insides of the rebel chiefs as the eyes of the dying stared into them. Those who'd known life in the prison, whose escape and rebellion had made it harder for those left behind, felt a surge of purpose that would rock the inner sanctum from below.

They entered the inner sanctum by removing bricks. They had good fortune in entering a chamber between the catacombs and the inner sanctum. It seemed to be a storage area of sorts, providing the rebels with a sanctuary to begin their attack. In this room, they discarded military gear and infiltrated the inner sanctum according to plan. The inner sanctum was so well fortified that no one inside was prepared for the bloody coup that followed. The rebels met with little resistance. There was no need to have infiltrated like spies. It was chaos and murder from the outset. The highest religious dignitaries were thrown over the railing, falling and breaking like eggs from the spires. After the coup, trials were held, during which time my father began to collaborate. Osim's mother died in the chambers of the catacombs. Only a few were nurtured back to health, and were deeply scarred by the ordeal. Deeply humiliated in one regime, they were honored in another. They were afforded every means of rising into the new bureaucracy and were among the most respected of the inner sanctum elite for what they had endured.

Now Osim looked away from me to my father who had stopped his babbling, seemingly to listen to Osim, although I doubted whether his look of understanding was any indication of lucidity as the term is used. It was nearly dawn. I could just make out the first sign of light on the horizon through the window. Osim looked at me and said it was time to make his purpose clear. While father knew much while he was raising Osim, such that he was forced to humil-iate the boy, father was accountable. But Osim said he felt strongly that children are able to endure what surrounds them, and accept it as the world because they know nothing else. The souls of children manage to contain the emotional elements to neutralize the acid that flows into them. He cherished much of his childhood despite being able to make comparisons then to what it might have been had father not adhered so strictly to agreements he never should have made. Osim rejected the concept of regret in that form. He couldn't change what was, and could only put all he had into chang-ing the present. He said the reason for his visit was simple. He want-ed to give the only people in the world he could call family a chance to choose a side. Obviously, father couldn't be held accountable. He was in no shape to be judged, but as far as I was concerned, Osim was offering me a chance to help. He called me brother. He said again the inner sanctum was slowly stripping away the nation, and unless something was done, my turn would come however ignorant or innocent I was. Father had been aware of that for a long time, he said. That is why he had been so certain of the dangers when Osim lived with us and the threat of his return. Osim had apparently taken it to heart as well, and had moved into the hideaway which was outside the village, effectively removing the threat. But the shadow of the juggernaut would by degrees block the rising sun and bury the world as I know it, he told me, adding that he'd given me everything I needed, and believing him or not was up to me.

All he needed was a signal from me that I sanctioned his sense of outrage at the current regime, that I concurred with and supported his purpose, but I said I didn't know what his purposes were. Some old history lessons, a cut-away look at an accumulation of bones, and a vague sense of impending doom, were no reasons to accept him as some kind of leader. When the span of life happens to tend to be shorter than a century, one must expect entire generations to die. In a nation such as ours, those bones would tend to pile up. If there were such a place as the catacombs. Merely seeing all those bones together would surely awaken some strange sensations, but to let such feelings launch one into a revolutionary posture was unjustified. I told him that he should understand that laws are necessary. The government of the inner sanctum wasn't perfect, no one said it was, but there are limits to allowing universal complaint because factions can be dangerous. It was thus natural to expect a government to impose some limitations in order to protect the order that exists. If some degree of complacency develops over the years, if the hearts of fervent rebels harden into paper-pushing statesmen, that is the price paid given the fact that time exacts a payment.

Osim's complaint was personal. He said he wanted to forgive, but actually, he was trying to set everything back in balance. Somehow he wanted to exonerate his father. Perhaps in his own mind, he felt he would have been a dignitary of some kind in the inner sanctum. Somehow his father would have rescued him from the bowels of the earth. But to my mind, he was a grown man complaining that his nursery wasn't good enough. There may not seem to be the means for ordinary citizens to make changes in society. There may not appear to be avenues for the common man to tweak this or that law for his own benefit. But when an ordinary citizen has a complaint the size of Osim's, the government has to say that no one man has the right to turn the world upside down. Desire to tweak the law is one thing. That can be tolerated. After all, everyone feels it, and so it doesn't need to be stated. But Osim was talking treason, and his past, however odious or difficult, was no justification for it. What made him think he had been assigned divine right for such a mission to save the world? What made him think he was God that he could return to offer forgiveness to us and a chance to join him in a cause deemed righteous by nobody but himself?

No, I told him, we would stay in the world as we have grown to understand it. Yes, I was a child that accepted the world and era in which I'd been born. I was not so arrogant to believe I was somehow chosen to modify that world at the high price of adding great numbers to an already huge, historical storehouse of bones.

Osim just looked at me. Then he said I was lost in too many personal matters to see that one man can have an effect. Perhaps I was too involved in the walls of one room, my own problems, intent on obtaining whatever gratification happened to be just beyond my reach, to see the bigger picture. "This hideaway is dwarfed by the size of the hideaway in your mind with all its own tunnels," he said. "But it's from there that we all must fight, dig in and begin to destroy the inner sanctum."

It took him a moment to calm down after that. He shook his head. He'd tried but had to be going. There was a big day ahead. The caravan was about to begin, and he didn't want to miss it.

So he had come to ask me for help in restoring the country to what he had decided was right, but he had to add that he could see I was far too wrapped up in self pity to understand the nature of the truth and have respect for it as well. Why couldn't he see that history was just a tale of so many coups and turns of events, piling a fresh barrage of bones on what is already the underlying foundation of the history of mankind? What made his truth greater than any cause that came before it? As for what I thought he could achieve, I reminded him that he was a wanted man, that whatever allowed him to wander the halls of the inner sanctum without being recognized would not serve him here. There was nothing he could accomplish, and certainly nothing he could achieve that he could expect the benefit of my help.

Osim shook his head even more. I added that if he ever avoided hurting us by staying in the hideaway, he was certainly endangering the whole community, perhaps the entire country, by showing up now. I suggested he give himself up. He laughed. Osim repeated I didn't understand. He said he had more reason to believe he could change the country than my mind in one night.

"Uncommon circumstances breed uncommon individuals," he said. "Take care of your father while I take care of mine."

As he opened the door to leave, father spoke. "I appreciate your visit, my son. You've brought a sense of peace to my world again."

"You are free, God be praised," Osim answered. "But may all hell move in and fester on what is left of my brother's dead soul." Then he shut the door behind him.

I trace the loss of my soul, eaten slowly into particles and swept away over the years since that night, to that exchange. There is a quality of Osim that has something to do with this. If I could crash through everything and control how the pieces fall together behind me; if remorselessness could serve somehow to defend my actions (just as guilt seems to betray mine), I'd be imitating him. But to follow Osim is to fail. I find his ways almost irresistible because they work for him, but whenever I have tried to live those ways, the way I am built obstructs progress. After his visit, I found myself in a state where I could not help but go in circles. He never seemed to make any effort to question his behavior, and in a strange sense, this sanctified it. My point is that under that influence, I have done things I would otherwise question in order to possess the same impunity, but I call upon every action to make an account of itself, but in this case, for some reason I cannot explain myself. Earlier in life, I made the mistake of believing and following him. Now I fear he has matured, that it may be right to follow him, but how can I know? My hope in reasoning through the story of my experiences with Osim is that I will be able to cleanse myself even for making the wrong choice, rationalize that if my behavior is called into question that I followed what I believed was the truth. But isn't this the same trap into which our fathers fell according to his account? Yet Osim has always pressed forward like a scientific force for congratulations on victory though he told lies to achieve it. It is as if he had a grasp on the nature of truth only to deceive. To meet his ends, he would drag everyone in even if it meant they would later all lie together under line upon line of stones. He would say it was their destiny.

It was morning. Osim was gone, and father was lucid for the first time since his torture in the inner sanctum. He was behaving in a manner consistent with how I remembered him before the ordeal that incapacitated him for the last several years. He was preparing to go out and watch the caravan. I tried to discuss matters with him, but he waved me off, mumbling I was a traitor and no son of his. I had already decided how I was going to handle Osim's return and the information he had divulged. I decided to inform the authorities. It was fortuitous that the caravan was about to take place that morning. I would have no hope of getting into the inner sanctum. In a sense, the inner sanctum was coming to me. All I had to do was find a way out to Bale's camel and explain the threat to him.

Bale was the highest dignitary of the inner sanctum. He had survived the ordeal of the prison of the catacombs, according to Osim, although no such information about his past survived. As far as what I had learned, the Bale family had always occupied the innermost sanctum circles, always closest to the high spires. I had no knowledge of the appropriate manner in which to address him. As I prepared to row out to the caravan, I was filled with uneasiness. I imagined myself just a bumbling idiot approaching our sovereign, neglectful of every respect and mannerism that is expected and reserved for high grace. I did not know the rituals.

It looked to be a perfect day for the great caravan, which came out only once a year to enjoy the desert air. It was also a show of strength, as if to say, the fortress is unnecessary, that they had no fear of coming out. The various camels were all still being assembled for the ride and yet as I walked down the mountain path to reach the plains, I could see the first signs that high dignitaries were arriving via the private path to the fortress. Servants were also readying for the main event. As I set my sights in on the main camel, some guards in the forming entourage saw me. I heard shouts, but I could not understand what they were saying. I was making straight for Bale's grand camel, and the closer I came, the more apparent it must have been that I might pose a threat. After all, the strictest security measures were kept to ensure that no harm would come to anyone in the caravan. All of us who lived outside the inner sanctum were kept at a strict distance. We could watch from the cliffs, but only after being carefully searched. Guards were stationed in front of every hideaway to ensure that everyone was being monitored.

Strange, but I hadn't even thought of myself as posing any kind of threat to the high dignitaries. Rather, I thought the information

I was bearing too important to fear what might happen if I was mistaken for some kind of assassin. It was as though my good intentions should be visible, when certainly, it was quite irregular that anyone should approach the caravan from the hills via an ordinary path, and apparently I was ignoring calls to identify myself.

I began to see that my approach was being taken seriously, and it was then that I woke to my plight. I stopped walking and watched for what was happening. I called out to Bale that I had a message. I saw the curtains part in the canopy that sat on the wondrous beast. A servant looked out. Behind him, I saw only a single light, and wondered what it was, although later I realized it was caused by the flame burning on Bale's head. Now several servants with rifles appeared on various camels behind the main entourage and took aim at me. I started to shout in my own defense, but one of them shot me in the shoulder. I fell down and rolled behind a rock. I heard more shots and then what sounded like blasts of thunder.

I peeked out from behind the rock, and to my shock, saw several canopies on fire. In the next instant, I saw Bale's camel actually explode. I dove back behind the rock to avoid being hit with falling debris. I heard the sound of thunder again. I looked out to the horror of seeing that most of the camels in the caravan were dead, the caravan in flames, and only then did I realize the source of the thunder. All along the cliffs, the hideaways were booming. Shells were exploding in the desert all around the caravan. The rising plumes braided in a swelling tangle toward heaven.

I crawled further back, found a safer area between several rocks and tried to catch my breath. Gasping and bleeding, I watched the furious fire in the desert rise over continuous explosions. I could feel the heat as far away as I was. The barrage from the hideaways continued for some time, and as the waves of fire danced in the smoke, I picked myself up and tried walking back to the path. Several soldiers with guns apprehended me, but I didn't recognize their uniforms. They wore patches that looked like piles of skulls. They tossed me rudely onto the ground. Several others walked through the smoke and started shooting. "You're lucky," one of them told me.

From my vantage point, I could see that the caravan was a total loss. Seeing the fall of the governmental body that had ruled the land as long as I'd been alive was a shock. It was slowly sinking in that Osim was behind all of it. I looked up at the hideaways in a mist from all the cannon smoke, and I saw father on the cliff applauding.

Many soldiers remained on the dunes, and I was taken up the path to the top of the cliffs, I heard the constant patter of guns behind me. No prisoners were being taken.

I was taken to the hideaway where Osim had lived, and there he stood again, looking out over the flames below, just as in my dream. They threw me down at his feet like a wet fish. "Like father, like son," he said.

"You almost killed me out there," I told him.

"No, you almost killed yourself."

"You could have warned me. You might have thought to tell me about the bombardment."

"If you had made the proper choice, there would have been no bombshell for you, my brother, but your life has always been a slow picking apart, a quiet execution, a slow burning, and watching your last flicker was pitiful from where I stand."

Then, as I looked up, for the first time in years I saw Lorelei again. No metaphor would be adequate to approximate the level of the joy I felt in seeing her alive. She had just come out of the hideaway, and she was simply beautiful. When we had been together, she had always worn lots of jewelry and makeup, but now she was absolutely plain, and she wore it well. I'd had a dream years earlier that she was attending to Osim's wounds, but now, like a dream come true, she attended to mine. I was taken into the back of the hideaway where she dressed my shoulder. She said I was lucky that the bullet had gone clean through. Everyone was calling attention to my good fortune. Lorelei was wearing a wedding ring. I was speechless and averted her eyes. If I was so fortunate, why did it seem that I was always on the downside of events?

Please excuse a lengthy digression, but I must confess that I have always roamed the tepid land between both hot and cold. My behavior has been consistent and predictable in this regard. I've never known either extreme except in avoidance. Too close to hot, I shut off to cool. Too close to cold, I seek heat, and so on, back and forth, back and forth. Looking back over my life, all I see is an endless race back and forth, a man standing on ground perfectly suited for him to find a place to relax, desperately driven instead to act as if either jumping up and down is meant to keep himself warm or to stop his feet from burning. Every way I move, I betray myself.

I must also confess that I had a dream about Lorelei shortly after seeing her. We were in a building that was undergoing many modifications. She had emerged from a restricted area, and we suddenly were standing face to face. We were happy to see one another, but now she had a family and very limited time to spend with me. I had a strong sense of how I would feel after the minutes had flown by, to be without her again, and it permeated every second of my being with her. It greased the clock and made time pass too quickly. I don't remember what we talked about, but she conveyed a feeling to me that it might have worked out for us if I had asserted myself and made decisions for a lifetime with her. Soon it was time for her to leave, and we searched for the exit, but most doors were blocked due to construction. She saw a break in the wall that she thought looked familiar, said goodbye and disappeared into it. I feared it was a dead-end, so I went the other way and found a stairway that led down into a huge meeting room filled with families. I realized her family was there, that this was her destination, so I walked around looking for her, but she was nowhere to be found. I went back up the stairs and tried to track her down in the walls of the building, but she was gone. I too became lost in the walls, but I felt certain that our paths would not cross again, and I woke depressed that I am so tepid.

Despite the frequency of facing either extreme and the constant activity, the endless, restless roaming, I have been nothing short of utterly tepid. Motivation and enthusiasm have always been just words to toss about. Hot and cold were what the lives of heroes were, but I could never make such commitment myself. I was too drawn by both sides, and so lived my life in neither one.

Could I draw out a plan and propose to inflict my personal dogma on mankind? It is for others in history, particularly the past, to choose sides and take action. The present is the culmination, and it is time that the great should be able to put down the arms and rest for awhile. Why should there be a battle over one side or the other when one can clearly see a blending of the two? History is nothing but the error of blind fools that have not seen the calm but opposing rivers reach their waterfalls and fall where mists rise in roaring clouds. They have failed to witness that the surge below these two falls is the place where fools rush in, ordered by these blind maniacs to swirl to their doom because it is deemed necessary by self-appointed leaders whose only call to rise in politics was that something snapped in their head.

I see political extremes not as rocks that cannot mix, but as I said, twin raging torrents that mix in the middle. I might swim in the tepid waters, but the drowning is real. I am doomed, and while I might think I am only bathing luxuriously at the culmination of an historical drama finally reaching its crescendo in me, my dead spirit has fallen with others over a cliff after having been pushed in a long drive downstream to face the enemy. I took no sides, and yet I drown in the basin of white water swirling over the rocks.

What swirling? As I survey my life, there's only an occasional drip of sand, not water. I live in an arid place, not where rivers converge. I look up. The water taps have been turned off in this region for thousands of years. Let's hear someone play Taps for the death of the taps. Nowhere can I see the mist rising. There is no steam, only my tepid heart at room temperature. It is the story of my life.

Life in the overall surge is just an endless mixing in, is it not? We're made to move along as we are ordered, aren't we? Aren't we fulfilling our purpose to pass freely in the seething moil, exchanging particles evenly along the way. There may be salt flats in the desert, talk of ancient oceans, and fear of a general and complete evaporation that will take the steam out of us and render us crystalline, but it's an unchanging stream that calls us to etch itself deep within us, and carries us along after promising fulfillment, scarring us instead to bleed rivers between the ever-widening banks.

But to some, another river, just as real, erodes the levies and rushes in. It came at me in the form of a man whose inward focus and division lay like a quaking fault in his breast; whose purposes flowed along this line, concentrated and elemental. His particles seemed more greatly charged and seemed to slowly rob the charge of mine. Alone, I thought I knew clarity, but with Osim, clouds erupted, and all my confidence and strength precipitated from billowing confusion. With him near, there was no call for heat, no leisure time for cool detachment. It was no use. Any nerves I had left hung stagnant in a tepid pool down to the roots gorging on the muck and lees. From that primordial slime, amphibious, evil thought is born.

There is no morality in taking control. Before a law is verified, its detractors will often say it is an immoral opinion, and such conflicts will be historical dramas. Morality is an issue until the coming of the new light, and then the abandoned position becomes just another museum piece to be viewed as if it were just a flaw in the heart that inevitably transcended it, and that it was necessary to kill it.

Are we inherently better now? Who is not ready to follow what he believes, to join the cause, even if later it is abandoned like a pregnancy drug that withers fetal limbs? One miracle becomes a parlor trick; an age of enlightenment becomes a dark time; a victory becomes a loss. Or does it? History is kind to the interests of its writer. That was no disaster, it says. That was a mere, minor setback, nothing else. Think of a powerful guild that is suddenly recognized in the process of hacking when the world fully believed it was sculpting. Everyone is surprised, especially those hacking away. A moment of silence for the limbless, then throw your hats up for the new dawn of insight. The guild, through disgrace, politically retains a slice of respect that it later clones to maintain its power. Behind closed doors, agents are procured, insurances are assured, and cash exchanges hands. The guild fortifies and secures its position. Its goal is impunity, which it can never reach because it is culpable, and so goes the cycle of rebirth and self-inflicted death blows.

"Educate me, prove me wrong," Osim used to say, "and next time I'll teach you." I agree. One right element shows the way to the next. Vacuums are seemingly full of air. A dead-end impedes. Once the light streams in, darkness is easily seen for what it is. But often, we camouflage our comas when we wake. Generations that lived in error sleep now, and we must press on. We are more prepared, in any event, we say, and they should not be blamed because they did not have the luxury of what we know now, thanks to their having given their lives for the resolution of the crisis. Let us be kind to both extremes as each was necessary for the conflict, and the end result is all that counts. Whatever the outcome might have been, we're left with something on which to build.

We may be kind to folly on a grand scale because it seems not to have affected us, but these impediments have exhausted humanity like a baby crying all night may drain the judge deciding our case. He climbs to the bench. He is worn out and angry. Surrounded by lunatics and bright self-serving idiots, he wants to be done with it. We tell him we have a good case on moral grounds. He explodes, "This case will be decided on facts!" In the long run, guilt and innocence will be considered facts under that law of trends. There will be parity, unification. They will be equal. The world will rejoice. Wonderful! There's even no more need to mourn the limbless in a moment's silence. A new tepid age is beginning, and all is well.

The best invention of such a world is the slate that never soils. The slate that cleaned itself was just a phase. When humanity looked at its defeat and said, "Let's start clean from here," it paid lip-service to the dust that was its downfall, and bleached it as best it could. This was the age of wiping the slate clean. Very primitive. During the slate that cleans itself stage, man looked the other way because orders said only, "Keep marching. Don't stop for those who fall out of the ranks, and whatever you do, don't look back."

Now imagine yourself as the caretaker of the slate that never soils. What are you but a marvel whose ingenious reappraisals show that the speck is in the eye of the beholder, not on the slate? You will realize that those with specks in their eyes are dangerous. Look again, and they are gone. This may be mistakenly seen as a slate wiping itself clean, but the slate was never soiled. For as in the case of those with specks in their eyes, soil utterly destroys, and the slate's intact. You see, what cannot see can't see itself as soiled.

And so it is with Osim. Look him in the eye when you accuse, and a blinding dust storm will rise and swirl around you. Even when

217

it settles, you won't be able to see, but based on what you hear, you'll know you're indelibly marked as tepid, while Osim is free and clear.

All that day, people from the villages streamed outward to the hideaways to see what had happened. When they saw Osim, they repeated excitedly over and over, "He lives, he lives, he lives." It was apparent that there was a general outpouring of thankfulness in the masses, and I was amazed that so few shared my sense of loss of political security in the current air of anarchy and uncertainty. All that day, the fire continued to burn in the desert, and all that night, the hideaways were lit up and seemed like a bright string of pearls along the ridge.

Also throughout the day, one could see clouds of smoke rising from the fortress of the inner sanctum. It was hard to see if the spires were there at all, the smoke so obscured the view by mid-afternoon. All through the night as well, there was a subtle glow in the distance as a fire of unknown size was burning.

It's origin became clear in the days that followed, for Osim filled in some details that I had obstructed or that he'd neglected to mention on the eve of the caravan. He'd harped on the fact that the nation was in danger of being stripped away. What he'd meant by that became clear, and it also explained the nature of his army.

Throughout our childhood, we had enjoyed playing in the ruins as though they were some kind of joke from the past, places built to keep people employed, mere foundations with no other purpose than to exist. What Osim told me of the truth of the ruins was difficult to accept, but in light of all the information pouring in, it began to make sense. We'd actually wondered about the truth as children. I remembered the conversation with father when he said the foundations couldn't be removed because they were made of rock and couldn't be built on again because that was against the law. Osim promised that the ruins could be restored in the new order.

The inner sanctum had actually never become comfortable in its rule after the war. Purging had become routine, so systematized that there was no mechanism for dismantling the departments devoted to its exercise. Thus, though the people might be maintained like sheep and be devoted to the letter of the law, the spirit that drove the wheels of justice had a sense that there would always be infractions by a percentage, and thus kept strict quotas.

The threat of losing an entire village was always present. The ruins were actually foundations of villages in which, it was rumored, there was a spirit of rebellion. There was no political sense in the people of what it would actually mean to be a traitor, so it was difficult to avoid, random at best, and once isolated, there was no defense. Every village had one informant planted whose duty it was to tread the fine line of being sure not to divulge anything that would endanger the community at the same time as seemingly being on the lookout for treasonable acts. At some point, when the number came up for the particular village, or cell as they were called, it was simply ripped up overnight and gone by morning.

That was a difficult thing to swallow. How could a village disappear overnight without being noticed by the next village? It might explain why establishments close to one another disappeared at the same time. Osim had an interesting explanation. From archives in the inner sanctum, he learned stories of how villages were turned to ruins in the early days. By the time Osim was a boy, most of it had been done. The children wouldn't remember, and adults wouldn't dare speak of it. It only happened to about a village a year after the early days, until Osim left the country. Then there were many uprisings and disappearances of villages. I wondered as I listened why our village had been spared, unless perhaps it was thought that its presence might lure Osim to return more than its absence.

In any case, Osim said that no one in the inner sanctum after the war was allowed to leave except during the caravan, and that itself was a privilege. Many children born in the inner sanctum had never been outside. They knew of it only by looking upward through the windows in the hall of spires, and from the legends that spoke of deep secrets howling in tunnels sealed at the surface. There were tales of discoveries that could not be explained, of fossilized footprints of dinosaurs that fell from the ceilings of catacombs. Yes, children listened with wonder to stories such as this, tales of huge, petrified, three-toed footprints causing such sensation that dignitaries

219

were lowered into the catacombs to verify it, only they never returned. They had escaped, but the children were told that the outside world was too dangerous, raising fears of what would emerge from below. They were told that only a caravan allowed anyone a chance to go out, and again, it was left to the dignitaries to leave the inner sanctum, and only to the camels after walking a protected path to the desert because crossing the mountains any other way was too dangerous. And what must the children of the inner sanctum be thinking now, I wondered as I looked to the glow of flames behind the distant walls of the sanctuary, to hear that the caravan has been destroyed? What footprints must these monsters be making in their minds now?

According to Osim, there was a record of a dignitary who escaped the inner sanctum and returned denying the story of any threat outside. Even he had believed the tales. He'd claimed there were quiet communities that lived in peace, but he made the mistake of going first to the higher, ruling dignitaries who already knew what was outside. By the time he was put on display before the people, all that was left was a pitiful sight. He was dead on a stretcher. His shirt was opened to display the incredible three-pronged scar made by a burning fossilized foot. The crowd dispersed. As an addendum, Osim said that before they'd branded him, he'd escaped and ran through the inner sanctum pounding on every door. Many would have recognized his voice, Osim thought, but still, his pleas were ignored door after door. Later that same day, they filed by his remains and were asked to believe that he'd been brought dead from the outside world. What kind of people would believe such tales? Osim guessed that they knew they were prisoners, and although he had found no documents yet to substantiate it, the same machinery within the inner sanctum was creating ruins of levels on the inside if necessary.

My first visit to the inner sanctum came when I was impressed into service to help bury the dead in the catacombs. The destruction of the caravan had the lives of the inner sanctum high dignitaries, but that was nothing compared to the carnage that followed. The fight for the inner sanctum was most bloody. Thousands had been killed. The work cost me quite a bit in terms of what I felt for peace inside. After handling so many of those bodies, moving them into the catacombs, piling them up and sealing tunnels into the new tombs , I was too numb to know what to make of it all.

Osim chose to participate in this gruesome labor and told me stories of his first visit to the inner sanctum. I remember that while we were lugging bodies into the catacombs he said that he had seen a funeral procession moving downward from one of the upper levels. It was then that he realized that he'd never seen a funeral come out of the inner sanctum to the cemetery during all the years when he was growing up. He was determined to follow it. He joined a train of commoners that attached itself at the back of the procession and followed as it entered into a passageway into an area of catacombs that seemed not only freshly excavated, but cut out to appear to be an inner sanctum in itself. He said the heart of an area of the catacombs had been cut out to create a sterile mausoleum in which graves were neatly arranged with marble tablets concealing the remains. These were engraved with names of the departed, including dates falling within the recent administration after the war. This model of the inner sanctum already had hundreds of dead, all neatly arranged, and he said it reminded him of the inner sanctum itself, only the cave was being filled with a dead bureaucracy. The ceremony was long. The dead high-level dignitary was deified as the long list of accomplishments was read, but Osim noted there were no echoes. Osim felt the catacombs awakened the life force in marvelous ways though they might appear to be terrible, but the more raw the better. He said one shouldn't try to sugarcoat the dead.

After we'd finished burying the casualties, friend and foe, Osim had the catacombs sealed. Commoners of the low levels who survived were free to go to the outer world for the first time. I called it exile, but they were quite overjoyed with the arrangement even if naive. Their entire lives had been spent as prisoners, and they'd longed for a chance to live outside the inner sanctum. They only wanted to witness the few executions of those high dignitaries who had not joined the fated caravan. Some had been ill. Others had stayed behind for reasons related to their professional obligations.

But there was also a large number of people who aspired to high-level life in the inner sanctum. The society had many rewards, and Osim said he could not call them innocent who were trying to raise themselves on the backs of others. They would also see stern justice.

When the rebels entered, they'd come through the catacombs as planned. The fire along the walls had been a diversion. There was a great resistance, but the surprise tactics were successful. There were many elements to sort out. Osim authorized several immediate executions of all high-level dignitaries found in the inner sanctum. He also agreed to the burial in the desert. It was deemed fitting they should join the caravan, even if a little late.

It disturbed me to see the common populace of the inner sanctum was sent out to make some kind of life on the outside. I felt they would soon feel the weight of the constant threat of exposure to the elements. I felt Osim was likely to continue the tradition of the ruins. The war would thus never end, and the cycle would continue. It was only a matter of time before a mark would appear by dusk on the door of every house in the village. No one would understand what the mark would mean, but that same night every hideaway would be destroyed and new ruins created.

The executions of ordinary citizens were hardest to bear. I felt they were found guilty for simply having lived in the inner sanctum; a crime for which they were no more culpable than for breathing. Once the mockery of justice started, when would it end? Osim explained to me later that I had no sense of the organization of life that existed in the inner sanctum and that it was not my place to make any comments about it. Better that I should not even think of it. For three years he had led a resistance movement that had done nothing except acquire a very keen understanding of what went on both on the inside and the outside of the inner sanctum. The new order began by addressing a long list of inner sanctum atrocities and would only end with the creation of a new inner sanctum.

At one of the trials, the story came out that when a particular cell was turned to ruins, everyone in the community was found guilty, but one man was mentally ill and incapable of standing trial. He knew nothing of what was happening, but it was the inner sanctum court's desire to see that justice was served on all the miscreants, and so the court ordered that a cure be administered. A doctor entered the court and gave the man a shot. There was no explanation of what kind of drug it was, and there were no signs of there being any effect, and yet the court made a decision on that basis. Without waiting for the results, once the cure was administered, he was judged fit to be executed and was sent off with all the others.

In that regard, I was coming around to accepting that there was a need for change. Osim had been planning for it all along, but he never left the country and faked his death to throw everyone off.

All accounts of Osim and his exploits already seemed to me to misrepresent his true nature. I could detect the direction it was going as in fashioning a hero out of his own sense of glory. After the starkness of the hideaways and the solemnity of the catacombs, Osim and his chosen few enjoyed the beautiful halls, luxury and marketplace atmosphere of the inner sanctum. Walking through it, they became filled with the same thoughts of the previous temporary inhabitants. They knew it was only a matter of time before it would be returned to its former glory, only now religious banners would fly above the fortress, which was being repaired and reinforced to ensure the new dynasty would stand a millennium.

I saw Lorelei with Osim on many occasions. In the society of the inner sanctum, women had to wear masks except when they were in their homes. If male guests were visiting the living quarters, masks were required. When Lorelei walked in the inner sanctum with Osim, she wore a mask, but she objected to the custom, and Osim lied to her that in time the practice would be abandoned.

The stories of how the takeover was accomplished spread quickly. It was a difficult labor to arm all of the hideaways with the old weaponry that was found derelict across the desert, but Osim nevertheless pursued a course of action to bring them to the mountains. Tunnels behind strategic hideaways had to be excavated, and the guns installed and positioned. My guess is that there was little technical understanding of the hideaways, and that there wasn't much hope that they could do serious harm to the caravan. There was plenty of time to create enough explosives, and obviously many people were involved, but what I find hard to understand is why he never sought anything from me except my loyalty, which he waited until the last possible moment to solicit.

The desert had the tendency to cough things up for a while after the bombardment. There were teams assigned to patrol the sands and bag any body parts that were found, a macabre assignment for which there was no lack of volunteers, apparently because there were fringe benefits. There was so much wealth in the caravan that the clean-up was a veritable treasure hunt. I was released the day after the caravan and was strolling the desert several days later when I came upon a bloated hand sticking up in the sand. Something reflecting sunlight is what caught my attention. It turned out to be quite a heavy gold ring on the dead hand, but what surprised me about it most of all was that there were twelve designs around the ring, face after face in relief, a very fine sculptured depiction of the faces of the high dignitaries of the inner sanctum around Bale's face in the center. Who but Bale would wear such a ring? As ill as it made me feel, I wrenched the ring from the finger, leaving only bone as the skin gave way from the base to the tip. It came off like some limp desert worm.

Although my father had shown lucidity and signs of recovery, it proved only to be a late surge, a welcome reminder of the man he once had been, but within a week he had a relapse and perished in a flurry of impassioned and painful gibberish. But I cherish those last few days because he did provide some explanations, verifying Osim's hard-to-accept history. Father couldn't explain the ring, however, but marveled at its beauty. The ring conveyed a message of peace to him, and as long as he twirled the ring in his hand, he seemed to be at peace, which made it easier for me to watch him die.

Before father died, he requested that I see to it that his remains be interred in the catacombs. He had already slipped somewhat by then into a rambling state, but I felt it was a request that should be honored. I conveyed father's death wish to Osim, and felt I had every reason to assume the request would be accepted. It was, after all, Osim's father as well. But Osim denied his last wish. At the time, he was directing numerous projects to restore order. I found I had to put everything I might have thought by the wayside, and that was ironic. When he came to the house on the night of the caravan, he asked me to put everything I knew aside. But whatever I might suppose would follow based on new truth would also be replaced. Didn't it follow that the catacombs would come to light? In fact, in the months that followed, Osim made it clear the country had endured enough pain. His explanation seemed somehow fabricated, but it couldn't be questioned. Osim's father had expected honorable interment in the catacombs, though he would not have chosen nor recommended it. Perhaps Osim denied my father's request after turning his father's position into a principle and then imposing it with the force of law. I believed that the bottom line was that he didn't think it absurd to request a burial in the catacombs. His father was denied access. Thus, the wishes of others would have to be rejected, even if they were the dying hopes of a second father.

All of our wounds went deep and would need to heal before such things as catacombs and prisons could be allowed to come to light. The thousands that had died in the fighting to win the inner sanctum would be placed in chambers there, and in time the cool cave breezes would cleanse their bones, but there was no call for more system shocks. Osim said that even in the days when the catacombs had been thriving, there hadn't been turnstiles that people could walk through. The place was managed. For some reason I imagined turnstiles painfully locking on a person at random who would not be able to escape. Others could not stop to help. They had to move on. The person would be left there to die. That was the legacy of the inner sanctum in my mind. If there was an opportune moment to reveal the truth, it would have to come through legend and parable.

I had other doubts of wishes being granted, and further disappointments were in the making. For example, wasn't it rational that I would presume that the fires in the inner sanctum were just the beginning of the effort to dismantle the citadel? Instead, all of us who lived outside were rounded up as a labor force to begin repairs and reinforcements. Most, if not all the others, went willingly.

There was a festive joy in the air that a new order of the people was being established. To now have rights to enter the inner sanctum and watch those who'd lived in the lowest levels emerge in ignominy was my people's bliss. But I knew everything from the history Osim had told me, and something was going terribly wrong.

One of Osim's projects was the commissioning of a monument to be erected at the end of the path that led to the desert from the inner sanctum. It was loosely based on one of the pieces that his father had written alluding to the blind men touching the elephant attempting to describe the creature. It was an intricate depiction of an elephant made up of blind men with their hands stretched out.

From a distance, it was only an elephant, exact in shape and form. There were to be many segments, each in themselves on close inspection to an image within the larger work. These figures were all interconnected to the whole, as if absorbed into the larger outline of what they were describing, which in turn, on closer inspection, was revealed to be themselves. Only the observer had the luxury of recognizing that it was not an elephant, but observing the sculpture from afar revealed the elephant.

This struck me as somehow ironic, although I find the reasons why, both vague and complex, and find it difficult to explain. The most interesting aspect of the piece is visible when one stands directly in front of it, and I believe it to be Osim's personal statement and neither that of Osim's father nor the artist. One blind man's head makes up the opened, lower lip of the elephant. He seems to have been thrown back dead, and his flailing arms downward make the tusks, two prongs usually seen thrust upward, not hanging down. Another blind man that one would expect to be feeling about like the others seems also dead on the elephant's head. Perhaps he is alive, but there is something lifeless in his position, but the most interesting thing is that he is feeling the elephant's eyes, one hand covering each. That is fine in itself, but from the front, the elephant could be interpreted as being blind as well, for after all, its eyes are covered, and while the hands of the blind men in the sculpture are iron outlines, the hands covering the elephant's eyes are solid as if to leave no doubt to the meaning.

I was angry at Osim for his rejecting father's wish to join the ossified army in the catacombs, but on the day my father was buried, there were mists blowing from the mountains, over the hideaways and out to the desert, making it a memorable day. Shortly afterwards, the truth was buried, and I was put in the inner sanctum labor pool. Those that left the inner sanctum were put to work in rebuilding some of the ruins. It seemed to be a fulfillment of my sense of what Osim's vision of the future should be, but there were so many people released from the inner sanctum that the homes we left did not provide enough room. The ruins provided foundations, so at least that portion of the construction work was done. It would speed the process of building villages, but I wondered about the future.

If there are foundations that are used to create new villages, what will the ruins be called after the new society rises? Ruins? Or will they be thought of as prefabrications reserved for explosions of population? There have been changes on the outside, and our work in the inner sanctum has effected some modifications, but I wonder that the maneuverings have taken place within a greater order that allows for the movements of inner elements but would otherwise say that everything has remained the same. In another major project, going by Osim's maps, all entrances to the catacombs were closed up, I never thought discussion of the catacombs would be forbidden, but everyone's lips were ordered sealed on the subject as well.

There were tremendous changes in society and in life. Everyone experienced tremendous upheaval. Within several months of the bombardment, I was busy in my new life in the inner sanctum as one of the lowest dignitaries. I recognized the ledge on which I walked as being just over the noses of the lowest populace, and while I suspected that I was made a low dignitary to keep me from mingling in the masses, I did not keep my nose in the air. I looked below the ledge from time to time, and recognized people from the outside world locked in with me. Seeing history repeating itself forced me to confront Osim on various anomalies of his new administration.

I remember it was at one of the first state dinners where all the newly installed dignitaries were being honored that I first spoke out. I asked first whether I was alone in thinking it odd that self-appointed leaders should gather to honor and admire themselves mutually. All of these people had been gathered by Osim, but what else distinguished them as individuals? They were rewarded for having served in the army, just as an earlier generation of catacomb prison survivors had risen in the ranks of the dignitaries, and yet what had they done more than that? What gave the newly-appointed dignitaries more right to rule than the thousands of commoners now imprisoned at the lowest level other than loyalty to Osim? I made a speech while they devoured legs of mutton and spilled wine from their mouths already overflowing with greasy food. They laughed at me, jeering my alluding to purity and righteousness. I had never joined the cause. I was ordered to sit down and shut my mouth because I was lucky to have been given any kind of place in the new order. Before sitting, I stated flatly that I found it odd that a new religious order would gag on words like righteousness. Someone said I could enjoy speaking freely at my level, but to watch my step. I knew too much and there were two ways of dealing with that fact. One was to give me some kind of rank, which is what they had done. The other would have been to ascertain perfect assurance of my silence by administering a noose around my neck. These comments led to laughter all around, and I sat down.

For the first time, I felt as I thought Osim must have when he first traversed the desert of bones in the catacombs, when he was inspired with purpose and a cause, but he had an opportunity and met with little opposition. I was dealing in politics. One cannot destroy an inner sanctum from within, at least not from where I was sitting. Osim had only the sensation of murmurs from an auditorium of bleached bones. I had a living mass of drunken authority and dared to question the root of power. The dead provide a quiet chorus to a revolution. The living are not quite as malleable.

These were things I could not conquer, but I felt it my duty to alert them to the notion. It might prove to balance the vision and render the rule more just. If I had learned anything, it was that I needed to conquer myself first. Given the freedom to do so, who could say what I might accomplish. Osim silenced the jeers that followed and pointedly said, "First you stand alone in objecting so strenuously to there being any need to change anything at all, and now you stand alone complaining that everything is the same while we merely enjoy a small celebration. Perhaps you should reflect on your own imbalances rather than impose them on us. If you cannot transfer your perception to the living; why don't you try raising an army of the dead?" A great cheer followed, and I left the assembly.

I thought my departure difficult but clean, and it never occurred to me that Osim would follow me. For reasons of vanity, I thought he was going to apologize, but instead he grabbed my shoulder and violently turned me around. He grabbed my hand, demanding to know where I'd gotten the ring. I'd started wearing it shortly after I'd taken it off the hand on the beach. I said I found it.

He was quite angry and demanded that I give it to him. "Consider it a confiscation by the authorities," he sneered as he wrenched it off my hand. I knew I had no real claim to it, but I didn't understand what gave Osim the interest in it or the right to it.

He said he had found mention of such a ring in his father's diaries. He'd seen it on my hand in the assembly, and it struck him that it was similar to the description he had read. Had he really had that clear a view of it from where he sat that he recognized it, or had he just become fanatic about whatever his father had written so as to see a need to put that world back together with whatever pieces struck him as having the shape he might force into place to complete his demented puzzle. Or perhaps he was transitioning to Bale.

As if imitating the unknown, man seems to build a world where no one can get all the answers. Osim walked off with the ring without knowing the story of how I'd obtained it. All I could think of was that hand in the sand. It kept me from giving him all the answers. I feel for certain that he wouldn't have explained it to me even if he understood how it might have gotten there. Neither of us has all the answers. We never will have them. It is as if we react to the enormity of the unknown by working with what dim light there is rather than grow intent on learning more and making it brighter. Why is that?

When Osim went back to the assembly, I heard a great cheer followed by laughter. My head was spinning. Why did I have no confidence in my own ideas? And yet, though I was meek, I expected others to think as I did. Was Osim any worse, forceful as he was, to expect others to share his views? He differed by making sure others agreed whether or not he was right. I thought my own views would take shape in those who thought about it, but there was nothing in history to suggest that the masses paid any attention to reason. When did they have time while wearing one yoke or another to think? Locked down by various men of action, who had time?

As for my position of great dignity in the new administration, I was also keeper of the nursery, of all things. My particular domain demanded that I supervise the children every afternoon while the great dignitaries assembled. The ages of the children ranged from infant to ten, and I considered every moment of it a torture beyond description. It was only when I learned recently that Lorelei was pregnant that I felt any degree of satisfaction, as I looked forward to the day that I might take care of Osim's child. It seems ironic after all that had passed, after father had taken care of him and kept things from him, that I might have the opportunity to fill Osim's child's mind with the truth. I relish the idea, and daydreaming the effect my influence might have on his son to eventually bring down his father fills my days. Actually, I have little hope of effecting any great changes in the universe, but thinking such thoughts helps me vent my frustration. I wish I could undergo an alteration, take religion to heart and believe in miracles everywhere, but I cannot seem to restore any sense of belief. I've grown numb to it all, and it's hatred that helps me through otherwise bleak afternoons, just as it was hatred that helped me survive other terrible times, only this hatred is new and all-consuming. I want to turn to dust quickly. For its power to eat away inside, hatred might be the fastest way.

When Osim first moved into the inner sanctum, he made it clear that he wanted every wall refortified. He had his eyes on the uppermost level by the spires, but until repairs were made, he was unable to rule from there. So biding his time, he supervised below with what seemed to me to be an obvious desire to ensure that his reign would be long and safe. One day I happened to ask him if he thought he was secure, and he answered that one must always be ready for a downfall, and if ready, one was actually floating between up and down. In such a position, one could really never rise, and one could really never be brought down. He pointed up to where the highest level in the sanctum used to be, which was now open sky, and said that his dream was realized when he could meditate in the uppermost chamber of the inner sanctum, but thoughts in the spire heights were no different than in hideaways, which is why those who think one way in the depths rise in the first place, and why their thinking has a character, that does not change. A character that does not change, I mused. Now didn't that epitomize Osim!

He warned me not to take too much to heart of the overall turn of events that brought us to the inner sanctum. "There are facts and there are interpretations," he told me. "Facts can be learned, but all interpretations are subject to evaluation by higher authority. You may interpret, but you may not have all the facts. Indeed, none of us has all the answers, so all the interpretations are suspect, and yet we feel somehow that some are better than others.

"Some people appear to be living out the purposes better than others because they seem unhindered by fear," he explained. "They do what is natural, and we find that easy to accept. At the same time, we may judge such individuals as not having the brains to contribute intellectually to the culture of our society. Somehow we place a high value on thought and judge others in light of what we consider to be the mark of thought, but isn't that largely subjective? Isn't it based on our own level of intellectual ability? Don't we consider ourselves as equally capable if not more empowered than most of our neighbors to do what is humanly possible because we too are human? It is pride. It is our eyes that are being covered.

"There are blind men all over us, and they all are the different sides of ourselves, and wherever we walk, like a wild elephant, we destroy whatever is in our path. The only place one should ever feel safe with humanity is in a cemetery or the catacombs, but there is something so generally unsettling about such places that we must seek the living tombs, though the world be riddled with hideaways sitting on top of a powder keg that sits on top of history's mass grave. I just pretended to light the fuse and everyone thought the explosion was perfectly controlled," he said. "When the smoke cleared, the news appeared to be the answer to everyone's prayers. Those on the inside got out, and those on the outside got in.

"Now we have the work to do that was once theirs. It may be a better era, but nothing can stop the build-up of the bone yard. It's just best to keep it hidden even if it isn't sought as a sanctuary, and even if it isn't being used as a prison. True, things begun in earnest may evolve, mutating into lies, but I intend that this be a quieter era. I've little control over more than my intentions. I just have the good fortune of having a good image from having been lucky in a daring, terribly risky assault. I feel your lack of trust, but doesn't this strike you as a decent posture? Given our recent history, and though nature promises horrors in the future over which we have little control, couldn't we use some peace for a change? I'm talking generally in political terminology while you're filled with personal uncertainties, driven by your own spirit to reason why you're alive.

"So concentrate on that. If it were given to you to have the world as you wanted it as long as you stood on guard, you'd abandon the post. Don't measure what we have with your vision of perfection. You'll waste away and never enjoy a moment, and who will listen and carry the torch for you should you try to pass it to others? They will think as they like, like us, in one or another random setting, influenced by many things, and by the one thing that binds all nature and guarantees the diversity. Be confident that you will discover wonderful things here in the inner sanctum, as luminous creatures are sometimes found in the darkness of caverns or in mines."

He took me by the shoulder and escorted me around various levels of the inner sanctum. He said that if we had time to walk around, by way of the cliffs and our old village, so that I could see the changes, I would be amazed how much the new populace had been able to build up the old ruins where we used to play as children. I would feel as if I were in another country.

We went to his uppermost chamber by the broken spires, and I was able to somewhat survey and verify his descriptions. Lorelei kissed him when we came in. She greeted me, but I was staring at my shoes. All the same, I couldn't help but see her marvelous feet and recall the days that she loved me. She was very attentive to Osim. I surmised their love was very great. He was able to relax with her, to give her song the space it needed to resound, and he exuded a complete confidence and trust in her. Why was I not able to keep thoughts like death and betrayal from muddling my enjoyment and capacity to appreciate not just the time I had with her, but be happy for them? I seemed to have to prove that life was sad by saddening myself as much as I could. I knew there were great forces like Osim out to prove me wrong. From Osim, I felt a sense that one could be fulfilled and live an abundant life even in the face of mortality. He had none of the hesitancy and death that filled me. He was all I wished that I could have been for Lorelei, but I was distanced from her just by that short space, which might as well have been an abyss, by thinking about it. Osim never gave such things a thought and thus stood beyond the threshold that for me was hundreds of miles through inner jungles, and so I never did find anyone to love me.

We gazed out the high windows. "They're writing the name Osim everywhere," he told me. He stood there rubbing the ring he had taken from me. It fit him quite perfectly actually. "When father was held up as an example and martyred, so many on the inside forgave him. They knew he was just a man and that his sins were no more than theirs. After his execution, when they were all exiled, he became a secret hero and a rallying call against the inner sanctum. They paid him homage by breaking the law and writing his name all over as a reminder, and equally kept alive the threat against themselves standing in opposition." Now he was turning the ring on his finger as if tightening a screw. "The children are now writing the name Osim on the walls . The reasons have changed, but it seems to have become a tradition. Isn't it strange that what happened with the father can now be attributed to the son? He fell, and I was raised. It's like this ring with the faces, each one coming into emphasis as the wheel turns. Even betrayal must have its day."

I told him that when he'd come out of the desert that night after having disappeared for three years, I'd thought father had found peace with God. "But it surprised me," I said, "that on that very next morning you set a battle in motion and by the end of day had the blood of thousands on your hands."

He twisted the ring on his finger. "It depends on how you see things, doesn't it?" he replied. "Every life will convey contradictions to the observer whose understanding is feeble. The perspective that allows for one to go through its box of alternate personalities has a sense of the faces we all wear, but how you measure others depends somewhat on your own temporary perspective, doesn't it? When you've reached wholeness and have words directly from God to offer the rest of us, I hope you'll also follow what you determine to be His personal directions despite how we might stand in your way. Don't confuse yourself judging the world by imposing barren principles without living them yourself. It really doesn't matter what you think of actions in motion, and even your hindsight is interpretation if you don't stand up for your sense of the truth, for without the principles taking root in you, you may throw them around, but in you they have no source to grow. They are like cut flowers that wither in your hands, for whose death you will not blame yourself. Rather, you will watch them die, and you'll conclude that they are lies, and what will you have then?"

Then he started laughing. When I pressed to know the reason for his amusement, he said he'd spent the afternoon in the catacombs at the site of Bale's grave, the body of which was missing a hand. There was discussion of the epitaph, and someone suggested, "He had a hand in death, and now the hand is gone." Someone else said, "Why not just, 'Here Lies Bale?'" Then Osim had the idea that won the day, which was *Here, Finally, Bale Does Not Lie.* We laughed. At least the new administration had a sense of humor.

While we were laughing, someone began shouting insults at Osim for his betrayal of the people. The man vented all his rage while Osim just stood quietly and listened. The principal complaint was that he had neglected his first duty which was to remove the walls of the fortress of the inner sanctum. Refortifying the walls merely perpetuated an order that would lead to continuing disorder. The killing was just done out of revenge, and maintaining division with the walls of the inner sanctum simply justified the killing, made the recent battle seem righteous in hindsight. Meanwhile, ruling class power of the inner sanctum prevailed.

He responded that he had such a hope of breaking down the inner sanctum fortifications in the beginning, but that there were a great many political tradeoffs that had to be made during the years of suffering and waiting in the catacombs.

"You should have gone across the desert and waited it out," I interrupted. "All that time hiding in the catacombs made you numb to death."

"Yes, if you want to put it that way, the catacombs did that to me, it's true. But my legacy will be of sacrifice and suffering. You have no idea what it was like for me during those days. There were great difficulties in gathering food and keeping a confidence level high. The inner sanctum may have had a sense of a growing rebellion, but obviously didn't feel that the threat was great enough to root it out. To the inner sanctum, it was probably treated like just another folie that would eventually be dealt with in its turn. Time was of the essence, and it took time to gather enough individuals whereby the inner sanctum could be overthrown. Also, I needed to devise a plan and implement it such that a lesser force might overwhelm one far greater. I was their leader, but deputies needed to be appointed, and the glue that congealed the force was violent hatred for the inner sanctum and the belief that power would soon be in our hands."

As we were talking, Osim motioned to some men who arrested the heckler and took him away. Osim continued his explanation by telling me that he recognized that this lust for power was wrong, but that the rage flowing in the blood of the people was necessary. It was not the time to talk sense but to make promises that one day they would take control and make the inner sanctum suffer. Preparations for war were not made with rational ideals but with strong emotion. He said that at first he planned by degrees to remove the walls of the inner sanctum, that he'd envisioned a free communing between the people on the outside and the inside, but he learned later that it would not just happen. There needed to be a plan for that as well. Walls on the inside of people needed to be broken down, and that was the greater difficulty. As it stood, the people on the outside were becoming acclimated to life on the outside, just as we would slowly grow accustomed to life in the inner sanctum. The danger, he said, was that too many would begin to prefer life on the inside so much that prejudice and fear of outsiders would grow out of all proportion. At the moment, everyone had a recollection of the previous state. It was equally dangerous, however, that the mixing of the two worlds would happen too late or too soon. There must be a time of healing, but there was a threat that walls of scar tissue would grow between the people, and he admitted that my fear of a continuing, cyclic disorder was justified, saying it was a necessary, natural order.

Osim had expressed all of these concerns at council meetings. There were many who believed, for example, that by giving the outsiders the right to reconstruct the ruins, they would quickly attempt to construct their own inner sanctum, and that this must be guarded against with the greatest vigilance. Some said it was foolish to even allow these people the right to build at all. Osim reminded the council that they had not taken over the inner sanctum to merely continue a reign of terror. There must be justice, and while these people may have had certain loyalties to the inner sanctum, the loyalty was based on fear. In any event, the new system would have greater appeal in its justice. While there was always a chance there would be a few enemies for whom the system must be vigilant, an open system would provide that the majority would be kind and just. Paranoia was natural, but Osim wanted things to simmer down. "To ensure that the boiling foam does not pour over the sides of the pot, someone must watch the fire underneath," he said.

At one point, Osim admitted to me that he'd come to see father and I before the caravan with a mind to gloat. At the time, he was, after all, on the verge of either great victory or defeat. It was his last chance to let the truth be known. So much of his life had been covered up in lies that he wanted the truth to be known no matter what might become of him. His original intention had been merely to inform us with joy, but when he encountered my resistance, he became angry and decided to tell me nothing. It pleased him to point out father's less-than-honorable role, and he regretted that his desire of reaching an understanding with me had gone by the wayside. There was too much emotion and uncertainty at that time, he told me, but now there was still a need for any wall between us to fall. Now more than ever, he needed my help and understanding. Osim said he wanted my idealism but needed my understanding of the compromises that are necessary to achieve those goals. The process needed to be political because it was not a case of the country having been divided again by a new war, but a continuation of the traditions of division that included war.

It was the first time that Osim ever approached me as a brother, and it was the first time I ever thought I'd seen a weakness in him. I know I was really seeing another sign of strength, but it was the first time that I felt he needed me, and my own sense of self-deprecation made me feel it must be weakness in him that would cause him to say he needed me. It was the first time I'd felt comfortable with him, and was the only inkling of hope I had for the new order.

That was three years ago, three long years ago, during which time I haven't budged from my lowest level ledge in the inner sanctum. I imagine I'll have a similarly low ledge to occupy in the catacombs, but the bones that I'll be tossed on, or the bones that will be tossed on me, will not likely be those of anyone I've known. Spelunkers or archaeologists who might come upon me in the distant future should remember I'll be just as horribly alone in the corridors of skulls as I've always been. But there has been a change in me. Whereas I would have been the only skeleton not urging them forward to fulfill some great enterprise that burns inside them. Give it up, would have been my cry. Now I'll urge them to continue. I've even a faint hope that my bones will swell the ossified throng's chorus to help Osim find his way through the catacombs in the future.

Most, if not all, of my early life was spent in restlessness and worry, with the cloud of Osim hovering over me. I feared that I would be forced into a state of being truly in his domain, under his watch, forced finally, as if to prepare for the place in the catacombs my bones one day will occupy, to reflect and meditate, asked to be somehow at peace, to accept the fact that this is where my future is, although I fear changes will come. Somehow it seems as if the call for everyone is to put the pieces of one's life together in a fashion where one can say, I am fine; I am at peace. What I found is that there are moments that generate an aura of peacefulness, such as my reconciliation with Osim, but somehow my spirit has its basis in restlessness nevertheless, Born to trouble, as the sparks fly upward.

In the final analysis, the speech that Osim made on his world of best possible intentions, when we surveyed that world through the windows of that highest chamber, could only take its place with all other experiences I have had with him. I have at numerous times found myself mollified by his eloquent explanations only to be awakened as a fool later. Somehow that is how I thought of myself in his inner sanctum domain. The fool! I couldn't amuse him, quite frankly, as I had no talent for that. If the power I had could be strengthened in focus and have the effect it might, it would rather be to depress him. I had wondered if he only kept me around as a means to detect that he was slipping. The day that I depressed him, he would withdraw for quick repairs.

But I have found that when I finally saw that Osim was confused and needed my help, that I had some vital and essential insights into my own confusion as well. It was this: Osim was always confused about his life. Somehow, I never fully understood that. When he'd figured out his life and betrayed signs of new confusion, I was disappointed in him. He'd always been human, but my jealousy was fed by a fear that he was superior, and its festering ate at me, making me less than I might have been.

Osim was never confused, but I was. He never spent so much time thinking little of other people, being petty and making himself less than he was. I realized when Osim admitted his weakness what I'd always feared, that he was the greater man all along, and that I was essentially what I had always been, a weaker human being.

This may seem simply to be a sorry tale of how I received the scars I bear. I feel needlessly embarrassed to say that to an extent, this is true. It is the story of the punishment I received. Had Osim been an inanimate danger, a fire, or a bush with thorns, I'd surely have avoided him. But Osim was one who was always present, ever threatening, and against whom there was no protection because he infiltrated my spirit. Looking back now, I feel that I was on the moon with only an umbrella to protect myself against meteors. Then, in awe of the dawn of Earth on a barren landscape, a meteor shower ripped through me. Later, broken, complaining about the universe, I found that the meteors had supposedly enriched and repaired me. Now I am the master of more than one world though I still have no control at all over myself or my own destiny.

In the meantime, Osim maintains his post at the helm as he always has, peering through the spires at the pinnacle of the inner sanctum, hoping that his vision will become real. He confided in me only yesterday that there were serious discussions of restoring the tradition of the annual caravan. He wanted to know what I thought about it. "This is not a choice," I told him. "It is how things must be. We are both looking through a microscope at a slide on which we see ourselves struggling to survive. To stop means to die."

That is when Osim informed me that several former high-level inner sanctum dignitaries had been captured on the outside, thanks to informers who recognized them disguised as ordinary people. Rather than executing them, they had been brought in to fill in a few gaps in knowledge. For example, they were proving to be instrumental in providing an accurate description of the rituals relating to the wearing of lit candles. Osim said it was fascinating, and that he had decided that incorporating some secular rituals was like an inoculation of protection against religious fanaticism. When I asked whether I might be allowed to wear a candle on my head, Osim said there were secrets reserved for a select few of the highest order. "You mean something like initiation and parading before the dead in the catacomb tunnels?" Osim nodded and expressed admiration for my intuitive grasp of inner sanctum rituals.

If one bases one's assessment of how one ought to behave in the world on the choices others have made, there are no limits. The great *Thou Shalt Nots* strike me personally as having landed at my feet, thrown in anger from the mountain and barely missing my head. In terms of what I've witnessed, I do not see that there is any universal recognition or adherence even to a minor degree. The propulsion system of the human being in its own element drives it the way it wants to go. Education is more like a hindrance during which time one is held back by others' ideas. Proposing to enrich, for some time, they only confuse. Experience proves the system gets tangled up in itself. The general drive is onward anyway, and whatever one might choose to do in trying to adhere to a sense of a great law or truth, one side of the human race has proceeded like a caravan the other is working to stop since the beginning of time.

My own experience has been a random accumulation of events that now reside in memory. Didn't everything that happened occur as a result of my disposition at a given time? Or did I never have control except in my review, my interpretation, or is even that suspect? Has not my own assembly of acceptance and rejection changed faces a thousand times? Purely partaken, isn't any reasonable idea merely ingested to be broken down by the enzymes of mood and passed out as so much refuse and gas? What meat of what mental muscle has been fortified by which philosophies forced down my throat? The truth is observable, discernable, but I cannot see it. I have inklings of what might be fathomed on the other side, but where I reside is a continuous history of bones disgorged by one party's lust to overthrow another. When will heaven intervene?

Given what has transpired in my life with the dominance of Osim, there isn't anything that can be said to inspire faith for my fellow man. My proper audience resides in the catacombs. The rest won't listen since the message is vague. The world wants its commentators to post only palatable perceptions to fuel it.

The truths the human race has seemed to be avoiding for centuries just might sink in if properly prepared. I've little chance of doing that, for my own sense of truth is in great disrepair. I've been largely shattered by experience and am now locked in the inner sanctum which is now Osim's domain. Ideas such as these have no sanctioned audience, and I often think my notion of reading to the bones in the catacombs is not so wild a thought. I'll be on a shelf there soon enough, and I have an itch to implant my vision in a book to represent what I've seen to those who'll come after, but I've become increasingly cynical of there being any interest in my view.

But there are only a few elements to tie together now to bring this account of Osim to a proper closing. It has come so far through our growing up together, his life in the hideaways, his disappearance, my surprise at discovering him on the desert, and his destruction of the caravan. My self-indulgent dwelling on myself was necessary because of what I became due to the impact of Osim. I was immoral and insensitive to everyone throughout my life, but now I am a low-level dignitary in the new inner sanctum.

Perhaps it has something less to do with capitulation. Was I ever in control? I raced as everyone does in youth, but I never lost the enthusiasm for being alive, and I thought my presence would ulti-mately have an impact. It's a sobering reality to see oneself as a mere extension like a coral flower that becomes part of the structure of bones, a part of one's total ancestry. One wonders at some point whether the purpose is for there to be a layer of life or a constant accumulation of bones, and in any case it doesn't matter because nature takes care of everything. We just do the babbling. But I real-ized after moving to the inner sanctum that I was substantially more bone in spirit than the living entity on the surface. Osim, despite the bones he sent to the catacombs, strikes me as being the life force, and that is why I've withdrawn, or rather withered into myself. My corporeal exile is not self-imposed. I cannot leave the inner sanctum. But my spiritual exile is voluntary, but strange how much I am mortified to remember small immoralities and petty mis-treatment of others even though it was normal behavior for a child. I would like to be alive again, but Osim spoiled that for me. I am like a monk now, quietly meditating over my sins in this rebuilt hideaway of spires. Perhaps it will make me something after all. I should have done this years ago, and doing it now, I'd like to pass along the sense of importance to the outside world, what used to be the populace of the inner sanctum now in exile on the cliffs, but I'm afraid they do not know the danger. It must be heaven to them to be in the wild after such a long imprisonment, but I fear the inner sanctum is the beast that will come and tear them apart some night, and now that it's beginning to cut its teeth, it gnaws on me.

A disturbing image haunts me. I see an entire generation born on the same day. There will be no births for twenty-five years. Then there will be a day on which another generation will be born. On this state birthday, every womb gives forth an ignorant babe that rides out on a wave of plaster. The child is caught, but the waves of plaster collect in a desert that descends into the catacombs where the previous generations were buried. It fills the tunnels and the caves to the stone vault, hardening for this generation of babes to come with picks and shovels to dig out holes for their parents.

It is a vision of a society of worms that tunnel into the same caverns into which their foreworm fathers once tunneled, filled by their own afterbirth. The day of birth is one during which all previous sins are concealed, which is at the same time a laying of new ground from which old truths will spring on the day of concealment. These creatures have instilled in their very nature a longing to bury the living truth and discover the old truth and keep it from dying. When they've buried their parents, and the excavation of the old truth is nearly complete, a new generation emerges and a new wave of plaster comes as a disaster, wiping out years of hard work in a swift wash cycle. The workers, too tired to start again, and distraught with the weight of their discoveries, wait patiently to take their place in the cycle, carrying along the heaps of dirty linen of lost hopes and broken dreams.

This image was born on a dream wave that washed over me in sleep, my first dream in several years. It was a significant moment to me that I should begin dreaming again. I used to dream constantly, but those were the days when my life existed in a state of prevalent possibilities. When the dreams died, it signified an emptiness ahead (as I look back). After the long, empty hiatus, I had this dream, and it brought with it a sense that I had reached the world of possibilities once again, and to that degree, I felt the hope of a child into which longed-for states could be directed. Without dreams, the world congealed, hardening around me until I grew so hard on myself and on others that I lost everyone and had nothing. Though this dream was in itself a gloomy vision, it was just a dream, and despite the rude awakening, I felt whole in the prospect of the possibilities awaiting a mere nod to begin to open around me.

It also bore a similarity to what happened after Lorelei left me. At first I couldn't stop thinking about her, and then when I thought I'd finally managed to put her out of my mind, all at once she started to fill my head with dreams about her every night.

In the same way, I thought I was finally putting thoughts of the catacombs and Osim's struggle out of my mind, and then I had this frightening dream full of symbols and foreboding. But while it was a nightmare that woke me in a terrible sweat, from which it took several minutes to calm down, it was also a victory for being a dream like those I had in the old days, bearing some hidden meaning in its clothing if I was willing to look through the pockets. The cyclic part with the plaster wasn't particularly important, but it struck me as redundant to a degree, more simplistic and allegorical, but forgivable in that I was out of practice in complex, comprehensive dreaming. I woke when a wave of plaster washed on me while wandering through a tunnel, an image wholly inconsistent with what I'd been feeling was the meaning of the dream.

But despite that, I sat up in bed pondering the images for a long time. A portion that preceded the flood of plaster particularly intrigued me. I'm not sure how, but everything I knew rotated into another position. The inner sanctum became Osim's hideaway into which we all were drawn. It had been armed for a caravan riding inward, and with the camels fully assembled, plaster began to spew from above, not just on the caravan but over our entire civilization, sealing everything, all while a sandstorm was developing to bury it. In time, when discovered, it will all be viewed not just as an extensive system of catacombs, but a model of all societies.

Although I knew that I was in the bowels of the inner sanctum at the time, a victim of the disaster, in the dream I had the privilege of witnessing the event from above. I watched as the inner sanctum erupted all at once with a tremendous force that blew upward in a billowing black mass. I knew it was due to the ignition of bones beneath the continent, that their burning fed the great plume of black smoke and sparks rising upward. I felt that the foundation of the shattered ruins would crumble within weeks as the impatient desert at last moved in, dousing the hissing embers like the sea and consigning the last traces of our lost city to the deep. Would anyone think they heard the sound of a bell tolling out in the dunes during sand storms? What would the sound signify and where would it lead other than to make a deep and poetic permanent impression?

From my vantage point, there was no crushing stampede of panic. I saw nothing except smoke and fire and felt the blaze as it roared through the catacombs beneath, feeding on centuries of bones like coal. When it finally caused complete subsidence, clouds of steam took the place of black smoke as the continent sank into the desert. With the last hiss, I turned away as one alone in the clouds.

It was not a peaceful sensation to behold this cataclysm, but I was gratefully above it all, and it was glorious to fly. Shortly thereafter, however, the torrent of plaster began. From what had seemed so natural on high, like someone in a plane, floating and watching the world unfold below with detachment, I woke like a rat washed out of its trance by the collected spit of the piper having played his tune. Sitting up in bed, shaking, waiting for explosions to begin all around me, I longed for a place in the sky, and had the strange sensation that I was cowering on a ledge somewhere, trapped inside a pipe.

But as I wonder what this all means to me now, I question whether there ever was a destiny for me, except in service to Osim's fulfilling his. It is difficult to reconcile events, and I've grown tired of the confusion. But for the first time in my life, I felt a true longing to be whole, functioning dutifully in society whatever may come. At first I thought that everything that would contribute to that wholeness had been stripped from me, but somehow he gave it back to me. I understand that if wholeness is going to come, it has to be achieved within. I must come to terms with myself, grow peaceful despite the isolation, with circumstances beyond my control, in a gathering weakness, facing inevitable dissolution and death, and somehow rise level by level in this inner sanctum to the very spires of peace, like Osim.

If ever there was a chance that I'd have been whole, it would have come by confronting sides of myself that I can say I've actually encountered. But fearing emptiness, I would always run away from these other selves, as if wholeness would come by putting them out of mind and behind me. I was only turning my back on growth, and now that they've caught up to me in my dead-end, they seem to be transparent, ghost-like shells of myself. I know they are necessary now, but they are not content to merely stay beside me as I would be willing to accept. They must surround and engulf me, and not just change me but turn my world into an empty, barren vista.

As for Osim's promises, he has tried to break the walls down. There have been some success in making changes. Osim has exerted a wonderful influence in council, and though at times he seems to be up against a mob, he has control, he has become master of the flower that grows in desolation, which provides one with a bit of water one needs to survive, and I believe that the walls of the fortress, though they are high and deep, will continue to fall. A doorway has been opened for visitation for families that have been separated, and a program has been instituted that allows people to exchange places to learn about the other side. The council only agreed to these programs in order to initially test them. They are a cynical bunch, and I feel that they are angry that the plan may be succeeding. Despite his adversaries, Osim is persistent. He has become a better politician, adept in making compromises while keeping everyone in line on a road heading in his direction.

All things considered, I fear that without an individual of Osim's capacity to turn thought into action, the world would once again adopt its original cycles, or should I say only that it feels better when the cycle is turned to one in your favor, not that one can ever hope the wheel will ever stop turning. Osim may even be a part of such cycles, an upward jutting or historical lift for all of us, a quirk that happens to provide a chance to prosper for those fortunate enough to be alive in the same era before the wheel resumes its steady course over and under the human spirit.

As the wheel turns, I sometimes feel like I'm in the center of a city, but from another perspective, even life is existence in a tomb, a quiet catacomb. I've put ashes from burnt bones on my forehead. It signifies that I'm playing out my time with the full awareness of its limited measure, and its seepage through my grasp. I have heard the words of Osim's father and understand the honor of interment in the catacombs. I know what it means to add my bones to the dead in advance of dying. The sands of time are slipping out of me. Something of me is being taken away, but something has been born that cannot be removed. Such submission is required to join the living.

The real world seems to live in my memory. It lies far off, containing millions whose mortality does not seem to affect me. They buzz about the ruins, surrounded by the desolation but not positively influenced by it, unable to place its puzzle piece into the overall focus and complete the picture. They seem to thrive and enjoy life, and I ache to participate, to forget as it were, but it is my duty to guard the light in the tunnel, and the bloom of the desert flower.

You see, I've been thrown not out into the cold, but into the heart of the truth by my experience. Transparent and ghost-like in mind, it has consolidated into the foundation of my life. It would have turned to ruins without a link within me to give me what is called a soul. Then I heard a faint sound, something like a bell clanging in an ancient tower that was sucked into quicksand, vaguely revealed itself when storms exposed it, though no one would dare venture out to see it clearly. It was a signal that I should cross the desert to rejoin the dead and exult in our mutual exhumation from the abyss. I stalled most of my life both in fear of drowning and in the hope that Osim and the rest of the living would notice my special talents, but that was why I was trapped. My boundaries were never a match for the open wilderness. In trying to call attention to myself dancing around the ruins, I never learned there were times I should have only been thankful, and down on my knees.

I learned that to make an escape, I would have to accept a model of reality where only a miracle that would take place inside would save me. I thought Osim was my great enemy and the world's, but he served as the catalyst for our mutual benefit. Even now, in my berth in the inner sanctum, like my future resting place, I rejoice that I heard the alarm, and I thank God for the will to heed the call, and I would counsel everyone to consider this carefully and do whatever is necessary to wake from the dead and be born.

Postscriptum: In the fifteenth year of Osim's reign, on the occasion of his twelfth caravan, the hills lit up with cannons ablaze and destroyed it. Rumors of a plan to obliterae Osim and other high dignitaries of the inner sanctum in the same way that he had taken power had been circulating for months. I was able to make my escape with Lorelei and their son through secret passages in the catacombs based on maps that Osim gave me to study.

In the aftermath of the bombardment, we were hunted, but Osim had managed a project that excavated a series of new catacombs extending below the desert for miles. Workers discovered an underground river, installed artificial lights and made a garden with animals and plants to feed many people. During the supposed destruction of the caravan, Osim and the others escaped into a secret tunnel, sealing it behind them. Osim understood they would scour the sands for the ring, then leave the desert, so he left a duplicate behind with the original depictions of Bale. The one he kept was altered with the faces of people important to him, those of our fathers, myself, Lorelei, his son and others who had served him.

And so we live in a new inner sanctum, cut off for now from the outside world. Osim has no doubt that his son will seek his revenge. The seeds are already planted for the wheel to turn again. The outside world always pulls at youth, and inner sanctums are ever under construction by older men. This is the yin and yang of power, of falling from grace, of reclaiming the garden, and of harvesting and distributing its forbidden fruit, and someday we will squeeze a few spires above ground and protect ourselves with a great fortress. Osim says we will see the day where battles will be between nations, won by hidden armies of the dead, so we are carrying the bones through the catacombs to be with us, singing, *As he ascended from a rattle of bones, so we descend into the catacombs.* In coming years, Osim's kingdom will extend everywhere: above, below, inside and out. Amen.

The Rock

A dying man was brought into the operating room where the team of doctors was waiting. As the anesthesiologist for the operation, I was getting prepared to put the patient under. The man pushed the mask away and said to everyone, "I know you're going to do your best, but it won't be good enough. I'm being forged right now. You see me convulsing and writhing in pain, but it isn't what you think. I'm being forged, pounded on the anvil of God. The sparks are flying, and I'm being shaped into something suitable for presence in a another state, into my final form. My spirit is being shaped, forged, right now on this table by God and His doctors who are the mechanics of the universe. Their operation is already in progress, and it takes precedence over yours."

The doctors ignored his ravings and continued to go about their business. I finally got the mask in place, and after the gas took effect, they proceeded with the operation. But he died on the table, just as he said he would. Later, as the doctors were washing up, I sat stupefied in front of my locker. I couldn't tell anyone because I knew that nobody would believe me, but I had actually seen the sparks flying. The man really was being hammered into shape on an anvil. I watched the whole process, and I knew from the manner in which the other doctors worked that they were oblivious to what I saw.

There is a high wall of rock in front of the hospital. I went outside and stood before it and made a promise to myself before the rock, the main thrust of which is loyalty to the rock. The rock is many things, and yet in most ways is a simple thing, a solid thing, and I told myself that the rock picked me, that it wanted my loyalty, and it was too far beyond me to question. And since my first visit to the rock, I have never questioned the arrangement because of the comfort the rock brings when I visit it at night and stand before it again, reaffirming my loyalty and thanking the rock for being there. But what I actually am and what I hold is inimical to the rock. I believe the rock has many enemies, as it were. The gasses, liquid agents, and the pills are all things that I don't just dabble in. I breathe them in. I swim in them. I ingest and distribute them all day long. They would knock me out, put me under, if it were not for the rock.

If the rock knew of any one of my infractions, it would crumble away and be gone. So I say nothing. I just stand in front of the rock, put my hand against it, feel its ridges and say, "Thanks for being here. I'm so glad you're here." I don't speak in any way of my betrayal, my constant betrayal, my swirling inner nature within to which the rock is blind. It is as if the rock is saying, "Stand here. Be loyal to me." I say, "I will." But I'm not in any way. I can make no claim at all to being worthy of the rock, but as I stumble for it in the darkness, as my eyes finally adjust to see its high walls, I am glad it's there. I need it. It provides a buffer within me to resist a complete disintegration into the gasses, liquid agents and pills that I wallow in all day. If I didn't have its firm support, I would stupify into a pool and wash away. I've always believed that the world is hard, that the ultimate goal is to be unified with the fluidity of the spirit that abounds in the universe. I thought that the hard world is a world of facts, that the facts displace the spirit and fortify the mind against spirit, and that the mind adopts this attitude as the preferred means to make sense of the world. Eventually it blocks out spirit in its various manifestations, so how does one find spirit again to adopt it as a means to displace the facts? Does it just walk into an operating room when you're gassing someone and allow you to witness what nobody else can see? After that, what must one do in order to prepare, so that one may see and tell of one's own forging when the time comes?

I believe the rock will keep me from going blind and fizzling away, that it will serve as an anvil over which my sparks will fly, but before anyone can stand loyally before it, one must believe that all souls need forging; some all at once, others along the way.

Swamped

Peter Steele abandoned his wife and children and took up teaching, his first love, in a small midwestern college. For Peter, it was about escaping an intensity he could not control. Before he was married, he'd felt secure in ideas, and when he felt the chaos of raising a family, the ideas always came back to mind, first as comfort in themselves, and finally as a concrete refuge of solitude that he thought a college teaching position would fortify.

A woman who taught in the same department had an office close to his, and she often knocked on his door to chat. Peter could see that she'd taken a shine to him, but he'd been as deliberately cold as one can be without actually insulting her. Margot was curious about his past. She wanted to know why he was single and solitary. She took a seat opposite his desk, looked around at the papers and the books and asked, "What do you get out of all these books beyond what you've gotten to pass on? You take the essence, try to make it live in others, but once you've harvested it, what comfort does it really give that you would sit as in a cold library? You need a life. How about we go out for a drink?"

"No, the thing about women is first you have a drink, then you throw a leg over her and the next thing you think you're in love. Thanks anyway, but I'm swamped here with papers to grade."

He thought that might get rid of her, but she laughed. "Throw a leg over one," she mocked, "like it's that easy. In your case, you would have to draw a line down the middle of the rock wall and make a door, open it and come out into the open. Before anyone would happily recline your way, you have to be happily inclined, if

250

you get my drift. I'm just curious what the books have that people don't. I got everything I wanted out of them by the time I was twenty-five. I love teaching, and I love history. I love ideas, and I think I've heard them all. So what's the idea that drives you? Let's test it against the others and see if it stands the test of quality and endurance. Is it worthwhile, universal and all that good stuff."

Peter looked up and saw she was smiling. No big deal, he thought. She's not serious. Still, he wondered if he could make a case, so he decided to let it spew and see if that would drive her away.

"Well let me tell you first, Margot, if I can trust you that anything I say to you will not go beyond these walls, that there is no line for a door, only the one I draw that you cannot cross if you expect me to trust you. Do you understand?" She nodded. "Good. Then the first thing is that ideas and life don't mix. It took me a while to figure that out. I was about twenty-five when I figured it all out, maybe had gotten all I needed as you say, and so I got married and had a family, which to me was like crashing on a glacier without provisions and clothing for the summer, let alone the winter.

"I remember when I decided to leave. There was an argument at the house at dinner, your typical misunderstanding that escalated into a shouting match. Despite my being the father, I was getting no respect from my teenage son. He was talking back, and my wife was defending him. I got my coat and hat and went out for a walk. They asked where I was going, and I said, 'Wherever I please!' and left.

"We lived near the city at the time, so there were lots of sounds. I heard sirens, jets in the sky, cars driving by, and my head was swimming with everything that just happened. It suddenly struck me how it all played together, the undecided game on television that has everyone hanging on the edge of their seats, the international political pressure, the responsibilities to the family, to work, to making a buck, and all of this was palpable, swirling around me like amniotic fluid. The sky was the color of that a fetus would see looking out from a mother's tummy. And there I was, about to be born.

"The first thing you have to understand is that I realized that there was no resolution. This is the state of life, the state of having a family, but at that moment I came to the realization that all of it

251

was exactly what I had to get away from in order to have peace in ideas, which ironically may be all about that, which may be about presenting that, explaining it and preserving it, but it had all gotten to me in a new way, which involved my chest. I thought I might have a heart attack. I was having trouble breathing. My anger and emotions were literally getting the better of me, and I saw that my wife and son were right about me. I had made it impossible for anyone to stand me because I had all these ideas telling me that it shouldn't be like that. I thought I would marry and have kids that would love me, who would gladly receive my knowledge and guidance, not constantly undermine me.

"All the ideas were telling me that it has to be like that, that it is like that, but in reality, having those ideas is different than living them. It is like the sun bursts with gigantic explosions, but at its distance from earth, it's very warm. So I thought about how I might put myself at a safe distance from life, and the ideas took over, that life can be this bombardment of things, the tension, the war, the anger, the murder, but none of it affects me. I'm able to philosophize about it and in a way not participate, but I do understand that I'm not above any of it. I just realized my limitations, that I couldn't involve myself and be questioned by a kid, whose mother was on his side. That was just a tip of the iceberg of the problems we had, but I decided I needed to be free of it. I had started the family, and it would be fine without me, so I left, and now I'm married to ideas."

Margot listened and was quiet after Peter finished. "So you could handle the ideas about life, but you couldn't handle life itself," she said. "That's very interesting. I'm surprised you haven't drunk yourself to death by now. You must be one in a million." Then she got up and left, which is what Peter had thought he hoped she would do, but now that she'd done it, he didn't feel so good about it. There is an idea about how any kind of sharing of personal information creates an expectation of validation. One doesn't merely tell a story in order to be blasted. Peter had done that, but he was reacting in accordance with the laws of nature to expect that Margot would react positively and try to understand.

There was a familiar murkiness in his feelings, similar to what he'd felt with his family, and he wanted to expunge it. Obviously, when dealing directly with people on a personal level, these kinds of upsets were inevitable, so he put on his jacket and went out for a walk. The campus sat close to the woods, which were full of the sounds of frogs having just emerged from hibernation.

As he listened to the frogs, he felt a sense of his always having been in a swamp, of coming from there, of still being in the middle of it, that predators were always there looking at him or looking for him. There were no sirens or planes or political tensions. All he needed to do was to keep things together, to hold the forces, but the only forces he could hold, ultimately, were ideas, which don't exist in the swamp. There was something else going on there.

He heard a noise and felt the eye of the predator, a sense of self preservation, and he heard a frog calling "Be a man, be a man." He stopped behind a bush and waited to hear the sound again. Then he realized he was most likely safe, being on a campus walking by houses. He thought of his father, grandfather and every other man as being forced to live in the swamp, how they heeded the call to "be a man." Whatever choices he would make, he would still be in the swamp, aware, awake, or maybe on the bottom hibernating, which is part of it too, in season, but otherwise one is armed, claws ready because it's a battle, a battle with ideas that motivate and carry one along. Ideas are weapons, and they are shields.

But in the murk and the deep, ideas didn't have a bearing. How one lives and dies, whether one survives is all instinctive. So it was a force of nature that drove him as he matured. He couldn't blame himself for leaving his family when he followed an inner force that is beyond anyone's endurance to fight. It hadn't driven him to make choices; rather it eliminated choices, leaving what was necessary.

As he was walking, he saw Margot going up the path to her house. He called to her. She stopped and waited for him. "Everyone talks about how the body of the chicken keeps moving when the head's cut off. But what about the head? It keeps talking, doesn't it? Blabbing away. *Brawk brawk*, more like whispers, which are empty ideas, so how about coffee and a chicken sandwich?" he asked.

"No thanks," she said. "I'm swamped. Besides, you're married."

The One-Eyed Fish

The adoption agency social worker told Mark that the boy he wanted to adopt was a one-eyed fish. While Mark was stunned that a professional would speak of a child in that manner, he didn't understand, so he asked what it meant. Tyler had two eyes after all, and while he certainly had greater difficulties than a normal 12-year-old boy, which included learning disabilities, he was good natured and wanted to be adopted.

Several people monitoring the adoption were not in favor of its going through, particularly in light of Tyler's problems. He'd been institutionalized most of his life. He'd been abused as a child, and he behaved badly with other children. These people felt that if Tyler were ever going to be adopted, it would have to be by someone who had experience with such children, and Mark was single. On the other hand, most of those who had a say in the matter were satisfied after evaluating Mark that he would make a fine parent, and many normal children only had one parent, and Mark had a nice home, and the school system in his neighborhood was quite good.

Mark was in the last stages of finalizing the adoption when he heard the fish comment, and because he wondered whether it was a test question designed to determine his reaction, he remained calm and inquired what the social worker meant. He answered that when a fish loses an eye in the ocean, other fish not only can detect the weakness, but they attack that very spot, and the fish, for obvious reasons, can't see it coming, nor can it do anything about it.

Mark said it was probably an unfair comment, but he promised to keep it in mind for whatever good it would do, adding that the school that Tyler would attend had strict rules that should ensure Tyler's safety. "Fish bide their time," the social worker said. "They will hang around looking at that hole in his head, that blind spot, and when given the opportunity, they'll move in for the kill."

Mark replied that the first thing that came to his mind when he thought of a fish with one eye was the flounder, a fish with no eyes on one side, which adapted by swimming flat on the bottom, essentially cutting off danger from that side. "It's a fish that is always looking up," he said. "I'll try to think of Tyler in that light."

"Flounder," the social worker muttered under his breath. "That's a good word for it. Thanks. The name helps my analogy a lot."

"You seem to need to put it all in a negative light," Mark said.

"Let me tell you something, Mr. Lamp," the social worker replied. "You can have all the faith in the world, and perhaps you are even very skilled at handling people. But there are no magic wands in these situations. Tyler's world is like the bottom of the sea where no weakness is allowed and where there is no pity. He'll sense it when it comes, and he'll react like a half-blind fish, which he is. Strange how we like to idealize arrangements to fit our ideas of the way we think things should be, but the way things are trumps that every time, leaving those who think they understand wondering how they could have been so completely blind. I'm only trying to help. I've seen this a thousand times. I guess you'll be like the other nine hundred and ninety-nine and realize I'm right when you bring Tyler back before the six-month trial period is over. Time will tell."

This conversation left Mark feeling so uncomfortable that he considered lodging a complaint, but as the adoption was so close to going through, it was just one of many minor negative experiences in a process that took several years including the major disappointment of having another adoption fall through in the last stage. So he counted his blessings and decided to leave it alone. It was only a matter of days before Tyler would finally be in his new home.

When the day came, Mark had a full schedule of things to do including good seats at a ball game. Tyler had a short attention span, and once he'd eaten his fill of food and gotten his first refusal to buy one more souvenir, he grew bored with the game and was begging to leave before the third inning. Mark didn't want to force the issue as Tyler was so loud with his complaints, so he left the stadium and took Tyler home where he teased the dog. Mark warned him to be gentle, but he was thrilled to bend its tail and pull its ears. Before the end of the afternoon, the pup was determined to keep its distance and ran to hide under a bed every time Tyler tried to play.

Mark coached a soccer team, and he wanted Tyler to come to a practice and perhaps join the team. Tyler was very happy to go, and while Mark went through calisthenics, Tyler set up pylons as Mark told him for dribbling drills. Somewhere along the line, however, someone must have said something to Tyler that upset him. Around the time that practice was ending, Mark was speaking to the team about the upcoming game. Every player had his own soccer ball, which Tyler quietly rounded up. He put them all in an empty equipment bag and waited until nobody was watching and walked to a lake on one side of the park and began kicking the balls out into the lake as far as he could. The wind was blowing out, so the balls were blowing to the far side.

Meanwhile, Mark passed out the schedules and let everyone go. Parents were arriving to take their kids home, and suddenly everyone realized the soccer balls were gone. Someone saw Tyler kicking balls into the lake, and the whole team ran over to get him. Mark didn't know what to do. He couldn't keep up with the kids, and Tyler heard them coming and dashed away before they got to the water. It took most of the boys the better part of an hour to go to the other side of the lake and wait for the balls to cross, and Mark couldn't find Tyler anywhere for at least another hour after everyone had left. Tyler didn't know the neighborhood, and Mark was worried that it would soon be dark, and he might not find him on his first day of adoption. Others got into the search, and finally a police officer found Tyler a couple of blocks away wandering around. He drove him back to the soccer field, and Mark thought that Tyler had a look about him that absolutely nothing had happened. Also, Mark was mentally exhausted, but Tyler was ready for whatever was next on the schedule. Mark wasn't even sure how to ask Tyler to explain what had transpired. By the time he saw Tyler in the police car, the relief he felt overwhelmed any urge to get to the bottom of it all in order to punish the boy. Tyler did admit that he'd gotten mad when one of the boys on the soccer team had called him a "retard," but he wouldn't describe the boy and ignored Mark's questions by saying he was starving. He started kicking the dashboard and demanding something to eat. Mark drove to a hamburger drive-in and accommodated him, but Tyler hardly touched the food Mark bought.

Back at the house, Tyler continued to tease the dog until it was time to go to bed, at which point he flatly refused to turn in. He said that after all the years in the orphanage of having to turn lights out at the same time every night, he wanted to stay up as late as he wanted on his first night of freedom. Mark explained that this new arrangement was not exactly freedom. Even if different in too many ways to count from his previous lifestyle, structure was still an important part of a every boy's growing up. Mark said because it was a special day, Tyler could stay up until 10 p.m. Tyler said midnight. Mark said 10:30, and they settled on 11, but by the time Tyler had changed into his pajamas, gotten a snack because suddenly he was hungry from not having dinner, brushed his teeth and found a game from his hand-held video game console, which he accused Mark of stealing, it was after midnight before Tyler finally climbed into bed. Then he wanted to read for a while, but Mark shut the light out and said, "Tomorrow's another day. This one's over."

"It's after midnight, so it's already tomorrow," Tyler answered.

"So you're not as dumb as you pretend to be," Mark snapped, tired as he was, and then instantly regretted it, expecting a violent reaction from Tyler, but there was only silence, and if Tyler didn't go to sleep rather quickly, he pretended that he did.

The next two weeks were brutal eye-openers for Mark as far as adopting a child with various problems. He bought Tyler a bicycle and signed him up for a summer afternoon program for kids at his church, which was more that a mile away. He walked Tyler there the first day, but after that, Tyler wanted to ride there by himself. Mark decided to let him go, then called the church to make sure Tyler arrived safely. He did, but Tyler was slow coming home, and

Mark started walking to meet him and saw Tyler coming on foot. The bike had been stolen because he'd forgotten to lock it. The next day, he drove Tyler, but he started a fight with a five-year-old and gave the little boy a black eye. The administrator banned Tyler from the program, and Mark had to cancel his work going forward several days because he had no activity for Tyler and had to stay home and watch him. School would start in a couple of weeks, but that was still too much time for Mark to take off, so he fumed.

Meanwhile, Tyler continued to tease the dog, accuse Mark of stealing things that would later turn up where Tyler had left them. He refused to pick up after himself or do any chores whatsoever, and he was mean to the neighborhood kids and hit another kid in the face. He was growing increasingly belligerent about bedtime and whining all the time of how bored he was. Mark told him that if he relaxed and settled into things, and could adapt to the adoption, that someday everything that Mark had including the house would be Tyler's. "Why would I want this junk?" he asked. "Someday I'm going to live on a submarine and torpedo every ship in the sea that I come across. I'll even send a cruise missile to blow you up."

The following morning, Mark called the adoption agency and said it wasn't taking. He had said as much to Tyler on several occasions that he was contemplating sending him back into the system, and Tyler said that would be fine and continued to watch cartoons.

A few days after that, Mark took Tyler back to the orphanage where he was met by several staff members including the social worker whose analogy had bothered Mark. Tyler got out of the car and walked straight into the building without ever looking back and saying goodbye. He had been busy playing a video game on the ride over and was aggravated to have to shut it off when they arrived.

Mark went in and signed some papers, thanked everyone, added an apology, and left. The social worker followed, winked and asked whether Tyler was a one-eyed flounder. "You've succeeded in transferring that to Tyler," Mark said, "made him believe he's a different species. He flew right back, so maybe a bird more than a fish, which makes you people what? Homing-pigeon trainers?"

Demon Pleas

As I laid back and the exorcism began, I felt connected to it at the outset, filled with rage at the words. I pulled with all my might at the restraints, and then it seemed as if I'd suddenly disconnected, that I wasn't listening anymore. The rage and pain dissipated, and I felt as if I'd slipped into a dream state. I felt almost drunk with a sense I remembered earlier in my life, like waking up from a good nap and connected to myself in a manner that was without any stress or fear. This desired state of mind became much more elusive as I grew older, until finally it disappeared altogether. Now I felt completely infused with it, and then I looked and saw something very strange, a kite across from me, with my face.

To say it looked like a kite is not completely accurate. It was actually more like a parachute filled with air, looking at it from under the canopy after landing on the ground, every part of it still connected by hundreds of strings to the jumper whose next move is to separate himself from it completely. I watched it wafting directly across from me, the face contorting, wincing uncontrollably, and then it surprised me when it opened its eyes and looked into mine.

"Make it stop," it said. "Stop listening to it. Take me back."

At first I wasn't sure what to make of it. Then I remembered the exorcism and wondered whether this was perhaps a manifestation of the demon that had possessed me. I followed the lines in to see how they were tied to me, and there was a kind of claw at every connection, something like an animal claw holding me at intervals. A few of the paws seemed to be relaxing their grip. One had let go entirely, but all the rest were tightly gripping me. It seemed as if the demon was also in a kind of dream state, but it was waking up to the fact that it was being forcefully disconnected from me, and now it was making a direct appeal to me, perhaps as a last resort.

"I don't know what I can do for you," I said. "If you are actually a demon, and we're being separated, I'm sure it's for the best."

"Without me you are nothing," the demon said. "I have given you elements of consciousness and personality that are the *sine qua non*, the elements without which you cannot make it in the world. Here, let me show you." Saying that, the wafting shape came over me like a blanket, immersing me in darkness. I felt awake again, filled with a sense of myself that I'd always known. There was no voice in my head, but I found myself wondering what was wrong with it, why anyone would want to change me, and it made me angry. Then something seared into me causing sharp pain, the words of the ritual exorcism, and the blanket blew off and away from me, taking shape across from me again as if filled with a strong wind, which pulled hard. Again I examined the connections. The gust had been sudden and hard, and the paws were all slightly less constricted. Two more had let go altogether so that a piece of the demon was altogether loose, wafting uncontrollably near its left cheek and having a discernable effect on its speech.

"There, did you feel that?" the demon asked. "I was a part of you again, inextricably so. You were yourself again for a moment, so you must remember now. If you don't do something soon, then everything you are will change forever. You must remember to draw me close. Think! Remember who and what you are!"

What he said made me think he was right, and just as quickly as that thought crossed my mind, I felt the approach of a large shadow. Looking up, the demon was right on top of me again. I heard mumbling somewhere. It was getting louder. I listened closely and recognized again the words of the rite in progress. I felt a pain in my head, and all at once it was gone. It was like the sun coming up. The shadow retreated, and again, I was face to face with my demon.

"I'm not sure that I can do anything for you," I said. "What's separating us appears too powerful to fight, beyond the control of either one of us. Whenever you are close to me, I can feel its presence."

"But it wasn't always like that," answered the demon. "We were together without any intervention, and we were doing fine. So how is it that when you were free that you did not object, and how can you be free if this is being forced upon you?"

"Do you hear the words?" I asked. "For some reason I hear nothing when we are separated."

The demon never stopped wincing but tried to calm his expression. "What are words anyway?" he asked. "They can't hurt me."

"Perhaps it is the spirit in the words then," I suggested. "What hurts you is a healthy delivery of too much truth."

"The truth is what you'll wake up to," the demon said, "when you realize that you've fallen asleep in church. That is where the words are coming from, and I am just the power of wakefulness. When I come close, you begin to wake. Since this is all just a dream, you'd be better off just letting me come close so you can wake."

"Or perhaps I should continue to hold you at bay and see what happens when you totally lose your grip," I snapped back.

The demon began to wince uncontrollably again, and another claw came loose. "You don't understand," he said in pain and desperation. "You need me in order to survive. Those are priests out there exorcising me from you for the simple reason that as long as I am ingrained in your heart, you are not responsible for your actions. I admit I have made you do some terrible things, but if we are separated, when you wake up, you will be deemed fit to stand trial for your many killings. So you will wake up clear and free, then you will be taken and put to death despite a clear conscience, and though you will remember nothing, the law will require you to die anyway, so if you let me go, you'll be waking up to a needle."

"You're contradicting yourself," I told him. "You're telling me different scenarios, which makes me realize you're not being straight with me. I also notice that each time you fail to convince me, another claw breaks loose, and you're beginning to fly loose of me. Even now if I do betray some slight misgiving about losing you, the way back is harder for you. The winds are stronger. You have less grip. You're grimacing more, which only means the words and their spirit are overpowering you, so I fear that we must both accept that

261

there is nothing either of us can do. We must wait for the outcome, and considering the look of your claws and the lies in your arguments, I have to believe that I'm receiving a cure here rather than losing the better part of me, so if my mental attitude has any force or bearing on the matter, then I'll take my chances. I release you."

With those words, the demon let out a shrill wail, and the paws started snapping loose from all around me. One cord held on while the whole spread collapsed. The wind blew past me, but I didn't feel it against my back. I only saw that the parachute or whatever it was was hanging onto me by a thread, and finally it broke, and up it went into the air, sailing toward the sun. It opened up as it went higher, and had the effect of putting the sun first into an eclipse for a moment, and then, just as it had covered me up, I saw it wrap around the sun just as everything went black.

I was awake. There were people talking. Someone asked whether it was over, whether the exorcism was a success. I felt a hand touching my eyes. "Can you see anything?" someone asked.

"No, I can't," I answered. "I'm blind. What happened?"

A man identified himself as a priest. He said they had just exorcised a demon from me. I said I had seen the demon and spoken with him, that he'd tried to fool me into letting him stay. I said I remembered seeing the sun go out, but I couldn't understand why I had woken up blind when my eyes had been good all my life.

Then someone else spoke up. It was my father. He said that I'd lost my sight in my childhood from a terrible fever, and not long after that, I regained my sight, which at first everyone thought was a miracle, but along with the sight there were other changes, terrible new aspects to my spirit, and over the years, it became more clear that I was probably possessed. Losing my vision again was a sign that my soul was restored, proof that the demon was gone.

"But why didn't the demon try to convince me not to let him go or I would go blind?" I asked.

The priest answered, "He wouldn't think of warning that you'd go blind without him because that is what he'd made you. He was too preoccupied with your sight coming back, which he knew was happening when you resisted him."

The Mosaic

I remember when I was a boy how mosaics were suddenly the rage of the women's club. My mother bought the tiles and a blank tray, and she began putting the pieces in using whatever grout or glue was supplied for the purpose. She worked both irritable and proud of herself, but when I saw the finished product, I wondered why there was no shape or recognizable pattern, why there was no scene depicted, no face or landscape, no tree or fountain. We'd studied ancient mosaics in school, and I mentioned that it was just another method, using tiles instead of paint, for example, to make a likeness of something else worth looking at. "Are you saying my tray isn't worth looking at?" she yelled, and then she started crying. Then she said how all her life she had never been creative, had never done well in art, had never done anything worthwhile, and it forced me to say how wonderful the tray was even though all she'd done was reach into the bag of tiles to pull out whatever she grabbed first, then put it in place, next to the last one. The result was very blue, I remember, and there was nothing wrong with a blue tray.

So she used it to serve cheese and crackers for many years, and when she died years later, I took the tray and kept it as a keepsake that my wife would stumble on from time to time and suggest I put it in the garbage because it was somewhat bent and useless as a tray after so many years. But it had become something else to me over those years, a piece of personal art if there is such a term, an object that brings forth more memory and meaning than the finest painting in any museum in the world, though of course, it totally lacks the necessary element of universality. But for me, I had to at least store it because even though she was dead, my mother would never forgive me for throwing it away. My keeping it was the only way to give credence to my sincerity when I told her that I liked it. It had stuck to me, maybe in my throat, since I had lied to her, and now it was a part of me that would follow me wherever I moved.

One day my father came over and saw the tray on the table. "You're mother made that, didn't she?" he asked. I nodded. "Well I want it. It should be mine. Bring it over to my house later, and I'll make some cheese and crackers for you, me and Arlene. But first you can use my tools and fix the fence. It needs some mending."

I took it over later that day. I went in the front door and called. They answered from the basement. I went down into a mosaic of an active life turned into a chart on the wall, a holding pattern of tools and anything else they could find. They had put it all on pegboard lining the whole basement. They must have taken everything out of drawers and put it all up. My father said, "Fix the fence first." I took a hammer and a box of nails from the pegboard, and he said, "Put it back when you're done, just like you found it."

"You mean like with they're being nothing anywhere, anywhere at all, if I set this one piece down somewhere, you don't think you would find it immediately and then see the one empty spot where it belongs and then simply stick it back up there? No, it has to be about teaching me that I can't be here and disrupt the perfect order that you've created, which in its own way is an abandoning of life's norm, a cocooning, what is it? You used to have stuff. You used to use stuff. Stuff was part of your life. It was in your life. It was all over the place, but it was being used. But now, you use nothing, but you have it all organized, and then when someone comes along, even they are a disruption, something off the chart, the pegboard, and they need to get it in the face that this is better. It's better this way. where you say, 'We're happier, god damnit. Leave us alone.'"

Then Arlene came over to me and said she was sorry for the way my father acted. She'd been drinking. It's what gives her colitis. I told her it was alright. "I shouldn't care," I said, "but look at all the fishing rods hung with such great care, none of whose tips will ever touch the water again."

"We use it, when we need it," my father said. "And then we put it back, and we always know where it is. My father did that, I'm doing it, and you should too."

"No, Dad," I told him. "You don't remember, but you lost all your father's tools because you never put them back. That's what boys do. When I was a boy, I remember how frustrated you'd get when I would use your tools and leave them out. You yelled at me a million times. But I'm forty-five years old now. If I use a tool, I'll put it back."

"Damn right you will, like you always leave the cup in the sink when I've told you a thousand times they get washed out and left on the towel for later use. You've never learned."

"I learned, but it seems more that you've forgotten how to go with the flow when people are around, like you're trying to spare yourself some horrible feeling. So you think you've eliminated it in your own mind by being organized, but look what remains. The mere touch of any single thing put into your gigantic mosaic initiates the big lecture delivered with the same emotion as when something did get lost. It's almost as if you actually like to scream before anything is misplaced because you miss it, and it doesn't happen anymore. You just need to dominate and control."

Arlene was rubbing my back, apologizing for him. She whispered that it would be better if I just put the tool back and not use it, that he'd be happier if I didn't, and she would go with me to the utility room. "Sure, why not?" I said. "He asks me to put a few nails in the fence outside and then stops me from doing it because taking a hammer from the precious pegboard breaks up the perfect order."

When I put it back in place, Arlene put her arms around my head and thanked me. "You don't know what it's like, how bad it is for me," she cried. "I'm so glad you're here. Don't let a little thing like that drive you out. Let the fence go. He won't care. But give me the mosaic tray your mother made." And then she kissed me on the lips.

Every other time she'd kissed me, it had been a welcome peck, but she pressed her face to mine and held my head against hers with her hand on the back of my neck. It started off like a grandmotherly kiss, but then it went where it shouldn't. I couldn't kiss like that, but I wasn't sure how to break away. She wouldn't let me. It grew deeper, more inappropriate and wrong. I started having feelings like "She's too old, but I'm getting old. She's dying, I'm going to die someday. I'm too old to be doing this. It's not the right relationship. She's my father's girlfriend. It's just wrong, and though there's a need to show love, the physical part of it is wrong."

As we embraced, my mind was racing. "There's a degree to which the ones with the testosterone boiling in them call the shots. I sure didn't have much left, and I knew my father had none, but over me he continued to fabricate the semblance of it to prolong control, but I knew it was all bluster, and I only obeyed him out of respect. But I started thinking about the life the hormone gives, how it gets the girls to line up on the shore, how it gets the men to jump ship and swim for them, and that's youth. And then there comes a point when it's over, when true love is just not going to happen on its own, and if it happens, then one forces it to happen, takes a mate out of convenience because there's too many associated thoughts in the brain for desire to get the upper hand. Intellectuality or experience breaks life up into so many thousands of pieces that the mind becomes a commentary on life, observing without participating. Being young and animalistic, driven by forces beyond your control, is acceptable. Everyone does that, and accepts it. But when you're an old man, you're going to kiss somebody for the wrong reasons, with your mind, not your heart, so it's the wrong kind of kiss, and there comes a time when the kiss of death is the only kiss left."

I broke off the kiss when I remembered the tray. I pulled away and asked why she needed it. "I want to destroy it to have your father back. I've lost him," she said. "Those tiles are all the days he lived with her, bright blue for sunny days, darker for stormy. She kept track, and what she made is a calendar in perfect sequence of the level of happiness of their marriage. If I were to do the same thing, I would have to lie to choose such lovely tiles, and the dark brick I'd present your father would never compare to your mother's, and now that he's seen it, he needs to know it's gone so there's no record of his love, and he'll forget her again."

I gave it to her and followed her upstairs and out the back door where she slammed it on the patio. The tiles flew all over the place.

I looked up at the kitchen window and saw father watching us. He looked down and seemed occupied with some activity in the sink. I couldn't tell, but he didn't look up again. Arlene swept the tiles, and I helped her pick up every last one of them. The hardest ones to find had gone into the grass, but most of those were right along the ridge where the bricks meet the yard.

After what Arlene had told me of my mother's making it a calendar, I felt like I was picking up my childhood days. I didn't know which days they were, but the tiles were mostly light blue, and when I found those, I remembered sunny days. When I found one that was darker, I remembered when it rained and I played indoors or looked for worms or floated popsicle sticks in the gutter down to the sewer. But those were good days too, and yet there was nothing like them in my current experience, and because I had no perfect recollection of the order of days as I lived them, just a general idea based on what year of school I happened to be in, I started to regret breaking the precious tray, which contained an accurate record of my parents' marriage but also days of my childhood, and now it was gone.

I handed Arlene a last batch, and she declared that she'd made a calculation which proved she had them all. But she didn't because I kept a handful of the nicer ones and put them in my pocket. Then she put the tiles in a bag, took it to the front curb and put it in the garbage can that would be picked up later that morning. Then we went inside where father greeted us with a spread of cheese and crackers on Arlene's finest glass tray. He set napkins down on the table and brought glasses. As we were sampling the various choices, father looked at me and said, "When this is done, you clean up, and don't forget to put everything away the way your mother likes it."

I looked at Arlene. She was crying. "What's with her?" he asked. I said I didn't know, but that I figured he wasn't supposed to mention my mother. He said that he meant Arlene, that I should look at her as my mother now and do everything for her. Arlene pushed her beautiful tray off the table and left the room. I cleaned up every last shard and left, stopping at the garbage can to collect the bag of tiles. Then I walked home with wonderful days of my youth bouncing in my pocket, thanking my mother for keeping such a record.

Interloper at the Halfway Point

Daniel (grandfather's name) Girard (father's mother's maiden name) Bastian (family name researched to an unmeritorious dead-end four generations previous) had labored under a great weight for so many years that he finally reached his own dead end by the time he was forty. It was all rather strange, and he chuckled as he put the rope around his neck that he'd reached the end at the halfway point, not just in his age but in his contribution to literature. He was tired of faking it, of knowing that there was something else necessary that he knew was out there, in other writer's works, but not in him to produce the kind of work deserving of the fame he'd already achieved, thanks to his father, who had pushed him into this and pulled all the strings that had brought him success. Too bad he wasn't there to pull the chair from under Daniel's feet. That would have made for an even bigger chuckle.

Edward Bastian had been a famous professor, respected by leaders in every field. He had pulled himself up out of nothing as his own father (Daniel's namesake) had immigrated and worked in a factory all his life. Edward wasn't disgusted by that, didn't push himself to escape. His success was more his father's doing with constant urging and reminding that he needed to pursue his education as a foundation, but it was who one knew that would make him someone worth knowing, so his father put his money away and got to know people who knew people at Philips Academy and got introduced to them. He did them favors, and they got him a job there, which paved the way for Edward's going to school there, and from there to Harvard where he met the friends his father foretold. Edward followed the advice almost by instinct, it had been inlaid so deeply into his unconsciousness. He married well and had the one son, Daniel Jr., one step removed, as he called him to his father. But Edward had a different plan for his son. Because he knew so many people, he could just grease the path, get him into good schools, even an exclusive kindergarten, and so Daniel just had it all handed to him, and while he showed brilliance in math, he was something of a slacker, disinterested in his father's plans for him, which were laid out from his childhood. "You'll be famous like me," Edward used to tell him.

But as is typical, Daniel was not impressed with his father's achievements. He didn't feel destined for greatness, and he preferred his grandfather's company over his father's. He used to spend summers at the old Bastian homestead, and his grandfather used to tell Daniel that he'd probably gone too far with trying to aim his son in the right direction, which was largely a course correction for himself, but was also something he couldn't do anything about given his circumstances, given that he had to come over on a boat without having finished his education and take a factory job, which is all anybody was able to do in the growing immigrant community of which he was a part. So when Edward was born, Daniel Sr., once removed, as he liked to call himself to his grandson, fed his son a daily diet of what he perceived was the lifestyle of the managers. They lived in nice houses on the hill. Their kids went to Philips and Exeter, then Harvard or Yale, and they went on to become leaders in their field. So he decided that if he could just get one foot in the door, then maybe he could push his son through the slot, drop him as a package on the other side, a little less random than leaving him in a basket on a doorstep, but ultimately he couldn't provide the things he coveted, though now, years later, he no longer saw them as anything worth seeking, and this is what his grandson admired.

Daniel saw his grandfather as being relaxed and accepting of anything he would want to be and found it preposterous to imagine that he was the type of father he described. He gave his grandson the opposite advice, to be what he wanted and not let his father interfere with his dreams. But whether it was a result of having everything handed to him or not, being lazy tended to put Daniel in the position of accepting what his father arranged for him. He used to sit at home while his father chatted on intellectual and political matters with colleagues and visiting dignitaries, unable to leave the room, his father insisting that he participate. He learned by listening how to echo what his father wanted to hear. He acquired an excellent vocabulary and mastered the subject matter, but what he really wanted was to sit back and not have to deal with any of it, and this is exactly what his grandfather offered, a safe refuge from ideas.

But when Daniel was in his early thirties, his grandfather's health began to fail. He had a problem that put him in the hospital for a couple of days, and everything was fine for a few months. Then he would have another episode that required hospitalization for a week. On getting out, everything wasn't quite as fine as was hoped. He called it "diminishing reruns" and by the fourth bout, he was back in the hospital within a week, and everyone could see the end was coming. Daniel first stayed at the homestead so he could be with his grandfather at his bedside during visiting hours, but in the last days he stayed overnight and left only to grab a bite to eat.

Those proved to be the most interesting days to Daniel and his grandfather's lucid ramblings provided the basis of the books he eventually wrote. It was as if there was something more in the ravings, something he could sense, transferred along the path cemented in place by the mixture of his feelings, the intensity of his focus, which made him unusually receptive. But it wasn't a gathering or harvesting of his grandfather's ideas; rather Daniel perceived that the most compelling part of the exchange was embedded in it, that what seemed like rambling was innately cogent, and this was the matrix that Daniel turned to as the means to satisfy his father's demand that he produce something that he could promote, only Daniel was never as satisfied with it as he was when he sat and listened to his grandfather.

One evening, his grandfather started talking about the rotunda effect, that when he'd visited the Capitol building in Washington he'd learned that standing in a specific spot across from another person, a private communication could be exchanged in whispers that were clearly discernable though the rotunda was crowded and noisy at the time. Since then, he said, there were many memories that lined themselves up in direct correspondence to his mind, whispering over a lifetime over the noise and commotion of life swirling around him. Daniel asked what kind of memories, to please give him an example, but his grandfather didn't seem to know he was there. Instead, he talked about how the rotunda was home, of how his life had slipped into it finally, that it had become a single event like the audio or video in a movie is an event, that he thought he would slip out of life, but instead he was slipping into an event within it, something like a track extant from everything that had been going on, that life is so many things together, but now he was aligned to one thing, but within it were new variations he had never witnessed or considered that explained the rest of it. It all took a new shape in his mind, but rooted totally in reality. And this reality was clear and comforting in every way because he was within it. But then all at once there were spots that came over his eyes, revealing instantly that he was a semblance that interpreted it, and a receptacle as well, full of things that he'd collected that couldn't be fixed, and these things were causing the spots.

Daniel was surprised to hear his grandfather talking this way considering that he'd never shown any interest or propensity for figurative language. Perhaps it was his own reaction to it that made it seem more cogent than it was. Grandfather went on to say that the spots were smaller in his childhood, and the fires they caused were distant and on the horizon. One couldn't even see or smell the smoke. By the time he was a young man, the spots were bigger, yet not an obstruction. The fires were visible but posed no threat, and only a light mist filled the valley. In middle age, he had to change his habits according to the behavior of the spots. He might break out with them and need to curtail his activities suddenly. But these kinds of flareups were infrequent. Meanwhile the fires had blocked his way out of the valley and were raging in the hills. Finally, by old age, it was all out of control. The fires were in the valley. He was all but blind with the spots, in a hospital bed, dying, listening to the sounds of construction since the hospital was undergoing an expansion, growing so much larger in anticipation of future needs. Once in a while, his eyes cleared up to see the workers outside the window, unaffected by the fire and smoke, pounding away as if they didn't even notice it, and grandfather said he realized the fires were all for him, that they were the spot on his semblance in the recognition of the event, a marker to the variations waiting to be experienced.

There was a train waiting outside that would take a route beyond the fires. A tunnel had been blasted through the mountain, and when he looked to see where the track led, he realized that the gravel came from the mountain. It was made of fossils, ground up beyond decoding, and the lost secrets were those he'd been searching for all his life, only he'd never considered that digging his way out of the valley into a new future would uncover the meaning of his past.

Daniel tried to get his grandfather's attention, but it proved futile. But toward the end, his grandfather sat up, looked at Daniel and told him to remember the strawberry credo, that all fruit have their seeds within except the strawberry, and it is the same for man. He started to say why the seeds of man were on the outside, but suddenly he was gripped by a convulsion. He had the presence of mind to grab Daniel's hand and look him in the eye, having a last moment of lucidity, but he was straining, as if holding on to life. Knowing the end was near, Daniel tried to comfort his grandfather. "It's alright, Grandfather," he said. "It's OK. You can let go. You can let go."

His grandfather was still straining, starting to shake, but he managed to reply with some difficulty, "They say 'let go' when you die, but there are things you hold onto, which are the things that link the things you let go of," and then he went limp, relaxing into a gentle heap, and Daniel stood close and listened to his breathing grow softer, fainter, until there was nothing, and Daniel immediately felt a presence as if somewhere in the commotion of his mind his grandfather stood on an exact spot for direct communication, and memories whispered through the tears that death was a good thing, that grandfather was happy. From that moment going forward, Daniel experienced the rotunda effect many times, not just in terms of his grandfather, but over many moments of his life, and he saw them as significant and learned to appreciate any memory that seemed to stand in relation to him and speak clearly across time.

Moreover, due to these experiences, Daniel appreciated his grandfather's ravings as being lucid, and for the first time, he was of a
mind to consider the underlying meaning in words and thought that
seemed to be abstract. He had a mind for math and a predisposition
for puzzles and word games. He thought he might try his hand at
writing, and grew even more determined when his father thought
the idea was preposterous, that Daniel should pursue a political
career because Edward knew so many people. But politics was something that had been thrown at Daniel all his life, and he knew from
imagining himself at a podium that he was too shy for such a career.

But writing suddenly appealed to him, and he told his father
about his grandfather's last hours, how compelling and strangely
lucid he was, but his father dismissed them as ridiculous ideas like
the Strawberry Credo. Evidently, Daniel pondered these things his
grandfather said beyond the limits of his father's patience. "Strawberry creed!?" Edward shouted in exasperation. "What the heck is
that supposed to mean? Look, people say a lot of things when they're
dying, and everyone looks into the words more than usual for meaning, but it ends up being nonsense to disinterested ears. If you didn't
say these were somebody's last words, who would care? And some of
it is just plain lousy, so if you're hoping there's some brilliance in
there to pass on, there isn't, so let it go. It isn't worth it. I hardly
remember anything he told me in life, so why should you worry
about some vain babblings of his in death?"

The next week, at Edward's regular gathering of intellectuals who
happened to be in town, Daniel waited for a lull in the conversation
ripe for a transition into a new subject, and he asked if those present
would mind his bouncing an idea off of them. All were willing, so
Daniel said there was an unfinished concept in his mind that began
with his grandfather's last words about the seeds of man growing on
the outside like a strawberry. Daniel suggested that man's seeds were
on the outside because there was too much commotion, acid and
struggling on the inside for seeds to grow, and so man's only hope
was to find the seeds on the outside of others, which could only be
shared and gathered with acquiescence, that seeds stolen or forced
are hollow, borne to fruition but never found whole and ripe. So to

spread seeds, man needs others not just to take them, but to need them, in which case the seeds become fertile when planted, but without others, we are nothing and die on the vine.

There was silence. Nobody knew what to make of any of it. Edward later upbraided his son for making a fool of himself and said the extended metaphor was ridiculous. Daniel agreed but didn't know how else to explain it. "How would one take a thought like that and express it well?" he asked his father. Edward didn't have an answer, unless it was that one knows when there is truth in the air, but it isn't quite so thick or dense or mixed with as much sugar as that. Daniel was embarrassed when he realized his father was right, but he still felt the potential in imagery and wanted to explore the possibilities, and he already had an idea for a novel.

It was to be an interweaving of ideas using stream of consciousness, a subtle divulgence of all of his ideas about life, but formed into a kind of knot, more of a tube that locks the mind when it pulls to escape. He had sat though enough classes in literature and read enough books to understand how a story line is sustained, and he never cared for discussions of tradition or criticism because he couldn't understand how there could honestly be any actual science of interpretation to separate good fiction from bad. He had read Goethe, remembered the phrase, "Genius is making the critic change his mind," from which he formulated a corollary, which was that fooling one critic might convince the others, which meant that if he could buy a good review, he could assume the role of writer and talk about the meaning of his book. He knew he could fake sincerity, though he wasn't going into it believing he was going to need to dissimulate. He just was picking up the pen without having "the calling" so to speak. But he didn't want to write adventures or pulp fiction. He wanted to be taken seriously, and he certainly had acquired enough knowledge to teach a variety of subjects. But writing seemed a fun way to make a living by thinking out loud.

When his first book was ready a year later, he brought the manuscript to his father and asked him to read it. Edward was astonished that his son had actually written a book, and he gathered from browsing it that it read fairly well. But he honestly didn't want to read the whole thing, so he merely called a friend in publishing and asked him for a favor. Several months later, Daniel had been signed to a publishing contract, and review copies of his book were already out. Edward saw to it that the key reviews were excellent, and that quickly, Daniel was a literary sensation.

He wrote a second novel, and he found the major magazines were eager to publish any stories and articles he wrote, and along the way of book tours and signings, he met a young lady with whom he fell in love and married her within a year. A short time after they were married, he was offered a teaching position in a small but prestigious college, and so he settled into his career seeming to have everything anyone could want who wanted to be a writer.

But Daniel was basically not happy with the arrangement. His students were all very excited to know him personally, and the college was happy with the benefits that came from having him on the faculty, but Daniel felt like he had fooled everyone. All he had done was to string together a lively series of disconnected images in a pattern that seemed to followed a man through his life, but he knew it was not genius though the critics said it was. He was disappointed that they could be bought like that. He realized what Goethe was really trying to say, that there is at times a critical blockade that is formed when there is a perception of how literature should be in a given time, and when a writer of genius comes along, it all falls down, and the critic becomes subservient to the writer. How many times in history have critics seemed to have the upper hand, and how many times have they been forced to see things differently? Daniel hadn't done anything like that, and as time went on he grew increasingly angry that it had been so easily achieved.

Some of the anger was directed toward his father, though it bounced back to him because he'd let him facilitate the deception, but most of it arrived by slight degrees as he immersed himself in teaching and began to understand the real nature of literature and something more of criticism. There was one critic who compared him to a television chef, whose delicasies are all prepared for the eye of the camera but are never meant to be touched or tasted. So his ingredients are not necessarily ingestible, and what may have the look of being tender and palatable is actually far removed from one's fork and plate, posing as nourishment, substituting mud for chocolate and concrete for flour. In short, the critic concluded, Bastian's creations were refined into semblances where real food for thought is required. There were also a few critics who had never been receptive to his work, who had written not quite scathing reviews, but intelligent evaluations that indicated to Daniel that he was well understood and dismissed in small circles that mattered, and his work would probably not survive in the long run. He was a flash in the pan, and he knew it, but he did want to do something about it to change the perception.

But anything he did would have to come on the heels of his other works and statements about art. He'd been interviewed on nationally-syndicated television shows. When he wrote his novels, there wasn't any pressure. It was all like a kind of serious jest, another one of Goethe's phrases, only now he was beginning to understand the real pressure of writing, the extreme difficulty in maintaining the necessary control over the work, all while the underlying structure was aesthetically correct. He wondered how he could ever approach the page again in the same way without feeling embarrassment. He sat at his desk and worried about writing, and when the bucket that was so full found the well empty, he began to despair.

The result of despair is often to go too far with self-dissection. Daniel began looking into himself as one runs his fingers through sand on a beach. He sifted through himself believing he was separate from the ocean in which he longed to immerse himself, that his sands had passed through the hourglass, and though he was only halfway through his life, he'd received accolades without deserving them. It was as if he'd stepped into the race full of energy when others were out of breath pacing themselves, and so he was able to sprint and appear superior, when in fact he wasn't worthy of attention because he wasn't a proper participant. He felt he needed to bow out, but he couldn't face the shame. Even though much of what he'd written was enjoyed by thousands of readers, he couldn't separate the fact that they had been magnetically trained to believe in advance that his work was worth their time. Had the reviews been honest, he figured he would have been lost in the heap with so many other writers vying for attention, honestly practicing their craft from start to finish whether they were successful or not.

He'd continued teaching until he was forty, but he was feeling burned out about that. The college wanted him to publish, and he'd been putting them off already for years with promises of a forthcoming book, and news on that had gotten old, turning from excitement to questions about whether it would ever come. He began to refuse interviews knowing that they would question him, and he tended to stammer when he felt defensive, and his last interview had gone very badly. Previously when interviewed, it was all role playing to him, and he always knew what to say that would make him look like he was on top of all the questions. But in this disaster, among other miscalculations, he admitted to having lost his love of teaching, which his students didn't like hearing. Several senior literature majors boldly questioned the merit of his work in one class. Another asked what the alternatives were for someone who started a journey halfway and found he couldn't finish, like a man who did not know how to fly being dropped into the cockpit of a plane already in flight, or someone who believed Xeno was right that you couldn't pass a certain point because there's a theoretical progress by going half the distance. What if someone just stood there and wouldn't budge? Was that a paradox, or was it just writer's cramp?

Daniel dismissed that class early and felt the whole charade was falling apart. As much as so many still wrote to say how much they loved his books, he felt like a fraud. He had stopped answering such letters months before. He thought of how many writers had just finally ended their lives, and he realized that it may be the only option for him. It somehow felt right to him under the circumstances. He would join an elite group of successful artists in the unique position of offering people some insight into the nature of what it means to live, whose own commentary, however illuminating, was somehow tainted by an ultimate contradiction. Some had said that the disparity between the message advocating life and the chosen method of departure must shed an unkind light on the teacher, for how can one assume the stewardship of the mind and then deliberately extinguish one's own light when there are those who endure a lifetime of torture and imprisonment rather than repudiate what they have stood for. Why didn't those people take the easy way out? Why didn't they repudiate it? Why didn't they leave people who believed in their work in shock and doubt?

Daniel knew the answer to those questions. He wasn't in the same league, and so he tied a rope around his neck one afternoon and jumped off the chair. As he leapt, he felt the rotunda effect one last time, realizing a significant aspect of the Strawberry Credo in his last moment of life. It was as if he felt his whole and ripe seeds disconnect from him at the moment he jumped, and he was able to watch as they fell and crashed in hollow fragility on the floor beneath his feet. He heard his grandfather whisper that his seeds were hollow too, that Daniel should not worry, and Daniel said, no, that grandfather's seeds were fertile, that he'd harvested and held them sacred. Hearing this displeased grandfather who said they were for planting, not for worship, and if they never took root, they were of no use. Daniel understood the Strawberry Credo only when he cast his own life into the balance, but with his own life, so also was the die cast from which there is no return, so Daniel's career ended that day. But the eulogies came in by the bundle, of how the world had lost such a great potential, and it was true, for every life resides on the husk of the great nut worth cracking, only it is a tough nut, about the thickness of a skull, which is to say it is equal to the task of standing up against the might of any one of us, try as we may to crack it, so let there be sympathy in our judgement.

Underworld at the Finish Line

There is nothing in the world, or the universe for that matter, that does not abide by fixed laws, some of which may need adjusting from our perspective depending on what transpires. For example, we may have determined certain limits and propounded a given law only to observe a variation that demands a modification to the law. But though we err in our determinations, we also know that anything and everything operates according to fixed laws and limits whether we have isolated them or only begin our approach to understanding what those limits may be.

But there is an undetermined degree to which, though everything abides the world, the world does nothing to reciprocate. There is a tale of an annual race that was run in the ancient world where the winner was pulled into the underworld at the finish line. The track ground swelled and opened just as the runner crossed the line, swallowing him up, it seemed, never to be heard from again. Then it happened that a young man of promising speed went way ahead of the pack but stopped before the finish line. All the other runners crossed ahead of him, but the ground did not open, and none was taken to the underworld.

This is just a myth, but it explains what would happen if we had a chance to react to what was waiting for us in supposed victory. As much as the tale distorts reality, it would be a distortion beyond belief to assume that runners would willingly cross the line and enter the underworld when the purpose of running is to enjoy the rewards on this side of the great continuum. There are tales of Mayan ball games where victors were honored with sacrifice, but how intense must have been the faith of those who participated knowing certain death awaited them should they win.

The real question is whether anyone can be so sure of the rewards on the other side of the finish line that are not of this world that he would give his all though he lose everything in the same last breath. A soldier may give his life to save others, but his effort is based on a desire to spare others from the same fate he willingly accepts. Perhaps the motivation in the Mayan games was to see the opponent as a teammate and strive to win in order that he might be spared. If the runner in the myth were to have stopped in order to let someone else cross into the underworld, he would have been branded a coward, but in effect, his stopping changed the rules, controverted the appearance of the underworld so as to demand an inquiry. So what would be the judgement against this runner?

First, it would be unlikely that the case would be heard in the underworld. Frankly, whatever lies beyond this world abides by a different set of rules, and whatever those may be, they generally tend to remain separate and distinct, so the hearing would be conducted in accordance with universal laws as they are understood on this side of the continuum, but at 30,000 feet. In this myth, the runner would be tried in a high court, literally, above the world, and he would be found guilty of stopping short of his destiny, which no man can do. As a result, he would face an immediate fall from grace and be dropped from 30,000 feet in the air to whatever awaited him.

Now, as he falls, he would reach terminal velocity, which is to say that he would fall according to given laws and no faster, though depending on how he spread his arms, the air might slow him down a bit. He might even be able to soar and fly through the air a bit. He might be expected to make peace with himself and his maker depending on his beliefs, but there are no preset rules for this, and it would be unlikely that the nature of his thoughts would be ascertainable unless he were to have a pen and paper to write something down before he hit the ground. Another question is whether he might expect the world in any way to intervene on his behalf, that as he "abides" the world as a falling object, obeying laws of nature, yet he is atypical, so might the world set aside its normal manner of receiving objects due to the fact that he carries spiritual content? Are there universal provisions that could be said to measure the internal content of a falling body so as to consider saving or salvaging the contents whatever else would happen to the container?

This is the question raised by the myth of the runner who avoided crossing the finish line only to be dropped to the face of the earth. As a runner, he was able to distinguish himself from his peers, but as a falling object, he is distinguishable from a rock in shape only. That would be the first thought in many observers on the ground. They would assume his fate to be a foregone conclusion.

But what if he were to pilot his body through the air and effect a safe landing? Hard as that may be to imagine, is it not a remote possibility, that perhaps there would be a soft, grassy hillside with just the right height and degree of slope that if he were to reach it at just the right angle of descent that he might slide down to a safe landing? It has actually happened that a woman who fell out of an airplane survived in this very way without trying, that she fell fully expecting to die but a hill intervened, swelled up and received her, swallowed her up, if you will, and presented her with a whole new but unexpected life. How much that must have changed her!

So it is with the underworld that awaits anyone in the race of life. We run against ourselves not knowing where the finish line is, only that when we get there, we will be swallowed up either into nothingness or somethingness, and either way, in accordance with laws that bind both sides of the continuum if there are two side, or laws that keep everything one sided so that the only result of crossing the finish line is that the race is over for us.

There is another story of a man who was dying in a hospital, being cared for by a homely nurse whose one desire was to someday be married. Knowing he is going to die, the man feels sympathy for the nurse, and in a gesture of good will, he offers to marry her so as to fulfill her dream to some small degree. She accepts his offer, and a chaplain is called to perform the ceremony. Afterwards, she attends to his every need with such care and an unforeseen focus that she ultimately manages to save him, and in a matter of only a few weeks, his health is restored. But the question becomes, how will he feel about a new lease on life with an unplanned, ugly wife? Will he not be a new person and fully appreciate, even love her for all she has done for him, or will his nature dictate that he would seek annulment of the marriage, or escape her clutches in another way? Ultimately it would seem that there are laws that govern the behavior of spirit, though we have only begun the approach to understanding how they govern us, and quite often when we think we know the parameters for our actions, we extend the playing field with an unanticipated move. Every man and woman taken all together, like every star in the sky, assists in formulating the spectrum of possibilities, and so we have a sense that there is some kind of universal limitation of action, meaning only that everything operates within boundaries, and whether or not they are clearly delineated is not the point. In the end, everything abides by the world, but again, the question is whether the world will listen to us.

When we are falling from 30,000 feet, will it hear us calling and provide a hillside slope that will save us? What is a miracle but the one chance in a billion coming up in its turn? Still, we tend to believe there is more as we put on our running shoes and prepare for the long race. We tend to put everything we have into the actual running, do we not? Or if we don't, we tend to hear from ourselves that we're not giving our maximum effort. We may ask why it matters, but we still press on, even though uncertainty awaits us at the finish line, and in our last steps, we tend to keep going right through and let the underworld have us. Whatever it is, we blast right through the tape and accept it as the reward even though we know we disappear from the face of the planet.

And if we could stop and prolong the inevitable by facing a short trial and a long fall to earth, would we have less fear from a sense that earth would welcome us, or that our spirit might learn to fly on such short notice? But we carry the underworld within, so we should not be concerned with what abides the world, where all things take care of themselves. In choosing to live, we may wonder what's on the other side, but we soar according to the constraints of boundless parameters toward the finish line, with a saving ugliness as our constant companion. How beautiful is that?

www.ingramcontent.com/pod-product-compliance
Lightning Source LLC
Chambersburg PA
CBHW021958010726
47494CB00003B/794

* 9 7 8 0 9 6 6 1 3 1 8 5 7 *